Nature
QUEST

junior devotional

An Exciting Voyage Through Creation

Nature Quest

JAMES & PRISCILLA TUCKER

Review and Herald® Publishing Association
Hagerstown, MD 21740

This book was
Edited by Gerald Wheeler
Designed by Patricia S. Wegh
Illustrations by Mary Rumford
Cover design by Ron J. Pride
Cover images provided by PhotoDisc © 1994
Typeset: 9.5/10 Journal

PRINTED IN U.S.A.

99 98 97 96 95 94 10 9 8 7 6 5 4 3 2 1

R&H Cataloging Service
Tucker, James A
Nature quest, by James A. Tucker and Priscilla Tucker.

1. Teenagers—Prayer books and devotions—English.
2. Devotional calendars—Juvenile literature.
3. Nature study—Stories. 4. Natural theology—Juvenile literature. I. Tucker, Priscilla, joint author. II. Title.

242.6

ISBN 0-8280-0865-5

Dedication

to Laurie,
Robert,
Jennifer,
Michael, and
Christopher

Authors

The authors, Jim and Cilla Tucker, live with their family in Berrien Springs, Michigan. Together they operate the Institute of Outdoor Ministry, which they founded to promote the use of nature as an effective means of illustrating the creative power and sustaining grace of Jesus Christ. The Institute publishes *Outdoor Ministry,* a monthly newsletter designed to help Christians use the study of nature and the outdoors as a way of getting better acquainted with Jesus. Many readers will remember the two previous devotional books authored by the Tuckers: *Windows on God's World* (1975) and *Glimpses of God's Love,* (1983).

Dr. Tucker is professor of educational psychology at Andrews University. As a teacher and consultant, he works with educators and school systems to improve the quality of instruction, especially for students who appear to have difficulty learning. Tucker demonstrates the value of using nature as an endless source of motivation to make learning interesting and successful.

Mrs. Tucker is a professional writer and editor. While working on her doctorate in education, she currently serves as managing editor of the *Journal of Research on Christian Education,* published by Andrews University. Mrs. Tucker is the author of two additional books, both on natural history themes: *The Return of the Bald Eagle* (1994) and *Nature Activities for Families* (in press). She specializes in practical things that parents and teachers can do with natural materials at home, in school, and in the educational programs of churches.

Dr. and Mrs. Tucker have spent more than 20 years developing methods and materials to assist parents and teachers. Their professional activities as well as their hobbies are nature-related and dedicated to glorifying Jesus Christ as Creator and Saviour.

Introduction

This is a book about God. It is about the power of God, and it is about the love of God. All nature beats to the rhythm of God's great heart. Everything in the universe illustrates the power of God's love.

You can say that God wrote a book so large that the universe cannot contain it. It is a book of laws—the laws that govern how the galaxies perform in inner space. And it is a book about love—the combined force of all of God's laws.

God gave us a miniature version of His book. We call it the Bible. In the Bible, we learn that God created our world to illustrate His love. We learn about the special creation of human beings. And we learn how God's special creation rejected Him. Then to show His love, God left His home and came to Earth. He came to reveal His power—the power of love. And He demonstrated that love by dying on a cross. As a result, God is now the author of another book, which He has promised to write in our hearts. "Looking unto Jesus the author and finisher of our faith" (Heb. 12:2). "I will put my laws into their mind, and write them in their hearts" (Heb. 8:10).

This devotional book is organized around the Creation Week. The first day is about light, the second day the atmosphere, the third day plants, the fourth about the starry heavens, the fifth about creatures of the air and water, and the sixth about land animals, including humans. And the seventh day tells of special features of creation that illustrate God's power and love. And this cycle is repeated 52 times, once for each week in the year.

We have taken some liberties with subjects for days two, five, and six. For example, we expanded the subject of the earth's atmosphere to include rocks, minerals, earthquakes, and volcanoes. We put butterflies on the fifth day because they fly in the air, even though we could have mentioned them on the sixth day as creeping things. Frogs, toads, and salamanders we discuss on the sixth day when they may have been part of the water creatures God created then.

There is much that we don't know about creation. But one thing we do know: God created the heavens and Earth and all living things therein. And we know that God sent His Son Jesus to die for each of us because of His great love for us. We believe in Him by faith, and nature is filled with illustrations that show us the characteristics of God and strengthen our faith in Him.

It is our prayer that as you take this journey with us through nature, the Holy Spirit will be your guide and you will learn of God's love by considering the wonders that are all around us.

t is the First Day of the week. We call it Sunday today, but it is not the sun's day. There will be no sun until the Fourth Day. One day it will become the resurrection day. It is the day when God brings the light of life to a world clothed in darkness.

Can you imagine that moment?

"And the earth was without form, and void; and darkness was upon the face of the deep" (Genesis 1:2). Darkness! No light of any kind—just darkness and silence.

Suddenly you sense power—power so great that the vacuum seems to pulsate. Waves of energy increase in frequency. Something is about to happen—something so profound that eternity will never be the same. God is coming to this place. For on the endless three-dimensional map of space, this is the place that the Creator has selected for the supreme declaration of His everlasting power.

"And the Spirit of God moved upon the face of the waters" (verse 2). "And God said, Let there be light," and suddenly, in a blinding microsecond of reality that would someday be called time, "there was light."

God, the Creator—one day to be called Jesus—had arrived! Later, when the world was enshrouded in another kind of darkness, He would say, "I am the light of the world: he that followeth me shall not walk in darkness, but shall have the light of life" (John 8:12).

And that light was the Light of life—yours, mine, and that of every other living thing on earth. When Jesus the eternal Creator arrived, He was light from the very center of the universe, light from the throne of God. It could not have been otherwise, because God is light. Where God is, darkness cannot exist.

"And God saw the light, that it was good: and God divided the light from the darkness. And God called the light Day, and the darkness he called Night. And the evening and the morning were the first day" (Genesis 1:4, 5).

Let There Be Life

A Word From Our Creator

In the beginning God created the heaven and the earth. . . . And God said, Let there be light: and there was light.
Genesis 1:1-3.

Let There Be a Firmament

It is the Second Day. We call it Monday, but it is not the moon's day. The moon will not grace the sky until the Fourth Day. The Second Day is the one that God has set aside to prepare the air. But this air is not air as we know it—sometimes too hot and sometimes too cold. Using an incredible process of insulation, the Creator provides a perfect environment for life.

Heavenly beings watch in wonder as the light of God's presence circles the globe. What was in darkness they now see as a vast expanse of water—endless waves of life-giving water. And again "the Spirit of God moved upon the face of the waters. . . . And God made the firmament, and divided the waters which were under the firmament from the waters which were above the firmament: and it was so" (Genesis 1:2-7).

On this day God produced a global envelope of atmosphere. He provided at least 5 quadrillion tons of air—a special combination of nitrogen (78 percent), oxygen (21 percent), argon (almost 1 percent), and tiny amounts of neon, helium, krypton, xenon, hydrogen, ozone, carbon dioxide, nitrous oxide, and methane.

The life-supporting oxygen was in just the right amount for the plants and animals that God had not yet created. And God caused the Earth to rotate, thereby creating winds that would keep the air circulating and fresh. The winds would bring oxygen for the animals to breathe and would carry away the carbon dioxide they exhaled. The plants would use the carbon dioxide to make food and release new oxygen.

Our God always provides for us in advance. Jesus gives us His Spirit, who, like the wind, provides us with spiritual breaths of fresh air in a world of darkness.

"And God called the firmament Heaven. And the evening and the morning were the second day" (verse 8).

A Word From Our Creator

And God said, Let there be a firmament in the midst of the waters, and let it divide the waters from the waters. Genesis 1:6.

t is the Third Day. But it is not the day to honor Tyn, the Norse god of war, from which we get the name Tuesday. The Third Day is when God lays the carpet in the new home that He is preparing on a planet called Earth. Before He can install that carpet, however, there has to be a floor.

"And God said, Let the waters under the heaven be gathered together unto one place, and let the dry land appear: and it was so. And God called the dry land Earth; and the gathering together of the waters called he Seas: and God saw that it was good" (Genesis 1:9, 10).

Can you imagine the gigantic operation that took place as this day began? God raised mountains of earth from under the water to build hills and valleys, and He hollowed out lake beds and stream beds. Then the wind moved gently across the resulting mud to dry it so that the special carpet could go down. And what a carpet that was!

"And the earth brought forth grass, and herb yielding seed after his kind, and the tree yielding fruit, whose seed was in itself, after his kind" (verse 12).

Do you suppose that Earth just burst forth in living green all at once? Or do you suppose that God started at one point on Earth, and as He swept His hand across the planet, unrolled a green carpet around the globe until vegetation covered the whole world?

Notice the new sounds. Wind rustling the leaves of trees, streams bubbling over rocks, and waves lapping at the edges of the lakes. But no bird calls fill the air, nor do we hear the voices of animals on land or the splash of fish in the water. Only plants rustle in the breeze. As Jesus looks out over the endless sea of grass, flowers, and trees, He is satisfied that His work is progressing well. He is building a special place for a special life form—you and me—and that place is beautiful!

"And God saw that it was good. And the evening and the morning were the third day" (verses 12, 13).

Let There Be a Living Carpet

A Word From Our Creator

And God said, Let the earth bring forth grass, the herb yielding seed, and the fruit tree yielding fruit after his kind, whose seed is in itself, upon the earth: and it was so. Genesis 1:11.

Let There Be Lights

It is the Fourth Day, the day on which God brought sunlight to earth to sustain life during the day and moonlight to brighten our paths at night. This is the day on which He also revealed the awesome majesty of the starry heavens created by "the breath of his mouth" (Psalm 33:6).

One night Napoleon was sailing the Mediterranean Sea with a contingent of his armed forces. As he paced the deck, his officers were standing nearby arguing against the existence of God. Napoleon is said to have suddenly interrupted their discussion with this statement: "That's all very well, gentlemen, but pray tell me, then, who made those stars?"

Who indeed! With all the talk these days about a big bang that occurred billions of years ago and resulted in all the starry hosts, humanity still finds itself caught up in the same argument. For the Christian, however, there is no question. Our faith in the fact that God created heaven and earth is not based on a theory, some possible explanation. Instead our faith rests on a deep and abiding belief that God is the source of all things.

Faith itself indicates that God exists. "Now faith is the . . . evidence of things not seen" (Hebrews 11:1). And the sun, moon, and stars represent perhaps the strongest and most indisputable representation of God's creative and sustaining power.

During the French Revolution an atheist said to a Christian peasant, "We are going to destroy Christianity. We will pull down your churches, burn your Bibles, and demolish everything that speaks to you of God." The peasant replied, "But you will leave us the stars." "And God set them in the firmament of the heaven to give light upon the earth, and to rule over the day and over the night, and to divide the light from the darkness: and God saw that it was good. And the evening and the morning were the fourth day" (Genesis 1:17-19).

A Word From Our Creator

And God said, Let there be lights in the firmament of the heaven to divide the day from the night; and let them be for signs, and for seasons, and for days, and years. Genesis 1:14.

t is the Fifth Day. The moon rises, then sets with the dawn. The sun peeks over the horizon, spreading its rays across a landscape more beautiful than our minds can comprehend. Except for the rustle of leaves and the sounds of water, we notice no movement or other sound. But if you were there, you could feel the energy of God's creative power as it builds for yet another day of miracles.

"And God said, *Let the waters bring forth!"*

Imagine the power of those words.

We don't know the exact response, of course, but perhaps it was like the rush of a mighty wind or like the rolling surge of a huge wave. In every direction—underwater and in the air—suddenly there was movement. How it must have thrilled the observing universe to see the flutter of millions of wings rising into earth's atmosphere and the swirl of fins flashing in its waters.

"And God created great whales, and every living creature that moveth, which the waters brought forth abundantly, after their kind, and every winged fowl after his kind" (Genesis 1:21). In the air it seemed as if the flowers had burst into flight and begun to sing, filling the sky with the color and sound of birds. And under water the lakes and streams sparkled with the reflected rays of the sun on myriads of brightly colored fish. The Creator's hand had produced a three-dimensional theme park animated with real living creatures that filled the water and the air.

And He made it all for you and for me. He made it all for every person that would ever live on earth. Like a father and mother preparing a special room for the child that is to be born, God prepared a special world just for us. It must have thrilled Him to realize how much joy all these creatures would bring to each human being.

"And God blessed them, saying, Be fruitful, and multiply, and fill the waters in the seas, and let fowl multiply in the earth. And the evening and the morning were the fifth day" (verse 22).

Let the Waters Bring Forth

A Word From Our Creator

And God said, Let the waters bring forth abundantly the moving creature that hath life, and fowl that may fly above the earth in the open firmament of heaven. Genesis 1:20.

Let Us Make Man

It is the Sixth Day. God has set the stage for the last act of Creation. Bird songs vibrate the air, and the water is a playground for fish. The wonder of what is about to happen can scarcely be imagined, but we can try.

The inhabitants of the universe look on in rapt attention. They seem almost to hold their breath as the Creator speaks.

"And God said, Let the earth bring forth the living creature after his kind, cattle, and creeping thing, and beast of the earth after his kind: and it was so" (Genesis 1:24).

Suddenly, from behind every tree and shrub, upon every hillside, and in every field, appear magnificent creatures of all sizes and shapes. Beings across the galaxies spot beasts of every kind—some in herds and some in pairs. Monkeys swing through the trees. Lions and tigers and bears romp and chase one another through the forest. Deer race gracefully across the meadows. And mice, rabbits, squirrels, bees, and butterflies explore every leaf, flower, and blade of grass, exulting in their wonderful new home.

Suddenly everything stops. The birds halt their singing. The fish cease swimming. The animals stop running, climbing, and digging. All eyes are on God Himself as He walks silently along a stream. He stops and kneels down. Scooping up dirt, He mixes it with water and begins forming something. What is it? It looks like a replica of the Creator Himself. But it is not moving. Wait! The Creator bends over His new creation.

"And the Lord God formed man of the dust of the ground, and breathed into his nostrils the breath of life; and man became a living soul." "So God created man in his own image, in the image of God created he him; male and female created he them" (Genesis 2:7; 1:27).

With this act God finished His work.

"And God saw every thing that he had made, and, behold, it was very good. And the evening and the morning were the sixth day" (Genesis 1:31).

A Word From Our Creator

And God said, Let us make man in our image, after our likeness: and let them have dominion . . . upon the earth.
Genesis 1:26.

The Seventh Day has arrived. As the moon rises and the cool of the night settles, God performs a very special act to seal forever the authority of His creative power on Earth. He sanctifies this day by setting it aside as a special day—a holy time—that will return again and again as a reminder of what He has done.

And thus was born the week—seven days, beginning with the light of the Creator's appearance and ending with a day of rest. In our time, we commemorate special events with holy days, or holidays. The Seventh Day of Creation is such a day: it is the birthday of the world.

The Lord of the universe has finished His finest creation: humanity. He placed man and woman in the midst of a garden home that He had prepared just for them, a garden where as far as the eye can see there is perfection. The trees are only four days old, the birds and fish are only two days old, and the animals—as well as Adam and Eve themselves—are only a day old. But the world looks like it has been in place forever. The character of God is represented on earth in what He has created and made.

Even in a paradise like this, God knows that human beings will occasionally need to stop pursuing their own interests in order to remember the Creator who made heaven and Earth. So He gave us a day, one in every seven—the Sabbath—to remind us every week that He is the Creator and that we are His creatures.

And the Creator spent that day visiting with Adam and Eve. What an occasion that must have been! Spread out before them was God's original lesson book—the book of nature—written in a language that only God can interpret. As eager students, Adam and Eve listened as Jesus used the abundance of natural wonders to teach them of His everlasting wisdom, power, and love. Today, as He did on that first Sabbath, Jesus still uses the things of nature to draw you close to Him.

JANUARY 7

And God Rested

A WORD FROM OUR CREATOR

And on the seventh day God ended his work which he had made; and he rested on the seventh day from all his work which he had made. And God blessed the seventh day, and sanctified it. Genesis 2:2, 3.

JANUARY 8

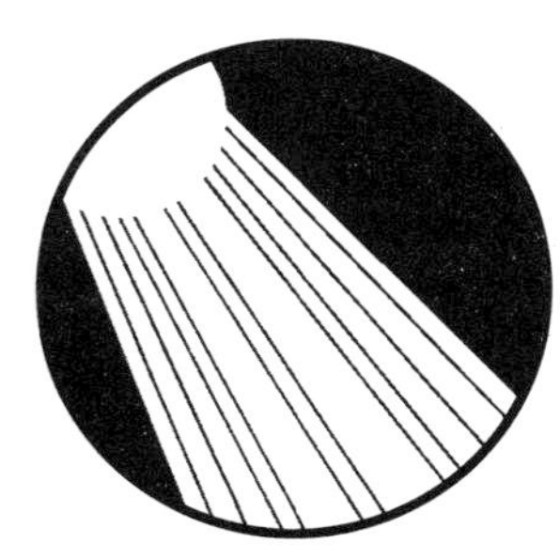

The Face of Jesus

When a firefly blinks on and off on a warm summer evening, what is that light? When the moon shines in the night sky, what is that light? And when a flashlight beam brightens the path ahead, what is that light? The firefly uses a chemical reaction to manufacture its glow. The moon reflects the rays of the sun. And the flashlight's power comes from electrical energy stored in a battery. All three sources of light are different, yet all three illuminate the darkness. But what *is* light?

Even though it is all around us, light is among the most difficult of all things to understand. Scientists spend lifetimes studying the properties of light, trying to understand what it is and how it works. At this point we have only theories, but the fact that we don't understand light doesn't keep us from using it.

What *do* we know about light? We know that it travels at a speed of 186,000 miles a second. That's fast—faster than a speeding bullet! The velocity of the swiftest rifle bullet is only about one mile per second.

Also we know that light consists of many colors. Sir Isaac Newton confirmed that fact in 1666 when he projected sunlight through a glass prism and saw the rainbow that resulted.

And we know that light travels in waves. But the waves are so tiny that even the longest ones pulsate a trillion times in an inch, and the shortest ones pulsate almost two trillion times in an inch.

It is difficult to understand completely something as complex as light. Isn't it great that we don't have to understand it to use it? We can use it without knowing anything about what causes it. Every time we look at something we are using light, because the light rays bouncing around in our environment interact with our eyes to send messages to our brain and allow us to see.

A blind man once went to Jesus to be healed. He had lived in total darkness all his life. When Jesus touched his eyes, the man could see. And what did he see? The face of Jesus, the Light of the world.

A WORD FROM OUR CREATOR

For God, who commanded the light to shine out of darkness, hath shined in our hearts, to give the light of the knowledge of the glory of God in the face of Jesus.
2 Corinthians 4:6.

In the story of Creation we read that "God formed man of the dust of the ground" (Genesis 2:7). How could God make a human being out of dust? In one way the answer is simple: He had to add water. Isaiah wrote, "We are the clay, and thou our potter" (Isaiah 64:8). Today we sing, "Thou art the potter; I am the clay." In order to form dust into anything, you have to add water. And that is what God did to make you.

You are 70 percent water! Your blood is 80 percent water and your muscles 75 percent water. Even your bones are 50 percent water. You have 15 to 40 billion brain cells, each about 80 percent water. No matter how you calculate it, you are a walking and talking container of water.

To keep you going, you must have the water replaced constantly. You need about two and a half quarts a day. This comes not only from the liquids you drink, but also from the food you eat. For example, an ear of corn is 70 percent water, a potato is 80 percent water, and a tomato is 95 percent water.

Water dissolves the nutrients from your food, carries them to all parts of your body, helps in the chemical reactions that turn food into energy, and transports your body's leftover waste products. You can live without food for about a month, but you can survive for only about a week without water.

If you took a bucket and put 30 parts dust in the bottom and then filled the bucket with 70 parts water and stirred it up, you wouldn't exactly have something that you could form into a figure, would you? All you would have is muddy water. You wouldn't even have clay. So how did God make a person who is mostly water? No wonder David was moved to exclaim, "I will praise thee; for I am fearfully and wonderfully made: marvellous are thy works; and that my soul knoweth right well" (Psalm 139:14).

Won't it be wonderful to drink from the river of life that flows from the throne of God? That water comes from Jesus, who quenches not only your physical thirst but your spiritual thirst as well.

Water of Life

A Word From Our Creator

And he showed me a pure river of water of life, clear as crystal, proceeding out of the throne of God and of the Lamb. Revelation 22:1.

January 10

Names

One of Adam's delightful jobs in the Garden of Eden was to name every living thing. Because of the marvels of natural adaptation within animal groups, we now have many more species of living things than Adam had to classify in the Garden. Naming plants and animals has always presented human beings with an interesting challenge.

When European biologists first attempted to use already-existing Greek and Roman names for the new plants and animals that explorers had found around the world, total chaos broke out. For example, when seventeenth-century biologists were presented with the carnation, a newly discovered plant, they gave it the following official name: *dianthus floribus solitariis, squamis calycinis subovatis brevissimis, corollis crenatis*. In English that translates to "the pink with solitary flowers, the scales of the cowlicks somewhat egg-shaped and very short, the petals scalloped"!

Fortunately, by 1753 a Swedish naturalist named Carolus Linnaeus had developed a better way to name things. His system, still used today, gives us what we call "scientific names" for every species of life in the world. The scientific name always consists of two Latin names of one word each—a genus name and a species name. So the carnation described above became *Dianthus caryophyllus*. The genus name, in this case *Dianthus*, is capitalized. The species name, *caryophyllus*, is not capitalized and can never be used for any other species in the genus *Dianthus*. Scientists might, however, use it as a name in another genus, for this would not create duplication in this new binomial (two-name) system. As long as scientists follow the rules that Linnaeus set down, no other species can have this name.

Using the system that Linnaeus developed means that we can use designated common English names, such as "northern cardinal," or colorful local names, such as "redbird." But to ornithologists, be they French, Russian, Chinese, or English, the bird is *Cardinalis cardinalis*.

How do you think Adam kept all the names straight? Do you think Adam used a binomial system?

A Word From Our Creator

And Adam gave names to all cattle, and to the fowl of the air, and to every beast of the field.
Genesis 2:20.

JANUARY 11

How Many Stars?

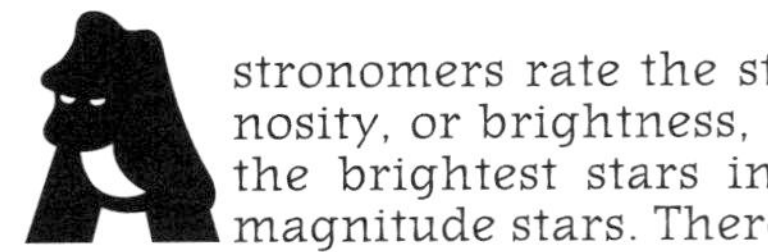

Astronomers rate the stars on a luminosity, or brightness, scale. They call the brightest stars in the sky first-magnitude stars. There are only 20 of those. The next-brightest stars are second-magnitude stars. Then come third-magnitude stars, and so on, to sixth-magnitude stars, the faintest ones that we can see with the unaided eye. From that point on, we can observe the stars only through a telescope, but the scale continues through the twentieth magnitude and beyond.

Early astronomers used crude instruments to measure the sky and to plot the stars. They counted exactly 5,119 stars—the number that we could see by the naked eye, the first-magnitude through sixth-magnitude stars.

In 1610, with the help of a crude telescope, Galileo discovered thousands of stars never before seen. From that day to this, newly discovered stars have increased the number from 5,119 to billions.

Astronomers estimate that our own galaxy—the Milky Way—has some 100 billion suns, or stars. Photographs of the night sky, taken from the largest telescopes, show at least 500 million other galaxies. Some estimates place the number at twice that—1 billion galaxies! Now, let's suppose that each galaxy has no more stars than our own has. That would mean that there are at least 100 billion billion stars. At this point it is safe to say that no matter how advanced our telescopic instruments may become, we will never be able to number the host of heaven.

If you are wondering how the number 100 billion billion is written, get a sheet of paper and put down a 1 with 20 zeros after it. The official name for that number is 100 quintillion. That's a lot of stars, and it's only a conservative estimate of what is out there.

Jeremiah, writing at the same time in history and without human instruments but with the aid of heavenly vision, declared that the "host of heaven cannot be numbered." What if every one of those stars has a planet or two, or five or nine, or more, to explore? Do you suppose there will be enough places to visit and things to do for eternity?

A WORD FROM OUR CREATOR

As the host of heaven cannot be numbered, neither the sand of the sea measured: so will I multiply the seed of David my servant, and the Levites that minister unto me. Jeremiah 33:22.

JANUARY 12

Pelorus Jack

It is sometimes nearly impossible to make some of life's decisions without the guidance of experience, and at times only the Holy Spirit knows the way we should go.

Pelorus Jack was a dolphin—a Risso's dolphin, to be exact. He was perhaps the world's most well-known dolphin other than Flipper, of television fame. However, Flipper was a created character portrayed by many trained dolphins, while Pelorus Jack was a "wild" dolphin that lived in New Zealand.

In 1888 Pelorus Jack began his life's work as a pilot. No one trained Pelorus Jack, yet somehow he knew that he could guide ships through the swirling waters of the treacherous 6-mile-long channel between the two islands that make up New Zealand. For 24 years Pelorus Jack led steamships through that channel. So great was Jack's fame that Mark Twain and Rudyard Kipling, two renowned writers, traveled to New Zealand just to be on a ship going through that channel. They wanted to see the dolphin and to join in the shout "Here comes Pelorus Jack!"

To perform his task, Pelorus Jack would wait at the mouth of the channel until a ship approached. Then he would carefully swim ahead of the ship, leading it this way and that on a safe course. When he had guided the ship safely through the passageway, Jack returned to the mouth of the channel to await the next one.

In 1904 the New Zealand government passed a law protecting Pelorus Jack. The fine for harming the dolphin was set at £100. But in 1912 Pelorus Jack disappeared. No one knows what happened to him.

Pelorus Jack never once asked for wages, went on strike, or was late for work. He was completely dependable for 24 years. What an incredibly dedicated helper he was! The only other pilot as dependable as Pelorus Jack is the one whom Jesus made available to guide us through the treacherous waters of life: the Holy Spirit. He has been on the job for much longer than 24 years and will continue to guide us forever. You can depend on Him.

A WORD FROM OUR CREATOR

Howbeit when he, the Spirit of truth, is come, he will guide you into all truth. John 16:13.

January 13

The Deer's Choice

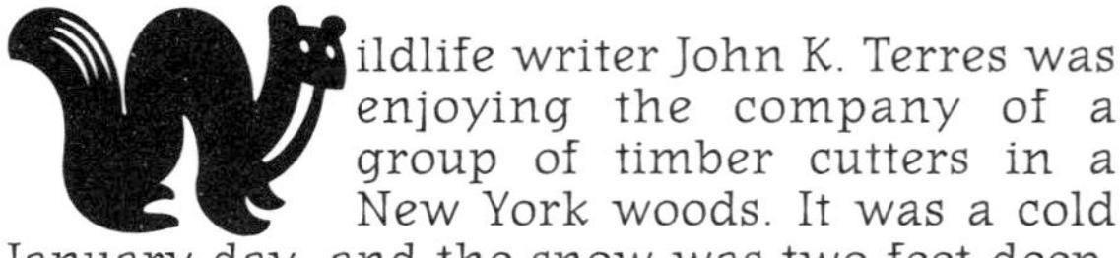

Wildlife writer John K. Terres was enjoying the company of a group of timber cutters in a New York woods. It was a cold January day, and the snow was two feet deep, with drifts reaching six feet. Having stopped for lunch, the men were standing in a loose circle around an open fire, eating and talking.

One of the men suddenly called for silence. From the distant but unmistakable sound of baying, the men guessed that hounds were after a deer. In deep snow dogs can wear a deer down and kill it with relative ease. The hounds seemed to be coming in their direction, and the men, most of whom were also hunters, instinctively reached for the ends of large sticks that they had placed into the open fire. They waited silently as the fire crackled.

A doe burst from the evergreens into the clearing. She was breathing heavily and bleating pitifully. The dogs came right behind her. In the natural order of the forest there seemed little hope for the doe. The deer struggled with each bound through the deep snow. She looked up, and for the first time seemed to realize the presence of the men and the fire. With no time to lose, she made what appeared to be an instinctive decision to act in a way that defies ordinary reasoning. Lunging toward the men, she slipped between two of them, and stopped by the fire within the circle. She was willing to throw herself on the mercy of men before she would trust herself to the mercy of the dogs. It was the right choice.

The men used their sticks to beat away the dogs, sending them howling back into the forest. The doe waited a moment by the fire, catching her breath. Then she moved slowly and deliberately back into the woods. John Terres refers to the doe's behavior as "perhaps a wild terror-ridden reasoning." What do you think?

A real enemy stalks each of us, "seeking whom he may devour" (1 Peter 5:8). And we cannot rely on our own strength, either to outrun him or to outsmart him. Our only hope is to move close to the Son of God, who will do battle in our behalf with that old dog, the devil.

A Word From Our Creator

Come unto me, all ye that labour and are heavy laden, and I will give you rest.
Matthew 11:28.

God's Other Book

Have you ever wondered how people who have not yet heard about Jesus can know Him? Is it fair to hold people accountable for their sins if no one has ever preached the gospel to them?

We find the answers to those questions in today's text. Creation is Jesus' original testament of Himself. For the past 3,500 years we have had the Word of God as expressed in the book that we call the Bible—first in the Old Testament, then also in the New Testament. But the book of nature is the oldest testament of all. It took God six days to write that book, and He dedicated the seventh day to its study.

This is not to say that we should not be taking the story of Jesus to the world, for He gave that great gospel commission to us Himself. But a God of love has made certain that everyone can know Him. The apostle Paul said the same thing in a different way to the Lycaonians in the city of Lystra: "Turn from these vanities unto the living God, which made heaven, and earth, and the sea, and all things that are therein. . . . He left not himself without witness, in that he did good, and gave us rain from heaven, and fruitful seasons, filling our hearts with food and gladness" (Acts 14:15-17).

However, when sin entered the world, another author—the devil—began to scribble on the pages of nature. He added all sorts of messages to confuse and frighten humanity, messages that included false theories about who God is, where we came from, and what we have to do to live forever. The gospel is the good news because it truthfully and simply answers all those questions.

And the gospel is really another Creation story. In Eden Jesus walked with Adam and Eve and taught them directly of His character as revealed in the world around them. Today Jesus walks with us through His Holy Spirit. And through us He tells the world about the new creation story—the fact that Jesus, the original Creator, died to save each of us from the natural result of sin. Jesus says, "Behold, I make all things new" (Revelation 21:5). That includes us.

A Word From Our Creator

For the invisible things of him from the creation of the world are clearly seen, being understood by the things that are made, . . . so that they are without excuse. Romans 1:20.

JANUARY 15

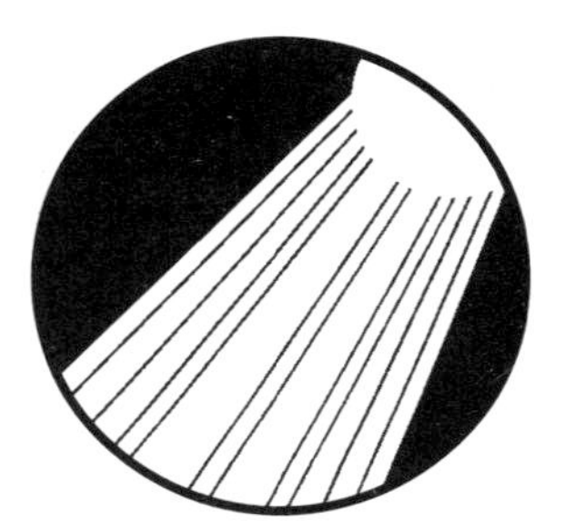

Light Is Atomic Energy

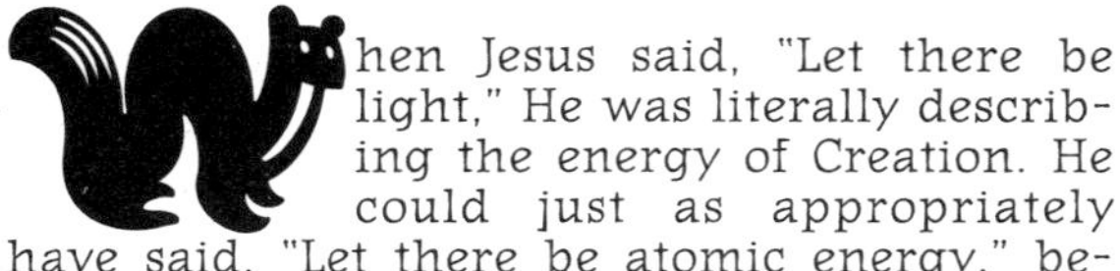

When Jesus said, "Let there be light," He was literally describing the energy of Creation. He could just as appropriately have said, "Let there be atomic energy," because that's what light is.

All forms of matter consist of atoms, and energy holds the atoms together—energy so powerful that even when only a little gets released, we have atomic explosions. Atomic power can be a destructive force, as in an atomic bomb, or a productive force, as in the generation of electricity. Under normal conditions the power of the atom does not escape with the force of a bomb or an atomic power plant. But we are almost constantly experiencing atomic power in the form of light energy.

Different kinds of atoms have different levels of energy. When an atom absorbs energy from an outside source, such as from heat, its energy level increases. As the absorbed energy is used up, the atom's activity level may drop back to normal. In the process it may release a small bundle of energy. You see that small bundle as light. Light occurs when the atom is losing energy. The process of gaining and losing energy happens so rapidly that we see it as a continuous flow of light, but light actually consists of pulses or waves of energy.

Different colors come from the different energy levels of atomic activity. Higher levels of atomic activity produce what we might call blue photons—short wavelengths. Lower levels of atomic activity create photons that have long wavelengths and appear to us as red light. When we heat a piece of iron to its highest temperature, you see it as white because it is emitting photons of all of the visible wavelengths, or colors. When you withdraw an energy source—heat, in this case—the iron begins to cool. As it does, you first see orange and then red wavelength photons as the atoms give off less and less energy.

So when Jesus said, "Let there be light," He was quite literally calling on the force of His own creative energy as the all-powerful God of the universe—the Light of the world. With a power like that to protect us, how can we ever be afraid?

A Word From Our Creator

The Lord is my light and my salvation; whom shall I fear? the Lord is the strength of my life; of whom shall I be afraid? Psalm 27:1.

Water: The Gift of God

Water is so important that God dedicated an entire day to its creation. We can't live without it. It is the universal solvent for keeping us clean, inside and out, and for supplying us nourishment. Not only is it impossible for us to live without water; it's as though God built our whole being out of the substance that He provided so abundantly.

Water has an unusual electrical characteristic that sets it apart from most other liquids. As you know, water's molecular makeup is H_2O, two hydrogen atoms connected to one oxygen atom. Because of this arrangement, every water molecule has a slight positive charge on one side and a slight negative charge on the other side, a feature that allows water molecules to hook up very easily with other nearby molecules.

Water dissolves and washes away dirt. It transports food to every cell of our bodies and then carries away the waste products of our body factories. Also water helps take oxygen as well as disease-fighting mechanisms to wherever our bodies need them. Besides lubricating our joints, it keeps our skin from drying out and shriveling up. In many ways water is our most essential nutrient.

We need at least six glasses of water a day, whether or not we feel thirsty. Thirst is not a good indicator of our need for water, however. It's a signal that often turns off before we've had enough to drink.

Just as we depend on water, we also depend on God, and many times Scripture uses water to illustrate our dependence on the Lord. God knew that we would understand the importance of water in our physical well-being, so He used that need to remind us of the importance of our spiritual dependence upon Him. The fact that we don't feel spiritually thirsty doesn't mean that we've had enough of the water that Jesus promises to provide in abundance. We need to drink deeply and daily of God's gift. So don't forget your water today—both physical and spiritual.

A Word From Our Creator

Jesus answered and said unto her, . . . thou wouldest have asked of him, and he would have given thee living water. John 4:10.

he Bible often uses trees as symbols of people. Sometimes they represent individuals, as in our text for today, and sometimes they stand for whole nations of people, as in the story of Nebuchadnezzer's mental illness (Daniel 4). The apostle Paul talks about the Christian church as being a holy tree (Romans 11). When we accept Jesus as our Saviour, we become branches on that holy tree.

In studying the old-growth forests of the northwestern United States, Oregon State University researchers have discovered one of the most amazing facts of nature, a fact that demonstrates one of the characteristics of being a member of the church that Jesus established.

The trees of the forest share nutrients with one another through their roots. A tree sends its roots far and wide through the soil on its never-ending search for more nourishment. Where the conditions are right, as they are in the old-growth forests, the roots of one tree encounter those of another. And here is where the miracle takes place. Growing in profusion in the lush soil of the virgin forest is a kind of fungus called *Mycorrhiza* (pronounced my-cor-RYE-za). The filaments of the Mycorrhiza fungi latch on to the roots of the living trees. The same fungus plant may have filaments attached to the roots of two or more trees.

Throughout the forest the Mycorrhiza fungi connect trees through their roots. These fungi form channels from one tree to another, passing nutrients through the forest from trees that receive more light to trees that receive less, and from trees growing where the soil is rich in certain essential nutrients to the trees growing where the soil can't provide those nutrients. By linking together the forest through the roots of the trees, the Mycorrhiza enables the entire forest to be a single unit, with every tree contributing as it can, and with every tree getting provided with sufficient food to meet its needs.

As members of God's church on earth, we share freely with one another from what God has given us. We pass on to each other the spiritual light that God gives us and the spiritual nourishment that we obtain from His Word.

Sharing Trees

A WORD FROM OUR CREATOR

And he shall be like a tree planted by the rivers of water, that bringeth forth his fruit in his season. Psalm 1:3.

Space Beings

What does the Bible say about the inhabitants of other worlds? It makes only a few references, but they clearly indicate the presence of extraterrestrial beings elsewhere in the universe. Today's text is the most direct reference to other beings in space. Paul also speaks of a "family in heaven and earth" (Ephesians 3:15). In the same letter he says that Jesus will restore unity to all things, "both which are in heaven, and which are on earth" (Ephesians 1:10). The Greek word translated "heaven" here is more accurately translated "the heavens." The only unity that Jesus came to restore was that of the family of God that humanity destroyed by sinning.

Do scientists believe that other worlds have inhabitants? Yes. A Harvard professor estimated that about 10 percent of all the stars are equivalent to our own sun and could therefore radiate the right amount of energy necessary to sustain life on planets like ours. Another scientist proposed that there are at least 10 million planets like Earth. To detect life in space, scientists have set up large radio telescopes to collect possible radio messages from intelligent life on other worlds.

The clearest evidence to me from the Bible about beings on other planets comes from an account in the book of Job that describes an extraterrestrial council. It says that "the sons of God came to present themselves before the Lord" (Job 1:6). Notice that they *came* from somewhere. Who were these sons of God? Luke writes that Adam was a son of God (Luke 3:38), so apparently "son of God" was a title given to the being in charge of a particular world. Later the book of Job tells us that at Creation "all the sons of God shouted for joy" (Job 38:7). After Adam sinned, Satan took upon himself the title of son of God and went to the council as the being in charge of our world. But when Jesus overcame Satan on the cross, He also redeemed the title of leadership on earth, and He is now the legitimate Son of God.

The most thrilling part of this story is that Jesus now includes us in that title: "But as many as received him, to them gave he power to become the sons of God" (John 1:12).

A Word From Our Creator

Therefore rejoice, ye heavens, and ye that dwell in them. Revelation 12:12.

January 19

Wavering Red Crabs

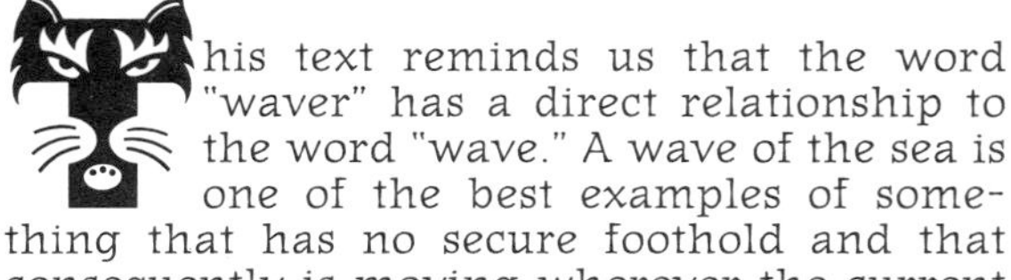

This text reminds us that the word "waver" has a direct relationship to the word "wave." A wave of the sea is one of the best examples of something that has no secure foothold and that consequently is moving wherever the current or wind flows.

One winter day the waters along the California coastline turned bright red as hundreds of thousands of tiny red crabs washed ashore. The crabs, only about two inches long, looked much like their hermit crab relatives.

The little red crabs usually live along the warm Mexican shoreline. Almost weightless, the helpless crustaceans are unable to break free of ocean currents that often carry large numbers of them away from their natural habitat. It is not uncommon to see large rafts of the little creatures far out at sea. But on this occasion the crabs got caught in an ocean current that took them northward from Mexico to the beaches of California. Once they reached California, strong ocean waves tossed the little crabs ashore.

There was no way to save the crabs. Throwing them back into the ocean did no good because the waves just dumped them back on the sand. So, seabirds, fish, and other coastal creatures feasted on the crabs, and people collected the crabs to cook and eat. The sea otters along the California coast were particularly delighted with having something easy to catch—and plenty of it.

For a week the crabs colored the ocean and covered the beaches. Then the ocean current returned to normal and no longer carried the little red crustaceans to the beaches of California. Scientists aren't sure what caused the unusual ocean current that "turned the ocean red," but they say that the phenomenon will probably happen again—although they can't predict when.

For a red crab, life is unpredictable. Its fate is at the mercy of the waves and the winds. You probably have heard the expression "Go with the flow." This little crustacean is a perfect example of what happens to people who allow themselves to be pushed along with the crowds whichever way the wind blows. But your faith can give you a strong foothold.

A Word From Our Creator

But let him ask in faith, nothing wavering. For he that wavereth is like a wave of the sea driven with the wind and tossed. James 1:6.

January 20

Bo to the Rescue

A major dog-food company conducts an annual contest to find the canine hero of the year. The stories of the nominees go to company headquarters, where judges review them and select the one example of heroism that they believe stands out above all the others. In 1982, the twenty-ninth year of the award, the honor went to a dog named Bo.

In the spring of 1982 Rob and Laurie Roberts and their Labrador retriever, Bo, were riding the rapids of the Colorado River when suddenly an eight-foot wave flipped the raft. The wave threw Rob downstream, free of the craft, but Laurie and Bo were trapped underneath it. Because Rob could not swim upstream against the current to rescue them, he could only watch helplessly as the raft bobbed along upside down with Laurie and the dog beneath it.

Bo's head bobbed up from under the raft, but only for an instant. In amazement, Rob watched as the dog dived back under the capsized raft. The next time Bo appeared, he was towing Laurie by her hair. After getting out from under the raft, Laurie grabbed Bo's tail, and he pulled her to shore across the incredibly strong current of the raging river.

Who can say what guided the actions of that courageous dog on that fateful day? Without Bo's efforts, Laurie would have drowned. Surely there is within the natural heart of creation a sense of the saving love of the Creator.

We are all aboard a flimsy craft on the raging rapids of time. But all is well, for on board with each of us is the Saviour, who, whenever wind and waves have threatened, has saved us helpless voyagers. "And he arose, and rebuked the wind, and said unto the sea, Peace, be still. And the wind ceased, and there was a great calm" (Mark 4:39).

A Word From Our Creator

God is our refuge and strength, a very present help in trouble. Therefore will not we fear, though the earth be removed. Psalm 46:1-3.

oday's text is God's very first promise of a Saviour for the human race. Adam and Eve had just experienced deception and defeat by Satan, who had come to them in the form of the serpent. God addressed the statement to that serpent, but only as it represents Satan. The symbol of a woman represents God's people on earth.

No one can question the superiority of a Great Horned Owl over a snake. As it flies on silent wings, the owl hears so well that even on a dark night it can follow the slightest sound directly to its prey. The owl then uses its razor-sharp claws to capture and kill its victim in one lethal motion. But even a bird as powerful as an owl can make a critical mistake.

A man in New England observed a Great Horned Owl that had captured a black snake. The owl's claws had not punctured any of the snake's vital organs, and the owl could not get to the snake's head before the snake's defensive reflex sprung into action. The snake wrapped itself around the owl so tightly that it left the bird helpless. The two creatures were locked in a death struggle. The owl—not the serpent—would have died if the man had not intervened. He killed the snake and set the owl free. But the struggle had weakened the owl, and it could not fly until it had rested to regain its strength.

The struggle between the owl and the snake is very much like our own struggle with Satan. If we think that we have the power to overcome the devil's wiles, we are as deceived as were Adam and Eve. We are locked in mortal combat with sin, facing certain death. But even though the serpent may have weakened us, God has said in today's text that He will take charge and conquer the serpent for us. In fact, He did just that on the cross, thus fulfilling His promise to Adam and Eve in the Garden of Eden.

Owl Versus Snake

A Word From Our Creator

And I will put enmity between thee and the woman, and between thy seed and her seed; it shall bruise thy head, and thou shalt bruise his heel.
Genesis 3:15.

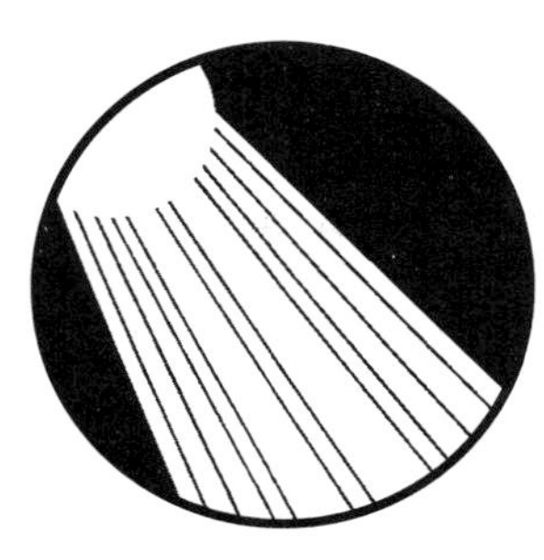

What Color Is a Polar Bear?

Answer this question: What color is a polar bear? Now, we didn't ask you what color the polar bear *appears* to be. Everybody knows—and every picture of a polar bear clearly shows—that the bear seems to be white except for its dark eyes, dark nose, and dark foot pads and claws. But this question is different. Regardless of what color the polar bear appears to be, what color is it really?

If you think that the polar bear is black, you're correct. Every polar bear is black from the tip of its nose to the tip of its very short tail. Now, how can something black look so white? There is a logical explanation. While the polar bear *appears* to be white, its skin is black. And polar bear hairs are hollow transparent tubes, so the fur has no white color at all!

Its fur is actually part of a complex and efficient system that enables the animal to survive the intense cold of its arctic home. The Creator has provided this bear with a combination parka and wetsuit to keep it warm in cold wind as well as in cold water. Starting from the outside is a thick mat of long, hollow, and colorless hairs that capture sunlight and channel it to the black skin that absorbs the heat. Dark clothing is warmer than white clothing for the same reason. Some of the sunlight bounces off the polar bear's hairs, and the reflection makes the bear look white. But most of the light rays pass *through* the hollow tubes and get absorbed by the bear's black skin.

Under the black skin is a thick layer of blubber that serves the same function as a wetsuit on a diver. The blubber may be as much as four inches thick in spots. It protects the bear's vital organs from the cold of the Arctic Ocean so thoroughly that the animal can swim in frigid water for hours at a time.

In our text God challenges Job to explain how he gets warmer when the cold north wind ceases and the south wind blows. We could ask a similar question about the polar bear. How would you provide the polar bear with the ability to survive the harshest of conditions? To start with, you'd have to use a solar-heating system in which light would be the primary source of heat. Where would you go from there?

A Word From Our Creator

Dost thou know . . . how thy garments are warm, when he quieteth the earth by the south wind? Job 37:16, 17.

ave you ever wondered about this text? Salt tastes salty, and it cannot taste anything but salty. So how can it lose its savor, or salty flavor?

When Jesus walked the countryside in Palestine, people collected salt from the marshes surrounding the Dead Sea and the Mediterranean Sea. As the salt-filled water of these bodies of water evaporated, a residue of salt collected on the marsh plants. The people gathered the crust and took it home to use on their food.

The salt had many impurities mixed with it. And here is where we find the answer to what Jesus meant in the text above. As long as you had plenty of salt, you wouldn't notice the impurities. But when you left salt in an open container, it absorbed the moisture in the air, ruining its flavor as it became a sticky mess.

The people of Jesus' time kept their containers of salt out in the air for a long time. Naturally the salt picked up moisture. Because many of the impurities were also white, there was no way to tell by looking at it whether the salt would still have a taste or not. There were no chemists to separate the real salt from the white impurities, so people assumed that after a while the salt lost its taste. And when that happened, they threw the remaining "salt" (actually the impurities) out onto the footpaths.

So Jesus meant exactly what He said in our text. People who look like Christians by all outward appearances may only be a collection of impurities. Jesus gives us the essence that makes us the salt of the earth. By staying close to Him, we won't lose that savor.

JANUARY 23

The Salt of the Earth

A WORD FROM OUR CREATOR

Ye are the salt of the earth: but if the salt have lost his savour, wherewith shall it be salted? it is thenceforth good for nothing. Matthew 5:13.

January 24

David Douglas and His Tree

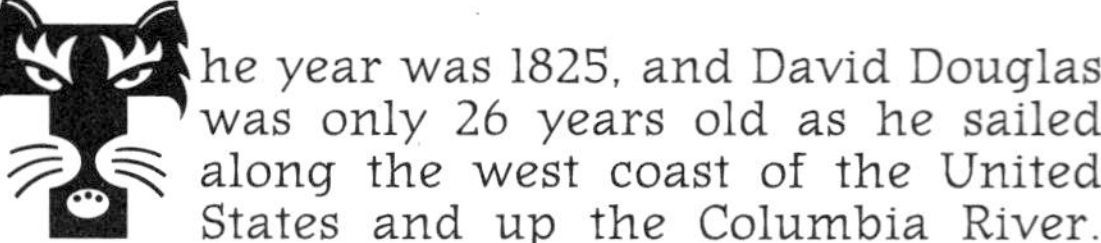

The year was 1825, and David Douglas was only 26 years old as he sailed along the west coast of the United States and up the Columbia River. The young botanist from London was on a quest. Since the age of 11 he had been obsessed with plants, and at the age of 21 he was appointed to the Royal Botanical Gardens in Scotland. Now, five years later, he was to examine the plant life of the New World.

As the ship approached land, one particular tree captivated David. As he reported later, "so pleased was I that I could scarcely see anything but it." He couldn't wait to see the tree up close, and when he did, he pronounced it "one of the most striking and truly graceful objects in nature." It was only fitting that the tree would later bear his name, as it does to this day—the Douglas fir.

David spent the next two years exploring the Northwest, finding new plants and shipping them back to England. His first shipment included 500 species, proving the words of William Hooker, one of the world's leading botanists, who described him as a man of "great activity, undaunted courage, singular abstemiousness, and energetic zeal." The Native Americans were immensely impressed with David's endurance, but they questioned his sanity. In fact, they called him "Man of Grass" because he would hike from first light to dark collecting plants that he couldn't eat.

On his 1829 trip to North America David made a discovery that eventually rocked the New World. While collecting plants in California, he pulled a plant from soil that contained gold. In fact, the sample had so much gold that flecks clung to the roots as he packed the plant for shipment. But David saw only the plant. That's the way that California gold was first discovered in 1831—not by Douglas in California, but by the botanists in London who unpacked the shipment of plants.

David Douglas had only one purpose in life. Nothing—not even gold—could distract him from his mission. And this mission was well established by the time he was 11 years of age. That is the sort of energetic zeal that God wants from youth today.

A Word From Our Creator

But this one thing I do, forgetting those things which are behind, and reaching forth unto those things which are before, I press toward the mark. Philippians 3:13, 14.

Scientists using radio telescopes are beginning to "unearth" discoveries that stretch human imagination to its limit—and sometimes beyond. For example, they recently discovered a string of galaxies stretching halfway across the sky. This is the largest "structure" ever found in the universe. Seven hundred million light-years long, it is 10 times larger, from end to end, than any cluster of galaxies previously found.

Furthermore, the newly discovered row of galaxies is a long way from Earth: the distance varies between 100 million and 200 million light-years from our planet. When you consider that one light-year, or the distance that light travels in a year, is about 6 trillion miles, and then multiply that figure by 700 million, you have, in miles, a 4 with 21 zeros after it. If you could travel at the speed of light—or 670 million miles per hour—you would spend 100 to 200 million years getting to the new galaxies. You could then journey for hundreds of millions of years back and forth along the string. And you could visit any of the billions of stars in each galaxy, not to mention the planets that may be circling each of those stars.

If you want an idea of how big this galaxy string looks, get your star map and go outside on a clear night. This huge celestial structure extends from Pegasus to the Big Dipper. The astronomers who discovered the string suspect that it may be much longer than it appears, perhaps stretching "all the way around the sky."

Just think, the mighty Creator of all those faraway stars loves you and me! That fact is even more difficult to understand sometimes than are the vast distances in space. Perhaps that's why so many people on this planet find it difficult to believe that Jesus is real. "But without faith it is impossible to please him: for he that cometh to God must believe that he is, and that he is a rewarder of them that diligently seek him" (Hebrews 11:6). "Lord, I believe; help thou mine unbelief" (Mark 9:24).

Galaxy String

A WORD FROM OUR CREATOR

When I consider thy heavens, . . . the moon and the stars, which thou hast ordained; what is man, that thou art mindful of him? and the son of man, that thou visitest him? Psalm 8:3, 4.

January 26

A Soaked Crow

You remember the story of the good Samaritan. The Samaritan was a social outcast, but that fact didn't stop him from providing loving service to someone in need. A story about a flock of crows illustrates the same type of service.

Other birds and human beings don't think much of crows because crows rob birds' nests of eggs and young, and they devour farmers' seeds and crops. As a result, crows are among the most hated of all birds.

The idea of a crow caring for an injured comrade is hard to imagine, yet F. B. Currier recorded an event that defies any other explanation. In the early 1900s Currier was watching crows in Massachusetts when one of the birds fell into the Merrimack River. The dunked denizen of field and forest immediately began to call out in distress.

Nearby crows quickly went to the aid of the fallen member of their flock. One of the crows flew down, used its claws to grab the half-submerged bird, and proceeded to drag it toward shore. When the first crow tired, another took over. And when that one tired, another took its place. The birds didn't give up until they got the soaked crow to the water's edge. Once there, the unfortunate crow crawled out of the water and spread its wings in the sun to dry them. Meanwhile, the attending crows stood by patiently until the wet bird had dried and preened its feathers. Then they all flew off together.

We may not consider crows to be the most honorable of birds, but we can certainly learn from their example in this case. It is not safe to judge others by their reputations. God's love sometimes is illustrated in the most unlikely places. As we consider the apparent concern of the crows in this story, we can remember these words: "Then Jesus said unto him, Go, and do thou likewise."

A Word From Our Creator

Which now of these three, thinkest thou, was neighbour unto him that fell among the thieves? And he said, He that shewed mercy on him. Luke 10:36, 37.

easuring six feet long and weighing 1,500 pounds, the leatherback turtle is one of the world's largest living reptiles. So it's not surprising that this enormous sea turtle has no natural enemies except the occasional hungry killer whale or shark.

What is amazing is that naturalists have classified the leatherback turtle as an endangered species. Only about 135,000 of them remain in the world—not a large number for an animal that has thousands of square miles of ocean in which to live, has plenty of food to eat, has few enemies, and lays hundreds of eggs each and every year.

The leatherback's upper shell is leathery and its under shell is soft. Its body shape is flattened compared to that of land turtles. Every year this streamlined sea turtle swims thousands of miles from its winter range in the North Atlantic to its summer nesting area along the Caribbean coastlines, and back again. Finding food is not a problem. The leatherback's diet consists mainly of large jellyfish, abundant in the turtle's range, so the creature has little competition for food.

The female leatherback must come ashore to lay her eggs in the sand. Then she returns to the sea. Two months later, three-inch babies hatch from the eggs and head for the water, but only one in a thousand newborn turtles grows up to be an adult leatherback. Although some of the hatchlings become prey for ocean creatures, the real danger is that human beings take most of the eggs from the nests and use them as food. Fortunately, recent programs designed to protect the eggs are helping to assure the survival of the leatherback turtle.

As she lays her eggs, the leatherback turtle cries real tears that, according to biologists, wash the beach sand from her eyes. But perhaps we could suggest that if Mrs. Leatherback knew what was to become of most of her babies—that human greed threatened her breed—she would have another reason for those tears. God's creatures work hard to survive in the way that He provides for them, and we humans are so quick to destroy the Creator's work. In the earth made new, things will be different.

The Leatherback Turtle

A Word From Our Creator

And God shall wipe away all tears from their eyes; and there shall be no more death, neither sorrow, nor crying, . . . for the former things are passed away. Revelation 21:4.

JANUARY 28

The Needle Always Obeys

Did you know that a sewing needle is more obedient than you or I can be? To prove this point, all you have to do is place a needle carefully on top of some water in a shallow pan or dish so that it floats. That floating needle will turn gently until it stops. When it does, the needle will *always* be pointing toward magnetic north! That's the rule, and the needle never disobeys it.

Airplane pilots and ship captains depend on the needle to keep the rule to tell them which way to go. If the needle disobeyed, they and their passengers might end up in all sorts of places they hadn't planned to be. They can depend on the needle to follow the rule and bring them safely to their destination.

Why don't you test the needle rule? Take a dish and put enough water into it so that it is at least a quarter-inch deep. Get a needle. Most needles are made of steel, which contains iron, and are slightly magnetic. Hold the needle lengthwise between your thumb and finger, as close to horizontal as possible, and place it carefully onto the water's surface. If the needle isn't exactly horizontal when you set it on the water, it will sink to the bottom, and you will have to take it out and start over. You may have to try several times, but eventually you will get the needle to float and then see it turn toward magnetic north, acting as a compass needle.

Good rules are very important. Wouldn't it be wonderful if people followed such rules as faithfully as the needle does? God's rules are always worth keeping, and when we follow them, those rules become very much like the needle, telling us which way is the right way to go.

Why do you suppose the Creator gave us the ability to choose whether or not we will follow His rules? He could have created us like the needle, which has no choice but to obey His laws. Why didn't He do that?

A WORD FROM OUR CREATOR

Blessed are they whose ways are blameless, who walk according to the law of the Lord. Blessed are they who keep his statutes and seek him with all their heart. Psalm 119:1, 2, NIV.

any years ago a boy lived in a large city. Very poor and with no family, he lived on the street. One of his favorite places was a huge cathedral with its beautiful stained-glass windows, each depicting a different saint from the tradition of the church.

The cathedral was always open as a place for people to come and pray. The boy did not even know how to pray, but he loved to slip into the church unnoticed in the middle of the day when lots of people were coming and going. Sitting in an isolated pew, he quietly stared in wonder at the figures depicted in glass. After a while he memorized every window so that he could picture every detail as he went to sleep at night in an alley. He could recall the figures of Matthew, Luke, Mark, John, Andrew, Peter, Paul—all of them. And he could have described all the details in each beautiful stained-glass window.

The leader of the church had noticed the ragged boy quietly sitting there, and his heart went out to him. He didn't know exactly what to say to him, but he decided to ask him a question about the pictures in the windows.

"Son," he said, "do you know what a saint is?"

The boy jumped at the sound of a voice speaking to him. He wasn't prepared for the question, but he had to answer something, and before he even knew what he was saying he blurted out, "Someone the light shines through, sir."

He was right. According to the Bible, a saint is anyone who has accepted Jesus as a personal Saviour. The apostle Paul (or Saint Paul, if you prefer) writes that he was going to "Jerusalem to minister unto the saints" (Romans 15:25). In the next verse he tells about an offering being taken up for "the poor saints which are at Jerusalem" (verse 26). The Bible calls all the followers of Jesus saints.

Jesus is the Light of the world, and if His light shines through us, then we, along with the faithful at Rome, are "called to be saints" (Romans 1:7). As the boy said, a saint is someone whom the Light shines through. Are you a saint?

A Light Shines Through It

A WORD FROM OUR CREATOR

But he that doeth truth cometh to the light, that his deeds may be made manifest, that they are wrought in God. John 3:21.

January 30

Water in the Sky

Through an amazing process provided by the Creator on the second day of Creation and revised at the time of the Flood, the waters above the earth are like canteens of water that float through the sky. Clouds are masses of droplets of water so tiny that it takes a microscope to see them. They are so light in weight that they float in the air. Even with all the water droplets, a cloud is still more than 99 percent pure air. It takes a million or more of these droplets to make a raindrop.

In the temperate zones raindrops start as ice crystals. It is many degrees below zero where raindrops form. A raindrop won't form until it has a tiny speck of something—usually dust—around which the water in the tiny droplets can gather to form an ice crystal. In a process hard to imagine, the freezing water droplets release heat into the air. Since warm air rises, the air around the developing ice crystals becomes warmer and also begins to rise, taking the tiny bits of ice along with it. As the crystals move upward, they bump into other tiny droplets that join the growing ice crystals.

The masses of frozen droplets become larger and heavier. Eventually the air cannot hold them up any longer, and they begin to fall. By the time the clumps of ice crystals reach the ground, however, they have melted into raindrops. Once in a while, in storm clouds called thunderheads, the hot summer air is already rising and the frozen water continues to rise until it grows into hailstones that are so large that they don't melt before they reach the ground.

Through a process called "cloud seeding," pilots drop tiny yellow crystals of a chemical called silver iodide into certain kinds of clouds. The crystals of this chemical are constructed very much like water crystals, or ice. When the yellow-colored crystals drop into the clouds, the tiny water droplets begin to attach themselves to the silver iodide to form ice crystals, which then makes rain.

Bible writers often used clouds, rain, and even hail to describe God's program on Earth. Can you remember some of the references? Check your concordance under "clouds," "rain," and "hail."

A Word From Our Creator

He bindeth up the waters in his thick clouds; and the cloud is not rent under them. Job 26:8.

 fully leaved fig tree at the time of year that Jesus came upon this one should have had an abundance of fruit. For some reason, however, this particular tree had lots of leaves but no fruit.

The purpose of a fruit tree is to bear fruit, not to have leaves. Certainly the leaves are an important step along the way toward fruit production. In fact, without them the tree would die. For example, the leaves produce food for the plant. The leaves are solar-powered factories that combine water (piped up through the stems from the roots) and carbon dioxide (breathed in from the air) to produce sugar, the basic substance in fruit production. But can you imagine a fruit farmer taking you for a walk in a grove or orchard to show you the leaves? Of course not!

There is a more important point to the story of the fig tree that Jesus cursed. The presence of leaves on a fig tree signals that fruit is present. Fig trees actually use food stored in the roots and stems to begin the production of fruit before the tree has many leaves. The leaves start their work in time to ripen the fruit. Jesus saw a fig tree with lots of leaves, and that tree was saying to the world, "You can tell by my many leaves that I am a fruit-filled fig tree."

Naturally such a tree attracted Jesus and His disciples. They expected to enjoy some delicious figs. But the tree had nothing but leaves. Something was fundamentally wrong with that tree. It could produce great-looking leaves that advertised fruit that it could not really grow.

Have you ever known people who claim to be what they're not? Is it possible to put on the appearance of being a fruit-bearing Christian but have nothing but leaves? Jesus said, "Ye shall know them by their fruits" (Matthew 7:16). If you don't already know what they are, you will find a list of those fruits in Galatians 5:22, 23.

JANUARY 31

Nothing But Leaves

A WORD FROM OUR CREATOR

And when he saw a fig tree in the way, he came to it, and found nothing thereon, but leaves only, and said unto it, Let no fruit grow on thee . . . the fig tree withered away. Matthew 21:19.

February 1

The Sun: An Everyday Hydrogen Bomb!

As stars go, our sun is medium-sized—yet it has a diameter of about 870,000 miles, more than 100 times that of Earth. And it's a close star—only 93 million miles away. The next nearest star is more than 25 quadrillion miles distant—almost 270,000 times as far away as our sun. The sun takes about 250 million years to make one revolution in its orbit around the center of the Milky Way—our galaxy.

A huge ball of gases, the sun consists of about 70 percent hydrogen and about 25 percent helium. Scientists first detected helium on the sun in 1868, before someone found it on Earth in 1895. The name of the gas comes from *helios*, the Greek sun god.

The temperature at the center of the sun is a hot 27,000,000 °F, and when it is that hot, things move around a lot. Thermonuclear reactions constantly take place in the sun's core. Hydrogen atoms crash into each other and combine to form helium atoms. This fusion of atoms releases energy in the form of heat and light. The energy radiates from the center of the sun to the surface, which is a sea of boiling gases about 200 miles thick where the temperature is a much cooler 10,000 °F. From there the sun's energy radiates throughout the universe. We get a tiny bit of it on Earth—just enough to keep our planet at the right temperature for life.

The hydrogen bomb releases its energy in the same way as the center of the sun does. But the most powerful hydrogen bomb would be considered less than the smallest popgun snap compared to the sun's output. Every day the sun converts 100 billion tons of mass into energy.

Certainly you and I are nothing compared to the massive amounts of energy that the Creator sustains and directs throughout the universe. Yet He sees the smallest sparrow fall. David exclaimed, "When I consider thy heavens, the work of thy fingers, the moon and the stars, which thou hast ordained; what is man, that thou art mindful of him?" (Psalm 8:3, 4). And then he sums it up: "O Lord our Lord, how excellent is thy name in all the earth!" (verse 9).

A Word From Our Creator

The Lord is thy keeper: the Lord is thy shade upon thy right hand. The sun shall not smite thee by day, nor the moon by night.
Psalm 121:5, 6.

A New Whale Is Found

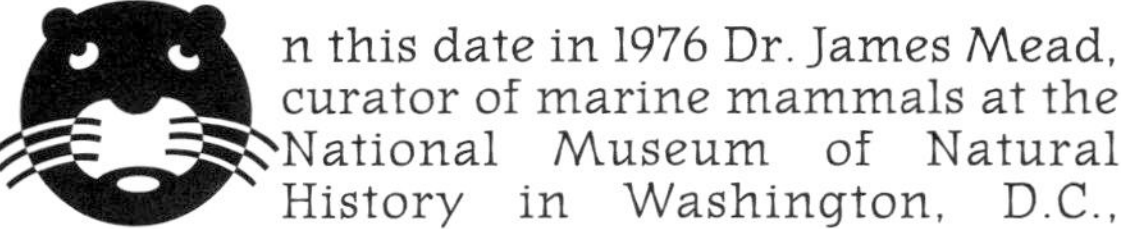

On this date in 1976 Dr. James Mead, curator of marine mammals at the National Museum of Natural History in Washington, D.C., walked along a beach on the coast of Peru. He was hoping to catch sight of some whales. On the beach Dr. Mead found a badly damaged skull of what he took to be a type of beaked whale. However, it was the smallest beaked-whale skull that Dr. Mead had ever seen, and he suspected that the skull belonged to a new species. After his discovery of the skull, Dr. Mead began his quest for additional evidence. It took 15 more years to prove that the creature actually existed.

Dr. Mead gave the new whale the scientific name *Mesoplodon peruvianus*. It doesn't have a common name, and you won't find it illustrated in a field guide to marine mammals. We will call it the Peruvian beaked whale for lack of an official common name.

As their name indicates, beaked whales have long snouts. They look somewhat like dolphins, but are much larger. Because they live far from shore and can spend up to an hour in very deep water, beaked whales are the hardest of all whales to see. In Dr. Mead's words, "If an animal that has those characteristics also doesn't like boats, you don't see it." As of 1991, when scientists accepted the existence of the Peruvian beaked whale, no one had yet seen a living example of the new species. Dr. Mead collected all or portions of 11 additional specimens. They were either caught in fishing nets or washed up on the beach, as did the original skull.

From these specimens Dr. Mead has concluded that the Peruvian beaked whale is indeed the smallest of the beaked whales. The largest specimen found was only 12 feet long—very small by whale standards. No one knows anything about the whale's range except that it occurs off the coast of Peru, although the creature may range both northward and southward along the coast of South America.

God's wonders continue to be discovered everywhere we look—from the tops of the mountains to the depths of the sea.

A Word From Our Creator

They that go down to the sea in ships, that do business in great waters; these see the works of the Lord, and his wonders in the deep. Psalm 107:23, 24.

FEBRUARY 3

Bandi-coots

Bandicoots are small marsupials that live in Australia, Tasmania, and New Guinea. Most of the 20 or so species eat a combination of animal and vegetable food, but some are strictly vegetarian, living on leaves, bulbs, fruit, and seeds. Others consume insects, snails and slugs, lizards, and mice.

At birth a tiny hairless baby bandicoot crawls into its mother's pouch, where it is protected and nursed until it can take care of itself. Unlike the kangaroo's pouch, the bandicoot's pocket opens to the rear so that no dirt can get inside when the mother digs for food.

Over the years the numbers of bandicoots have decreased steadily. People have collected them for their fur and destroyed their habitat. Traps and poison set out to eliminate the rabbits that destroy farm crops have killed still others.

Recently, however, environmentalists and farmers have realized that although bandicoots eat a few bulbs and potatoes, they also eat millions of destructive beetle larvae and other insects. As a result, at least one species of bandicoot has benefited from a well-organized protection program.

Several years ago people found a population of eastern barred bandicoot living in abandoned cars at the Hamilton, Australia, city dump. When the city council decided to clean up the dump area by removing the rusty cars, a man named Peter Brown spearheaded a "Bring Back the Bandicoot" program. Supporters of the program built temporary "hotels" made of concrete pipes to house the bandicoots until more natural homes could be provided. Farmers let bushes and weeds grow along the fencelines, children planted bushes, and scientists began to breed bandicoots in a local park. Drivers were cautioned to watch for bandicoots crossing roads, and people made sure that their cats, which had been killing bandicoots, stayed in at night. Naturalists are now moving eastern barred bandicoots to other good habitat areas in Australia.

Because of sin, we, like the bandicoots, lost our home on Earth. Compared to Eden, living on Earth today is like dwelling in a dump. Jesus became our champion. He has gone to prepare a place for us.

A WORD FROM OUR CREATOR

In my Father's house are many mansions: if it were not so, I would have told you. I go to prepare a place for you. John 14:2.

In this final verse of the book of Hosea, the prophet sums up all his teachings in one statement. It is very easy to assume that because we have always done something in a certain way, we should continue to do it the same way.

One morning at camp I was sitting at the breakfast table with a friend whom I had come to respect for his practical wisdom. As you will soon understand, he was a master teacher.

As part of our breakfast fare we each had a banana. While my friend watched, I unsuspectingly took my banana and started to peel it. The teacher spoke quickly.

"Wait," he said. "Are you sure that you know how to peel that banana?"

"Of course," I replied. "Why?" Seeing the twinkle in his eye and knowing what that usually meant, I had the feeling that I was about to learn something.

"Well," he said, "if you had ever observed a monkey peeling a banana, you'd know that you're doing it upside down. You're trying to open the banana at the stem end, where the peel is strongest. So the chances are good that you'll have trouble breaking the peel to start with. Then when you do, you'll very likely smash the end of the banana in the process of peeling it."

My friend, the master teacher, then proceeded to show me how monkeys peel a banana—just flip it end for end and pinch off the tip opposite to the stem end instead. The peel is weak at that end and easily breaks open.

The next time you peel a banana, try doing it the "new" way. And let each banana that you peel remind you that doing something the same way time after time doesn't make that way the right one. We have a heavenly Master Teacher who is even more eager to give us helpful direction than was my friend at camp.

Peeling a Banana

A WORD FROM OUR CREATOR

Who is wise, and he shall understand these things? . . . for the ways of the Lord are right, and the just shall walk in them.
Hosea 14:9.

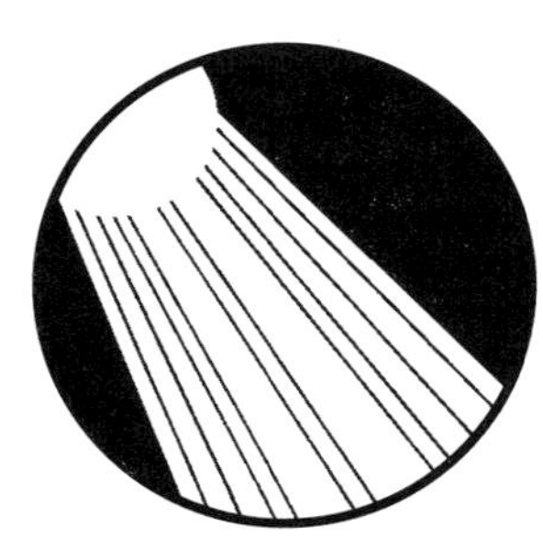

Light in Their Homes

It was the occasion of the ninth plague of Egypt. The Pharaoh and his people had resisted God in spite of blood in their drinking water, frogs in their beds, lice in their hair, flies in their faces, death to all their cattle, boils on their bodies, and locusts that ate up anything green left after hail had shredded their crops. Pharaoh was a difficult man to convince. In the end, even after he had lost his firstborn child, Pharaoh still pursued his wicked course and lost his army in the Red Sea. But on this day darkness covered Egypt.

Just what is darkness? It has no definition other than as a comparison to light. You may define darkness as the absence of light, but you can't turn that statement around to say that light is the absence of darkness. Light has substance. We can define it as something real. Because light is a physical result of the release of energy in the transformation of matter. Darkness, on the other hand, is nothing but nothing.

Light is the most obvious result of God's creative power. That's why when the Creator arrived on the first day of Creation, "*there was light*"! Wherever God is present, light is also present. Because we live on a lighted planet, we take light for granted. So when Pharaoh sat in darkness for three days, God was trying to tell him something.

We don't know how God caused that darkness, but we have a hint. When the Israelites camped by the Red Sea and Pharaoh's army came after them, "the angel of God" that went before Israel in the cloudlike pillar moved between the two camps. Scripture tells us that the cloud was darkness to the Egyptians and light for the Israelites—just as it was in the ninth plague.

Throughout the Bible light reveals the presence of God, while the absence of light indicates that His presence has departed. Pharaoh, the Egyptian king, was too proud to realize what the darkness signified, but it is comforting to remember that during all of that darkness the homes of Israel had light. No matter how dark our world becomes, Jesus, the Light of the world, has promised to provide light. Without Him there is only darkness—nothing but nothing.

A Word From Our Creator

They saw not one another, neither rose any from his place for three days: but all the children of Israel had light in their dwellings. Exodus 10:23.

Earth's Air-cooled Blanket

If you keep going upward into the air, will you get warmer or cooler as you ascend? If you said "cooler," you're right. But if you also said "warmer," you're also correct. How can that be?

Meteorologists divide our atmosphere into four regions: the troposphere, the stratosphere, the mesosphere, and the thermosphere.

The troposphere, which includes most of what we call our weather, extends up to about 10 miles above sea level at the Equator, and it tapers down to only five miles above sea level at the poles. It is the region where airplanes fly. As you climb through the troposphere, the temperature gets cooler until it reaches an average of about -70° F.

The stratosphere extends from the top of the troposphere up to about 30 miles. Weather balloons ascend into its upper reaches. Contrary to what happens in the troposphere, the temperature increases as you go higher into the stratosphere—to about 45° F. We have now left behind most of the water vapor with its cooling effect and can now feel the sun's direct heating power.

The mesosphere rises above the stratosphere for another 20 miles to an altitude of about 50 miles and includes the ozone layer. Ozone is a gas that blocks the sun's dangerous ultraviolet rays from penetrating through the atmosphere. Due in large part to the presence of the ozone, the temperature falls again as you climb through the mesosphere. Here we encounter the coldest part of the atmosphere with the temperature dropping to as low as -120° F.

The thermosphere stretches above the mesosphere for another 50 miles or so until we can detect no atmospheric gases at all. The temperature in the thermosphere starts to go up again, and it continues to climb rapidly to well beyond 2000° F because there's nothing to deflect the searing heat of the sun.

Without our atmosphere the sun would scorch the Earth during the day at a temperature of about 180°F, while at night the temperature would drop to -220° F. Our atmosphere is a marvel of thermonuclear engineering that only a powerful and loving God could have provided.

A Word From Our Creator

Hast thou with him spread out the sky, which is strong, and as a molten looking glass? Job 37:18.

February 7

Clean-Air Machines

We are all aware of the warnings that dangerous chemicals fill our air, water, and soil. Pollutants spew from factory chimneys and automobile exhausts to poison the air. When these chemical toxins settle in the soil, they affect not only the soil itself but also get washed into rivers and streams, converting clean water into liquid poison. Pesticides used to control destructive insects settle in the ground, remain on the food being grown, and kill beneficial insects, birds, and other wildlife.

Indoors we face other substances that threaten our well-being. Industry uses such solvents as trichloroethylene (pronounced TRY-clor-o-ETH-el-een) and chloroform. Benzene appears in the dyes coloring drapes, upholstery, and carpets. And formaldehyde is a component in plastics and insulation. All three chemicals release invisible vapors that cause reactions ranging from allergies to cancer in our bodies.

While industry has started to put into place practices intended to eliminate—over the next several decades—existing and future pollution, nature is already at work doing its part to clean up the mess. As trees and plants take in air they use the carbon dioxide and store the pollutants in their cells. Then they release pure, clean oxygen back into the atmosphere. Each tree and plant is a clean-air machine.

Luckily, we can take advantage of the natural filtering system of plants to clean the air in our homes. Aloe vera, azalea, and philodendron plants absorb formaldehyde from the air. Peace lilies, chrysanthemums, and corn plants capture benzene. And English ivy and dracaena collect trichloroethylene. All of these plants are inexpensive and easy to grow, and it takes only two medium-sized plants for every 100 square feet of floor space to remove the pollutants from a room.

Isn't it exciting to know that even now, before the new earth described in today's text, leaves provide healing?

A Word From Our Creator

In the midst of the street of it, and on either side of the river, was there the tree of life . . . : and the leaves of the tree were for the healing of the nations.
Revelation 22:2.

February 8

Raw Materials of the Solar System

Today's text states that God created something visible out of something invisible. It doesn't say that He created the visible things out of a substance that doesn't exist—it just says that we can't see that substance. This Bible passage presents a fact that's consistent with the most up-to-date understanding of the laws of physics.

Whatever can be seen and can occupy space we call matter. But matter is just organized energy, and matter can convert into energy and back again into matter. Although we have only theories to explain these things, the evidence for this fact is convincing, and the theories are consistent with the statement in today's text. A physical law called the *conservation of matter* explains this: Matter and energy may not be created or destroyed, but each may be converted into the other. That is another way of saying that things that are seen can be made from things that are not seen. Matter is seen—energy is not.

Consider the matter that forms the solar system. Everything in space consists of basic substances called elements, and although more than a hundred different elements exist, only eight of them make up most of the universe.

By far the most common element in the universe is hydrogen. For every million hydrogen atoms we find the following number of atoms from the seven other most common elements: 85,000 helium, 661 oxygen, 331 carbon, 91 nitrogen, 83 neon, 33 silicon, and 26 magnesium. But if you could see into the very essence of these elements—into the atomic structure of the things that can be seen—you would find only energy, no substance.

It stretches the imagination to understand how everything that we see and feel, including the chairs we sit on and the food we eat, is nothing more than organized bits of energy that present themselves as matter for our use. In fact, our physical bodies consist of the same matter which is organized energy.

And it is by faith that we believe that God, as the Creator, is the organizer of energy into the things that we see around us.

A Word From Our Creator

Through faith we understand that the worlds were framed by the word of God, so that things which are seen were not made of things which do appear. Hebrews 11:3.

February 9

Homing Pigeons

Take a horseshoe magnet and hold your finger between the prongs. Do you feel anything? Does the magnet attract your finger? Does it pull it to one side or the other? Probably not, unless you have some iron on or in the finger. Yet, whether you can feel it or not, a magnetic force is being exerted on your finger.

Now imagine putting your finger between the prongs of a magnet hundreds of times weaker than the usual horseshoe magnet. If you didn't feel anything with a stronger magnet, there is no possible way for you to sense anything with a weaker one. But it may surprise you to learn that pigeons, and perhaps other birds, are sensitive to the magnetic field created by the earth—magnetism that is hundreds of times weaker than that of a horseshoe magnet.

Through experiments, ornithologists at Cornell University have established beyond doubt that homing pigeons know exactly where they are on our planet simply by lining up their magnetic sense with the magnetic force of the world. As you know, the world exerts a magnetic force that causes a compass needle to point to magnetic north. Apparently the pigeons can always sense this magnetic field. They have a built-in compass that almost never fails. Birds released near enormous iron-ore deposits, which disrupt the magnetic forcefield in the area, get disoriented.

Although not yet proven as fact, some evidence suggests that homing pigeons have iron-containing tissue in their heads. We could duplicate this characteristic by implanting iron filings under the skin of a finger, then placing it between the prongs of the horseshoe magnet. With iron in our finger we could feel the magnet's pull.

Christians easily feel the pull of Jesus. His Holy Spirit is calling softly to each of us. When our minds and hearts focus on Jesus, we will be as true to Him as the compass needle is to the magnetic pole. We will always know the way home.

A Word From Our Creator

That they should seek the Lord, if haply they might feel after him, and find him, though he be not far from every one of us. Acts 17:27.

February 10

The Leopard's Spots

If leopards could change their spots, a lot more of them would be alive today. Their fur has become so popular that hunters kill many thousands of the lovely cats every year to provide pelts for leopard-skin coats. Even though naturalists have placed the leopard on the endangered species list, illegal hunting and trading go on, and the animal's numbers continue to drop at an alarming rate.

Found throughout most of Africa as well as in all of the forested lands westward to Korea, Japan, Ceylon, and Java, the leopard is the most widespread species of the world's wild cats. While usually dwelling in wooded areas, leopards also live in grasslands and scrublands, where they capture their prey on the run and then typically drag it up into a tree for safekeeping. They are long and low, averaging a little more than two feet high at the shoulder and seven and a half feet long. Leopards are incredibly strong. While the largest males weigh no more than about 160 pounds, people have found carcasses of their prey weighing up to 150 pounds in trees 12 or more feet above the ground.

Rudyard Kipling recounts the legend of how the leopard got its spots. In the story, a friend wanted to help the leopard blend into the countryside where it lived, so the friend touched the leopard's fur with his fingers. Wherever the five fingers touched the fur, rosettes of five black spots remained.

Although Kipling's story is a fable, perhaps there is some truth to it. The Creator of all things is the leopard's friend. He certainly colored the leopard to blend in with its surroundings. But now those beautiful spots have become its downfall. If only the leopard could change those spots—get rid of them—he would be safe to roam freely again. But the leopard can't change its spots. Only the Creator can do that.

What about us? If we could change our ways without help, wouldn't we do so? As human beings on planet Earth, we are certainly endangered. The same Creator who gave the leopard its spots and can change them can also transform us. Jesus is the only way to survive.

A Word From Our Creator

Can the Ethiopian change his skin, or the leopard his spots? then may ye also do good, that are accustomed to do evil. Jeremiah 13:23.

A Hug a Day Keeps the Doctor Away

You go to the medical office for your annual checkup. After examining you, the doctor takes out a pad and writes a prescription that says, "One hug four times a day—breakfast, lunch, dinner, and bedtime." Would you take the prescription seriously? Dr. David Bresler, director of the Pain Control Unit at the UCLA Medical Center in Los Angeles, sometimes writes just such a prescription. And he has evidence that this treatment works wonders.

"The type of hugging I recommend is the bear hug," says Dr. Bresler. "Use both arms, face your partner, and perform a full embrace."

Medical research has demonstrated that hugging can make you live longer by helping to guard against many forms of illness, especially stress-related diseases like mental depression and hypertension. This simple therapy can also assist you in falling asleep without taking pills, and it can strengthen family bonds. Dr. Harold Voth of the Menninger Foundation, in Topeka, Kansas, says, "In the home, daily hugging will strengthen relationships and significantly reduce friction." Pamela McCoy, a registered nurse who trains nurses at Grant Hospital in Columbus, Ohio, says, "We found that people who are hugged or touched can often stop taking medication to get to sleep."

The body actually responds physically to touch. According to Helen Colton, author of *The Joy of Touching*, researchers have found that "when a person is touched, the amount of hemoglobin in their blood increases significantly." When that happens, more oxygen gets from the lungs to the blood to be transported throughout the body.

In some cultures hugging has become a lost response except with babies and small children. That's too bad. Of course, it wouldn't be appropriate to go around hugging anyone and everyone in sight, but maybe we should think about the text for today and ask, "When is the season for hugging in our house?"

A Word From Our Creator

To every thing there is a season, and a time to every purpose under the heaven: . . . a time to embrace, and a time to refrain from embracing. Ecclesiastes 3:1-5.

Unless you live in the right place on Earth and look for it at the right time of year under the right conditions, you have probably never seen the zodiacal light. The zodiacal light follows the zodiac—the stream of 12 constellations that appear to move across the sky during the night on the same path that the sun follows during the day. It first appears about two hours after sunset, where for those of us in North America, its position is just above the southwestern horizon. As the sky darkens, the light becomes more defined, assuming the shape of a faint gigantic pyramid with rounded corners.

The zodiacal light is brighter when it is near the horizon, but it never is more than a foglike glow in the night sky. As the western zodiacal light rises, it gets dimmer until it all but fades from view just before midnight. Shortly thereafter, you can look farther along the path of the zodiac and see the eastern zodiacal light come into view and brighten as it moves down toward the eastern horizon.

The zodiacal light results from the reflection of the sun's rays on a cloud of space dust that surrounds the sun all the way out to the orbit of Mars. The particles of dust range in size from microscopic dust grains to asteroids a few feet in diameter.

The best place on Earth to see the zodiacal light is anywhere along the equator, but you can also spot it from the mid-northern latitudes and the mid-southern latitudes. To start with, the months of January, February, and March are the best months for viewing. The second-best months are October, November, and December, but even during those months you can't see the zodiacal light if the moon is shining or if there are any other lights around you. The sky has to be completely dark. Even the bright light from Venus and Jupiter can make it very difficult to find the zodiacal light. The best place to be is on a hilltop where you can see the entire sky.

The heavens declare the glory of God even on darkest nights.

The Zodiacal Light

A Word From Our Creator

The heavens declare the glory of God; and the firmament sheweth his handywork. Day unto day uttereth speech, and night unto night sheweth knowledge.
Psalm 19:1, 2.

FEBRUARY 13

Frozen Water

God is here asking Job if he can create rain, dew, ice, or frost. The text is a perfect description of frozen water: a frozen raindrop is ice, and frozen dew is frost. When water is in its liquid state, it flows. When it is in its gaseous state, it rises as the vapor we call steam. But water in its solid state is ice.

Ice can fall from the sky as hail, sleet, or snow. It can also form on solid objects when dew, the water that condenses out of the air, becomes frost. And ice can occur in standing water as the water temperature falls below 32°F. When ice and snow melt and then freeze again, we sometimes get icicles. Most of earth's fresh water is frozen, and 90 percent of earth's ice forms the ice sheet that almost completely covers the continent of Antarctica. There is so much ice stored there, that if you could cut it into huge cubic-mile ice cubes you would end up with six million cubes. Should all of that ice melt, it would raise the sea level over the entire world by 260 feet. Not only that, but the ice is so heavy that it has pushed the continent itself down several hundred feet.

And all of that ice began as snowflakes—delicate crystals of frozen water. Sometimes hundreds of snowflakes get together to form giant flakes several inches across. The largest snowflake ever reported developed during a winter in Siberia. It had a diameter of 8 inches by 11 inches.

The other delicate crystal form of water is frost. When you get the chance, use a magnifying glass to look at the frost on a window. It looks like lace with an ever-changing pattern of beauty. How can just plain water be so beautiful?

How would you go about creating a substance that is colorless, occurs as a solid, a liquid, or a gas, and makes some of the most beautiful natural art in all of creation?

A WORD FROM OUR CREATOR

Hath the rain a father? or who hath begotten the drops of dew? Out of whose womb came the ice? and the hoary frost of heaven, who hath gendered it? Job 38:28, 29.

FEBRUARY 14

The "Cow of China"

Our world has some amazing foods—foods that have uses we have only begun to explore. Take the soybean, for example. This well-known member of the legume, or bean family, represents one of the most nutritious foods known to humanity. The soybean has three times more protein than meat or eggs and 11 times more than milk. Also it contains all of the amino acids needed to keep us healthy.

The Chinese cultivated the soybean 3,000 years ago. They used the sprouts as food and developed soy sauce, cooking oil, flour, and milk from the beans. In fact, the milk was so nutritious that the soybean became known as the "cow of China." More recently the Chinese used the soybean to develop what was originally called *doufu*, or bean curd. Now known as "tofu" in many cultures, bean curd has become a primary substitute for meat in many dishes.

The soybean became a popular plant for experimental agriculture in the United States in the 1920s and 1930s. With about 10,000 varieties, it seemed that this amazing plant could provide a substitute for just about anything. One of the foremost proponents of soybean products was Henry Ford, the automaker. Mr. Ford planted hundreds of varieties of soybeans on his farm in Michigan. He extracted the oil to produce paint and plastics, and he ground the bean into meal to make horn buttons, instrument knobs, and accelerator pedals for automobiles. Ford, who even had thread made from soybean fibers, is said to have worn a suit made from such fibers, complete with shirt and tie and topped off with a soybean hat. But when a goat ate the Illinois license plate made of soybean fiberboard, it dashed his hope of making a vegetable car!

Today soybean products include adhesives, skin creams, paints, printing ink, plastics, insulation, fire-extinguisher foam, soap, and prescription drugs. Drug companies grow the antibiotic called streptomycin in soybean broth. One writer suggested that the soybean must have been the bean that inspired the fable "Jack and the Beanstalk." But a plant such as the soybean is no fairy tale. It is a very real example of the power of our Creator to bring forth wonders out of the earth.

A WORD FROM OUR CREATOR

He causeth the grass to grow for the cattle, and herb for the service of man; that he may bring forth food out of the earth. Psalm 104:14.

FEBRUARY 15

Space Pioneer

Someone has named our text today God's telephone number: JER-3303. When you dial a friend on the telephone, how long does it take for the call to go through? It doesn't take long, does it? How quickly does it take to reach the Lord? The psalmist once said, "Hear my prayer, O Lord. . . . When I call, answer me speedily" (Psalm 102:1, 2).

How long do you think it takes for our heavenly Father to hear our prayers? The angel sent to answer the prophet Daniel's prayer said, "At the beginning of thy supplications the commandment came forth, and I am come to shew thee" (Daniel 9:23). God heard Daniel's prayer instantly. To the prophet Isaiah, God said, "Before they call, I will answer; and while they are yet speaking, I will hear" (Isaiah 65:24).

At a cost of hundreds of millions of dollars the United States launched a series of small spacecraft, each named *Pioneer* and numbered in the order of their launch, to explore our solar system. *Pioneer 10*, for example, weighing only 570 pounds, blasted off into space on March 3, 1972. It was intended to operate only 21 months—just long enough to fly by Jupiter and send back photographs of the giant planet that we know so little about. As it turns out, this tiny nuclear-powered spacecraft did its job and kept on going into space, still sending back messages. In 1983 *Pioneer 10* became the first human-made object to leave our solar system. Traveling at 28,900 miles per hour, *Pioneer 10*, now more than 5 billion miles from Earth, continues to transmit precious data back to eager scientists. Each transmission of data takes seven and a half hours to reach Earth and requires only eight watts of electrical power. When NASA's Deep Space Network of antennas receives the transmission, the power of the signal measures only 4.2 billionths of one trillionth of one watt. And the scientists around the world can read and use the message!

How do you suppose our prayers are transmitted to God's throne instantaneously though the billions of light-years of space?

A WORD FROM OUR CREATOR

Call unto me, and I will answer thee.
Jeremiah 33:3.

FEBRUARY 16

Bird Memory

By studying the amazing phenomenon of bird memory, scientists have learned that some species can recall the exact spots where they stashed food. In fact, they can remember the locations of hundreds—perhaps even thousands—of such storage spots. The brains of such food-storing birds seem to retain an actual picture, or map, of the countryside where they live. Using their special map, each bird is able to pinpoint the location of a buried peanut or other morsel, returning to that spot long after it first placed the food in the ground. And there's more!

Bird thieves are also out looking for stored food. The longer the food stays stored, the greater the chance that another creature will find it. However, food-storing birds remember the order in which they stored food in various spots. So when they get hungry they go directly to the most recently buried cache—the one least likely to have been taken by another bird. After eating what's there (if it has not already been located by another bird), they go to the food that was stored next to last, then to the food hidden just before that, and so on. They save the food stored first for last. And there's still more!

Apparently the method that birds use to remember where they have put food is very similar to using photography. They virtually "take pictures" of each storage location and file these photographs in their memories. To prove this theory, researchers covered one eye of each of a number of food-storing birds. Then they released the birds to collect and bury food. If they kept the same eye covered when it came time for the birds to find the stored food, the creatures could locate their caches. However, if the scientists covered the other eye instead, the birds could not find the food.

What a magnificent memory God has given to these birds. Have you ever felt forgotten—that no one knew or cared where you were? If you ever get tempted by such a fear, remember the birds with such precise memory. The God who gave the birds that ability certainly knows where you are and what you need at all times. Just ask Him for help, and He will be there.

A WORD FROM OUR CREATOR

Who remembereth us in our low estate: for his mercy endureth for ever. Psalm 136:23.

FEBRUARY 17

Thank God for the Bugs

A WORD FROM OUR CREATOR

And God made . . . every thing that creepeth upon the earth after his kind: and God saw that it was good. Genesis 1:25.

We usually think of bugs and other creeping things—cockroaches, spiders, silverfish, ants, caterpillars, potato bugs, cucumber beetles, tomato worms, and the like—as being pests. You probably already know that there are *lots* of each kind of creeping thing. Have you ever seen just *one* ant at a picnic or just *one* Japanese beetle in a garden or just *one* wasp at a nest? But have you ever thought about how many different *kinds* of insects live on earth?

Scientists have named almost a *million* different kinds of insects, and they believe that to be only about *one tenth* of the total number of species that actually exist. Naturalists have found more than 15,000 insect species just in and around New York City, so you need not travel to the tropics, where insects are particularly abundant, to find a wide variety of them. When you know these few facts, it is easy to understand that insects make up the largest group of animals in the world.

However, it may surprise you to learn that only 1 percent of the world's insects are destructive and cause much loss of property and crops. That 1 percent of the world's insects destroys about 10 percent of our crops. Since this small number gets the most publicity, we often forget about the other 99 percent.

Where would we be without the majority of the insects—those that are beneficial? Without them to pollinate flowers, we would have few fruits and vegetables. There would be almost no clover and much less cotton. And of course we would have no honey. The list of food and products that could not exist without the aid of insects would be very long. And we haven't even considered being without the beauty of moths and butterflies.

When you consider the balance between beneficial and harmful insects, 99 percent clearly wins out over 1 percent. And when you also consider that proportion with respect to sin, you might realize that the devil hasn't been as successful as he'd like to be.

February 18

When Did the Skunk Receive Its Odor?

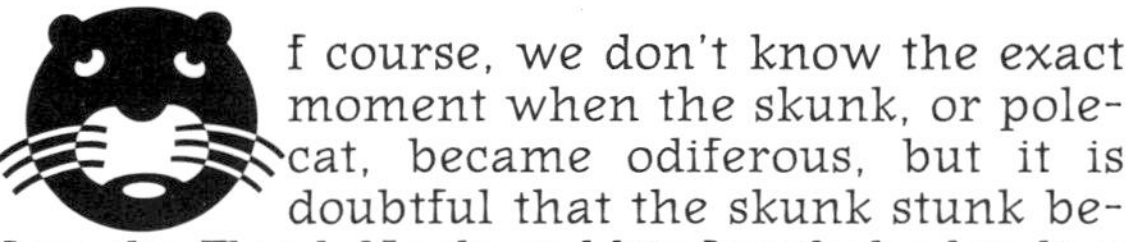

f course, we don't know the exact moment when the skunk, or polecat, became odiferous, but it is doubtful that the skunk stunk before the Flood. Noah and his family had to live for a long time in the ark with two skunks, and interactions with all of those other animals would surely have caused one of them to get miffed at least once. And once would have been enough.

One night when I was a boy, my dog cornered a skunk on our front porch. I can't begin to tell you about the problems that caused. A year later you could still detect the scent on the doorpost.

Several years ago, when we lived in Texas, we had a local skunk that decided to spend the winter under our house. After exploring such alternatives as traps and bait to no avail, we had to take drastic measures. It is one thing to have a skunk spray the outside of your house, but when essence of polecat is permeating your house, you must act.

We hired a duo of brave lads who agreed (for a handsome fee) to go in after the skunk. With one holding a rifle and the other a flashlight, they spotted the black-and-white tail and shot twice, demolishing the animal. Then they dragged the carcass out from under the house. That's when they noticed that they had bravely shot a dead skunk! Sometime during the winter the skunk had died—whereupon the local 'possum had consumed it. But even dead, the skunk had made its presence known. After the boys had collected their fee, they told us what they had found. All of us laughed and breathed a sigh of fresh air.

Actually, when you remove the scent glands from baby skunks, the furry creatures make great pets. We don't know *when* the skunk became odiferous, but this is our theory about *why*. Since it's such a furry and cuddly little animal and since it naturally seems to like being around humans, God knew that placing the "fear of you" upon the skunk would not be enough. God had to give the polecat something special to keep us from bothering it. It's not a very good theory, but we can't think of a better one. Can you?

A Word From Our Creator

And the fear of you and the dread of you shall be upon every beast of the earth, . . . into your hand are they delivered.
Genesis 9:2.

FEBRUARY 19

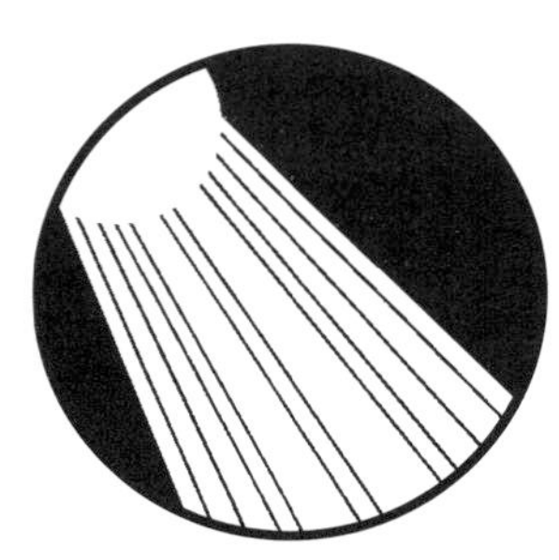

Light and Words

This text is straightforward. It says that even a simple-minded person can gain understanding from God's Word. But if we turned the text around, it would teach another equally important truth that's just as scientifically correct: "The entrance of thy light giveth words." If that sounds confusing, remember that if it were not for light from some source, you could not read the words on this page. So light has to enter the picture in order for the human eye to read printed words.

The process works like this: A source of radiation, such as the sun, a lightbulb, or a fire emit particles of energy called photons. Those photons hit the page of this book. Most of the photons that strike the page where there is black print get absorbed and converted into heat. (The amount of heat is so small that you don't feel it.) However, most of the photons that hit the white background bounce back into the air—something we term reflection.

Since light travels in a straight line, the photons reflect the images that are left after the black print absorbs the other photons. The reflected image goes through the lens of your eye, which focuses it on the retina at the rear of your eyeball. The retina then translates the image into nerve impulses that the optic nerve carries to your brain, and you "see" words. We call the process "reading," and it is really quite wonderful.

Photons of light get organized into nerve impulses that send messages to your brain. You could say that the light teaches you the words. Not only is that the way you read—it is also the way that you see everything. Light arrives, reflects off of the surfaces around you, and enters your eye to send a message to your brain about what's there. It happens so automatically that we take it for granted.

Jesus said, "I am the light of the world" (John 9:5). When the light from Jesus enters your life, you get a new understanding of things. Do you suppose that might be why Jesus is also called the Word that "was made flesh and dwelt among us"? (John 1:14).

A Word From Our Creator

The entrance of thy words giveth light; it giveth understanding unto the simple.
Psalm 119:130.

FEBRUARY 20

Volcanoes From Cannons

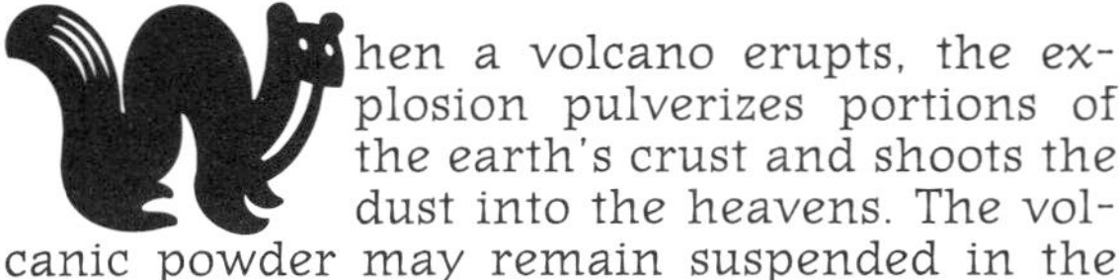

When a volcano erupts, the explosion pulverizes portions of the earth's crust and shoots the dust into the heavens. The volcanic powder may remain suspended in the air for years. If enough dust gets thrown into the atmosphere, it affects the world's weather.

When Mount Tambora erupted in Indonesia in 1815, two hundred megatons of dust enshrouded the entire globe for several years. The dust deflected the sun's warming rays, and history books describe the summer of 1816 as the "summer that never came."

When Mount Pinatubo erupted in the Philippines in June 1991, it sent 20 megatons of dust and gas into the upper atmosphere. As a result, it deflected about 1 percent of the sun's radiant heat back into outer space, reducing the global temperature by an average of about one degree—more in some places, and less in others. Since that eruption, scientists have begun to think about some very interesting possibilities.

For example, if humanity's damage to the earth's atmosphere is causing global warming, more volcanic eruptions could reverse the effect. But that doesn't sound like such a good solution, because volcanoes are unpredictable and often erupt in places that put people and property at risk. Besides, human beings have not learned how to cause a volcano to explode. Or have we?

Believe it or not, some scientists are actually considering an alternative. They are proposing to use large cannons to fire cartridges of dust high into the sky to try to duplicate the cooling effects of volcanic dust. It is estimated that such a project would cost about $30 billion per year. But, say the scientists, if the world is in the process of warming up to temperatures that no life could endure, then such a drastic measure will be necessary just to survive, and no cost would be too great.

Do you remember the last time on earth when human beings thought to protect themselves from the elements of the atmosphere? "And they said, Go to, let us build . . . a tower, whose top may reach unto heaven" (Genesis 11:4). What was the result?

A WORD FROM OUR CREATOR

Who hath measured the waters in the hollow of his hand, and meted out heaven with the span, and comprehended the dust of the earth in a measure . . . ? Isaiah 40:12.

Natural Healing From Bogs

A bog forms when a waterlogged area builds up thick layers of densely packed, partly decayed plant life called peat. Although the conditions sound simple—lots of water plus lots of plant life minus adequate drainage—the creation of a bog takes hundreds of years. The thick, wet turf covering a bog has so little air in it that only certain specialized plants can grow there. For example, the thick leaves of some plants help to conserve nutrients that they must produce above ground through photosynthesis rather than drawing them from the soil. Plants that thrive in the highly acidic turf release nutrients for their less-hardy neighbors to use.

Perhaps the most common plant growing in bogs is sphagnum moss. Vast stretches of this simple plant carpet many bogs and eventually mix with other plant life, then decays to become "peat moss." We can burn peat for fuel, and often add it to sandy soil to increase the soil's water-holding capacity. American Indians cut the absorbent stuff into strips to use as diapers.

Peat also has medicinal purposes. Ancient peoples used many of the plants growing in a peat bog (including cranberries) for healing. Even now one Russian factory produces an ointment from peat for the treatment of eczema, ulcers, and burns. During World War I peat moss served as surgical dressing for wounds because something in the moss seemed to control infection.

One surprising use for peat moss is in "mud" baths, first taken to treat rheumatism in 19th-century Europe. Since the 1950s a German doctor has used peat baths with amputees and injured athletes. People can take peat baths at higher temperatures than water baths because of the way in which the peat distributes the heat. A person who takes a 30-minute, 118-degree peat bath raises his body temperature by one degree, which in turn dramatically increases blood circulation to speed healing and reduce pain.

With all of our human formulas for healing and comfort, sometimes the best ways are still the natural ones.

A Word From Our Creator

Heal me, O Lord, and I shall be healed; save me, and I shall be saved. Jeremiah 17:14.

Early civilizations looked to the heavens as the playground of their gods. With their vivid imaginations, they decided that the arrangements of stars represented figures from their religious stories, called myths. For those early stargazers the sky was a stage for their mythical players.

We call each of these groups of stars a constellation, a name based on the Latin word *stella*, or star. The ancient Greeks had 48 named constellations. By the year 1600 astronomers listed 60. Today the official catalog of constellations recognizes 88. The cast includes 13 humans along with 19 land animals, 10 water creatures, nine birds, two centaurs, a dragon, a unicorn, and a hairy head.

It is hard to imagine a bear represented by a group of stars that more greatly resembles a dipper. Today it has become more common to refer to these two groups of stars as the Big Dipper and the Little Dipper rather than as the Big Bear and the Little Bear.

With the possible exception of the Big Dipper, Orion is the most well known of the constellations. It is somewhat easier to see the image of Orion, the hunter, since one star shows as the left shoulder and one serves as the right, one represents his head, three for his belt, three more for his sword, one for each knee. More stars outline his raised club.

Also it is fairly easy to imagine Cygnus, the swan, flying with outstretched neck through the night sky, but it is even easier to see the stars as forming a cross. Modern stargazers now call the constellation the Northern Cross. (By the way, the Southern Hemisphere has a Southern Cross.)

We humans have named a few stars and constellations. Astronomers even have detailed a numbering system that they use to map the sky. But how do you suppose we could ever name—let alone remember the names of—the billions and trillions of stars that God has made? Can there be any question that He knows each of us by name and asks each of us to join Him soon among the stars?

Players on a Celestial Stage

A WORD FROM OUR CREATOR

He telleth the number of the stars; he calleth them all by their names. Psalm 147:4.

FEBRUARY 23

The Owl Butterfly

In Central America and South America lives a large butterfly with an eight-inch wingspan. For birds that eat butterflies, this very large specimen would make a delightful dinner—except for one thing. On the underside of the hind wings of the butterfly are two large, round "eyes"—that is, marks that look like eyes. In fact, combined with the other markings on the butterfly's wings, the "eyes" make the insect look almost exactly like the tropical screech-owl, a small owl inhabiting the same jungle growth where the butterfly lives.

Birds that would normally make a meal of the large, juicy butterfly see only those "owl eyes," and they stay away. Each "owl eye" even has a small patch of white highlighting on the upper side of what appears to be the dark, dilated pupil.

With such protective coloration, the butterfly doesn't have to worry about anything disturbing it even when it's sleeping, because the "owl eyes" never close. Consequently, the butterfly has the equivalent of a permanent guard on duty at all times, day and night. Some people would tell us that patterns such as the perfectly designed "owl eyes" on butterfly wings happened by chance. Well, the chance that the butterfly's protection is accidental is so small that we surely wouldn't want to bet on it.

The Creator, who made everything in the first place, gave all His creatures ways of coping with the danger that began when Adam and Eve sinned in the Garden of Eden. Undoubtedly He established simple laws of protective coloration that came into play as soon as the effects of sin began to appear around the world.

That same Creator has given each of us the same assurance of protection against sin and its ultimate result, eternal death.

A WORD FROM OUR CREATOR

Thou shalt not be afraid for the terror by night; nor for the arrow that flieth by day; nor for the pestilence that walketh in darkness. Psalm 91:5, 6.

February 24

The Other Otter

Animal shows often feature the playful antics of the river otter. But still another otter, the sea otter, lives along the Pacific coast of North America from California to Alaska and down the Pacific coast of Asia to the Commander Islands of Russia. The largest of all otter species, the sea otter grows to a length of five feet and to a weight of 80 pounds.

The sea otter's pelt was at one time among the most highly prized of all furs. During the height of the fur trade era in the early 1900s a single pelt was worth as much as $2,500. Unfortunately for their survival, these adorable sea mammals are naturally friendly to people, so they didn't stand a chance against greedy fur traders. Within a few short years the number of sea otters became so low that the animal was perilously close to extinction. Hunters slaughtered them by the thousands until 1911. In that year Russia, Japan, Great Britain, and the United States entered into an international treaty that made it illegal to kill any more of them.

An expert swimmer, the sea otter often dives 100 feet below the ocean's surface to find a sea urchin, a clam, an abalone, or some other kind of shellfish to eat. When it has grabbed a tasty seafood dinner, the creature swims to the surface, rolls over onto its back, and spreads out its food on its chest and belly. If the meal is a clam, the otter places the shell on its chest, picks up a handy rock, and hammers away until the shell cracks open.

Sea otters mate for life. Home is a bed of kelp, a type of giant seaweed that grows thick enough to provide a mattress for the pup and to protect the otters from killer whales. The whales can't swim through the kelp.

But the pup's favorite place is on its mother's tummy, where it is safe from just about everything but a marauding bald eagle. The mother's abdomen is the pup's sleeping crib, feeding place, and playpen for eight or more months. Often the mother throws the pup into the air and catches it again on her chest in a game that certainly looks like fun. To protect her pup, the mother sea otter stays in the thick kelp beds and watches for the bald eagle. Aren't you glad God made mothers?

A Word From Our Creator

As one whom his mother comforteth, so will I comfort you. Isaiah 66:13.

FEBRUARY 25

T Cells and Secret Codes

A WORD FROM OUR CREATOR

Not every one that saith unto me, Lord, Lord, shall enter into the kingdom of heaven; but he that doeth the will of my Father which is in heaven. Matthew 7:21.

e know about some of the mechanisms that our bodies use to defend us against disease. For example, sometime ago science discovered the leukocytes, or white blood cells, that our bones store until we need them to fight invading germs. Every year we are discovering more ways in which our bodies work to protect us.

One of the latest findings concerning the natural defenses of our bodies is the discovery of T cells. Acting as guards, these ultra microscopic cells come equipped with secret codes, like passwords, that they use to test every new thing they encounter. The secret codes are chains of chemicals that match up perfectly with the chemicals of those elements of our bodies that belong there. The chemical makeup of a disease germ or a foreign cell won't match the code. By some as-yet-undiscovered method, the T cells then sound the alarm that an intruder has entered the body. Down in the bone marrow, the leukocytes wait like firefighters at a fire station. Once the T-cell alarm sends out its signal, the leukocytes leap into action and rush by the nearest artery to the battle area where the invasion is taking place. Without such safety features as the T cells with their secret protection codes, you and I would not live long on this earth.

The Bible refers to God's people on earth as the body of Jesus. When Jesus is our personal Friend and Saviour, we too have a secret code that helps Him to recognize us and to receive us unto Himself. We are born as invaders in the body of Jesus, but through a wonderful process that we don't understand, He makes us new in Him. Jesus gives us a clean heart and a right spirit.

ince light is a form of energy, it is only fitting that the Creator should be clothed with it. After all, Scripture calls Him "the light of the world" (John 2:12). He is the Word that "was made flesh" (John 1:14), and that Word is a light shining on our life paths (Psalm 119:105). What do you suppose God's garment of light looks like? If you could see God, how bright would He appear? Would He be different colors? Would lightning flashes emanate from His form? We can't be certain of the answers to those questions, but the Bible does have some clues.

When God appeared to Israel from Mount Sinai, "the sight of the glory of the Lord was like devouring fire on the top of the mount in the eyes of the children of Israel" (Exodus 24:17). Then God called Moses to climb that mountain and meet with Him there. Can you imagine that—an audience with God, the Creator of the universe? How do you think Moses felt? How would *you* feel? Moses had been in the presence of this fire before when he had met Jesus at the burning bush.

John saw Jesus in vision and wrote that "his countenance was as the sun shining in his strength" (Revelation 1:16). From these and other texts we can deduce that the light that God wears appears like a burning, white-hot fire—somewhat like the sun.

When Moses asked to see God's glory, the Lord placed him in a cave and covered him with His hand as He passed by so that the power of His brightness would not destroy him. As Moses came down from Sinai, "the skin of his face shone" with that radiant energy (Exodus 34:30). His face glowed so brightly that he had to veil it to keep from frightening the people.

The light of God's coat is so bright that when He returns in the clouds of heaven, "every eye shall see him" (Revelation 1:7), and the wicked shall be destroyed "with the brightness of his coming" (2 Thessalonians 2:8). This is the same Jesus who said on the first day of Creation week "Let there be light!" As Jesus speaks, the very elements tremble—not in fright, but with the excitement of raw energy. He is the source of all energy, and He loves you.

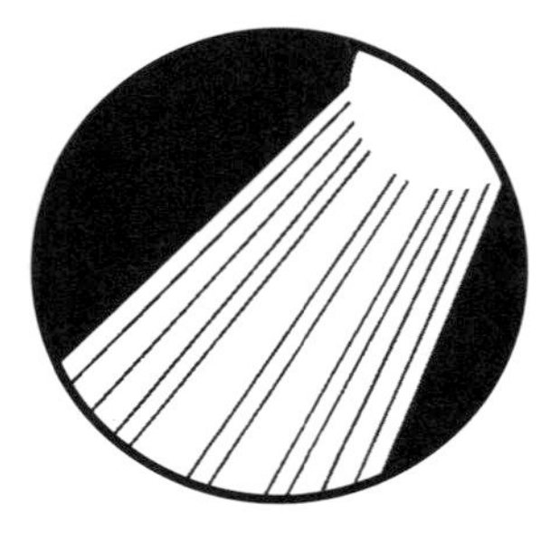

God's Coat of Light

A Word From Our Creator

Who coverest thyself with light as with a garment: who stretchest out the heavens like a curtain.
Psalm 104:2.

February 27

Peat and Fire

One of the greatest energy reserves on earth for heating homes is peat. For example, scientists estimated that in Minnesota alone the more than two million acres of bogs contain enough peat to supply that state with energy for more than 50 years.

As we saw before, peat is the thick, decayed material that lies under a swamp or bog. It consists primarily of decomposed plant matter, but animals that die in the bog also become part of the resulting fuel. It can accumulate in depths from several inches to 30 feet or more.

Peat moss provides a good example of how peat forms. As we learned earlier, one of the main plants growing above a peat bog is sphagnum moss. The carpet of living green sphagnum moss on the surface of the bog is made up of healthy plants that continue growing upward, leaving below the old dead and decaying stalks and leaves. These stalks and leaves compress to become the peat moss used by gardeners to enrich their soil.

Those who harvest the peat for fuel scrape away the living material from the top of the bog, dredge the peat from the bog, drain off the water, and dry the remains. Dry peat catches fire easily. Sometimes when a drought has dried up the peat bogs, lightning or a careless person's match ignites the dry moss. Such fires may burn for years because they are almost impossible to extinguish. Only a soaking rain can put out a peat fire.

As Christians, we are always growing upward toward the sunlight of Jesus' love. And when He comes, we will be taken from this world, leaving below the death and destruction of sin to be ignited later into a fire that humanity will not be able to extinguish. Only the creative energy of Jesus—as He makes all things new—will be able to control the power of that fire.

A Word From Our Creator

But the heavens and the earth, which are now, by the same word are kept in store, reserved unto fire against the day of judgment. 2 Peter 3:7.

hen I moved from Massachusetts to Texas, people told me that the very large trees in downtown Austin were oak trees—live oaks, to be exact. That posed a problem for me. Massachusetts has several kinds of oaks. All are huge, majestic, and mighty! They represent strength and provide symbols for poets. But they all have pointed leaves—or at least leaves with some sort of interesting shape. So when someone showed me the live oak, something seemed very wrong—it didn't have "oak" leaves, so it couldn't be a "real" oak.

Accustomed to seeing white oaks with long, rounded lobes on the leaves; pin oaks, with lobed leaves with pointed bristle tips; black oaks, another species with sharp tips to the lobes; and chestnut oaks, the leaves of which are at least toothed if not actually lobed or tipped with points—it had always been obvious to me that the leaves of "real" oaks were not smooth-edged and leathery as are those of the live oak. "Real" oak leaves also turn brilliant colors in fall, while live oaks are evergreens. Either live oaks were misnamed—or something was wrong with my definition of an oak tree.

As it turned out, I was looking at the wrong characteristics in trying to judge an oak. It doesn't matter whether or not the leaves are lobed. Nor does it matter whether or not the leaves change color in fall or drop in the winter. All oaks share one feature—their fruit! No matter what else may be true, if the tree bears acorns, it is *a real oak*.

So often we look at the outward appearance of people and judge them by our standards of what we think is appropriate. Fortunately for us, God sees what we often can't: He observes the qualities of our heart and how we manifest them. The next time that you deal with someone who doesn't appear and act like *your* idea of a Christian, look closer. You may be making the mistake of trying to identify an oak by its leaves—instead of by its fruit.

"Real" Oaks

A WORD FROM OUR CREATOR

Wherefore by their fruits ye shall know them. Matthew 7:20.

The Universe Is Stretched Out

People hotly debate about the nature of the universe. Some believe that it began with a big bang and has been increasing in size continuously since then. Others hold that the size and organization of the universe are set and do not change. The subject seems to be one that scientists enjoy discussing at great length. It is interesting that God rarely figures in their discussions and that they almost never use the Bible as a source of information when it comes to the nature of the universe.

For those of us who believe that the Bible, as the Word of God, contains truth presented by the Creator of the universe, it is amazing to note that the Bible authors, writing some 3,000 years ago, presented a consistent description of the universe—a description that is as accurate as any current theory. Text after text describes the universe as expansive and expanding. Scholars translate the descriptive term that the Bible uses as "stretched out."

"I, even my hands, have *stretched out* the heavens, and all their host have I commanded" (Isaiah 45:12).

"He hath established the world by his wisdom, and hath *stretched out* the heavens by his discretion" (Jeremiah 10:12).

"The burden of the word of the Lord for Israel, saith the Lord, which *stretcheth forth* the heavens, and layeth the foundation of the earth, and formeth the spirit of man" (Zechariah 12:1).

Among many similar texts, those four illustrate an important point. "Stretched out" is past, "stretchest out" is present, and "stretcheth forth" is future. It seems that the Bible writers make it clear that the heavens are ever-expanding: they have been growing since God created them, and they will continue to do so forever.

Dr. Allen Hynek, an astronomer at Northwestern University, wrote that "the whole of space seems to be expanding or stretching out in all directions." All the evidence from recent explorations in space supports the idea of an expanding, orderly universe—just as the Bible describes.

A Word From Our Creator

Thus saith God the Lord, he that created the heavens, and stretched them out. Isaiah 42:5.

The brown pelican alternates flapping and soaring over the ocean as it looks for food. When it spots a fish, the big bird folds its wings and dives bill-first to scoop up the fish—plus three or more gallons of water—in its expandable pouch. Then the pelican bobs to the surface and opens its bill and points it downward to let the water drain out before gulping down the fish.

To a hungry pelican, all fish are fair game—even someone else's. One day a woman fishing along the Florida coast landed a large snapper on the pavement bordering the oceanfront. A sharp-eyed brown pelican saw the flopping fish, swooped down, and grabbed it—taking off with not only the fish but also with the hook and line still attached to it. The surprised woman watched open-mouthed for a few seconds, then gave the line a yank. She pulled the snapper from the pelican's bill, reeled it in, removed the hook, and quickly dropped it into a bucket.

The pelican retaliated. As the woman bent over to put the lid on the bucket that held *his* fish, the pelican pecked her on the backside. The woman shrieked and accidentally kicked over the bucket, which set the coveted fish free again. The pelican grabbed the fish and carried it to a nearby piling and swallowed it.

But just as the brown pelican watches for a chance to take an easy meal from a human angler, so two other kinds of birds keep an eye on the pelican to pirate its catch. While the pelican sits with its bill open to let the water pour out, laughing gulls sometimes perch on the edges of the bill, reach in, and take their pick.

The Magnificent Frigate Bird employs another method of piracy. A pelican must swallow fish headfirst, and sometimes the fish doesn't cooperate by lying in the bird's pouch in this position. When all else fails, the pelican resorts to tossing the fish into the air and catching it headfirst. When the pelican flips the fish, the frigate bird swoops down and uses its long sharp-tipped bill to catch its meal in midair.

Such illustrations of thievery are humorous because they represent a natural part of the life of the birds. Stealing for personal gain, however, is not funny.

MARCH 2

Magnificent Thieves

A WORD FROM OUR CREATOR

Men do not despise a thief, if he steal to satisfy his soul when he is hungry. Proverbs 6:30.

March 3

Thorny Devil

Deception works two ways. Sometimes things look harm*less* when they're not, and other times things appear harm*ful* when they're not.

North America has several species of horned lizards (often mistakenly called "horned toads"). The horns of these short-tailed, fat-bodied reptiles vary in size and number, but no matter how many or how prominent the horns on their heads and on their bodies, horned lizards are extremely unappealing to their enemies. Their ugliness protects them. For further protection, the horned lizard stands completely still and flattens out its body to become nearly invisible as it blends in with its surroundings. The lizard can also quickly bury itself in sand. If something does pick up a horned lizard, the reptile can inflate its body by gulping air, jab with its horns, and even spurt blood from a small opening at the base of its third eyelid.

The thorny devil of Australia is even uglier than its American relatives. For one thing, it has a long tail—and thus more surface area to cover with projections. It has even brighter colors, with war-paint-like black, reddish-brown, and yellow markings. But most frightening of all is the fact that huge thorns cover the lizard from its nose to the tip of its tail. When approached by a potential predator, all the thorny devil has to do is tuck its head between its front legs and arch its back to form a tiny mound of unappetizing spikes.

Horned lizards—including thorny devils—are not the monsters that they appear to be. Their looks are deceptive. They appear fierce and aggressive, but actually they are shy, and would rather escape than defend themselves.

Deception had its beginning in the Garden of Eden. Satan is the arch-deceiver. But he does not present himself as a thorny devil—ugly, with horns, a long tail, and a pitchfork. That would immediately put us on our guard. Inspiration warns us that in the last days Satan will appear as an angel of light accompanied by false prophets as he attempts to "deceive the very elect" (Matthew 24:24). Only by really knowing Jesus can we avoid being tricked by Satan's appearances and recognize him as the *real* "thorny devil."

A Word From Our Creator

For such are false apostles, . . . transforming themselves into the apostles of Christ. And no marvel; for Satan himself is transformed into an angel of light.
2 Corinthians 11:13, 14.

uring the past century most of the native animals of Bible lands have either become extinct or have had their populations reduced to such an extent that they are now endangered species. Using the Bible as its guidebook, in 1963 the government of Israel established the Nature Reserve Authority to reestablish the animals of the Bible in their native haunts. As far as possible, government officials want to bring all of the creatures studied by King Solomon back for today's schoolchildren to observe as well. For example, the fallow deer, whose meat Solomon's servants served on his table every day, no longer existed in Israel until its reintroduction some years ago.

A flood in 1966 swept away the last known Middle Eastern ostrich (the ostrich of the Bible). The onager, better known as the wild ass, had been hunted to extinction in Bible lands by the 1930s. In 1973 explorers discovered a herd of onagers in a remote area of Ethiopia. This find created great excitement because a species thought to be extinct still existed. By a means reminiscent of Noah's ark, naturalists captured seven of the animals and transported them by a giant Hercules transport plane, along with 12 Ethiopian ostriches, to Israel.

The Ethiopian habitat of the new variety of ostrich was similar enough to Israel to provide hope that the bird would once again be a native creature of Bible lands. Both the reintroduced onagers and the transplanted ostriches are doing well. In fact, the onagers might be doing too well. Because they range widely and can gallop at 45 miles per hour, the animals are difficult to control. They sometimes wander to areas where they aren't welcome, such as into Jordan, where people shoot them. Based on the words of the Bible, it sounds like onagers haven't changed much since God described their habits to Job:

"Who hath sent out the wild ass free? or who hath loosed the bands of the wild ass? Whose house I have made the wilderness, and the barren land his dwellings. He scorneth the multitude of the city, neither regardeth he the crying of the driver. The range of the mountains is his pasture, and he searcheth after every green thing" (Job 39:5-8).

The Bible Zoo

A WORD FROM OUR CREATOR

And God gave Solomon wisdom and understanding exceeding much. . . . And he spake of trees . . . : he spake also of beasts, and of fowl, and of creeping things, and of fishes.
1 Kings 4:29-33.

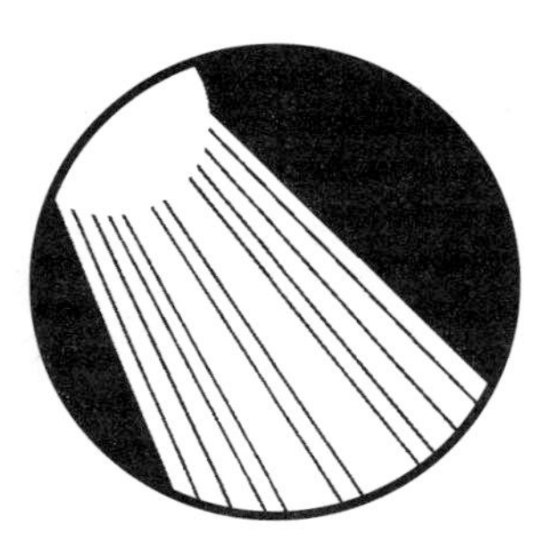

An Angstrom

What's an angstrom? Here's the first clue: It's very small. In fact, a string of 250 million of them would be only an inch long. Here's the second clue: You can't see it. Now that's not surprising because it's obviously too small to see. But even if you had a pile of billions and billions of them, you still couldn't see them. Actually that's a trick clue, because it leads you to think that an angstrom is something tangible but invisible. So here's the third and final clue in the form of a question: Can you see a millimeter?

An angstrom is a unit of linear measurement—that is, scientists use it to measure distance. But why would anyone want to measure distances as short as 250 millionths of an inch? Good question. Scientists employ angstroms as a way of measuring very small distances, such as the diameter of an atom or the thickness of soap film on a bubble. Most commonly, angstroms serve as the measurement for wavelengths of light.

The wavelengths of visible light range from about 4,000 angstroms for a blue-violet light to about 7,000 angstroms for deep-red light. But even 7,000 angstroms equal only 28 millionths of an inch. Angstroms would not be a good measure of your height, but we can use your height to help you understand just how small an angstrom is. If you and a friend are each five feet tall, then you are each 15 billion angstroms high. Now suppose that you shrink to a height of one angstrom, while your friend stays the same size. Your friend would now be 15 billion times taller than you.

When we measure tiny distances like the wavelengths of light, we need a very small unit of measure. But when we measure the height of a person, we take a medium unit of measure like feet or meters. And when we measure great distances such as those in space, we have to have a large unit of measure such as the light-year—the distance light travels in one year. But that is looking at the world and the universe from our perspective. God can see the universe from the inside of an atom, where angstroms represent a great distance, or from beyond the planets, where even light-years fail to measure the vast space adequately.

A Word From Our Creator

But, beloved, be not ignorant of this one thing, that one day is with the Lord as a thousand years, and a thousand years as one day. 2 Peter 3:8.

MARCH 6

Thunders and Lightnings

What a morning that must have been when the power of God moved to the mountaintop, thereby creating an awesome meteorological display. Mighty flashes of lightning and great roars of thunder would have been the natural response of the heat in the cloud meeting the cool air at the top of the mountain.

In order for lightning to occur naturally, a massive cloud formation called a "thunderhead" has to form. A thunderhead builds when warm air from the earth's surface rises. (That's why some of the fiercest lightning storms form over desert areas with their hot rocks and soil.) As the hot air rises, it cools. If the air is moist, as it is when it results from a breeze blowing in from the sea, water condenses, freezes, and begins to fall as ice-crystals that may grow into hail. The hotter the air below, the faster the air rises, often pushing the ice formations back up into the cloud so that they collide with those falling from above.

The collisions in the center of the thunderhead are so powerful that they shear electrons from otherwise stable atoms. The electrons begin to collect as masses of negative electrical charges. When enough of them collect in one place, they are attracted to another part of the cloud or to the ground as a flow of electrons (electricity) that appears to us as lightning.

You can imagine how awesome the display was that morning in the camp of Israel when God made Himself known to the people. The children of Israel had not yet learned about the love of God—they saw only His power, and they were afraid.

When you see lightning and hear thunder, what thoughts about God come to your mind? Are you afraid, or do you marvel at the love of a God with such power? The God of the universe has the power to snap His fingers and eliminate the earth with all its heartache and degradation. Instead, "God so loved the world, that he gave his only begotten Son, that whosoever believeth in him should not perish, but have everlasting life" (John 3:16).

A WORD FROM OUR CREATOR

And it came to pass on the third day in the morning, that there were thunders and lightnings. Exodus 19:16.

March 7

Birch Bark

Did you know that within the past 200 years American Indians were still making boats the same way that Noah constructed the ark? The type of wood is different in each case, but the process is the same—right down to sealing the boat with pitch. In fact, the word for ship and the word for tree bark come from the same root in a number of languages. The source of the English word "disembark" is obvious.

In most tree species—for examples, the oaks, maples, and pines—the increasing size of the growing tree forces the bark of its trunk to split. The once-smooth trunk and branches of the young saplings soon become cracked and rough as the outer bark tries to stretch to accommodate the growth. But some trees maintain a smooth, nonfurrowed bark over most of their trunk surface. Examples include the sycamore, the basswood, and the birches. These trees add layers of bark on the outside for several years, and then the outer layers split and fall away from the wood underneath.

In birch trees, for example, the bark remains smooth, flaking off in some species and peeling in strips in others. Birch trees grow quickly, but they reach only 30 to 80 feet tall—medium-tall for trees. Birches also have relatively short life spans. Three of the 40 or so kinds—the paper birch, the gray birch, and the European white birch—have white bark. The stark white of the birch trunks against the dark green of a northern forest is a dramatic sight. In earlier times people used the bark from birch trees as we do writing paper today. In fact, the English word "birch" comes from the Sanskrit word *bhurga*, "the tree whose bark is used for writing upon."

More recently, American Indians used the bark of paper birches to make canoes. They first built a frame from a tree with a soft wood, such as cedar. Then they took the long, slender roots of the tamarack, an evergreen tree, to sew sheets of birch bark together to cover the frame. Finally they waterproofed the canoe by sealing its seams with the sticky pitch from pine or balsam trees. As you can see, the entire boat was made from natural tree products—just as thousands of years ago God instructed Noah to build an ark out of gopher wood.

A Word From Our Creator

Make thee an ark of gopher wood; rooms shalt thou make in the ark, and shalt pitch it within and without with pitch.
Genesis 6:14.

That statement was written some 3,500 years ago, long before modern astronomy had discovered the details that we now know about the heavens. But the accuracy of the inspired Word of God continues to go unchallenged as we discover more and more facts about the universe. Mazzaroth is another term for the 12 constellations, commonly called the "signs" of the zodiac. The ancients used the positions of these constellations as we do a calendar. They knew that while events on Earth were highly unpredictable, the path and schedule of the constellations through the heavens was dependable. In our text for today, God challenges Job to duplicate such exactness—as if he could.

That brings us to Arcturus. It is quite extraordinary that the author of today's text would compare the unchanging qualities of the zodiac with the unique aspects of a single star known as Arcturus. It is the fourth-brightest star that we see in the Northern Hemisphere, 22 times larger than the sun, and traveling through space at the incredible speed of 85 miles a second—that's more than 300,000 miles an hour! Our sun is journeying through space at "only" 12.5 miles a second. Long ago Sir Isaac Newton calculated that, in general, the stars move at controlled speeds that do not exceed 25 miles a second. Arcturus is one of a very few stars that break this rule.

The unaided eyes of ancient astronomers could not have detected that Arcturus is actually a "runaway" sun. Since the star is 32.6 light-years away from us, even the great speed at which it moves would have gone unnoticed to them. In 100 years the star shifts across our sky only one eighth of the apparent diameter of the moon.

Why not take a look at Arcturus tonight? It is not hard to find, for the two stars at the end of the handle of the Big Dipper point almost directly to Arcturus. As you watch this star, imagine, if you can, the speed at which it is traveling. Could *you* guide something that big going that fast?

Arcturus

A Word From Our Creator

Canst thou bring forth Mazzaroth in his season? or canst thou guide Arcturus with his sons?
Job 38:32.

Lobster Claws

The northern lobster, which lives along North America's east coast, starts life as a translucent newborn less than half an inch long. At this stage the crustacean's five pairs of legs all have the same weak, slender form. Six weeks later, though, after growing rapidly, the front pair of legs develops into two large claws.

Each of the lobster's front claws is designed to serve a special purpose. When hunting, the lobster uses the cutter claw, the smaller of the two and edged with many small teeth, to quickly grasp a passing fish. The lobster uses the other claw, the larger and stronger crusher, to break open clams, mussels, and other hard-shelled ocean creatures. Many people enjoy the meat of the northern lobster's claws. As a result, trapping lobsters is a major industry along the Atlantic Coast. In order to increase each lobster's value, biologists tried to induce lobsters to develop two crushers instead of one crusher and one cutter. They first determined that a lobster needs to exercise its claws to develop a crusher. Only six of every 26 lobsters raised on smooth-bottomed aquariums developed a crusher, while most of those raised on a bed of broken shells, mud, or even plastic buttons developed one. If a lobster had even one chip of shell to grasp and pinch, it was likely to develop a crusher claw.

Biologists assumed that if exercising one claw caused it to become a crusher, then exercising both claws equally would result in two. The scientists designed a program in which each lobster's right claw received as much exercise as its left. But as if in total protest against the biologist's efforts, the lobsters in this group failed to develop even the one usual crusher. Eventually the scientists determined that when it comes to making crusher claws, it doesn't matter how much exercise the claws get—only that one claw gets more of a workout than the other.

The development of humans, as well as of lobsters, follows a pattern set down by the Creator. He designed us to form a balanced character—physical, mental, and spiritual. Attempts to overemphasize the physical aspect always leads to the shutdown of the natural development of our overall character.

A Word From Our Creator

Exercise thyself rather unto godliness. For bodily exercise profiteth little: but godliness is profitable unto all things.
1 Timothy 4:7, 8.

magine that you're an insect trying to get safely through a section of grass in a field. Every acre of grassland contains as many as 2 million spiders—that's a spider for every three square inches—and every spider is waiting for you to take a false step. Everywhere you turn, a pair of hungry jaws lies in wait. What chance do you have to get through that jungle?

One type of spider lives underground with its web spread out in all directions like a deceptive welcome mat. The spider waits at the bottom of its tunnel, ready to spring with the first quiver that your feet cause when you step on its web. Another type of spider moves about silently, hoping to pounce on you before you're aware of any danger. A third species of spider swings a strand of silk with a weight on the end. If the strand touches you, the force of the weight causes the string to quickly wrap around you and hold fast. And if you intend to use your wings to escape from all those enemies lurking in the grass, spiders that have spread their webs as invisible nets in the air may catch you.

You know, in a very real sense, we all confront danger that's not very different from what we would face if we were insects. In today's text David is referring to the wicked who lie in wait to hurt the poor. It's interesting that he uses two different examples in the same sentence. Lions stalk their prey and don't use nets, while spiders do. But both predators lie in wait. Can you imagine a huge web/net with a spider the size of a lion lying in wait for its prey? That's about how David felt when he, as a lonely servant of God, found himself up against the wiles of the wicked. But David, of all people, understood the source of power in such a situation. He had no trouble with Goliath, and it was David who wrote, "Yea, though I walk through the valley of the shadow of death, I will fear no evil: for thou art with me" (Psalm 23:4).

Lying in Wait

A WORD FROM OUR CREATOR

He lieth in wait secretly as a lion in his den: he lieth in wait to catch the poor: he doth catch the poor, when he draweth him into his net. Psalm 10:9.

MARCH 11

Feet

Your feet are important to how you behave as a Christian. The Bible is full of instruction about how God's people should walk as they follow Jesus. For example, God said to Isaiah, "Thine ears shall hear a word behind thee, saying, This is the way, walk ye in it" (Isaiah 30:21). And Jesus said, "I am the light of the world: he that followeth me shall not walk in darkness, but shall have the light of life" (John 8:12). God has given us that light in Himself and in His Word: "Thy word is a lamp unto my feet, and a light unto my path" (Psalm 119:105).

Where our feet go is very important, because they cannot go anywhere without the rest of us. And God, in His wondrous way, never asks us to do things that He doesn't give us the power to do. So because He wants us to watch where our feet take us, He made sure that we have good feet.

Each foot is a structural miracle with 26 bones, 30 joints, more than 100 ligaments, 31 tendons, and 18 muscles. About 25 percent of the bones of your body are in your feet. Each foot is like a tripod formed by the heel, the base of the little toe, and the base of the big toe. As you take a step, the foot that you put forward bears the weight of your body. Each step starts at the heel, moves to the outside of the foot (base of the little toe), and then shifts to the base of the big toe. About that time the other foot moves forward to start the process all over again. All the bones, muscles, and tendons work together with those of the ankle and calf to keep you balanced and moving as you walk. Your feet take you 8,000 to 10,000 steps a day over all sorts of surfaces. To help your feet accomplish all of that work, each of them has yards of blood vessels, miles of nerves, and about 125,000 sweat glands!

And yet, with all of that miraculous action, your feet do not decide where to take you—your mind does that. "But if we walk in the light, as he is in the light, we have fellowship one with another, and the blood of Jesus Christ his Son cleanseth us from all sin" (1 John 1:7).

A WORD FROM OUR CREATOR

I have refrained my feet from every evil way, that I might keep thy word. Psalm 119:101.

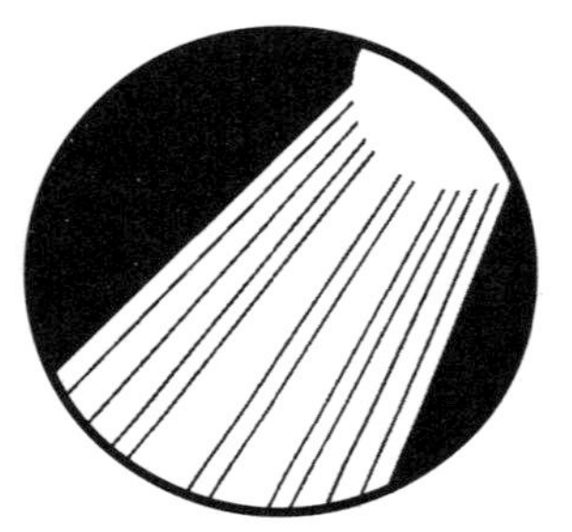

The Source of Rays

Visible and invisible rays constantly surround us. In fact, human beings can see only the rays of visible light. All the rest—cosmic-rays, ultraviolet rays, X-rays, and gamma rays, to name a few—cannot be detected by the human eye.

A light ray is a stream of photons from an energy source. The source may be the sun, but it may also be an electric light, a glowing fire, or even a star in deep space. Photons are particles of energy so small that we can only speculate about their size, but they travel in waves, and we can measure the lengths of those waves. Photon wave lengths are so short that scientists have—as we saw in an earlier reading—coined the term "angstrom" as their unit of measure for radiation wavelengths. The shortest wavelength of visible light, for example, is about 4,000 angstroms, while the longest is about 7,000 angstroms. You can put about 250 million angstroms in an inch. So watching light waves is not exactly like watching waves on a lake—unless you can imagine up to 62,500 little wavelets in every inch of the lake's surface. And those wavelengths are very long compared to those of some of the invisible rays.

As the photons move through space in waves, they also vibrate at different speeds. That means that they bounce up and down at great speeds as they move along in the stream. Scientists call the frequency of this bounce *hertz* (cycles per second). So photons move in waves measured in angstroms, and they vibrate at a frequency called hertz.

It is the vibration frequency, or hertz, that indicates the amount of energy in a stream of radiation. Rays with short wavelengths have more power than those with longer wavelengths. X-rays, for example, have a very short wavelength, less than 100 angstroms, and they vibrate at 30 billion billion hertz. That is why they are so dangerous. Rays with long wavelengths vibrate more slowly and scientists do not call them rays—instead they refer to them as waves, like radio waves.

When the Creator said "Let there be light," it is hard to imagine the great amount of energy that He released. You could definitely say that He made waves that day.

A WORD FROM OUR CREATOR

Ah Lord God! behold, thou hast made the heaven and the earth by thy great power and stretched out arm, and there is nothing too hard for thee.
Jeremiah 32:17.

MARCH 13

The Night 5 Million Birds Died

A WORD FROM OUR CREATOR

For yourselves know perfectly that the day of the Lord so cometh as a thief in the night. For when they shall say, Peace and safety; then sudden destruction cometh. 1 Thessalonians 5:2, 3.

It was late on the afternoon of March 13, 1904, when across the prairies of Iowa and Nebraska vast flocks of Lapland longspurs took to the skyways. The call of their ancestral breeding grounds was overwhelming, and like clouds of leaves before a storm and with an intensity that would drive them northward on a nonstop flight through the night, they filled the air.

How could they know that some 200 miles to the north and west a gigantic blizzard was bearing down upon them? The advancing swarms of birds met the advancing line of storm clouds somewhere over northern Iowa and Nebraska. Their urge to go northward overcame any natural instincts about the danger of the approaching storm. They attempted to fly through it.

As the blizzard hit, farmers and townspeople in southern Minnesota struggled through the night to reduce the storm damage. Early in the storm they began to hear the twitters of struggling birds. Then the birds began to fall from the sky—at first in small numbers, then by the thousands. In Worthington, Minnesota, where more than 2 million longspurs fell to their deaths, the tragedy became known as "the great bird shower." And the tragedy repeated itself in towns over an area radiating out from there for 25 to 30 miles, covering about 1,500 square miles in southwestern Minnesota and southeastern South Dakota.

A farmer just outside of Worthington was startled the next morning to find several of the exhausted longspurs still alive. He picked up the birds and took them into his house, where he and his wife kept them in their window garden for two weeks, feeding them until they regained their strength. When released, the longspurs took to the air and set a course northward. They were going home.

It would be hard to find a more graphic description of "sudden destruction." Jesus is coming soon, and He has given us advance notice. Our natural instincts may tell us to ignore the warnings, but He has also promised to save us from destruction and to set us on the right course for home—the home that He has gone to prepare for us.

MARCH 14

Roots

Notice in this text the phrase "rooted and grounded." Roots do two things for a plant: they feed it and hold it in place. These two purposes work together. In order for the roots to hold the plant in place, they must be alive. And in order to stay alive, the roots must continue to feed the part of the plant that's above ground so the leaves can produce food. In turn, the food manufactured in the leaves supplies nutrients to the cells in the roots, which obtain more water and raw materials for the leaves. This cycle of interdependence is endless.

The parts of the root system get smaller and smaller as they penetrate deeper into the soil. Rootlets grow from the main roots, and tiny root hairs grow from the rootlets. A botanist studied the root production of one winter rye plant growing in two cubic feet of soil. When the plant was 4 months old, the scientist washed away the soil around its roots. Then, with the aid of a microscope, he began to count and measure. He found 13,800,000 rootlets and root hairs, which if placed end to end, would stretch 387 miles. That means that that one little rye plant had produced roots at the rate of three miles per day, or 660 feet per hour, or 11 feet per minute. That plant was definitely rooted and grounded.

Looking at a tree won't tell you whether it's rooted deeply in the ground or if its root system is shallow. But when a storm comes along and the wind pushes against the tree, what happens then will often reveal quickly whether the tree is rooted *and* grounded. A strong wind will more easily blow over trees with shallow roots.

Plants that get too much water will grow shallow root systems—they don't dig deeply into the soil to find a permanent water supply. Such plants are like people who get their spiritual water passively, perhaps by only going to church once a week or by listening to spiritual recordings every day. When the storms of life blow, they fall easily.

To develop strong spiritual roots we must dig deeply into God's Word in personal study. Only those of us who are rooted *and* grounded will survive. How are your roots?

A WORD FROM OUR CREATOR

That Christ may dwell in your hearts by faith; that ye, being rooted and grounded in love, may be able to comprehend . . . the love of Christ. Ephesians 3:17-19.

The Galactic Force

Today's passage, which appears in the song of Deborah and Barak, is a poetic statement of God's assistance in overcoming Sisera, the evil Canaanite commander. Sisera was the man who made the mistake of taking a nap in Heber's tent. You probably remember how Heber's wife, Jael, took advantage of the opportunity and put a tent stake through Sisera's head, ending a period of oppression by the Canaanites. The Israelites had a grand celebration, and the song of Deborah and Barak commemorated the victory of those two faithful judges. Deborah and Barak realized full well who had won the battle, and their song gives God all the glory and honor.

Sisera's army had been formidable. The Bible says that he had 900 chariots under his command. With no chariots of their own, how could the Israelites possibly overcome such a force? The solution was simple, but it didn't involve anything that they could have mustered themselves. According to the song, the forces of nature fought against Sisera and his army. Verse 21 tells us that the Kishon River swept them away. All that required was a rainstorm. The ground turned to sticky mud, the chariots got stuck, and a flash flood swept them downstream.

As impressive as the victory was, it's also very interesting that the authors of the victory song knew about the courses of the stars. Every star in the heavens is in orbit, moving silently yet powerfully through space on a course determined by the gravity of an awesome force in the center of that orbit. Just as planets in the solar system circle the sun, the other suns and their families of planets orbit the center of the galaxy.

Astronomers call the time that it takes a sun to revolve around the center of its galaxy its galactic year. Our sun's galactic year is 225 million years. Galaxies, in turn, orbit around an unseen center in clusters. And all the galaxy groups in the universe revolve around an unknown force—perhaps the center of the universe. Find that center, and, we believe, you will find God—all-powerful, all-knowing, and everlasting.

A Word From Our Creator

They fought from heaven; the stars in their courses fought against Sisera. Judges 5:20.

March 16

Buzzard Day

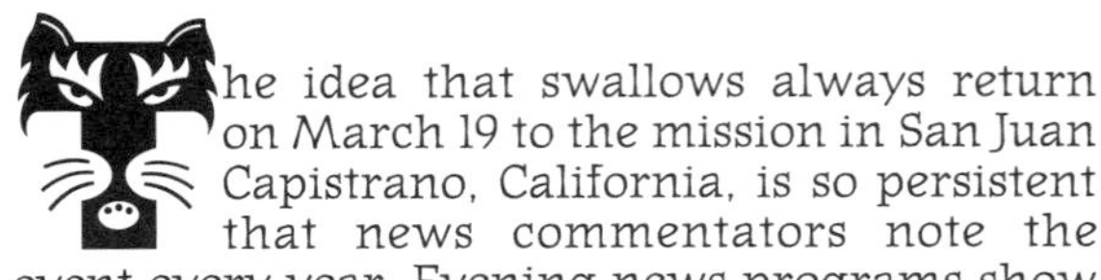

The idea that swallows always return on March 19 to the mission in San Juan Capistrano, California, is so persistent that news commentators note the event every year. Evening news programs show the swallows streaming into the mission on that date, and everyone says, "Isn't that amazing!" But people rarely question the report.

The same thing happens with the "buzzards," or vultures, in Hinckley, Ohio. According to legend, the vultures that have been wintering in the south return to Hinckley on a certain day in mid-March. The town has capitalized on the legend. They used to call the event Buzzard Day, but in order to take advantage of the weekend, townspeople have arbitrarily declared the date as the first Sunday after March 15. Now they call it Buzzard Sunday.

A banner over the town announces the date well in advance. The annual buzzard contest awards a prize to the person who can guess the exact time that the first buzzard will arrive. Children decorate their schools with paper buzzards. The town makes plans for a buzzard festival with a big pancake breakfast to feed those who gather to await the first buzzard. When the day arrives, more than 35,000 people may gather for the early-morning buzzard watch. Each person hopes to be the first to see one of the famous birds. The television cameras are in place. Someone shouts. There it is—a mere speck in the distance. The cameras roll, and the evening news reports that the buzzards arrived right on schedule. And no one seems to question the authenticity of the event.

The truth is that neither the swallows of Capistrano nor the vultures of Hinckley pay any attention to the dates that human myths have established. The swallows usually arrive days before March 19. Likewise in Hinckley, the vultures have been there for days.

People have set many dates for Jesus' return, but He told us plainly that the date is not known. Besides, we don't need to wait for a particular day, because Jesus also said that "now is the day of salvation" (2 Corinthians 6:2).

A Word From Our Creator

But of that day and that hour knoweth no man, no, not the angels which are in heaven, neither the Son, but the Father. Mark 13:32.

March 17

Guinea Pigs

These adorable little creatures aren't really pigs, of course, and they certainly aren't related to guinea fowl. Furthermore, they don't come from the African country of Guinea or the South Pacific island of New Guinea, so why would anyone ever have called them guinea pigs?

Guinea pigs are members of the cavy family, a large South American family of rodents. Cavies live in colonies with extensive burrow systems. They are mainly nocturnal, and farmers often consider them a nuisance. But it is reported that every Indian family in Bolivia keeps cavies as pets.

For several thousand years the people of South America have been raising guinea pigs. None of them live in the wild any longer. In the mid-1500s European explorers took some of them home as pets, and before long people all over Europe had guinea pigs. Merchants sold them for a gold English coin called a guinea. Since the grunts and squeals of the little creatures sounded like those of pigs, they became known as the little pigs that you could buy for a guinea—*guinea pigs*. The coin was named after the country that served as the source of the gold—Guinea. So in a roundabout way, the guinea pigs were named for an African country in which they have never lived. By the way, pigs do live in Guinea, but they aren't guinea pigs.

At birth guinea pigs are small enough to fit into a teaspoon. They come into the world with their eyes wide open and with a full coat of hair. After licking themselves dry, they begin to eat and grow for four weeks, by which time they have attained their full length of 8 to 12 inches. They have no tails at all, which has somehow given rise to the folk saying that if you pick up a guinea pig by its tail, its eyes will fall out.

Guinea pigs are among the most adorable little creatures in the world. They are naturally tame, and when you hold them, they snuggle down in your hand or in the crook of your arm and peek out at the world through unblinking black eyes. They are comical to watch as they go about their business. Aren't you glad that God made cute little animals, as well as those that are big and strong?

A Word From Our Creator

I have made the earth, the man and the beast that are upon the ground, by my great power and by my outstretched arm, and have given it unto whom it seemed meet unto me. Jeremiah 27:5.

March 18

33-kDA

This promise relates to the spiritual life that Jesus develops in us as we turn our lives over to Him, but we can find a biological truth here also. Who better to complete the re-creation of our character than the Creator Himself—the One who made us in the first place?

Your external features and the functions of your internal organs are controlled by the set of coded messages, or genes, that you inherited from your parents. Genes make up the 23 pairs of chromosomes that exist in the nucleus of almost every cell in your body.

Some genes work only in specific parts of your body. Through a highly complex process that we are only beginning to understand, the genes that regulate the growth and operation of different parts of your body are activated only in those parts. For example, certain genes produce your liver, and other genes cause it to function. And even though those liver genes appear in almost every other cell in your body, they do their work *only* in your liver. You have liver genes in your big toe, and you have big-toe genes in your liver. But the genes function only in the area where they are supposed to work. If the big-toe genes did their work throughout your body, you would be nothing but a collection of big toes.

A gene that operates in every cell in your body is the "on/off" switch gene. Discovered by scientists at Stanford University, this is the gene that switches on when you hurt yourself, such as when you cut your finger. New tissue, including skin with your own personal fingerprint, must form to replace the damaged tissue. Scientists have cataloged this gene as number 33-kDA. As a number, it doesn't mean much, but as an important element of your body, it is a matter of life and death. The Creator put within Adam and Eve gene number 33-kDA, and every human being since that time has received an exact copy of 33-kDA.

If Jesus can provide such an amazing way for our bodies to fix themselves when we get hurt, He certainly can complete the spiritual work that He has begun in us. The difference, in this case, however, is that the "on/off" switch is our power of choice. We decide—and He does the rest.

A Word From Our Creator

Being confident of this very thing, that he which hath begun a good work in you will perform it until the day of Jesus Christ. Philippians 1:6.

March 19

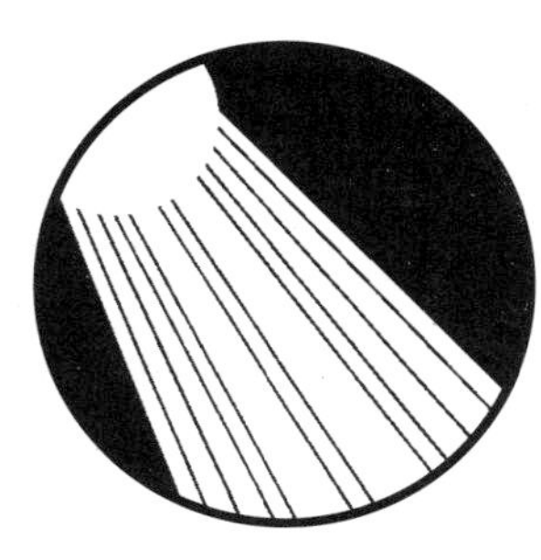

Sparkling Lights

While on a walk in South Carolina, a woman and her friends approached the edge of a pond. On the far side of the pond she could see what appeared to be sparkling lights of all different colors. As she called to her friends to look, the lights almost immediately began to go out. But as they watched quietly, the sparkling water-lights began to reappear. Someone called them "dancing lights," for they appeared to be bouncing around on the water's surface. Others said they looked like little tongues of fire or lights on a Christmas tree.

The lights mystified the group. Some of the people were certain that the reflection of sunlight on the backs of a school of fish caused them, while others were just as sure that they were the result of the sun's reflection on the wind-rippled water. Since none of them could get to the other side of the pond, the mystery continued. The woman asked everyone she knew about the lights, but nobody had an explanation.

One day she was standing by another pond when the lights appeared again. This time there was a canoe and someone to go out and check on what was causing the sparkling lights. To their amazement, they found that small water bugs were somehow creating the lights. But we still don't know what kind of water bugs they are, or what makes the light. The water bugs sparkle only when undisturbed.

It is wonderful to discover mysterious things in the natural world. They give us another indication of the kind of Creator we have: He has created enough mystery to keep us busy looking for answers for all eternity.

As Christians we shine as mysterious lights in a dark world. Our light, which comes from Jesus, the light that lighteth every man (John 1:9), will attract people to Him.

A Word From Our Creator

That ye may be blameless and harmless, the sons of God, without rebuke, in the midst of a crooked and perverse nation, among whom ye shine as lights in the world. Philippians 2:15.

March 20

The Earth's Four Corners

Usually we assume that John the revelator is speaking only symbolically in our text. That may be the case, but a recent discovery proves that the earth actually has four corners of sorts. For reasons yet to be explained, four points on earth have a sea level some 220 feet higher than everywhere else. As it happens, each point is over an area of ocean.

Scientists at the Johns Hopkins Applied Physics Laboratory in Silver Spring, Maryland, were working on a world-mapping project for the U.S. Navy. Using satellites to get a precise measurement of the earth's surface, they discovered that four high points existed over an otherwise sea-level ocean.

The four points at which the surface of the water is elevated in this unexplained way occur over the following approximate areas:

1. From Ireland north toward the North Pole.
2. From New Guinea north toward Japan.
3. About midway between Africa and Antarctica.
4. Just west of South America.

If you plot these points on a globe, you'll notice that the resulting figure produces a pyramid-type design of earth. Of course, a mere 200 or so feet of increased elevation does not cause a very obvious difference on a round earth that is 25,000 miles in diameter, but the phenomenon is significant enough to cause some researchers to wonder why such a strange condition exists.

It is also interesting to note that between these high points on earth are several low points more than 250 feet lower than one would expect if the earth were precisely round. Since we know that wind is generally what pushes water around on earth's oceans, we may be tempted to wonder whether or not four prevailing winds are shoving the ocean into huge piles of water, thereby causing these four "points." Furthermore, we could also wonder what might happen if the prevailing pattern of winds changed in some way. What do you think?

A Word From Our Creator

And after these things I saw four angels standing on the four corners of the earth, holding the four winds of the earth. Revelation 7:1.

March 21

Skunk Cabbage: A Warm-blooded Plant

A Word From Our Creator

He giveth snow like wool: he scattereth the hoarfrost like ashes. . . . who can stand before his cold? He sendeth out his word and melteth them. Psalm 147:16-18.

Well before the snow has melted and weeks before most plants of spring have put forth their tender shoots, the skunk cabbage is sending up its ugly, stinking flower. Other plants freeze in the snow- and ice-laden marshes of this plant's range in eastern and central North America, but the skunk cabbage flourishes. Why?

The skunk cabbage belongs to the aroid family, the only plants on earth that come with built-in heaters. Botanists still don't know fully how the heat production works, but as one science writer put it, skunk cabbage and its relatives "behave more like skunks than cabbages." They break down fat into carbohydrates, which the flower cells in turn burn to produce the heat. The amount of heat generated in the skunk cabbage flower not only melts away the snow but also keeps the flower at a constant 72°F for the two weeks that it blooms.

The philodendrons, common decorative plants, are also members of the aroid family. One philodendron adds another wrinkle to the aroid mystery: it burns fat directly without first converting it into carbohydrates. The temperature in the flower of this aroid may reach 100°F during the two nights that it blooms. The plant's heat production is so efficient that Dan Walker, a botanist from the University of California, says that the "fuel is chewed up at a phenomenal rate, approaching that used by a hummingbird's wing muscle and heart muscle."

One theory about the hot blossoms is that the heat attracts insects that could not move if they were too cold. By finding a warm place in and around the warm flowers, the insects keep cozy as they move from flower to flower, pollinating the plants in the process.

The aroids teach us that the Word of God, Jesus, is capable of providing a warm, safe haven for us, His followers, even when our own righteousness is more like the smell of skunk cabbage (Isaiah 64:6).

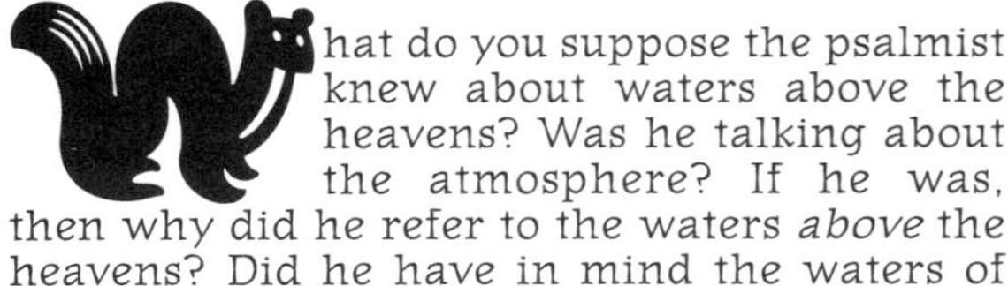

What do you suppose the psalmist knew about waters above the heavens? Was he talking about the atmosphere? If he was, then why did he refer to the waters *above* the heavens? Did he have in mind the waters of the river of life in heaven, where God's throne is? We can't know for sure, but it is possible that here again, through the miracle of inspiration, the Bible relates to a truth that even its authors may not have understood.

Astronomers do find water above the heavens. Racing through space at incredible speeds are huge balls of ice, crystallized water. In fact, if they had known about them, ancient star gazers might have had the gods participating in a celestial snowball fight. We now know these snowballs in space as comets.

During the last fly by of Halley's Comet in 1985-1986, scientists sent several probes into space to study it. Thus we learned that Halley's Comet is an oblong ball of ice, nine miles long and five miles wide, covered with a blackened crust of space debris. As the comet gets close to the sun, it heats up and the ice begins to melt and boil away through the crust, releasing steam and other gases into space.

When photons streaming through space from the sun encounter the comet, they bombard the escaping gases, pushing them away from the sun in a visible lighted stream. That means that when the comet is going away from the sun, its tail will point out in front of it.

A comet leaves behind floating dust particles. When Earth's orbital path passes through these areas of dust, we see a meteoric shower as the dust particles burn up in our atmosphere.

As a comet encounters a planet's atmosphere or comes too close to the sun, it sometimes breaks up into two or more smaller comets, or, on rare occasions, it might totally disintegrate. What do you suppose would happen if the earth collided head-on with a comet? Would the comet break up into chunks of ice that would rain down upon earth? Is it possible that John the revelator saw such a situation in vision when he wrote, "And there fell upon men a great hail out of heaven, every stone about the weight of a talent" (Rev. 16:21)?

Space Snowballs

A Word From Our Creator

Praise him, ye heavens of heavens, and ye waters that be above the heavens. Psalm 148:4.

The Perfect Flying Machine

We take birds for granted, yet they represent one of the most impossible miracles of engineering genius on earth. If you received the task of designing and building a bird, where would you start?

First, you would have to construct a creature that weighed almost nothing, but was sturdy enough to withstand strong winds. You couldn't use thin sticks like those we use for kites, because they break at the first contact with a tree, so you'd have to think of something else.

Second, you would need a covering that was wind-efficient and insulating to prevent the first rain or snow from grounding the bird. And the covering would need to replace itself several times a year because of the beating that it would take in flying.

Third, you would have to have an efficient engine that would hold enough fuel to sustain flight over long distances without refueling and yet without adding a lot of weight to the body. It would require a lightweight fuel that burns slowly.

We could list more specifications, but let's stop and consider whether or not you're ready to bid on the job. Can you imagine the task that confronted the Creator as He designed His idea called "bird"?

Consider just one of the features: the strong lightweight structure for the creature. And let's use the Magnificent Frigate Bird as our example. This large bird of the tropics has a seven-foot wingspread. It can soar for hours without ever appearing to move a feather, and only a structure that weighs no more than a kite could do that. In fact, as ornithologist Robert Cushman Murphy reports, the entire skeleton of the frigate bird weighs only seven ounces! Even the bird's feathers weigh more than that. And yet science tells us that those bones are so perfectly designed in terms of mechanical laws that they have a tensile strength close to that of cast iron.

If God can make a bird, He can certainly make you into the special person that He wants you to be.

A WORD FROM OUR CREATOR

Ah Lord God! behold, thou hast made the heaven and the earth by thy great power and stretched out arm, and there is nothing too hard for thee. Jeremiah 32:17.

ou have about 650 muscles in your body, 650 motors that give you the ability to move. A person who just lies around all day instead of getting his muscles working is often compared to the sloth, an animal that creeps so slowly that you have to watch closely to make sure that it really is moving. Slow movement is normal for the sloth, but it's not normal for you.

Sitting or lying around and watching TV all day is a good example of slothful behavior. About the only exercise you get is dashing for a snack during the advertisements. And that's not enough to keep several things from happening.

Unused muscles quickly begin to lose their size and power. If inactive long enough, they will stop functioning altogether. For example, if you strap your arm to your side, eventually you won't be able to use it at all, even if you take away the strap. But you're not going to do that, of course. You're more likely to pick up lazy habits that will keep you from getting the kind of exercise that keeps your muscles strong.

Lack of exercise also affects the way you think and the way you feel. In fact, depression is a common result of slothful living. According to a health scientist named Paffenbarger, if you are more active, you're more likely to have a happy outlook. The reason for this is simple—exercise helps the blood flow to your brain.

Your brain makes up only about 2 percent of your body's total weight, but it uses 25 percent of the oxygen that your body takes in. It's also eight times more dependent on oxygen than any other organ in your body. When you don't exercise, your blood accumulates in your abdomen, and your brain becomes starved for oxygen. If the brain is short on oxygen, it cannot function efficiently. You aren't able to understand things clearly or to make appropriate judgments. Also, you will feel unhappy and irritable.

The inevitable result of such body abuse is a shorter life span. God made you to move, and "in him we live, and move, and have our being" (Acts 17:28).

650 Muscles

A WORD FROM OUR CREATOR

The desire of the slothful killeth him; for his hands refuse to labour. Proverbs 21:25.

March 25

Border Collies and Aleutian Geese

The border collie is a gentle, medium-sized dog valued for its ability to herd sheep. A border collie may be black and white or gray and white, or it may be a combination of black, white, and tan. People do not breed the border collie to meet accepted physical standards of color and form but instead for intelligence and trainability. Since 1873 the border collie has demonstrated its talents in sheepherding trials. The dog works by responding immediately to the whistled commands of its trainer, commands that tell the dog to retrieve a wandering sheep, to circle the flock to keep it together in a tight group, and to divide and combine flocks. Recently, people have used the border collie's gentleness and intelligence to round up a group of a different type.

By 1975 foxes had destroyed all the Canada geese on the Aleutian Islands except 800 birds on Buldir. U.S. Fish and Wildlife Service personnel decided to rid the islands of the foxes and transplant some of the geese from Buldir to other islands. Armed with nets, wildlife biologists raced after the geese on Buldir. And the geese usually outran the biologists. After three weeks of chasing over the rocky terrain, tripping, and sometimes injuring themselves and the birds, the scientists had netted only 120 geese.

In hopes of finding a more efficient way of capturing the Aleutian geese, the scientists asked an Oregon dog trainer for help. The trainer and his two border collies, Cap and Lass, joined the roundup. Cap and Lass, following the whistled signals of their trainer, proved to be just what the scientists needed. In only four days the dogs found and cornered 143 geese. The geese "froze" when they saw the dogs, so the scientists only had to walk up to them and pick them up. The long and patient work of the trainer was certainly obvious as the collies performed eagerly and effectively.

By careful training that begins when they are young, border collies learn to use their intelligence and gentleness in valuable ways. Our parents have the God-given responsibility to train us to respond, not as dogs to whistles but as responsive children of the Creator, eager to use the talents that He has given us.

A Word From Our Creator

Train up a child in the way he should go: and when he is old, he will not depart from it. Proverbs 22:6.

March 26

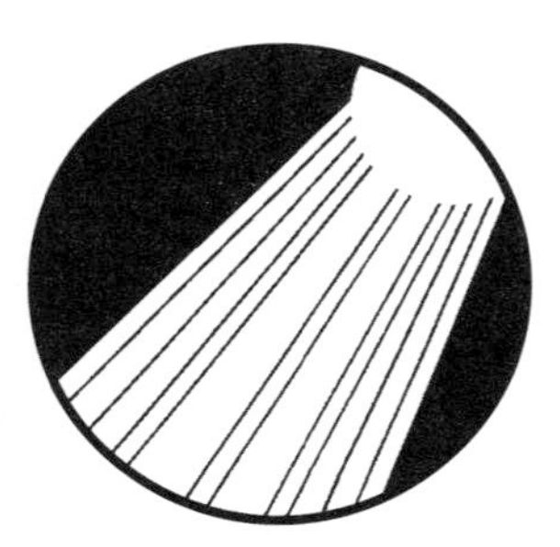

Light of the Eyes

You have probably heard sayings such as "her eyes sparkled," "his eyes lit up," or "they are bright-eyed and bushy-tailed." These phrases have come down to us through history from a time when human beings believed that light actually came from our eyes. After all, when you look at a person, you always see a spot of light there. Don't you?

Four hundred years before Christ, the Greek philosopher Plato taught that we can see because our eyes spray out particles of light that interact with objects and allow us to see. Democritus, another Greek philosopher of that time, disagreed with Plato. According to Democritus, light came from the objects in the form of tiny particles that invade the eye and cause us to see. Yet another Greek thinker, Aristotle, argued that light, wherever it comes from, travels not in particles, but in waves like the ripples on a pond.

As it turned out, all three men were partly right. Plato was right about the particles, Democritus about the particles coming from objects, even though he did not know that the particles actually originated from a light source and bounced off the objects, and Aristotle about light traveling in waves. It is really quite amazing that these men could sit around and talk about these things and come to such scientifically correct conclusions without using modern instruments. How do you suppose they did that?

Now let's go back to our text. We know that there is not really a light in our eyes, but when we are happy we tend to hold our heads up. This allows your eyes to catch the reflection of whatever light is around you.

Let's suppose that you are moping around with your head down and feeling sad or discouraged. Suddenly you learn something that makes you glad and hopeful. Your head snaps up, and the reflection of the light source in your eyes is visible to your friends. They will say something like, "Did you see those eyes light up?"

So the light in our eyes is not what Greek philosophers thought it was, but it does indicate when we are happy or sad. As David learned, when we are discouraged we can depend upon the Lord to renew the light in our eyes.

A Word From Our Creator

My heart panteth, my strength faileth me: as for the light of mine eyes, it also is gone from me. Psalm 38:10.

MARCH 27

The Waters of Earth

It is hard to imagine how much water our planet really has. The amount is so great that it is easier to measure it in cubic miles—that is as a cube, like an ice cube, one mile high, one mile wide, and one mile deep. One cubic mile of water holds more than a trillion gallons. If you want to write that number, start with a 1 and add 12 zeros. Remember that is the number of gallons in just *one* cubic mile of water.

Earth has about 326 million cubic miles of water. Measured in gallons, that's 326 million, million, million gallons, or 326 sextillion gallons.

About 97 percent of earth's water is salt water in the seas and oceans of the world, and about 2 percent is bound up in glaciers and polar icecaps, leaving only about 1 percent for all the freshwater in lakes, rivers, streams, and under ground. What about water in the atmosphere? The air above the earth contains only about one-thousandth of 1 percent of the available water on Earth.

About 4 trillion gallons of water falls as rain on the United States every day of the year. About 70 percent of that gets used by plants or evaporates back into the air. Of the remaining 30 percent, people use about 6 percent. The rest flows by streams and rivers into the sea.

The hydrologic cycle, by which water evaporates into the air and returns again as rain or dew, is so efficient that every drop of water on earth has been recycled so many times that you literally are drinking the same water molecules that have been drunk by others for thousands of years. Some of the water you bathed in yesterday may have been flowing several months ago in the Jordan River. And it is possible that John the Baptist baptized Jesus in that same water 2,000 years ago.

Because of the water cycle in nature, we probably still have the same amount of water on earth now as when God created this world, and it is the same water now as it was then. God provided water in abundance, and then He established methods by which to store it for permanent use for as long as our planet should last.

A WORD FROM OUR CREATOR

He gathereth the waters of the sea together as an heap: he layeth up the depth in storehouses. Psalm 33:7.

Rio Frio is a very small town a few miles south of Leakey and just west of Utopia in western Texas. Rio Frio received its name from the nearby river of cold water that flows down from the Edwards Plateau and into the Rio Grande to the south. The Rio Frio is a beautiful little river bordered by some very large trees, such as bald cypress and live oak.

The history of the entire area revolves around one of those oaks, the Rio Frio Landmark Oak. A combination church and school built in the late 1860s nestled behind this old tree. Preachers of all Protestant denominations came to speak in this little building, and the town conducted elections here and judges held court here. Picnics and weddings took place in the shade of the ancient oak's branches.

When it came time to make an official survey of the land for the landowners in the community, the highest point of a nearby mountain and the old oak tree in front of the school were designated as the most permanent landmarks in the territory. The tree served as the bearing point for the first town lot, and all future deed descriptions in the community were tied to that landmark. In a very real sense, that oak has served as the cornerstone for the town of Rio Frio.

The Landmark Oak still stands along Farm Road 1120 on the east side of the Rio Frio. But a blight has begun to attack the live oaks of Texas, and someday the Landmark Oak may fall to the disease. It will be a sad day when that ancient giant among trees falls to the unseen hand of a blight creeping across the land.

This earth has also seen giants among men. Some have served as steady and stately examples for others, but the Bible clearly states that "all have sinned." It is only by establishing our connection to Jesus, who is the only absolutely true cornerstone, or landmark, that we can be sure of our standing before God.

March 28

The Rio Frio Landmark Oak

A Word From Our Creator

[We] are built upon the foundation of the apostles and prophets, Jesus Christ himself being the chief corner stone. Ephesians 2:20.

March 29

Orion

Is it possible that in today's text God was giving Job clues to some of the secrets of the universe, secrets waiting for astronomers to reveal at the end of time—our time?

What is Orion's band? To ancient stargazers, the constellation represented a hunter named Orion who moved gracefully across the heavens. The three stars that make up the hunter's belt represent Orion's "band." Each of these three stars, which together are part of a pattern, is actually traveling at three different speeds in three different directions. In fact, each star that forms the constellation of Orion is traveling on a course independent of all the rest. The bands that appear to connect the separate stars into a whole have been loosed, as it were.

Yet the most beautiful aspect of Orion is not the speed and direction of its many stars; rather, it is the beauty and purpose of one particular star—the middle star in Orion's sword—hanging down from the belt. Astronomers know this star as the Great Nebula of Orion. Take a look at it through binoculars. You will see that it is not a star, but a glowing cloudlike structure of cosmic gases and dust shining with the reflected glory of many stars. In fact, the Orion nebula contains within it what appears to be a gigantic cavern in space, if you can imagine that—a space of indescribable beauty 19 trillion miles across and 51 trillion miles deep. It almost appears to be the entrance to an unseen section of space.

For centuries mankind has wondered about this star. Garrett P. Serviss, author of *Curiosities of the Sky*, wrote, "Is there not some vast mystery concealed in that part of the heavens?" The poet Tennyson, who called it a "mystery star," wrote, "I never gazed upon it but I dreamt of some vast charm concluded in that star to make fame nothing." And Ellen White described a vision in which she saw the Holy City coming down through the open space of Orion to its final resting place on earth.

Could it be that behind the Great Nebula of Orion is the entrance to the power base of the universe? What do you think?

A Word From Our Creator

Canst thou . . . loose the bands of Orion? Job 38:31.

The hoatzin (pronounced WHAT-seen) is one of the world's most unusual birds. Once thought to be most closely related to the chickenlike birds, ornithologists now consider the hoatzin to be a close relative to the cuckoos. Hoatzins live in small colonies of 10 to 50 birds in the jungles of northeastern South America. They are poor fliers, using their wings mainly for gliding. Their call is a noisy, croaking sound often heard at night. Hoatzins also have a strong, disagreeable odor that's earned them the name "stink bird."

A pair of hoatzins builds a platform nest of sticks in river shrubbery 5 to 20 feet above water. Then the female lays two or three brown-spotted white eggs in the nest. Those eggs are ordinary-looking enough, but the dark, leathery-skinned chicks that hatch out are exceptionally ugly. The naked newborns appear helpless, but shortly after they hatch, the strange-looking little hoatzins begin clambering about the bushes in which they live—and if they fall into the river, they swim!

At the "elbow" bend on each wing, the hoatzin chick has two strong claws that it uses, along with its feet, to climb from branch to branch. If threatened by a predator, such as a snake or marauding monkey, the baby hoatzin dives into the water and swims underwater to escape. Then it simply uses its wing claws and feet to slowly and deliberately climb back up into its tree. After about two or three weeks—when it begins to learn to fly—the chick loses its wing claws and its capacity to swim.

The Creator has given the hoatzin chick the ability to "depart from the snares of death." As children of the same Creator, we also receive what we need to survive. You have heard the saying "It's a jungle out there." To survive spiritually, all we have to do is ask for the special spiritual adaptations that God has promised to help us live in *this* world while we look forward to living in perfect peace and safety with Him in heaven.

Hoatzins

A Word From Our Creator

In the fear of the Lord is strong confidence: and his children shall have a place of refuge. The fear of the Lord is a fountain of life, to depart from the snares of death. Proverbs 14:26, 27.

The "Killer Squirrel"

Seventy-five-year-old Mrs. Frisbee was walking along the sidewalk near her son's home in Austin, Texas, when a vicious animal attacked her from behind. The savage assault came from nothing less than a resident gray squirrel. It naturally frightened Mrs. Frisbee when the rodent began biting her legs. She tried to run, but the animal chased her, grabbed her, and climbed up her coat, biting his way up to her shoulders. Pulling the coat over her head, she ran to a neighbor's house for safety. Somewhere along the way the squirrel jumped off and disappeared.

The authorities summoned a state health department veterinarian to the scene. Wanting to get the squirrel to check it for rabies as quickly as possible, he brought his gun. Soon a posse roamed the neighborhood, looking for the "killer squirrel" that, as it turned out, also had bitten other people besides Mrs. Frisbee. Two motorcycle police officers joined the search, and soon one of them yelled, "Hey, I think I have him!" And sure enough, there was the squirrel—but it wasn't clear just who had whom. The small beast was attacking the officer—biting right through his boots!

Needless to say, the squirrel didn't live long, and the vet took its body to the lab for the rabies check. Tests found no sign of disease. The only explanation anyone could offer for the squirrel's behavior was that mating season had arrived and that this was one extremely territorial squirrel. It attacked anything and anybody that came into its area.

We could say that the squirrel was only doing what it believed to be right, but that wouldn't make its actions any more desirable. There is sometimes a limit to what we can do in the name of what is right. We have to use common sense in defending even right causes. Often we can hurt others by being tactless or too forceful.

A WORD FROM OUR CREATOR

For all the law is fulfilled in one word, . . . Thou shalt love thy neighbour as thyself. But if ye bite and devour one another, take heed that ye be not consumed. Galatians 5:14, 15.

n *Arnie the Darling Starling* you can read the remarkable story of the baby Eurasian starling that Margaret Corbo rescued from a daisy patch one spring day in 1979. Mrs. Corbo returned the bird to his nest several times, but he wouldn't stay, so she decided to raise him herself. Since he sort of reminded her of Arnold Schwarzenegger, Margaret called him Arnold, or Arnie.

For weeks Arnie didn't make a sound—not even a chirp to beg for food. He just sat silently and watched the world and listened. Margaret was passing him one day when she heard someone call, "Arnold." The voice sounded like her own.

"Arnold!" the voice said again, in a scolding tone this time.

As Margaret stared at the bird in disbelief, he tilted his head to one side and said, "Arnold?" as though asking for confirmation of his name.

Sure now of her attention, Arnie repeated his name once more. "Arnold."

That was only the beginning. Before he died at the ripe old bird age of almost 4, Arnie could not only talk, but he also learned to sing—well, whistle is more accurate. He could whistle "Mary Had a Little Lamb," "Michael, Row the Boat Ashore," and the opening bars of Beethoven's Fifth Symphony.

Starlings are known for their ability to mimic the sounds that they hear, but usually they repeat the calls of other birds. Few people appreciate this ability of the starling, however, because the species is among the most detested of all birds. Starlings are raucous and mean. Ever since their introduction from Europe in 1890, they have been contributing to the decline of some of America's favorite birds by moving into the nesting cavities used by species like bluebirds and swallows.

But Mrs. Corbo didn't care if the baby starling in the daisy patch was one of a hated breed. He was a baby bird in need, and she cared—she cared enough to save him. In the process Arnie learned new songs, and one day, after Margaret had said it to him many times, he lit on her shoulder and said in a soft voice, "I love you."

Arnold

A WORD FROM OUR CREATOR

And they sung as it were a new song before the throne . . . : and no man could learn that song but the hundred and forty and four thousand. Revelation 14:3.

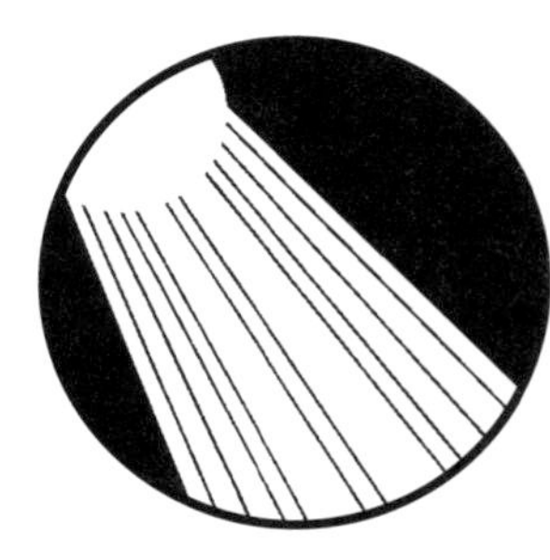

Mirrors and Reflections

A Word From Our Creator

But we all, with open face beholding as in a glass the glory of the Lord, are changed into the same image from glory to glory even as by the Spirit of the Lord. 2 Corinthians 3:18.

How would you like to live without a mirror? You would never have to see yourself as others do, and you would never know if your hair was combed or if your face was dirty. You might think that would be a great idea—at first. Would you want to look at other people who couldn't see their own appearance and didn't fix themselves up to be neat and attractive? A mirror is extremely useful. But for a mirror to work, there has to be light.

Any smooth surface that reflects an image is a mirror. Light coming from most sources is diffused. That means that the light rays bounce off of so many surfaces that they spread around to totally bathe an area in light. When you look into a mirror, light rays from everywhere around you hit the mirror's surface. Enough of them get reflected straight into the pupils of your eyes to let you receive an image of yourself.

The flatness or curvature of the mirror's surface affects how you will see yourself. If the mirror is flat, you appear the same size as you really are, but you seem to be twice as far away as you really are because the light rays are bouncing from you to the mirror and back to your eye before you see them. If the mirror's surface is curved, it distorts your image, and you may appear larger or smaller than you really are.

In order for the mirror to do you any good, you have to have some idea of what you should look like, and then, in your mind, you compare what you see in the mirror with that ideal mental image. If you notice a difference between the two images, then you work at getting the reflection in the mirror to match the picture in your mind.

Today's text refers to the mirror as a "glass." As a Christian, you have a spiritual mirror that reflects you as you really are. And in your mind, with the aid of the Holy Spirit, you see Jesus. You have heard the word "reflection" used in the sense of thinking about something. Through reflection, your mind's eye picks up the rays of Jesus, the Light of the world, and you see the difference between yourself and Him. Then you let the Holy Spirit help you become like Jesus.

APRIL 3

The Tides

As early as A.D. 77 the Romans recognized the relationship between the tides and the movement of the moon. But not until 1687 did Isaac Newton develop the idea that the universal law of gravitation causes the tides. The earth draws toward its center everything within its reach, including the sun and moon. With gravities of their own, the sun and moon also tug on the earth, causing the fluid oceans to respond with four daily tides.

Tides operate on a 24-hour-and-52-minute cycle. That's why high tide and low tide are almost an hour later each day than they were the day before. The main tidal cycle divides into four subcycles, each of which is six hours and 13 minutes long, to produce two high tides and two low tides each day. To describe the daily cycle, we start with what is called high-high tide when the water comes farthest up on the beach. From high-high tide the water level falls to its lowest point in the cycle—low-low tide. Then, six hours and 13 minutes later, the water has risen to high tide again, but since this high tide does not advance as far up the shore as the first one, it is called low-high tide. Now the water level drops again to a low tide, but one that is not as low as the low-low tide, so we term it high-low tide. After another six hours and 13 minutes the water has pushed back to the original high-high tide level. In summary, the pattern is high-high, low-low, low-high, high-low, and back to high-high to restart the cycle.

We call tidal flow toward the coast flood tide. When the water rushes away from the coast, we label it ebb tide. The rapid flow of the incoming flood tide often causes a visible wave known as a tidal bore. In Nova Scotia the tide from the Bay of Fundy up the Petitcodiac River pushes a four-foot-high tidal bore in a daily tidal current that sometimes rises and falls more than 50 feet!

The tides provide a magnificent illustration of the perfect precision with which our Creator controls the elements of nature.

A WORD FROM OUR CREATOR

And they feared exceedingly, and said one to another, What manner of man is this, that even the wind and sea obey him? Mark 4:41.

Dandelions and Goldenrod

It is easy to judge a flower (or a person) by its common reputation. For example, two of the most beautiful wildflowers in North America are generally hated and considered pests. People see the golden-yellow dandelion blossoms that dot spring lawns not as beautiful wildflowers but as pesky weeds that they need to eliminate at all cost. The equally beautiful goldenrod that gilds the roadsides and meadows every fall we usually despise as a source of allergies, even though it isn't to blame at all.

Those persistent dandelions that lawn owners battle today provided a rich and much-needed source of vitamins for early American settlers. Because of the food that it stores in its taproot, the dandelion plant stays green well into winter and blooms with the first warm spring sunshine. Pioneers used the greens as a spring tonic—a dose of the vitamins and minerals that the plant provided really did make people feel better after a winter-long lack of green vegetables. They also used it as a vegetable, boiling the older, less-tender leaves before eating them and using the young leaves in salads. And they roasted the roots to make a coffeelike drink and made wine from the flowers.

The more than 100 varieties of goldenrod native to North America constituted a gold mine in colonial times. People considered goldenrod such a useful herb that they sent shiploads back to England where others sold the dried leaves to make medicine. The genetic name of goldenrod, *Solidago*, refers to the ability of the plants to make a person well, or "solid."

When we accept Jesus, we become flowers in His garden, bringing joy and happiness to the world and glory to His name. But, as with the wildflowers, we are welcomed by some people and perhaps despised by others. However, it is not the job of one flower in the garden to judge another's value. God's garden has room for everyone, and He alone is the gardener who will judge where we belong and what our work shall be.

A WORD FROM OUR CREATOR

Of a truth I perceive that God is no respecter of persons. Acts 10:34.

A major problem that astronomers have had is seeing clearly through Earth's atmosphere. For years scientists dreamed of peeking above our atmosphere, where air molecules would not distort the light from space. Not long ago that dream came true.

In 1990 astronauts aboard the NASA space shuttle *Discovery* launched the Hubble Space Telescope. Hubble, as scientists call the telescope, has a primary mirror almost eight feet in diameter. That mirror reflects an image from space to a smaller secondary mirror, then back through a hole in the center of the primary mirror and into a camera. From the camera, the image goes by radio signal to laboratories on Earth.

While scientists at first had problems with the relationship between the two mirrors, they have apparently solved most of these difficulties. Hubble has revealed things that would be impossible to observe from Earth.

Focusing on a galaxy called M87, a galaxy 52 million light-years away in the constellation Virgo, Hubble has detected evidence of a black hole about 5 billion times the mass of the sun. A black hole isn't a hole at all. Rather, it's an object so massive that its gravity drags everything, including light, toward its center. At the center of M87 the stars are 300 times closer to each other than expected. This indicates that something extremely powerful is pulling them toward the center of the galaxy. The only theory available to explain such a force is the existence of a black hole.

Hubble has given us the best pictures yet of the planet Pluto and its giant moon, Charon. Charon is almost half the size of the planet around which it revolves, giving rise to the theory that Pluto is a double planet. Charon orbits about 12,000 miles above Pluto's surface.

Hubble has found evidence of a new solar system only 56 light-years away, with the star Beta Pictoris at its center. The telescope has sent back information about what appear to be comets hurtling toward Beta Pictoris on paths apparently affected by the gravity of other unseen objects with at least the mass of the moon. Could those objects be planets?

Hubble Space Telescope

A WORD FROM OUR CREATOR

And the heavens shall praise thy wonders, O Lord: thy faithfulness also in the congregation of the saints.
Psalm 89:5.

Killer Cones

Cone shells form a large family of many-whorled mollusks living among the rocks and corals of tropical oceans. Of the world's 500 cone species, only one dwells along the west coast of the United States, and only about 15 inhabit the south Atlantic Coast and the Gulf of Mexico.

Cones are well-known for their beauty. Their shells display a wide variety of colors and patterns. But cones also have another characteristic that's not so beautiful. Some members of the family that live in South Pacific and Indian Ocean waters have poison glands. Venom passes from these glands through a tiny tube to the radula (RAD-u-la), a type of scraper with many tiny teeth. The radula, used for tearing up food into smaller pieces, is located in a long mouthlike organ called a proboscis (pro-BOS-is). In some cones, however, several of the little teeth on the radula are like tiny arrows filled with poison, and the animals use them to kill prey.

Most poisonous cones eat only marine worms, while others prey on other cones. With their powerful poison, they can defend themselves from octopuses and other potential enemies if they have to. And the poison of fish-eating cones is strong enough to kill a human who comes in contact with it.

A cone shell lies buried in the sand on the ocean floor—and waits. When an unsuspecting ocean creature swims close enough, the cone extends its proboscis and shoots one of its tiny arrows into the victim, instantly paralyzing the fish or other animal. Then the cone stretches its mouth open wide and swallows the food whole. Another arrow moves into place, and the shell is ready to shoot its next victim.

Our world is full of agents of death. Some are sudden and devastating, like the killing darts of the cone shells, while others are little habits that control our lives. Sometimes we become ensnared in problems that seem impossible to overcome. But God promises that if we take "the shield of faith, . . . [we] shall be able to quench all the fiery darts of the wicked" (Ephesians 6:16).

A Word From Our Creator

For, lo, the wicked bend their bow, they make ready their arrow upon the string, that they may privily shoot at the upright in heart. Psalm 11:2.

April 7

Sociable Spiders

The idea of spiders being sociable is almost a contradiction in terms. Spiders are among the most efficient of all of Earth's predators, trapping and devouring other spiders just as readily as they catch and eat an insect. So the thought of spiders that are friendly to other spiders and prefer to live together in spacious and extensive colonies may take some getting used to. In any case, of the 35,000 or so different kinds of spiders in the world, a few of them—about 35—are very sociable.

Colonial spiders share a particular tree, cactus plant, parallel strands of telephone wire, or some other structure allowing them enough space to erect their deadly nets side by side. Such colonies may contain as many as 10,000 individual spiders. That's quite a condominium of death for the myriads of flying insects in the area!

The spiders adapt the size of their individual webs to the amount of food available. If food is scarce, neighbors spread out and allow more web space per spider. On the other hand, if food is plentiful, the spiders crowd much closer together and have smaller webs.

Spiders that dwell in colonies have at least two advantages over those that live alone. First, because all of the webs are interconnected, they have a fail-safe early-warning system. When a predator attempts to enter the web, the spidergram immediately alerts all the spiders throughout the entire colony. Second, the more spiders there are, the better the catch. The extensive web system traps insects that would have avoided the web of a single individual.

But whether it is one individual or a colony of thousands, the purpose in life for spiders remains the same. They live to catch the unsuspecting insects that stumble into their traps. You've heard the expression "thick as thieves"? There's sometimes a false sense of friendship when association is based on mistrust.

When the love of Jesus converts thieves (or other sinners), their lives change and they no longer feel any kinship with their former friends. They have new life, a new Friend, and a new family of friends with whom to walk a new life.

A Word From Our Creator

Can two walk together, except they be agreed? Amos 3:3.

April 8

Pain

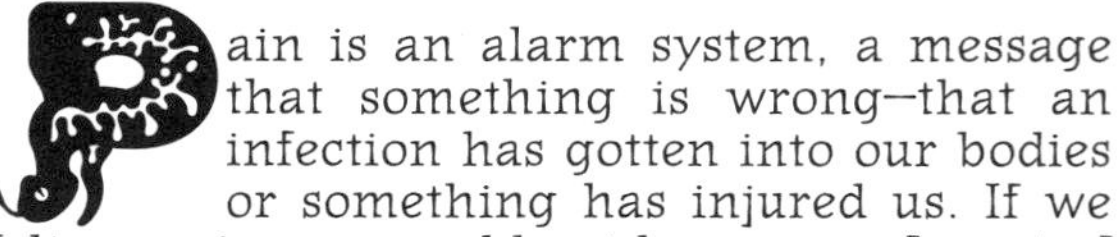

Pain is an alarm system, a message that something is wrong—that an infection has gotten into our bodies or something has injured us. If we felt no pain, we would not be aware of most of the problems that our bodies face, and we would not seek medical care. But the fact that pain is a good thing is no reason for us to enjoy it. In fact, we spend a great deal of effort to get rid of pain.

Pain is the most common reason for seeing a doctor and for taking medicine. Dr. John Bonica, of the International Association for the Study of Pain, estimates that people spend $70 billion a year for pain relief.

We know very little about the nature of pain—what causes it, why some people feel it more severely than others, and what makes it go away. However, we do know that body chemicals go into action the minute that something injures us. These chemicals activate the part of the nervous system that causes us to feel pain within seconds of receiving the injury. The body also produces chemicals that are natural painkillers. The threshold of tolerable pain is different in each person and may be determined by the ability of the body to produce these natural pain relievers.

More amazing than anything else we know about pain, however, is the fact that our attitude may determine how often and how strongly we feel pain. For example, in a Harvard study, sugar pills relieved pain in one third of the people being treated. If the patients believed that they were taking a real medicine, the pain went away. Simple peace of mind was enough for the body to produce its own painkiller.

Jesus brings the greatest peace of mind that we can know. "And the peace of God, which passeth all understanding, shall keep your hearts and minds through Christ Jesus" (Philippians 4:7).

A Word From Our Creator

And God shall wipe away all tears from their eyes; and . . . neither shall there be any more pain: for the former things are passed away. Revelation 21:4.

April 9

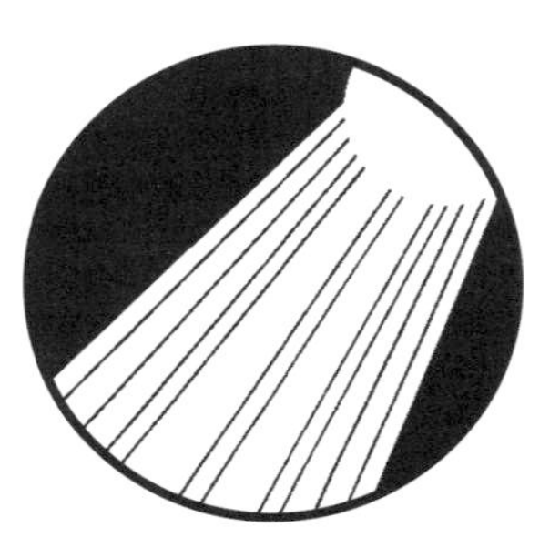

A Prism: Color From Clear

Visible light contains all the colors of the rainbow. The raindrops in a rainbow break up the light rays into bands of color that form the spectrum. If you want to study the spectrum, you don't have to wait for a rainbow, though. All you need is a prism.

A prism can be any one of a number of specific shapes of a solid three-dimensional object, but the most common shape is a three-sided bar with flat ends. When a prism is made of transparent material, such as glass, it separates the light into the full spectrum of colors. How can a piece of clear glass do that?

Unobstructed light rays travel in a straight line. But when those light rays have to pass through something, such as a piece of glass, the light is bent. Hold a prism up to the sunlight. Sunlight is called "white" light because the "color" white includes all the colors of the spectrum. As the sunlight passes through a glass prism the prism bends the rays of each color as they go through. Violet rays are bent the most and red rays the least. All the other colors spread out between those two. As a result, the light emerging from the prism is a full spectrum of all the rainbow colors. If you want to, you can take another prism and reverse the spectrum back into white light.

The spectrum, as projected through a prism, is a marvel of beauty and artistic wonder. Each color blends perfectly into the next in a continuous flow from where the violet rays become visible through blue, green, yellow, orange, and red to where the rays become invisible again. Artists and printers have tried to match the perfection of the spectrum. It is safe to say that they never will, for the spectrum is an example of the perfect work of the Creator.

When Jesus came to Earth as the Light of the world, He also served as a prism. Through Himself He presented the light from heaven to humanity. He showed how we ourselves can let His light shine from us in good deeds that demonstrate that He has lighted our hearts with His love.

A Word From Our Creator

Let your light so shine before men, that they may see your good works, and glorify your Father which is in heaven. Matthew 5:16.

April 10

Caves

Caves have provided shelter and hiding places for people for thousands of years. Some caves form when volcanic lava cools, and pounding waves that carve openings in the rocks along the shore produce others. But most caves result from the action of underground water.

As water seeps down through cracks in rock, the rock slowly dissolves until it leaves a channel large enough for more water to rush through. The water washes away more and more particles of rock and carves out a cave. At first the water fills the cave, but later the water level drops and air moves in. Water continues to seep down through cracks in the rock that eventually forms the ceiling and walls of the cave. With the water come dissolved minerals, which create stalactites hanging from the ceiling, stalagmites that rise from the floor, and columns when the two forms meet in the middle.

We call the study of caves speleology (pronounced spee-lee-OL-uh-gee). Exploring caves is fun, but it can also be a very dangerous hobby if you're not extremely careful. It's best to start your exploration by visiting nearby commercial caves and then joining a club of cave enthusiasts, called spelunkers.

The world is full of many wonderful caves. For example, Mammoth Cave in Kentucky contains rivers, waterfalls, and two lakes, plus fantastic mineral formations. The Eisreisenwelt Caves of Austria house glaciers and fantastic ice formations. The Singing Cave in Iceland—a lava cave—was named for the wonderful sounds that echo from it when people sing into it. The Blue Grotto, on the island of Capri in the Mediterranean Sea, is a wave-formed sea cave filled with sapphire-blue water. The deepest cave in the world is the Gouffre Berger in France, where an underground river has cut a channel more than 3,000 feet below the surface.

Throughout history God has used water to provide hiding places for mankind, and He continues to use water to create spectacular sights in caves. Can you name an instance where Jesus used water to illustrate how He saves us? John 4:5-30 tells such a story.

A Word From Our Creator

When the men of Israel saw that they were in a strait, (for the people were distressed,) then the people did hide themselves in caves. 1 Samuel 13:6.

"A Rose by Any Other Name Would Smell as Sweet"

A Word From Our Creator

The wilderness and the solitary place shall be glad for them; and the desert shall rejoice, and blossom as the rose. It shall blossom abundantly. Isaiah 35:1, 2.

The rose in our text is possibly a sweet-smelling yellow-and-white narcissus that grows in Israel. The flower that we commonly call a rose belongs to the apple family. Although they're different flowers, the scriptural rose and the cultivated rose share a common trait: people value each for its scent. Yet, if you judge a rose by its smell, as Shakespeare did in the quote used in our title, you may be surprised to learn that most of the thousands of varieties of cultivated roses have no odor at all.

The practice of breeding roses goes back about 5,000 years, when the Chinese began experimenting with the flower. Since the late 1700s, breeders have developed more than 20,000 varieties of roses. Rose breeders continue in their quest to produce a rosebush that not only can bloom abundantly throughout spring and summer but can also survive disease, insects, and harsh climates. They want it to produce blossoms that retain their beauty even when shipped long distances as cut flowers. And they also want the flowers to stay fresh for a week when put into a vase. Naturally, breeders would also like to have flowers that smell good, but accomplishing this presents a problem.

Roses, like people, are the result of hundreds of thousands of genes inherited from their parents. When breeders scientifically mix the genes to produce more petals or better color, the genes that determine a rose's scent are also affected. In trying to produce a stronger and more beautiful rose, breeders have for the most part lost or changed its smell.

Attempts to put the fragrance back into the rose have produced roses that smell like nasturtiums, violets, and even cloves. At times breeders have taken two fragrant parent roses and wound up with roses that have no scent or—even worse!—smell like sewer water.

God put the fragrance in flowers. Why would human beings want to change God's plan? Fragrance attracts the insects that pollinate the flowers and thereby guarantee the following year's blossoms. It's a simple system, and it works. For thousands of years humanity has tried to "improve" the rose. Can we really improve on what God has created?

APRIL 12

Mercury

If you were leaving the sun to visit all the planets in our solar system, the first one you'd come to is Mercury, 36 million miles from the sun. And if you could hop a photon freighter traveling at the speed of light, it would take you just over three minutes to get there. That might be enough time to learn that:

1. Mercury is the only planet that's not tilted. It spins on an axis almost perpendicular to its orbital path. That means it wouldn't have seasons as we know them.

2. Mercury is one of two planets—the other being Pluto—with an elliptical, or egg-shaped, orbital path. Their orbits are not circular.

3. Mercury is about 3,000 miles in diameter. Only Pluto is smaller.

4. It takes almost two Earth months for Mercury to turn from one day to the next. A Mercury week would last nearly 14 Earth months, but

5. Of all the planets, Mercury travels the fastest, moving on its orbital path at more than 100,000 miles an hour. It circles the sun four times in less than one Earth year. If you were to grow up on Mercury and count years as we do—the time it takes your planet to orbit the sun—you would be more than four times as old as you are now.

6. Mercury's gravity is 38 percent of what it is on Earth, so if you weigh 80 pounds here, you would weigh 30 pounds on Mercury.

For your visit to Mercury you would need a lot of very special clothes. The planet has no atmosphere to temper the extremes of heat and cold. A typical day begins with the temperature at almost -300°F. As the sun rises, though, the temperature begins to climb rapidly to 800°F or higher, the highest surface temperature of any planet. With no atmosphere on Mercury, you would also have to take along all the air needed for your stay.

The Mercury landscape is one continuous mass of craters, and you'd never know when another incoming meteorite would crash into the surface, sending up a huge splash of dust and boulders. And since the planet has no atmosphere to conduct sound waves, you wouldn't even hear the whoosh and thud of the meteor.

A WORD FROM OUR CREATOR

O give thanks unto the God of heaven: for his mercy endureth for ever. Psalm 136:26.

April 13

The Amazing Sharks

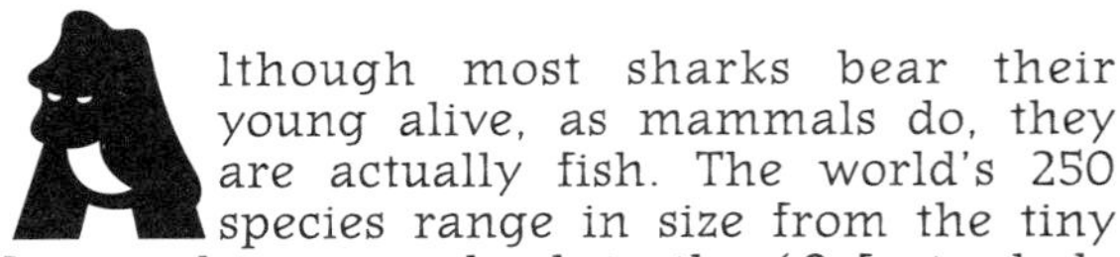

Although most sharks bear their young alive, as mammals do, they are actually fish. The world's 250 species range in size from the tiny four-inch pygmy shark to the 60-foot whale shark. Most large sharks have minute teeth and live mainly on plankton, small squid, crustaceans, and small fish. On the other hand, small and midsized sharks have larger teeth and prey on fish (even other sharks), squid, octopuses, seals—just about anything.

Sharks are well designed for their lifestyle. Their torpedo-shaped bodies allow them to use quick bursts of speed. Their powerful tails are perfect for propelling them. And their inflexible fins are great for steering but not for quick stops or backing up. When sharks hit their target, they do so with such force that they can break off teeth or stun themselves, especially if the object of their attack is a boat.

Except for the plankton-eaters, which use their teeth to strain food from mouthfuls of water, sharks' teeth are designed for seizing, cutting, piercing, and crunching. The teeth grow in rows around the jaws, and more than a single row may be in use at one time. Behind the functioning rows of teeth wait several reserve rows lying flat against the inner surface of the jaws like shingles on a roof, all pointing backward. The reserve rows of teeth move forward to replace worn-out ones.

Although well-equipped for killing, sharks usually eat only when hungry. Smaller fishes seem to be able to tell when they're in danger. Food fishes, such as mackerel, usually hurry away when a shark approaches. But schools of mackerel also have been seen to open a pathway to let a potential predator pass peacefully through.

When we set aside the deadly realities of sharks in today's sin-cursed world, we can see that they are among the most beautiful creatures on Earth. What were the waters of Eden like with the ancestors of sharks—beautifully streamlined—moving peacefully about among the other fish, exhibiting occasional bursts of speed—perhaps just for the joy of being there?

A Word From Our Creator

And God created . . . every living creature that moveth, which the waters brought forth abundantly. *Genesis 1:21.*

April 14

Three Powerful Words

It is about 2:30 in the afternoon. All eyes watch the priest as he prepares to slay the Passover lamb. Behind the priest in all its splendor rises Herod's Temple. The open doors make the Holy Place visible not only from the Court of the Priests but also from the Court of the Men and from the Court of the Women. Everyone gathered to celebrate the Passover can see into the sanctuary all the way to the veil that hides the Most Holy Place from view. This tapestry is 29 feet wide by 87½ feet high and several inches thick. The space behind this veil represents the throne of God, and no man or woman—not even the priests—may go behind the curtain. Only the high priest is permitted to enter the Holy of Holies, and then only once a year on the Day of Atonement.

Meanwhile on a hill outside the city, a hanging is taking place—the Romans are hanging three men on crosses as common criminals. One of the men, however, is different, and He has been the subject of much debate and a series of huge demonstrations over the past week. Some hoped that He was the Messiah who would become king and overthrow the Roman occupiers. Others accused Him of being an imposter and demanded His death when He stated that He was the king of the Jews. To satisfy the Jewish leaders at the time of their holiday, the Roman governor, Pilate, had told them to do with Jesus whatever they wished. So now He was being crucified in shame.

A hush falls over the crowd at the Temple as the priest raises his knife. The Passover lamb is about to die. Suddenly something is wrong. There is motion at the back of the Holy Place, and a sound reaches the priest's ears. Instinctively, he turns his head toward the veil. The knife drops from his hand. The lamb escapes, but no one notices. The eyes of every worshiper watch as the mighty veil begins to tear all by itself from the top to the bottom. As it rips, the ground begins to move back and forth. And then all is quiet.

The Man on the cross outside of town—the One who claimed to be the king of the Jews—has just uttered three words: "It is finished!" (John 19:30). A Lamb—the Lamb of God—has died.

A Word From Our Creator

And behold, the veil of the temple was rent in twain from the top to the bottom; and the earth did quake, and the rocks rent. Matthew 27:51.

esus is dead and buried! After a night of little sleep the followers of Jesus spend Sabbath in stunned disbelief. Just a week earlier, the Man whom they took to be their Saviour had ridden triumphantly into Jerusalem, surrounded by throngs of people shouting, "Hosanna to the son of David: Blessed is he that cometh in the name of the Lord; Hosanna in the highest" (Matthew 21:9). Now fear and despondency grip the hearts of every disciple. Torn apart with anguish, they keep asking each other "Why?" "What went wrong?" "We trusted that it had been he which should have redeemed Israel" (Luke 24:21). Instead of celebrating, the disciples are hiding in fear.

But fear also grips the hearts of the chief priests and the Pharisees. In Jerusalem word that the veil has ripped from top to bottom has spread like wildfire. The holiest of all holy places now stands revealed for all to see, and there is no light there—just darkness. The glory of the Lord has departed. Refusing to believe what they know in their hearts to be the truth, some of the Jewish leaders resort to the only solution they know—power politics. While the Jewish nation rests on the Sabbath, according to the law, these leaders request an audience with Pilate. Imagine that—they go on the Sabbath day to the hated Romans for protection from the power of God. They request and get a seal on Jesus' tomb and a round-the-clock guard of Roman soldiers.

It is indeed a dark day. The Creator of the universe is dead. The Sun of righteousness (Malachi 4:2) has set, and darkness—spiritual this time—is again "upon the face of the deep" (Genesis 1:2). The Bright and Morning Star has ceased to give His light (Revelation 22:16). The Light of the world has gone out. The sun shines in the sky, but its light is somehow dim, and the blood runs cold in the veins of all the people.

Little do they know that the greatest victory ever has been won. If they had only been listening, they would have known what was about to happen. The world is resting, waiting for a new week, when the glory of God will break through the darkness and restore hope to all who believe. If someone could just tell them, "Wait until tomorrow!"

APRIL 15

Earth's Darkest Day

A WORD FROM OUR CREATOR

And the light shineth in darkness; and the darkness comprehended it not. . . . He was in the world, and . . . the world knew him not.
John 1:5-10.

April 16

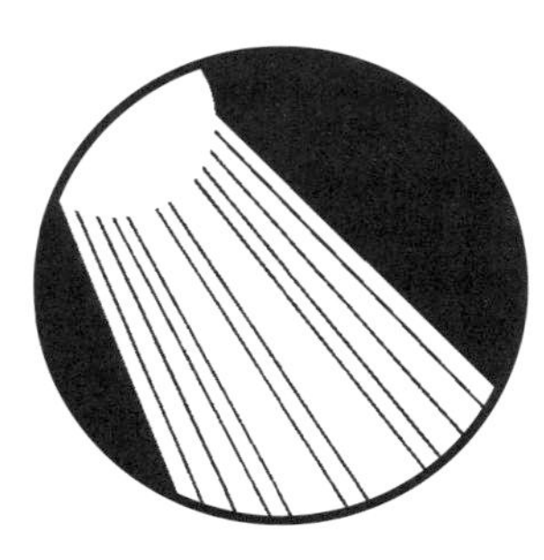

An Angel of Light

A Word From Our Creator

And, behold, there was a great earthquake: for the angel of the Lord descended from heaven, . . . His countenance was like lightning, and his raiment white as snow.
Matthew 28:2, 3.

It is impossible to overemphasize the impact of this event in the history of the universe. Beings from unnumbered worlds had looked on in amazement as the Creator—their Creator as well as ours—had willingly allowed Himself to be ridiculed, shamed, and finally crucified on the previous Friday. The Lord's own angel, Gabriel, who had always been Jesus' chief agent and protector, had to stand helplessly by while the Master of the universe gave His life for you and me.

All Jesus would have had to do is call out, "Gabriel, these people don't appreciate what I'm doing. Even My best friends have left Me. Take Me home to My Father." How long do you think it would have taken the angel to rush to the aid of Jesus? Gabriel would have been at His side in a split second, and with the same blinding flash that characterized his arrival on Resurrection morning.

But by His own command Jesus had forbidden all the heavenly angels to come to His aid while His death secured our salvation. But then, in the predawn hours of the first day, after Jesus had rested in the tomb over the Sabbath, the Lord's angel arrived to bring Jesus home. Can you imagine Gabriel's joy as He called his beloved Master from the tomb?

The earth began to shake. The Roman guards looked about in terror. Something supernatural was happening. Like a meteor from heaven the light came. Like a bolt of lightning it struck in their midst. The huge stone sealing shut the tomb rolled away as if it were a pebble, and Jesus strode forth clothed in the splendor of heaven. The guards fell over like dead men.

The power that was there that morning was the same power that existed thousands of years earlier when the Creator said, "Let there be light." And, as before, it was the Light of the world. The Creator had risen from the tomb—victorious over death. It was the first day of a new world in Christ Jesus.

A Typhoon Is a Hurricane Is a Cyclone

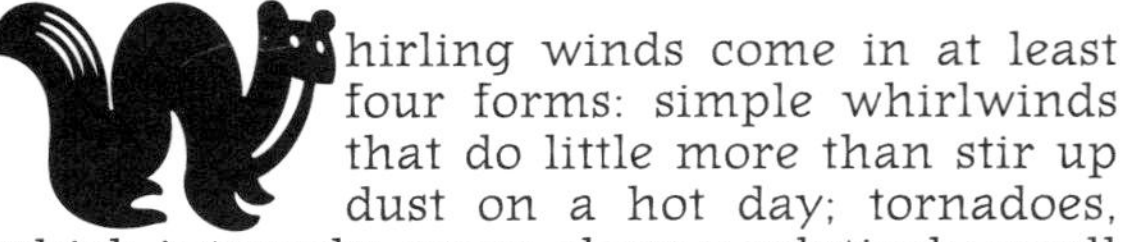

Whirling winds come in at least four forms: simple whirlwinds that do little more than stir up dust on a hot day; tornadoes, which intensely sweep along a relatively small path; hurricanes, which are vast swirling storms covering many square miles; and regular low-pressure weather patterns representing the common but not-so-dangerous storms that occur routinely. Traditionally we have used the word "cyclone" to describe any type of tempest that consists of dangerous twisting winds. But the word originated in the Old World, where the only "twisters" were what we refer to in North America as hurricanes. Consequently, "cyclone" has come to mean one of the large storms (like our hurricanes) that swirl out of the Indian Ocean and affect the weather of Europe and western Asia. So a "cyclone" is a hurricane in the Indian Ocean.

New World explorers replaced the word "cyclone" with "hurricane," a variation of the West Indian word for the storms. The word "hurricane" now refers only to large cyclonic storms that swirl out of the tropical Atlantic Ocean.

That leaves the Pacific Ocean. Can you figure out the word for hurricane-type storms in the Pacific? It's "typhoon", a word that has its origins in the languages of the South Pacific.

So a hurricane is a cyclone in the Atlantic Ocean, a typhoon is a cyclone in the Pacific Ocean, and the only place where the word "cyclone" is still commonly used as it was originally intended is in the Indian Ocean.

By the way, in the Northern Hemisphere, cyclones whirl in a counterclockwise direction, whereas in the Southern Hemisphere they whirl clockwise. Scientists believe such storms regulate heat on earth and help equalize the natural precipitation that makes our planet such a perfect place for life. So, in a way, the storms are a necessary part of our existence in the world as we know it. When do you suppose cyclones began to appear on earth, and why?

A WORD FROM OUR CREATOR

Out of the south cometh the whirlwind: and cold out of the north. Job 37:9.

April 18

Poppies and War

The Creator has provided us with abundant evidence of His love and His promise to save His people. Poppies provide a special example of humanity's response to God's saving grace. Wherever poppies occur naturally, they grow in abundance, covering acres of ground with a brilliant display of color. It is hard to see a field of poppies and not have your spirits raised.

Yet for many people, poppies have led to pain and degradation. In fact, poppies have on more than one occasion been the subject of human beings' most destructive behavior toward one another—war!

As you probably know, one variety of poppy, the opium poppy, is the source of two of the world's most addictive drugs—opium and heroin. In the early 1800s addiction to opium reached epidemic proportions in China. The Chinese government passed laws banning the import and use of the drug, but the laws did little to help. Most of China's opium came from India, which was then under British control. In 1839 Chinese warships opened fire on British opium ships from India, setting off what became known as the Opium War. The British claimed that they were just defending their trade rights, but the Chinese thought it best that opium not be one of the goods entering their country—trade rights or no trade rights. Unfortunately, Britain won the war in 1842, and China had to pay Britain for the cost of the war and for the opium that it had confiscated and destroyed.

During the past several decades war veterans have often raised funds by selling small artificial poppies. These plastic flowers symbolize the lives lost in Flanders, the site of one of the bloodiest battles of World War I. Masses of bright red corn poppies covered those battlefields on the border of Belgium and France.

While God offers peace, it often seems that people would rather fight. This is the way it has been and the way it will be until Jesus comes back. "The grass withereth, the flower fadeth; but the word of our God shall stand for ever" (Isaiah 40:8).

A Word From Our Creator

And they shall beat their swords into plowshares, and their spears into pruninghooks: nation shall not lift up sword against nation, neither shall they learn war any more. Isaiah 2:4.

April 19

Stardust

When you see a shooting star streaking like a banner of light across the sky, you're supposed to make a wish. If you complete your wish before the star disappears, tradition says the wish will come true. Such superstition illustrates how people, even in recent times, have attributed supernatural powers to phenomena in the night sky. Actually a shooting star begins as a *meteoroid*—a piece of space debris. As it encounters earth's atmosphere, friction causes the meteoroid to burn at white heat (above 4,000°F). It is now a *meteor*, which may last only a second or so.

Astronomers say that as many as 200 million visible meteors enter earth's atmosphere each day. Most of them burn up in the atmosphere, but enough of them make it to earth's surface to add as much as 1,000 tons of rocky material to our planet's mass every day. Astronomers call meteors that reach the ground *meteorites*.

Meteoroids that become meteors range in size from those that are only grains of dust up to those that measure more than 30 feet across. Most meteors are dust-grain-sized pieces of rock or metal. The really large ones occur only once in about 1,000 years. The largest known meteorite is one that weighs 66 tons and fell in Namibia. As the earth and its atmosphere travels through space, it runs into this stardust, and we see one or even a shower of shooting stars. On most nights, if you are away from city lights, you can see about five meteors an hour. But at certain times during the year, when earth's path passes through sections of the solar system that contain a lot of meteoroids, you may see a spectacular shower.

The most famous meteor shower in history took place on the night of November 13, 1833. One person said that the stars fell like flakes of snow. Millions of people, terrified by the spectacle, took to the streets. Some believed that there would be no stars in the sky the next night. On the other hand, thousands of Christians felt a thrill at the realization that the event was a fulfillment of Bible prophecy, a sign of the second coming of Jesus.

A Word From Our Creator

He brought me to the banqueting house, and his banner over me was love.
Song of Solomon 2:4.

April 20

Hearing Is for the Birds

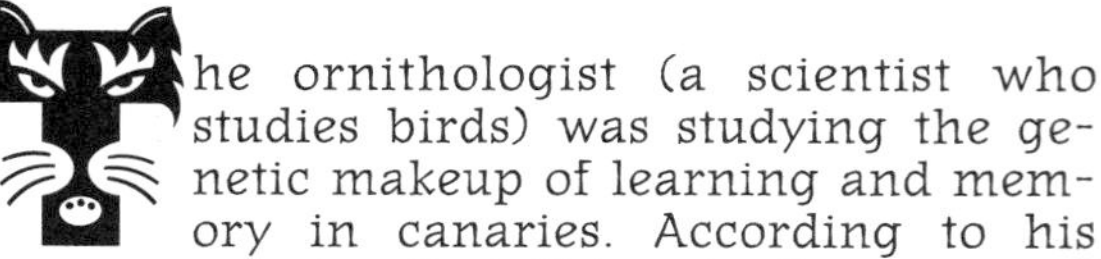

The ornithologist (a scientist who studies birds) was studying the genetic makeup of learning and memory in canaries. According to his theory, canaries that listen to the songs of other canaries—sounds that were familiar to them—develop a greater amount of a particular protein in the brain than do canaries that listen to unfamiliar sounds. This protein somehow is associated with learning and memory. To test his theory, the scientist placed ordinary canaries in isolation and subjected them to recorded sounds. About 50 percent of the canaries heard the sounds of other canaries singing. The others heard noises that would be meaningless to the canaries, such as the songs of other species of birds.

The scientist's idea was this: When a canary hears something familiar, certain genes in its brain cells become active and produce a coded message that triggers the production of the special protein. For instance, when the canary hears a sound that it prefers, like that of other canaries singing, the code in the canary's brain says, "I want to remember that sound, and I'm going to store the sound in coded form in my memory."

Now back to the experiment. As it turned out, the canaries that had listened to recordings of other canaries singing produced 10 times more of the particular protein than did those exposed to the songs of unrelated birds or to a series of random tones.

So by some means yet to be discovered, the special brain protein appears to store the memory of the sound, and the more the bird hears the familiar sound, the more of the memory protein its brain produces. This is the first time that researchers have discovered a genetic trigger associated with learning and memory.

Could it be that we have the same trigger? It would explain why you get an emotional feeling when you hear certain familiar sounds, such as a favorite song or your mother's voice on the other end of the telephone after you haven't seen her for a while. It could also explain why Paul wrote to the Romans that faith is increased by hearing. The more we listen to the words of God, the more faith we store up in our character.

A Word From Our Creator

So then faith cometh by hearing, and hearing by the word of God. Romans 10:17.

If you are ever tempted to think that God can't fulfill His promises, consider the tree frogs. They all require water in which to raise their young, yet they live in the trees, sometimes far from water.

A first sign of spring in North America is the sound of the male gray tree frogs, also called spring peepers, advertising for a mate. First one peeper inflates its throat and gives its high-pitched chirp, then other males join in.

Whereas most frogs live on land or in water, the more than 500 species of tree frogs spend most of their time high in treetops. Sticky pads on the tree frog's toes allow the little creature to clamber around the tree and cling to vertical trunks, horizontal branches, and even the undersides of leaves. Many species, such as the North American peepers, do climb down from their leafy habitat long enough to congregate near a lake or marsh to breed and lay eggs. If you want to see a tree frog, this is the best time to do so. Find the wet area where the peepers are calling. As you approach they will fall silent, but if you stand very quietly, they will start up again. Then switch on your flashlight—the light doesn't seem to bother them—and watch the peepers peeping.

Spring peepers find water readily available on the ground, but other tree frogs never leave the trees. Since they need water in which to lay their eggs, the Creator has given them a number of unique methods for providing a watery place for the eggs to hatch and the tadpoles to develop. One species lays its eggs in bubble nests of its own making, while still another kind deposits its eggs in special pockets on the female frog's back.

The Amazonian tree frog, one of those species that stays in the trees throughout its life, builds its own pool in which to lay its eggs and raise its tadpoles. First the tree frog finds a hollow tree trunk that's open at the top to catch the rain. Then it gathers beeswax from a nearby hive to line the hole. When the waterproof hole has filled with rainwater, the tree frog lays her eggs.

For our God, nothing is too difficult—water in the desert or a waterproof container in the tropics.

Tree Frogs

A Word From Our Creator

And he said unto me, It is done, I am Alpha and Omega, the beginning and the end. I will give unto him that is athirst of the fountain of the water of life freely. Revelation 21:6.

Walnuts and Strawberries

Not long ago Helen Snyder, of Ojai, California, had a problem. Whenever she raised strawberries, the birds in her garden ate the fruit about as fast as it ripened. Ms. Snyder enjoyed having birds in her garden, but since she also liked eating strawberries, she didn't want to face another growing season plagued by feathered thieves pecking away at her berries. What could she do?

The plan that she came up with is so nifty that it's worth knowing for its practical value as well as for the lessons it teaches. Before strawberry season began, Ms. Snyder gathered about five dozen black walnuts. She washed the nuts, then dipped them in bright-red all-weather paint. Then when the strawberries started putting out leaves, she scattered the bright-red walnuts on the ground around the plants.

When the birds saw what they thought were red berries, they gathered to enjoy a strawberry feast. But they quickly learned that the berries in that patch were impossible to eat. So the birds decided to leave Ms. Snyder's patch alone.

When the real strawberries finally became ripe, the creatures didn't bother them at all. They were convinced that the strawberries would be as hard as the painted walnuts and went elsewhere for dessert.

Have you noticed that when people who often lie finally tell the truth, nobody believes them? Is it possible to get so accustomed to the presence of fakes in this life that when the real thing comes along, we don't recognize its worth? Satan would like nothing better than for us to reject the fruit of the Spirit because we believed it to be fake. So he presents his own false version of the Spirit and confuses people. Let us pray for the wisdom of discernment to recognize the truth when God presents it.

A Word From Our Creator

Having eyes, see ye not? and having ears, hear ye not? and do ye not remember? Mark 8:18.

Early one morning, on a trail high in the mountains of the American Northwest, we learned a wonderful truth about the Creator. All around us for as far as we could see stretched cedar, fir, and spruce trees. All of them were growing straight and tall, looking like millions of cathedral spires pointing to the God of heaven.

In order for them to grow upward as they do, trees have to defy the constant pull of gravity every moment of their lives. The natural pull of this world called earth is toward its center, while the growth of trees, as well as of all plants, is exactly and directly opposite to that gravitational force.

Yet, while struggling to grow upward, plants also obey the downward pull of gravity. Scientists call this positive attraction to the earth's gravitational pull *thigmotropism* (pronounced THIG-mo-TRO-pizum). The thigmotropism of all plants causes them to send their roots downward in harmony with the natural pull of gravity, so, in order for a plant to grow upward, it has to defy its own thigmotropism. Botanists (scientists who study plants) describe this growth away from earth as *negative* thigmotropism.

Plants also respond to other natural forces. One of them is light. Attraction to light is called *phototropism* (pronounced FO-to-TRO-pizum), and plants have a natural tendency to respond to the sunlight. So, while gravity's natural pull is downward, the natural pull of sunlight works to overcome that downward pull. Only when a tree dies and loses its capacity to respond to the sun's light does it become completely subject to the laws of gravity. Then it falls, decays, and becomes part of the soil where it once grew.

Jesus is the Light of the world, and His light is the only power strong enough to overcome the natural pull of earthly attractions. As we respond to His love, our faith in Him grows stronger and straighter, and we, like the trees on a thousand mountains, point to Jesus, our Creator and Saviour.

APRIL 23

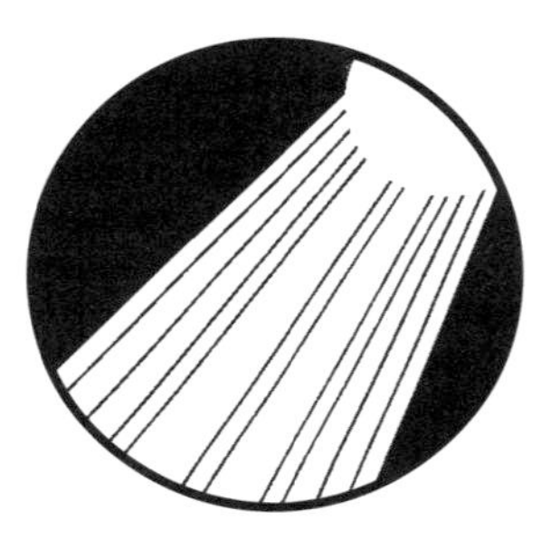

Anti-gravity

A WORD FROM OUR CREATOR

For whatsoever is born of God overcometh the world: and this is the victory that overcometh the world, even our faith.
1 John 5:4.

APRIL 24

Circadian Faith

Jesus told the people to renew their faith every day by following His example of serving others. The rhythm of the day and the night in our lives helps us to understand what this text means.

As I write this I'm flying from Baltimore to Atlanta. The sun is sinking in the west. The airplane is just skimming the tops of the clouds. The blue sky stretches from horizon to horizon, and it arches like a huge bowl overhead with a golden fireball blazing on one side and reflecting in the shimmering and filmy mist of the cloud cover below.

People on the ground below cannot see the sun. The cloud cover is too thick. But I know that no one down there would doubt for a second that the sun is blazing in the sky above the clouds. People are going about their daily routines, routines governed by the rhythm of the rising and setting sun—the light and the darkness. Scientists call that routine the circadian rhythm.

Even if clouds hide the sun for days, weeks, or even months, as happens in some places, everyone continues to act according to an innate daily rhythm. We may prefer the sunshine to the clouds—and the world somehow seems a more positive place when the sun is shining—but the clouds and even the rain do not stop us, partly because we know by faith that the sun is up there and that eventually it will shine through the clouds.

Several years ago I heard a Native American tribal leader speak of time, clocks, and the daily rhythm. For Mr. Two Moons the daily routine is simple: the day is for helping people, and the night is for sleeping. There's wisdom in his statement. God intends the day to be for service, and He gave us the sun to light our way. Then He offers us the night to rest so that our bodies can prepare for service again.

When the clouds of life obscure the face of Jesus—"the Sun of righteousness" (Malachi 4:2)—and when we temporarily lose sight of our reason for being, we still know by faith that Jesus will make everything all right. Following a daily routine of dependence on Jesus through prayer, Bible study, and service will strengthen our faith to help us survive even the thickest cloud cover of life's difficulties.

A WORD FROM OUR CREATOR

And he said to them all, If any man will come after me, let him deny himself, and take up his cross daily, and follow me. Luke 9:23.

Each of the 50 states has adopted a state flower, and the choices range from Maine's hardy white pine cone to California's brilliant golden poppy. Each state carefully chose the plant to represent what it saw as its character.

It is ironic, then, that several state flowers are not native to North America. Alabama's camellia, Alaska's forget-me-not, Indiana's peony, New Hampshire's purple lilac, Ohio's red carnation, and Tennessee's purple iris all came to America from Europe and Asia.

School children in Alabama voted that the goldenrod, a native plant, be designated the state flower. In 1929 the state legislature duly adopted it as such. However, it seems that the more popular camellia replaced the goldenrod in 1959.

In 1919 Tennessee's schoolchildren voted for the native passionflower, which for many years served as the unofficial floral emblem of the state. However, when the state legislature finally took action in 1933, it adopted the purple iris instead.

The hardy purple lilac is New Hampshire's European import, adopted in 1919. Brought to America by early settlers, the shrub flourished and now reminds us of the colonists—who were also transplanted and also flourished.

Ohio adopted the red carnation—twice! Both times—in 1904 and in 1953—the state designated the flower as a token of love and reverence for President William McKinley, a native of Ohio, who was assassinated while in office. The carnation was his favorite flower.

Humans are a fickle lot when it comes to expressing our preferences and intentions. Like flowers, human promises often fade with time, so it is comforting to know that we have a Saviour on whom we can depend. Like a never-fading flower, His love will never vanish. He said, "I am the rose of Sharon, and the lily of the valleys" (Song of Solomon 2:1), and He added, "For I am the Lord, I *change not*" (Malachi 3:6).

Choosing State Flowers

A Word From Our Creator

The grass withereth, the flower fadeth: but the word of our God shall stand for ever.
Isaiah 40:8.

April 26

Morning Stars and Evening Stars

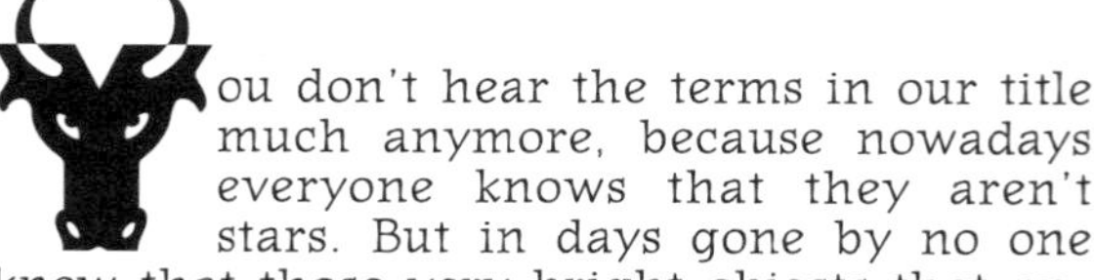

You don't hear the terms in our title much anymore, because nowadays everyone knows that they aren't stars. But in days gone by no one knew that those very bright objects that appeared in the evening sky just after sunset and in the morning sky just before sunrise were actually planets. Neither did they know that the evening stars were the same heavenly bodies as the morning stars.

Two planets, Venus and Mercury, have been most often represented as morning and evening stars. Because the orbits of both Venus and Mercury are closer to the sun than Earth's, we can see them only by looking in the direction of the sun. Therefore, the only time we can view either planet is just after sunset in the western sky or just before sunrise in the eastern sky. Since people could view them only at those times, they considered them special stars.

The Greeks and Romans had different names for what they believed to be four wandering stars. The Greeks called Venus *Hesperus* when it was the evening star and *Phosphorus* as the morning star. The Romans named Venus *Vesper* in the evening and *Lucifer* in the morning. Both the Romans and the Greeks called Mercury *Mercury* in the evening and *Apollo* in the morning.

The Bible makes use of the term *morning star* in three different places. In the first, when He is telling Job about the creation of the Earth, God reports that "the morning stars sang together" (Job 38:7). It is highly unlikely that the author of the story of Job was referring to Venus and Mercury. Rather, it is more likely that the author had in mind an order of beings, because in other biblical instances the term relates the morning star to Jesus.

The bright morning star is really a planet, and planets do not have light of their own. They shine with the reflected light of the sun. Malachi 4:2 refers to God as "the Sun of righteousness." When Jesus walked as a man among human beings, He said, "The Son can do nothing of himself, but what he seeth the Father do" (John 5:19). As our example, Jesus reflected the will of His Father. He is the Bright and Morning Star.

A Word From Our Creator

I Jesus have sent mine angel to testify unto you these things in the churches. I am the root and the offspring of David, and the bright and morning star. Revelation 22:16.

April 27

Battling Butterflies

We usually think of butterflies as symbols of gentleness and beauty. Yet butterflies are among the fiercest of Earth's creatures. For example, the tiny one-inch American copper establishes a territory and then drives every other moving thing away, darting out at other butterflies, cats and dogs, birds, squirrels, Frisbees, airplane shadows—and butterfly collectors.

When butterflies battle each other, sometimes three or four rise into the air together and try to buffet each other to the ground. The males of Minor's swallowtail, a species of the American Southwest, are so aggressive that they start killing each other from the moment of birth. As they emerge from the chrysalis, they tear each other to shreds. Given this kind of behavior, it's a wonder that this species survives at all! Other species, such as some of the blues, don't even wait until they are fully grown before they begin to do battle. The caterpillars fight each other!

Most butterflies fight silently. Calicoes, however, click at their opponents when attacking. They produce the sound, which can be heard at a distance of more than 100 feet, by snapping two body segments together. The caterpillars of other butterfly species make squeaking noises, and still others produce grating noises. Whoever would have thought that butterflies made sounds?

Because they're so beautiful, we find it hard to think of butterflies making war, but they fight to protect their territories—their "land." Human history is full of stories of nations warring against each other because two groups of people wanted the same piece of land. Fighting for territory seems to be a natural characteristic of this world. Aren't you thankful that we have a Saviour who went to battle for us and won for us the right to a place in heaven and the new earth?

A Word From Our Creator

And all this assembly shall know that the Lord saveth not with sword and spear: for the battle is the Lord's, and he will give you into our hands.
1 Samuel 17:47.

APRIL 28

An Ant That's a Spider That's a Fly

Based on the lives of two tiny garden creatures, our text could accurately be revised to read, "Beware of false prophets, which appear unto you as ants, but inwardly they are ravening spiders." Not long ago, while weeding our garden, we came upon what appeared to be an ant. But it jumped, and it ran much faster than any ant could. Having seen this creature before, we immediately realized that we were observing one of the many examples in nature of *look-alike* creatures. The "ant" was a spider!

This particular spider resembles an ant so much that you must look at it very closely to see that it really isn't. The ant-spider, as we will call it, has what appear to be three parts to its body. By definition, spiders have only two body sections, while insects have three. But the ant-spider has a constricted area in the middle of one of its two segments, making it appear that there are three. Many a tiny insect has been tricked by this spider and has become its dinner.

Another look-alike is a small fly that lives in southeastern Arizona. Looking just like a spider, it has what appear to be only *two* body parts and eight legs. (Insects have only six legs, of course). What appear to be the spider's eight legs are actually dark lines in the colorless wings of the fly. The "head" of the "spider" is really the fly's orange abdomen. Two black spots on the abdomen look just like eyes. The deception is so complete that Tom Eisner, a biologist who has photographed this fly, was at first fooled by its appearance. And not only does the fly *look* like the spider, it *acts* like one, too, moving about in a spiderlike zigzag pattern.

There are many look-alikes in nature, so keep an eye out for them. In light of our text, what do you think each of these creatures gains by its charade? And what do you think these creatures teach us?

A WORD FROM OUR CREATOR

Beware of false prophets, which come to you in sheep's clothing, but inwardly they are ravening wolves. Matthew 7:15.

April 29

Saved by a Dolphin

Bangladesh is a small country located on the upper end of the Bay of Bengal at the northern part of the Indian Ocean. Most of Bangladesh is low coastal plain with an elevation of less than 50 feet. Because this tiny country lies so near the ocean, the people of Bangladesh live in fear of the tropical storms that they call cyclones and that we call hurricanes.

On April 30, 1991, a cyclone swept up from the Indian Ocean, moved through the Bay of Bengal, and slammed ashore along the coast of Bangladesh. The storm caused immeasurable property damage, but the loss of life best describes the tragedy of the day. The tidal wave that accompanied the storm washed away entire villages.

Although that storm created unending misery for thousands of people in the region, one breathtaking story stands out as a witness to the love and mercy of a Creator God who has not forgotten His children. Abjullah al-Noman, the state minister for the environment for Bangladesh, relates the miraculous tale.

Among those lost in the coastal village of Ukhia was a baby swept out to sea by the waters of the cyclone. What chance would a helpless baby have against a raging storm that was ripping up trees and washing away villages?

Swimming along at just the right time was a dolphin—a wild creature of the sea. It was just an ordinary dolphin, but something told it to take hold of that helpless baby and to begin swimming toward a safe haven farther up the coast. No one knows how the dolphin kept the baby from drowning, but it did.

The dolphin brought the baby to the shoreline at a point 18 miles from Ukhia! People took the baby gently from the dolphin's mouth and rushed it to a nearby hospital, where it recovered.

Suppose you had been that baby and suppose you were rescued by a dolphin. How would you feel? What would you think about dolphins? Wouldn't you want to tell everybody on earth what the dolphin had done for you? Isn't that what Jesus has done for you?

A Word From Our Creator

Wherefore he is able also to save them to the uttermost that come unto God by him, seeing he ever liveth to make intercession for them. Hebrews 7:25.

April 30

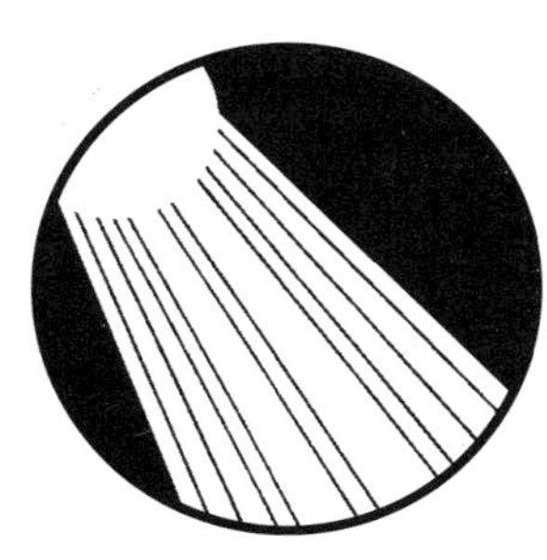

Lightning

Basically lightning is a stream of electrons moving through space at a very high speed. An example of lightning is the spark that you get when you walk on carpet and touch a metal doorknob. You see and feel a spark, and you hear the snap that it makes. Lightning is a gigantic spark of the same sort, and thunder is the sound made by that spark.

We experience lightning and thunder as two separate events because sound travels slower than light. When a streak of lightning occurs, light waves and sound waves start out at the same time. The light speeds to your eye at 186,000 miles a second, while the sound travels to your ear at the leisurely rate of about 1,000 feet, or one fifth of a mile, a second.

A "streak" of lightning usually begins as a downstroke from a cloud to earth. The downstroke is not very strong, and it travels at a speed of only about 60 miles a second—not fast at all compared to the speed of the return stroke. Measured in electrical power, the first downstroke may carry only 500 amperes and produce almost no light. It creates an electrically charged path for a series of upstrokes that will follow from any conductor, such as a lightning rod or a person standing out in the rain. The result is an ultrapowerful upstroke from earth to cloud that carries an average of 30,000 amperes traveling almost half the speed of light and heating up the air to as much as 60,000° F—five times the surface temperature of the sun. It is this stroke that we see and call lightning. The heat produced by lightning expands the air at supersonic speeds and produces the sonic boom called thunder.

It's hard to imagine the amount of raw power in a thunderstorm. Meteorologists tell us that the energy released by an average thunderstorm is equal to the power of about ten atomic bombs.

And so it will be when Jesus comes again—an awesome display of power as the King of kings arrives on a chariot of clouds with millions of angels to take us back to heaven with Him.

A Word From Our Creator

For as the lightning cometh out of the east, and shineth even unto the west; so shall also the coming of the Son of man be. Matthew 24:27.

May 1

Not So Fresh Water

What you are about to read is depressing—but it does have a happy ending. We live in a world suffering from thousands of years of sin, a terminal disease that the earth cannot survive without the help of Jesus, the great physician. As a result we are rapidly approaching a time when we will have little pure water left on our planet. Human beings are dumping enormous quantities of industrial wastes into the world's lakes, rivers, and streams. Thus an increasingly potent chemical soup is replacing our fresh drinking water. People have to dig deeper and deeper wells to find pure water.

At the same time, industrialists are drilling thousands of wells to hold toxic wastes that they pump directly into the ground. This practice pollutes the vast quantities of water stored underground in natural holding tanks called aquifers. Consequently, more than half of the earth's underground water is now contaminated with either disease-producing bacteria or poisonous wastes.

But industry isn't responsible for all water pollution. Think of all of the pollutants that come from our houses and towns and farms, pollutants such as detergents, drain cleaners, salt to melt ice and snow, insecticides, and chemical fertilizers. Lead dissolves into the water from old pipes, and petroleum leaks from underground tanks. The list goes on and on, and the water continues to accumulate the residue.

We used to be able to collect rain as the purest form of water. Water naturally distilled by the sun leaves all its impurities behind when it evaporates into clouds that condense into rain. But now even rain is polluted. As it falls it bonds with acid molecules in the air. By the time it reaches the ground, the rain itself has become a toxic pollutant.

Are you worried? You needn't be. We have God's promise that "He that walketh righteously, . . . his waters shall be sure" (Isaiah 33:15, 16). Furthermore, God will "make all things new" (Revelation 21:5), and in vision John saw "a pure river of water of life, clear as crystal, proceeding out of the throne of God" (Revelation 22:1).

A Word From Our Creator

Take heed to yourselves, that your heart be not deceived, and ye turn aside, and serve other gods, . . . and then the Lord's wrath be kindled against you, and he shut up the heaven. Deuteronomy 11:16, 17.

Venus's-flytrap

Venus's-flytrap is a member of the sundew family, a group of insect-eating plants that grow in sunny, moist areas such as bogs and wet sand. This unusual foot-high plant lives only along the coasts of North Carolina and South Carolina in the eastern United States. The small white flowers of the Venus's-flytrap form at the top of a stalk. Each leaf has two parts: the lower portion is long and narrow, but the upper part has two lobes hinged together at the center, like a book with rounded edges. The lobes are edged with bristles and covered with reddish hairs that secrete a gluelike substance. In addition, three trigger hairs grow on each lobe.

The sticky goo that oozes from the tiny leaf hairs attracts insects. When a bee, fly, or other insect lands on a leaf and touches the trigger hairs, the gluelike substance holds the insect while cells along the outside of the leaf quickly expand to push the halves together. The outer bristles interlock, forming a cage with bars. At that point the captured creature has no way of escape. The leaf presses against the insect and secretes juices to digest it. When the plant has finished eating, the leaf reopens, setting the trap again. The plant uses the nourishment gained from its prey to produce more leaves, for when a Venus's-flytrap leaf has caught several insects, it dies.

For the unsuspecting fly, Venus's restaurant spreads a table of promising fare—all those glistening droplets of potential dessert are irresistible. But by giving in to its appetite, the fly triggers the trap and is soon digested history. Plant geneticists have put the Venus's-flytrap's sticky hairs to good use by genetically engineering a potato plant with leaf hairs that attract and trap insects harmful to the potato's growth. The plant protects itself by destroying its enemies. Additional research may help us to protect other plants, as well.

A quick glance at our text may tempt you to believe that David is seeking vengeance against his enemies for all the trials that he endured at their hands. But if you read on, you'll see that what he really has in mind is the protection of the kingdom of God. David is calling for an end to God's enemies.

A Word From Our Creator

Let their table become a snare before them: and that which should have been for their welfare, let it become a trap. Psalm 69:22.

May 3

Venus

At the speed of light, it would take us six minutes to travel the 67 million miles from the sun to Venus, the second planet from the sun. That would give us just enough time to learn that:

1. Venus is the closest to Earth in size in our solar system—its diameter is about 7,500 miles, compared to Earth's 7,900 miles.
2. The planet rotates backward—that is, the sun rises in the west and sets in the east! Venus turns at a speed of only four miles per hour, so if you walked eastward at that speed, the sun would appear not to move at all. One Venus day lasts 243 earth days.
3. Traveling at a speed of 79,000 miles per hour, Venus orbits the sun in less time than it takes to rotate completely around—only 225 Earth days. In Earth terms, on Venus a day is longer than a year. If you were to grow up on Venus and count years as we do—the time it takes to orbit the sun—you would be more than one and a half times your current earth age, but you would be even fewer days old!
4. On Venus the gravity is 90 percent of what it is on Earth, so if you weigh 80 pounds here, you'd weigh 72 pounds there.
5. The surface of Venus reminds us of how artists have depicted hell. The temperature is a hot 860°F. The atmosphere consists mostly of carbon dioxide, and the clouds overhead are composed of poisonous sulfuric acid with constant lightning and thunder. The atmospheric pressure is more than 90 times as great as it is on Earth—about the same as it would be about a half mile down in the ocean. The atmosphere is so thick that the wind, blowing at about six miles per hour, would sweep you along as if you were in a river current.

Venus is the third-brightest object in the sky. The brightest of the planets, it is seven times brighter than Sirius, the brightest star. Scripture calls angels stars, and today's text tells us that Lucifer used to be the brightest of all the stars in heaven. In fact, his very name meant "shining one" or "brilliant one." Perhaps his brilliance went to his head. It is interesting that the Romans saw Venus as a morning star and called it Lucifer.

A Word From Our Creator

How art thou fallen from heaven, O Lucifer, son of the morning! how art thou cut down to the ground, which didst weaken the nations! Isaiah 14:12.

May 4

Was He Stubborn or Was He Persistent?

A Word From Our Creator

And Jesus answered and said unto her, Martha, Martha, thou art careful and troubled about many things: but . . . Mary hath chosen that good part. Luke 10:41, 42.

Our neighbor Mrs. Norris told the story of a pair of eastern bluebirds that nested in a birdhouse near her chicken pen. The pen always had lots of chicken feathers, and Mr. and Mrs. Bluebird were quick to make good use of them to line their nest. One year Mrs. Norris and her husband watched as the bluebirds put the final touches on their nest.

Both bluebirds went to the chicken yard and each picked out a feather. Then both of them returned to the nest. Politely Mr. Bluebird let Mrs. Bluebird take her feather into the birdhouse first. He then followed her with his carefully chosen feather. Soon Mrs. Bluebird emerged without her feather, flying off to get another one. Mr. Bluebird then came out with his feather still clutched in his bill. He flew up to a wire and sat there waiting.

Mrs. Bluebird quickly returned with another feather and entered the birdhouse. As before, Mr. Bluebird followed her into the house, still carrying his feather. Before long Mrs. Bluebird left to go after another feather. Mr. Bluebird popped out again—*still carrying his feather*. He returned to the wire above and waited.

A third time Mrs. Bluebird arrived with a carefully chosen feather. Once again Mr. Bluebird followed her into the birdhouse with his own feather. This behavior went on for more than an hour, and Mr. Bluebird never left his feather in the house.

It's tempting to think that Mr. Bluebird was lazy, but since bluebirds are industrious birds, it's more likely that Mrs. Bluebird just didn't want the feather that Mr. Bluebird brought. He continued to offer her his contribution to the nest, and she continued to refuse it. Can't you almost hear her asking, "Blue, how many times do I have to tell you that I don't want that feather? Get it out of here!"

Jesus isn't offering us a feather, but what He offers is just what we need. Do you suppose that it is possible to tell Him, by not accepting His offer, that we don't want His gift?

robably no game develops patience as much as the game of golf. People play it around the world, and its fans number in the millions. Many stories tell how birds and animals have created trouble for golfers. The *Golfer's Handbook*, published in Scotland, records a number of such incidents, but the best is probably of the crow that carried away 30 golf balls from a golf course in New South Wales! After being hit by a golf ball, a goose in Massachusetts kicked the ball into the water trap. In that instance I am sure that the player viewed the situation as one of tribulation—he certainly had an opportunity to learn a lot of patience.

Sometimes, however, the story goes the other way. Mr. McGregor, an Ontario golfer, had putted his golf ball to the very edge of a hole, where the ball stopped. A grasshopper immediately jumped onto the ball and tapped it in. Did Mr. McGregor get credit for the putt? Yes indeed. The rules allow for natural occurrences over which the player has no control. In that case, it was Mr. McGregor's opponent who received the opportunity to learn some patience.

One of the strangest examples of animal interference on a golf course happened to a pair of golfers named Clark and King. When they arrived at the rough where Clark's ball had landed, they found a cow eating the ball. The next day, at the same hole, Mr. King hit his ball into the same rough. He hurried to reach the ball and placed his woolen hat over it, saying, "I'll make sure the cow doesn't eat mine." When it was his turn to play, Mr. King returned to the spot—only to find that the cow had eaten not only the ball but his hat, as well! That was heavy tribulation for Mr. King, and he too had the chance to learn some patience.

Paul wasn't talking about playing golf, of course. It is not just in the playing of a game that we can learn patience. Tribulation can come in whatever we do. The important thing is how we react to that tribulation. Reacting in the right way helps us develop patience.

The Cow That Ate Golf Balls

A Word From Our Creator

And not only so, but we glory in tribulations also: knowing that tribulation worketh patience. Romans 5:3.

Perkins National Forest

When they migrate, hundreds of millions of small songbirds fly great distances over open water. Because they have no place to land while traveling over the water, the birds must make it to the distant shore on the energy that they stored before they began their flight. Sometimes birds fly into unexpected storms and head winds that make it difficult for them to fly. During these emergencies the birds draw heavily on their energy reserves, and many do not reach land. They drop into the sea, and hungry fish quickly consume them.

On the Great Lakes sailors and passengers aboard ships have reported seeing hundreds of exhausted birds fall into the water or onto the decks during stormy weather.

John P. Perkins, of Conneaut, Ohio, worked on an ore-carrying ship crossing the Great Lakes. When Mr. Perkins noticed that tired birds often landed on his ship, he decided that they would feel more at home if they had some trees in which to rest. So the next time the ship docked, Mr. Perkins bought several evergreen trees planted in large wooden tubs. Then he placed them on the deck of the ship. Sure enough, the birds loved the trees. Mr. Perkins had provided a haven of refuge for the birds flying across the lakes. Before long his shipmates had named the small grove of trees "Perkins National Forest."

When Jesus and His disciples were in a boat crossing a lake, a fierce storm blew up. Like the migrating birds, the disciples could make no headway against the wind. Their energy was simply not enough to match that of the wind and the waves. Do you remember what happened? Jesus "arose, and rebuked the wind, and said unto the sea, Peace be still. And the wind ceased, and there was a great calm" (Mark 4:39). Jesus was a haven of safety on that small ship—a "tree of life"—just as were the trees that Mr. Perkins placed on his ship.

A Word From Our Creator

Come unto me, all ye that labour and are heavy laden, and I will give you rest. Matthew 11:28.

oes today's title seem overwhelming? Well, what you may not know is that that phrase is the long version of a word that is in everyday use today but did not exist before about 1960. The word is LASER, the acronym formed by using the first letter of each of the main words in the phrase made by today's title.

Perhaps the best way to describe the difference between an ordinary light beam and a laser beam is to compare the movement of the photons to a parade. Ordinary light resembles a mass of people moving along at different speeds and in different directions—some strolling this way and others hurrying that way. In contrast, a laser beam is like a platoon of well-drilled soldiers—all marching in step.

The production of laser light is a complicated electrochemical process, but we can simply describe the result as a stream of photons each with exactly the same wavelength and each going in exactly the same direction. Since individual photons move in a straight line, a laser provides a powerful and concentrated light that can travel a great distance without losing its focus.

For example, no ordinary light source on earth is powerful enough to reach the moon. The photons from ordinary light, such as from a lightbulb or a beacon, head off in all directions, so the light loses its strength. By using mirrors and lenses, like those on a car's headlights, we can focus beams of ordinary light somewhat, but these beams still consist of a mass of disorganized photons, each with a mind of its own, so to speak. On the other hand, scientists can direct a laser beam from earth to light up a section of the moon only two miles in diameter—incredible precision after having journeyed 240,000 miles.

The Bible uses the word *light* interchangeably to describe both physical light and mental understanding. In today's text, Daniel is thanking God that He can reveal and explain the king's dream. God, the source of light, can illuminate the world if that's what it takes to reveal His will. Or He can provide just the right amount of light concentrated on a single point so that we can see and understand Him.

MAY 7

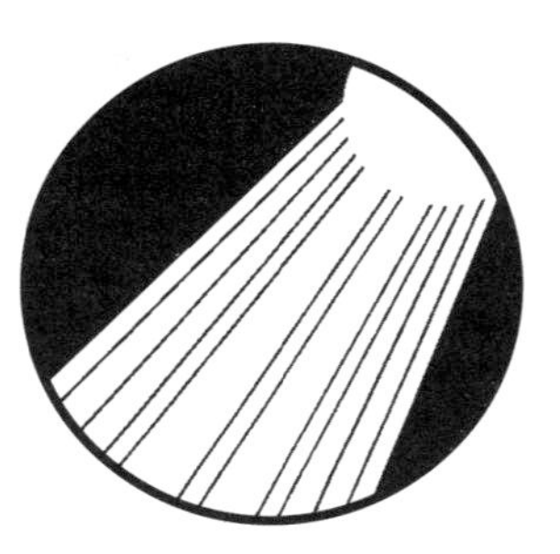

Light Amplification by Stimulated Emission of Radiation

A WORD FROM OUR CREATOR

He revealeth the deep and secret things: he knoweth what is in the darkness, and the light dwelleth with him. Daniel 2:22.

May 8

The Hidden Beauty of Caves

Every cave is like a well-kept secret, and visiting a new cave is like exploring a new land. We never know what we're going to see.

Not long ago we visited a cave in Texas. When we entered it, a guide took us on a 20-minute hike through a desolate part of the cavern that was nothing but dry, bare rock. The guide referred to that section as being dead. As we moved from drab room to drab room, the guide turned on lights ahead of us and switched off lights behind us. The presence of light, even electric lights in a cave, causes the growth of simple plants like algae, fungi, mosses, and ferns. So to keep the cave true to its natural state, it was necessary to maintain the darkness.

After trudging along for a while and wondering why we had decided to visit a dead cave, suddenly we entered the living portion of the cave. As we went from room to room, the lights would come on, and we would gasp in wonder and awe at a new and dazzling display of formations: stalactites, stalagmites, and columns in many different forms and in many different colors. Crystals of various minerals growing in delicate shapes formed a fantasyland.

We thought about how this cave had been there for thousands of years before anyone had found it. All of that beauty was quietly being prepared for the day when someone would discover and reveal it to the world. How many other splendor-filled caves still remain hidden in the ground?

And then we thought about ourselves. We are like the cave. Our inner beauty is the product of the Creator—working slowly and steadily where no one but Jesus can see it. The character of Jesus is growing in His people in the darkness of this world. And it is the Light of the world who reveals that beauty. "Arise, shine; for thy light is come, and the glory of the Lord is risen upon thee" (Isaiah 60:1). Many others await the revelation of the inner beauty that God has been developing in you.

A Word From Our Creator

That thine alms may be in secret: and thy Father which seeth in secret himself shall reward thee openly. Matthew 6:4.

ave you ever waited until the last minute to prepare for a test? You try to cram as much information as possible into your brain in the shortest possible time. For a while you may remember it, but you will soon forget most of what you try to learn. Learning is a natural procedure, and God made a person able to acquire only so much new information at any one time.

The rules of learning are much the same as those that govern farming. We have to do more to grow a crop successfully than choosing what we would like to plant. Let's imagine a ridiculous farming example of cramming.

It's spring and time to get the ground ready for planting. But the farmer decides to work on his tractor in the warm barn rather than plow the land out in the crisp cold. He reasons that the harvest is months away and that it's important to have a well-running tractor. There's plenty of time for plowing. So he enjoys days of getting his tractor running just right. Those days stretch into weeks as he continues to reason that he still has plenty of time left to get the plowing and the planting done. After all, it takes only a day or two to plow and plant the entire field.

So the farmer orders books on tractor maintenance. He attends seminars sponsored by a local farm equipment company on how to make sure his tractor is in the best-possible condition. Spring passes quickly and summer is drawing to a close when the farmer finally decides that it's time to do the plowing. Realizing that he has only a short time, the farmer crams all the spring and summer fieldwork into a few short days. His tractor runs at top efficiency. After carefully preparing the ground, he plants the crop in straight rows. His work completed, he waits for the harvest—with just a month left in the growing season. The necessary spring rains have long gone and the hot summer sun beats down on the field. The few seeds that sprout and struggle through the soil are baked by the sun. Some of the sprouts are half grown when drenching late-summer thunderstorms beat them to the ground. The end result is no harvest at all.

How is this story like putting off studying until the last minute?

Cramming Is Not Natural

A Word From Our Creator

Be not deceived; God is not mocked: for whatsoever a man soweth, that shall he also reap. Galatians 6:7.

The Deist

W hat a question! When David looked at the sky at night, the awesome display of God's power filled him with wonder. How could God possibly be interested in people on our tiny planet, especially when they were rebelling against Him? David's response in the rest of the psalm doesn't really answer the question. It didn't really receive an answer until God Himself answered it 1,000 years later.

You don't have to be an astronomer to be amazed by what little we know about the stars and other aspects of the universe. Take outer space, for instance. Where does it end? Our most powerful telescopes have now revealed galaxies billions of light-years from earth, and many of them are traveling away from us, farther into space. Where are they going? What is out there? Is there a point where there are no more stars, planets, or moons—just space? And how far does that space go? Forever, you say? How far is forever? Can you picture it?

For thousands of years people have tried to explain the universe scientifically without giving God any credit. But we seem to know in our hearts that the only logical explanation for space and all that it holds is a supreme intelligence called God. Even so, rather than accept a loving God who cares for us, some people propose that while there is a God, He's an uncaring God. This philosophy is called deism (pronounced DEE-ism).

The deist looks at the order of the universe and says "There has to be a God," but then denies that God has any personal interest in what's going on here on earth. For the deist, creating things is no more than God's hobby. Once He has made something, the deist's God has no further interest in it. Well, that's not the God whom we serve, is it?

In Jesus, God answers David's question once and for all. "For God so loved the world, that he gave his only begotten Son, that whosoever believeth in him should not perish, but have everlasting life" (John 3:16). That's the answer to the question—God loves! He loves you, and Jesus proved it.

A Word From Our Creator

When I consider thy heavens, the work of thy fingers, the moon and the stars, which thou hast ordained; what is man, that thou art mindful of him? Psalm 8:3.

May 11

The Wood Thrush and the Cowbird

For reasons that we really don't understand, brown-headed cowbirds are apparently too lazy to build their own nests and raise their own young. The female cowbird's only claim to motherhood is the fact that she lays the egg from which her babies will hatch. But with that act her motherhood ends, because she lays each of her eggs in the nest of another bird.

When a cowbird's egg hatches, the foster parents usually adopt the nestling. And when the foster parents feed and care for the newly hatched cowbird, they do so at the expense of their own offspring. Typically, the young cowbird is larger and grows faster than the natural babies in the nest. Soon the foster mother's real children may get crowded out, trampled, or starved to death—while the young cowbird thrives.

But the cowbird nestling does not deceive the mother wood thrush, even though the baby cowbird looks much like the young thrushes. How does the mother thrush know that there's a stranger in the nest with her own three or four babies? The difference is plain to see as soon as the babies open their mouths to beg for food. Each young wood thrush has a yellow lining to its mouth, whereas the lining of the brown-headed cowbird's mouth is red. Mrs. Wood Thrush puts food only into yellow mouths.

No matter how often or loudly or long the cowbird begs, it gets no food from Mrs. Wood Thrush. She doesn't hear the call produced by a red mouth. The fate of the baby cowbird may seem harsh to you, but what lesson does this story teach in a very direct way?

Do you remember what Jesus said about asking for things in His name? Many texts in the Bible tell us that God hears and answers the prayers of those who pray in faith, and that God does not hear and therefore cannot answer the prayers of those who ask in selfishness.

A Word From Our Creator

If I regard iniquity in my heart, the Lord will not hear me: but verily God hath heard me; he hath attended to the voice of my prayer. Psalm 66:18, 19.

The Wood Turtle Stomps for Its Supper

To illustrate this text, we are going to describe one of the feeding habits of the wood turtle, a resident of the Northeastern and Midwestern states. When this turtle hasn't found enough food by just walking around, it resorts to rustling up its grub in a more creative way. The hungry turtle stomps its front feet to create a vibration in the ground. Earthworms, apparently disturbed by the activity, travel to the surface of the soil, and the turtle snaps them up.

When the turtle stomps, it does so at a rhythm of about a stomp a second. Each stomp is more forceful than the previous one. Then the turtle switches to the other foot and repeats the maneuver. Selecting a damp or muddy spot, such as a creek bank or forest floor, the turtle usually stomps for a period of a half hour to two hours. Worms emerge only inches from the turtle's feet. A naturalist studying the stomping behavior of wood turtles tapped on the soil, duplicating the rhythm and force of the turtle's legs. He brought four worms to the surface in 15 seconds!

Earthworms respond to a variety of other vibrations, also, such as those caused by children jumping on a lawn, a power mower left running, and the running of a robin's feet. One theory is that the vibrations may sound like moles, which are underground worm eaters, tunneling through the ground. The worms then head for the surface to escape the moles. Another theory is that the vibrations may mimic those of raindrops, and worms crawl to the surface to avoid drowning in their tunnels. In any case, the worms respond instinctively. Unable to analyze the situation and the possible consequences of their action, they just crawl to the surface when they feel the vibrations. When the turtle stomps, the worms emerge.

We may be tempted to think that worms are stupid, but sometimes people also respond without thinking. Is it possible to be drawn irresistibly to the rhythm of a beat only to be consumed by the influences that have produced that beat?

A Word From Our Creator

But I was like a lamb or an ox that is brought to the slaughter; and I knew not that they had devised devices against me. Jeremiah 11:19.

May 13

No More AIDS

Among the most tragic results of sin are the diseases that have taken the lives of billions of people. In modern times we often feel confident that science and technology can find a solution for virtually all of the illnesses that may attack us. But it seems that every time we find a cure for widespread killers like bubonic plague, tuberculosis, and polio, along comes an even worse killer that defies everything that we know. Cancer was once such a disease. At one time a diagnosis of cancer doubled as a death notice. But we've seen evidence within the past few years that we may be able to cure and even prevent most forms of cancer. Then along came AIDS.

The complete name of the disease is *a*cquired *i*mmuno*d*eficiency *s*yndrome, but most people know it as simply AIDS. Scientists have theories about how AIDS works its deadly ways. Some believe that a virus, the *h*uman *i*mmunodeficiency *v*irus (HIV), attacks and weakens the natural defenses of the body until it can't fight off any disease—even relatively common and otherwise nonthreatening ones like pneumonia. A more recent theory holds that this virus is capable of changing into so many forms that the body is unable to defend itself against the variety of diseases that result. Let's describe this theory in terms of a computer game.

If you enjoy computer games such as Super Mario Brothers, you know that the game producers construct each succeeding level with ever more challenging situations. As players become proficient enough to master the most advanced level, the game producers have to come out with even tougher challenges. But suppose the producers came out with a game level that had so many different foes to conquer and so many different pitfalls to avoid that you simply couldn't win—no matter how good you were.

God constructed your body to outwit invading diseases. But if you play Satan's game, the sin producer has figured out a way to attack your body with so many diseases at once that your natural defenses can't win. Jesus has given us rules to live by that increase our health, and He has promised us an eternal life that's disease-free.

A Word From Our Creator

And the inhabitant shall not say, I am sick: the people that dwell therein shall be forgiven their iniquity. Isaiah 33:24.

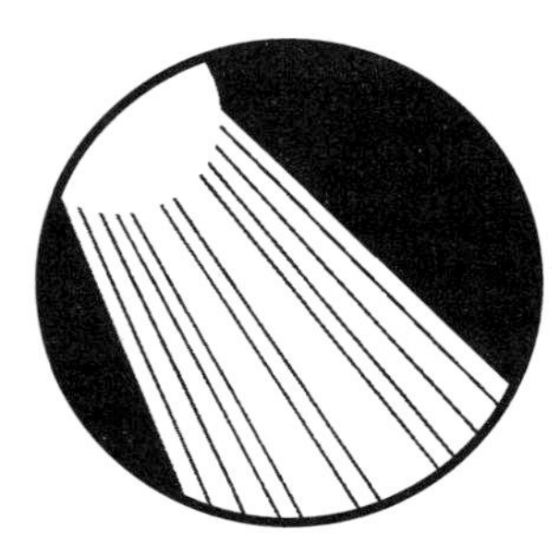

Absolute Darkness

Not long ago scientists discovered an amazing community of animals at the bottom of the Pacific Ocean. Some of these creatures live beside hot-water vents 8,000 feet below the surface near the Galápagos Islands. According to scientists from the University of California who have visited the area in a special submarine, the animals are unlike any others on earth. For example, they found new forms of crabs, clams, mussels, and tube worms. They are different in their appearance to be sure, but the major difference is in their capacity to exist without any apparent link to sunlight.

The production of food by plants supports virtually every other form of animal and plant life on earth. Even other deep-sea creatures exist by scavenging from the refuse that falls to the ocean floor from above where it grew with the aid of sunlight. But near the vents of the Galápagos Rift, where no light has penetrated since the ocean formed, the creatures derive their energy directly from the minerals that spew from volcanic cracks in the ocean floor. The water there is rich in sulfides, compounds of sulfur and oxygen. Many of the creatures host special bacteria that can take the sulfides and make the carbohydrates, proteins, and lipids necessary to build bodies and sustain life. So, while all the rest of the creatures in the world depend on the photosynthesis of plants for energy and building materials, sulfide-metabolizing bacteria sustain these creatures. As a consequence, some of the vent animals do not have a digestive system. In fact, the tube worms don't even need a mouth, since they do not eat.

As we have said, these creatures do not depend on sunlight. But the heat that produces the sulfides would not be possible without the existence of gravity. The sun's gravity affects how the crust of the earth moves and lets molten rock escape to the surface. While the direct light of the sun supports most life on earth, the sun's gravity makes it possible for the others to survive as well. God sustains all of His children on earth—even those who haven't yet seen the light of the Sun of righteousness (see Malachi 4:2).

A Word From Our Creator

Through the tender mercy of our God; whereby the dayspring from on high hath visited us, to give light to them that sit in darkness and in the shadow of death. Luke 1:78, 79.

May 15

If Ice Is Hard, How Can It Flow?

Frozen water (ice) covers one tenth of earth's surface, including the entire Arctic Ocean and most of the Antarctic continent. Ice is an amazing thing. Did you know, for example, that just about everything gets smaller when it freezes but that water expands when it turns to ice?

Unlike just about every other substance on earth, ice is less dense as a solid than as a liquid. That's why ice cubes bob to the top in a glass of water and icebergs float in the ocean. It's also why lakes and rivers don't freeze from the bottom up. (If you like to ice-skate, you should be glad of this!) While fresh water freezes at 32°F, salt water, with its high mineral content, freezes at the slightly lower temperature of 28.7°F. In both cases, the layer of ice on a river, pond, or ocean acts as a barrier against cold air and helps keep the temperature of the water underneath warmer than the air above and protect water life from colder temperatures.

We recognize ice in several natural forms. For example, beautiful snowflakes, which are frozen, crystallized water drops, are a form of ice. Where the snow doesn't melt, it compresses and becomes a glacier. A glacier is solid ice, but because of the immense pressure that exists within the ice, it actually flows—very slowly, of course—like a river of solid water. If the snow falls faster than the glacier takes it away, the glacier grows from year to year. But if it doesn't get enough snow to sustain it, the glacier will shrink in size over time. The chunks of a glacier that break off into the ocean we call icebergs.

Sleet is another form of ice, consisting of frozen water droplets. Especially in powerful thunderstorms, frozen droplets can add layers of ice to become hailstones as they pass through supercooled water on their way to earth. These balls of ice may travel at speeds of up to 90 miles per hour, damaging crops, buildings, and automobiles when they finally hit.

As harsh a substance as ice seems to be, the Creator has often used it as a way of protecting life, a means of keeping living things warm. Who but the Creator could think of such a thing?

A Word From Our Creator

Out of whose womb came the ice? and the hoary frost of heaven, who hath gendered it? Job 38:29.

May 16

Are You a Weed or a Wild-flower?

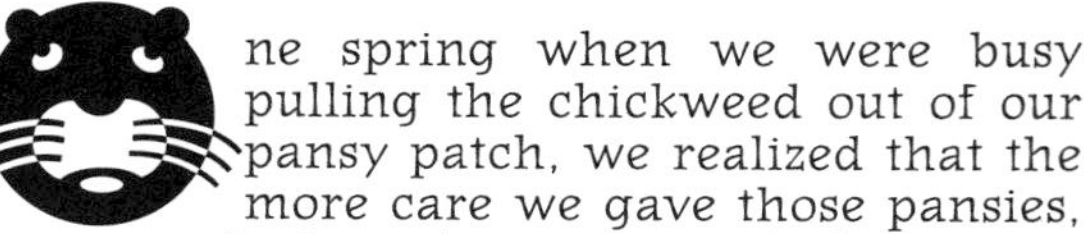

One spring when we were busy pulling the chickweed out of our pansy patch, we realized that the more care we gave those pansies, the more chickweed we nurtured! Chickweed seemed to be taking over our yard and our garden. It grew not only in the soil around and between the pansy plants but even between the individual pansy stems.

Common chickweed has a pretty little five-petaled white flower. Its graceful stems can grow up to 32 inches long, with short leaves growing along them. Unlike some of the other varieties of chickweed that prefer woodlands, meadows, swamps, and rocky areas, common chickweed thrives along roadsides, in waste places, and *in gardens*. If chickweed is an attractive wildflower and grows so easily, why were we pulling it up all spring to make room for the more showy pansies that are no more than hybrid descendants of wild European violets, which in turn were once considered weeds of grainfields and gardens?

When is a wildflower a weed? If it grows in the wrong place, we consider it a weed. Or if it crowds out desirable plants, we call it a weed. Should it cause runny noses and swollen eyes in some people, they would condemn it as a harmful weed. Is chickweed a weed or a wildflower?

Chickweed is an important food source for birds, prevents soil erosion on roadside banks, and makes a quick-growing no-maintenance ground cover. (Why else were local garden supply centers selling it for 79 cents a pot during the same time that we were pulling it up by the roots to get rid of it?)

We are all like weeds until Jesus gives us a purpose in life. Is it possible that we could be judging others as weeds when they are actually misplaced wildflowers? It would be hard to imagine Jesus seeing any wildflower as a weed. Does He see the potential wildflower in every weed? What do you think?

A Word From Our Creator

And if ye call on the Father, who without respect of persons judgeth according to every man's work, pass the time of your sojourning here in fear.
1 Peter 1:17.

he secret to hanging the Earth upon nothing lies in the power of gravity. The power of gravitational force is easy to see and it is easy to experience, but just what it is and how it works has been a mystery for centuries. We define gravity as the force that acts on all objects because of their mass. On our planet, it causes things to fall toward the Earth.

Sir Isaac Newton first proposed the idea of gravity about 300 years ago. Legend says he saw an apple fall from a tree and suddenly realized that the same force that made the apple drop also holds the moon in place. Scientists later determined that the sun's gravity is the force that keeps the Earth and all of the other planets of our solar system together in space.

By calculating the mass of each planet and its distance from the sun, astronomers were able to observe the gravitational force acting on the planets. They also noted that the mass of the planets in the solar system affected the orbits of the other planets circling the sun. Everything pulls on everything else, holding each celestial body in position in space and keeping it from colliding with the others. As a result, the behavior of planets—such as their speed of rotation and path of revolution—is predictable.

As astronomers observed the exact orbit of Uranus, once believed to be the outermost planet, they noticed that it wobbled in its path around the sun. Astronomers working in the 1800s calculated that only the gravitational force of an unknown, more distant planet could cause it, and soon two men using a telescope found Neptune. Many, many years passed while astronomers watched Neptune as it proceeded along its orbital path. Again they noticed that the planet's movements were irregular at times. They proposed the existence of yet another planet and discovered Pluto.

The sun holds the planets in place, and an unseen force at the center of the galaxy prevents the sun from drifting off by itself. And all of the galaxies appear to be revolving around the center of the universe. We know that gravity is the force that holds the universe together, but we don't know what gravity is. What do you think it is?

Hanging in Space

A Word From Our Creator

He stretcheth out the north over the empty place, and hangeth the earth upon nothing. Job 26:7.

My Yard Partners

A WORD FROM OUR CREATOR

Give us this day our daily bread. Matthew 6:11.

If you live in the southeastern United States, as we did for several years, you've undoubtedly seen cattle egrets. These small white members of the heron family spend their days around cattle and horses, feeding on the insects kicked up by the hooves of grazing livestock. The long-legged birds even perch on the backs of the animals to wait and watch for their dinner.

When I mowed the grass in our Texas farmyard, birds came eagerly to benefit from my labor. All summer long a pair of scissor-tailed flycatchers, a family of eastern bluebirds, and a pair of mockingbirds seemed to welcome the sound of the mower. Before I had finished even my first trip around the yard, the birds would appear.

The personalities of these different species were fun to compare. Mockingbirds are by nature somewhat belligerent. They seemed to ignore me, but they stayed just close enough to pick up any stray insect stirred up by the passing mower. The bluebirds brought the whole family and sat on the utility wires, watching. Then, taking turns, each one dropped to the ground, picked up a bug, and returned to its perch.

The scissor-tailed flycatchers were the tamest of all. One of them actually came down and waited in the grass, as a cattle egret would. The flycatchers seemed to have no fear of the noise and size of the lawn mower. Either they had learned that they had nothing to fear or they were so hungry that they were willing to risk the danger of a confrontation with that noisy mechanical monster.

In their natural state, all God's creatures depend upon their instincts for survival. Science offers all sorts of explanations for the behavior of my avian lawn partners, but I like to think that we had developed a trusting relationship. I gave them a source of food, and they brought me pleasure and companionship.

Isn't my relationship with those birds like our relationship with our heavenly Provider? He is the provider, and we give Him pleasure and companionship. We can trust Him even more than the birds in my yard trusted me.

umans spend millions of dollars every year trying to kill mosquitoes—vicious little monsters that are only about a quarter of an inch long and rarely survive longer than 30 days. Nevertheless, they are among the world's most harmful creatures. About 2,500 species of mosquitoes live worldwide, including the Arctic, and many of them spread some of our deadliest diseases.

A female mosquito may lay as many as 300 eggs at a time in or near water. Using her hind legs, she pushes the individual eggs into a group and sticks them together with a glue-like substance from her body. The raft of eggs floats until the larvae, called wigglers, emerge. After busily feeding on small plants and animals for several days, the wigglers enter the pupa stage. The pupae, or tumblers, do not eat, but roll and bounce around in the water for two to four days. Then they emerge from the pupal shell as adults.

Male mosquitoes sip nectar. Only the females suck the blood of cold-blooded animals such as frogs and snakes or warm-blooded animals such as birds and mammals—and people. The blood provides the nutrients needed by the eggs developing in the female's body.

A mosquito stabs its victim's skin with needlelike stylets, then sends saliva into the punctures. The saliva keeps the victim's blood from clotting and causes the allergic reaction that makes most people itch. When a mosquito "bites" a diseased animal or person, it sucks up some of the disease-causing organisms. Then it passes some of them on to anyone or anything else it attacks. Mosquitoes spread many kinds of encephalitis, which can cause seizures, brain damage, and death; dengue fever, a painful disease that can be fatal; malaria; and yellow fever, and can trigger life-threatening allergic reactions.

You can take precautions to prevent mosquito attacks. Stay away from stagnant water where insects breed, use an insect repellent, burn citronella candles when sitting outdoors in the evening, and wear white or light-colored clothing.

In Christian living, we should avoid ungodly associates, resist the devil, and put on the robe of Christ's righteousness.

Mosquitoes

A WORD FROM OUR CREATOR

Blessed is the man that walketh not in the counsel of the ungodly, nor standeth in the way of sinners, nor sitteth in the seat of the scornful. Psalm 1:1.

Klip-springer Devotion

Klipsprringers are small antelopes that live on the cliffs and rocky crags of southern and central Africa. They are not quite two feet tall at the shoulder and weigh no more than 35 pounds. Their name, which comes from the Afrikaans language, means "cliff hopper"—a term certainly descriptive of their antics!

The pair-bonding that occurs between a male and female klipspringer is among the strongest of any species in the world. For the klipspringer, it is a matter of life and death that there always be a pair. So, when you see one, you can be sure that another will always be nearby, standing watch. Predators are common, and no klipspringer can afford to remain unguarded for a second. The pair has a special ritual for the changing of the guard. The one that has been feeding approaches the mate that is watching for predators. By much nuzzling of muzzles, the one on guard becomes convinced that it is safe to take a feeding break and let the other one assume sentry duty.

Robin Dunbar, who has studied klipspringers extensively for many years, tells the story of one pair where the male had a difficult time getting enough to eat. The male had probably lost his mate because his new mate was a young female that was not yet wise to the ways of survival. But she knew about the nuzzling part. After feeding for a while, the female would approach the male and give him the nuzzle treatment, letting him know that she was ready to assume the sentry post, and that he was free to feed. So he would descend from the lookout point and begin feeding. Very soon thereafter, however, the female would lose interest in guard duty and wander down for some more feeding. Immediately the male would bound up to the lookout point and take up the guard post again. Back would come the female with more nuzzling, and the whole procedure would happen again. Mr. Dunbar reports that the male hardly got his quota of food that day. For him it was more important to guard the pair than to get enough to eat.

What a perfect example of our relationship with Jesus. He has promised never to leave us, never to forsake us.

A Word From Our Creator

Be strong and of a good courage, fear not, nor be afraid of them: for the Lord thy God, he it is that doth go with thee; he will not fail thee, nor forsake thee. Deuteronomy 31:6.

Let There Be Sound

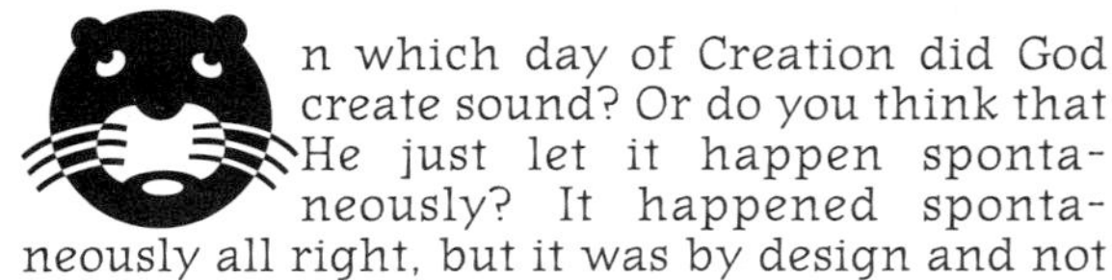

On which day of Creation did God create sound? Or do you think that He just let it happen spontaneously? It happened spontaneously all right, but it was by design and not by accident.

We need to agree on what we mean by sound. An old riddle asks the following question: If a tree falls in a forest, does it make any sound if no one is around to hear it? The reason this is a riddle is that there are two definitions of sound. One of them regards sound as the effect of vibrations on the ear of a listener. According to this definition, sound can occur only if someone hears it. The second definition considers the vibrations themselves as sound. The argument will never be resolved because the answer to the question is not a matter of science—it's a matter of language and opinion. The way to get around the argument is to call the vibrations sound waves and to forget about whether they produce sound or not.

Sound waves are not the same as light waves. The movement of photons in a stream produces light waves, while a disturbance of the molecules in a substance, as in air, water, or metal, causes sound waves. When you throw a stone into water, you see a series of ripples. The ripples are waves, and they show how sound works.

Anything that causes a substance to vibrate produces sound waves. Consequently, if you don't have a substance that can vibrate, you can't have sound waves. For example, in a vacuum (a space without matter), sound waves cannot exist because there is no substance that can receive and transmit the vibrations. Therefore, sound can't travel through outer space, because it is a vacuum. If you were on a planet with no atmosphere and you said something to a friend a few feet away from you, your friend would see your lips move, but wouldn't hear anything.

So to answer the question about when sound was created, we can say for certain that sound waves appeared as soon as there was something to make them and something within which the waves could vibrate. Genesis 1:2 tells us that "the Spirit of God moved upon the face of the waters." Movement on water could have caused sound waves. That was on the first day.

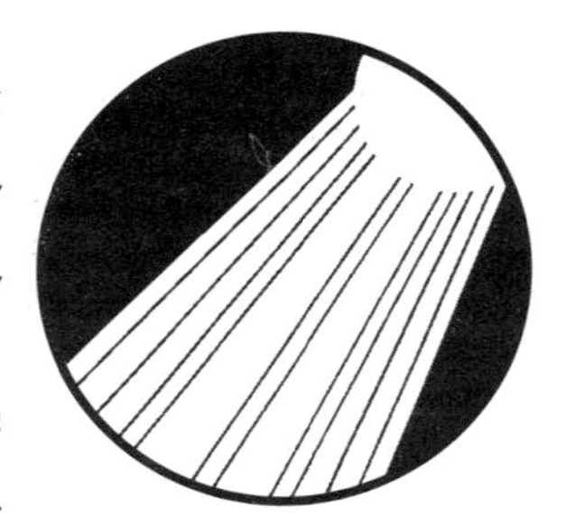

A WORD FROM OUR CREATOR

And suddenly there came a sound from heaven as of a rushing mighty wind, and it filled all the house where they were sitting. Acts 2:2.

May 22

Higher Than the Mountains

High in the Andes Mountains of South America, more than 18,000 feet above sea level, the act of taking a breath of air brings into your lungs only half of the amount of oxygen that it does at sea level. For those of us who have spent our lives near sea level, it would take weeks to adjust to the thin air at "only" 15,000 feet so that we could breathe comfortably. Even climbers who have conditioned themselves to exist at high altitudes will face life-threatening complications from oxygen shortage if they go above 18,000 feet faster than their bodies can adapt.

Indian children living in the highlands grow and mature more slowly if they live above an elevation of two miles. Many of those who spend their lives at even higher elevations suffer from dangerously enlarged hearts and chronic altitude sickness—nausea, headache, and gasping for breath at night.

Yet in the Andes thousands of Indians live at or above 12,000 feet and work at elevations of up to 18,000 feet—and have done so for centuries. Once people thought that they were genetically adapted to this severe environment. However, researchers have found that any lowlander can adjust to these same conditions if given enough time, and that a highlander who spends too long at sea level must readapt when he returns to higher elevations.

But a highlander may be born with at least one unique trait—the presence of more capillaries in his fingers and toes. Because of the increased blood supply to these parts of his body, a highland Indian, dressed in layers of llama wool but gloveless and barefoot, has warm hands even in freezing weather and can break ice with his feet to launch his reed boat. If night overtakes him on his way home, he can go to sleep without fear of waking up with frostbitten fingers and toes.

When we rise to join Jesus in His house "in the top of the mountains," we won't have to be concerned about adjusting to a higher altitude. The God who created us—the God who gave us the breath of life—will also give us instant heavenly lungs.

A Word From Our Creator

And it shall come to pass in the last days, that the mountain of the Lord's house shall be established in the top of the mountains. Isaiah 2:2.

his text is actually a statement of traditional rules that the Jews had about touching things. But it is a perfect introduction for a discussion about one of North America's poisonous plants.

Nearly everyone in North America has had a run-in with poison ivy. When the plant occurs in bushy form, it's called poison oak, and when it appears in vine form it's labeled poison ivy—but it is the same plant. We're taught as children to recognize the vine with leaves that come in threes. The old saying "Leaflets three, let it be" reminds us to stay clear of the poisonous plant.

Most parts of the poison ivy plant contain the toxic oil that causes a rash with swelling, itching, and blisters. Some people say that they get the rash by just being near the plant, but most authorities say that the oil must come into direct contact with the skin to do any damage. To be on the safe side, stay well away from vines with three leaflets.

Remedies for treating the rash caused by poison ivy vary from taking injections to washing with soap and water. But when I was a boy, I accidentally discovered the best of all cures. It was my job to wash dishes. Because I spent so much time out in the woods, I often had poison ivy on my hands and arms. After I had had my hands in the hot dishwater for a few seconds, the itching disappeared. As I used this remedy to relieve the itching, I discovered that as an added benefit the rash dried up in a few days. I thought that I'd discovered a new cure. Years later, however, I read about "my" remedy in a book of folk medicine. Hot water may be the oldest known treatment for poison ivy, and it is still the best one in most cases.

While we have been warned about touching poison ivy, it is almost impossible to go through life in North America without encountering the plant. I am thankful that I know how to treat the poison.

Our experience with sin is very much like our encounters with poison ivy. With sin, it *is* impossible to go through life without participating in it either accidentally or on purpose. But while we cannot escape its presence and its results, there is a sure cure for it. Jesus is the treatment.

Poison Ivy

A Word From Our Creator

Touch not; taste not; handle not. Colossians 2:21.

May 24

Let's Get Out of Here

A Word From Our Creator

Then we which are alive and remain shall be caught up together with them in the clouds, to meet the Lord in the air: and so shall we ever be with the Lord.
1 Thessalonians 4:17.

Suppose you want to get off this planet. What would it take? Space travel has become so common that we have almost stopped wondering at the difficulty in getting astronauts into space. Yet space travel is still a dangerous and incredibly expensive thing.

To escape earth's pull, you have to board a rocket ship that produces enough thrust to propel you in the opposite direction of the pull of gravity. The amount of thrust we calculate in g's, or multiples of the force of gravity. The more g's of thrust that you can get from your rocket, the faster you get away from earth. But a human can withstand only a limited number of g's. As the g force increases, you begin to feel heavier, and your body begins to lose its ability to function. After only several seconds at five g's, for instance, your vision dims and you lose consciousness. You could survive up to about nine g's perhaps, but only for a few seconds. So astronauts use rockets that accelerate to only two or three g's. But to escape from earth at low g levels requires more time and therefore a larger rocket with much more fuel—an extremely expensive system that can carry only a few people.

As you leave the surface of this planet, the atmosphere becomes thinner, which means that there is less of it to press upon you as it does here on the surface. If you aren't wearing a pressurized space suit, at about 100,000 feet above the earth's surface your body fluids will begin to boil. So you definitely need a space suit and containers of compressed air to maintain the proper pressure against your body.

And then there is the matter of zero gravity in space. No one knows how long you can survive in space in a state of weightlessness. Also, you have to contend with temperature problems—either extreme cold or extreme heat, depending on the various conditions. Radiation will kill you unless you have a shield. We haven't mentioned food and water, all of which you have to take with you somehow, because you won't find any vending machines in space.

So, how are you going to escape from this world?

n recent years the series of *Jaws* movies has been exciting, frightening, and in some cases disgusting to those who see the films. The movies capitalize on what are really quite infrequent occurrences in North Atlantic waters: man-eating white sharks attacking swimmers on a coastal beach. People who have seen one or more of the movies sometimes leave with such fear that some refuse to swim in the ocean again. The danger is real, but the fear is an overreaction.

Sharks *do* attack people. But of the 250 of the world's species of sharks, only 24 have been known to do so. Most shark attacks are unprovoked and end in death. And the white shark of *Jaws* fame *is* a killer. But the chances of a swimmer getting attacked are extremely low.

Sharks are unpredictable. Shiny objects and things with contrasting colors attract them. They can't see sharp details but are smell-minded, so the scent of blood lures them. Attacks on humans probably result when the curious shark confuses humans, especially those in wet suits, with large fish or marine mammals. The shark may also be defending its territory. Or attracted by the smell of blood from a skin diver's speared fish or a swimmer's fresh body cut, the shark may move in on the human being. Usually the shark realizes its mistake when it inflicts its first nonfatal bite, and then swims away.

In North America, where the white shark is our most dangerous species, lifeguards warn swimmers when a shark is present and advise them to stay out of the water until the prowler has gone elsewhere. In the unlikely event that a swimmer gets caught by surprise and is the first to see the shark, he or she should very calmly leave the water. Thrashing around may excite an otherwise peacefully inquisitive shark.

The same can be said for the Christian's reaction to the dangers of sin. The danger is real, but with Jesus as our protection we have no need to get anxious. The Lord says, "Be still, and know that I am God" (Psalm 46:10). We can calmly trust in Him—He will take care of us.

"Shark!"

A WORD FROM OUR CREATOR

Fear ye not, stand still, and see the salvation of the Lord, which he will shew you to day. Exodus 14:13.

May 26

Tapir Fish Bait

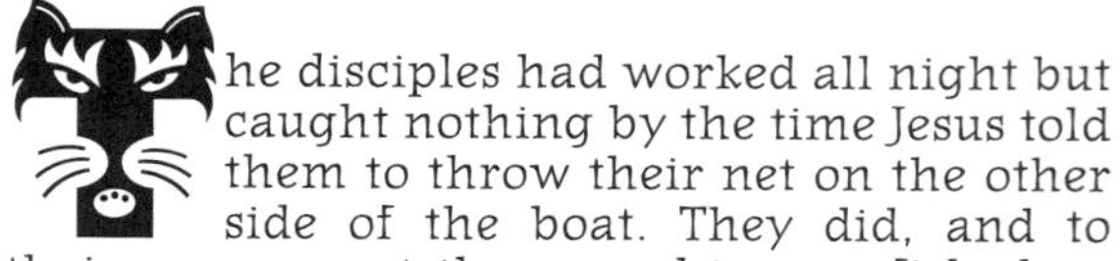

The disciples had worked all night but caught nothing by the time Jesus told them to throw their net on the other side of the boat. They did, and to their amazement they caught more fish than they could easily handle. The South American adventurer Henri Charrière relates an experience that reminds us of this Bible story.

Finding food in the jungles of Venezuela can be a challenge, and one of the best ways to survive is to learn from the creatures that live there. This story involves a tapir—a tropical animal that looks somewhat like a large pig with a much longer snout.

One day while sitting quietly beside a stream, Mr. Charrière watched a tapir emerge from the jungle to eat the leaves from a nearby vine. After eating lots of leaves, the animal waded into the stream and belched up some of the partially digested leaves and stirred them into the water with its head. After a few minutes, fish began to appear on the surface—bellies up and moving slowly as though drugged. The tapir calmly proceeded to eat the fish, one after the other, until it had had its fill.

Curious, Mr. Charrière picked some of the leaves from the vine, crushed them between some rocks, and collected the juice in a gourd. He then poured the juice onto a calm stretch of water and stirred it around. To his surprise, fish began appearing on the surface, knocked out by the substance. Mr. Charrière was able to supply his entire camp with fish from that time on.

Do you suppose that Jesus knew a secret about fish that even today we do not know—something about where to find them and how to attract them? One thing is sure: the disciples learned that good results always came from following Jesus' commands. The Creator has given us a number of them. If we follow those directives, we will lead better lives, and we will enjoy eternal life. Jesus said, "I am the vine, ye are the branches: . . . without me ye can do nothing" (John 15:5). He also said, "Follow me, and I will make you fishers of men" (Matthew 4:19). The miracle that Jesus performed for the fishermen and the miracles that He does in our lives are as easy for Him as it was for the tapir to catch fish.

A Word From Our Creator

And he said unto them, Cast the net on the right side of the ship, and ye shall find. They cast therefore, and now they were not able to draw it for the multitude of fishes. John 21:6.

May 27

Forget-me-not

The forget-me-not, a tiny flower brought to North America from Europe, has a name rooted in legend. The story is that a heavily armored knight drowned while trying to retrieve his ladylove's silk handkerchief from a river. With his dying breath he cried out, "Forget me not!" and a plant with hundreds of tiny blue flowers suddenly sprang up on the riverbank to preserve his memory. For the rest of her life the knight's lady watered the flowers with her tears. In 1917 the people of Alaska designated the forget-me-not as their territorial flower to remind them that although Alaska "awakened in a day," it "came to stay."

Putting romance aside still leaves the little blue flower with an important place in scientific history. Most members of the forget-me-not family have hairy stems that keep ants from crawling up to the flowers to sip the nectar. The plants need the nectar to attract bees and other flying insects, which in turn pollinate the plants.

An eighteenth-century German botanist named Sprengel wondered if the yellow circle in the middle of the forget-me-not served a special purpose. After spending a great deal of time studying the flowers, he concluded that the color scheme was designed to attract insects to the heart of the flower, where pollination takes place. The forget-me-not's flower is a miniature target, and pollinating insects naturally aim for the bull's-eye. From this one example, Sprengel went on to study the designs of other flowers. Science credits him with being the man who worked out the first theory about ways in which flowers and insects work together for their common good.

Having answered his question about the forget-me-not, Sprengel realized that he had seen an important relationship in the natural world, and he turned all his attention to learning all that he could about that subject. He found something to do, and he did it with all his might. In doing so, the botanist helped us to see how the yellow center of this tiny blue flower serves a very specific purpose besides being delicately beautiful. In addition to the earthy legend about the flower, forget-me-nots remind us that our heavenly Knight did not die in vain.

A Word From Our Creator

Whatsoever thy hand findeth to do, do it with thy might. Ecclesiastes 9:10.

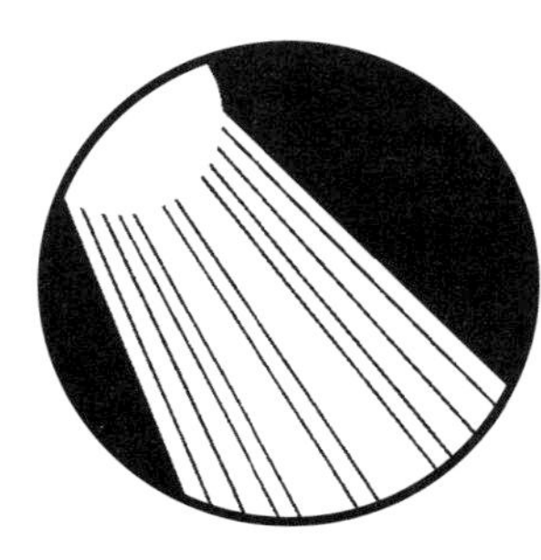

Brighter Than the Sun

Because this story takes place in the middle of the day and because the light was brighter than the sun, we can assume that it did not come from the sun. Its impact blinded Saul, and he fell to the ground. And then a voice said, "I am Jesus whom thou persecutest" (Acts 26:15). Here is another instance where light accompanied Jesus' arrival. Because light is a by-product of atomic nuclear reactions and because a very powerful and very bright light always seems to accompany the Creator, it is reasonable to assume that the Creator and Sustainer of the universe would move about in a cloak of high atomic energy.

During the past 50 years science has discovered a lot about the power of atomic energy. For example, we've learned that when an atom releases nuclear energy, the resulting power can heal, or it can kill. The nuclear explosion of an atomic bomb takes about one millionth of a second, and in that amount of time 2 septillion (that's a two with 24 zeros) uranium atoms split, releasing energy equivalent to thousands of tons of the explosive TNT. And that power is nothing compared with the nuclear explosion of a hydrogen bomb, which can release the energy of millions of tons of TNT.

Apparently, while in human form Jesus was able to lay aside His all-powerful creative energy. But as God He has a problem. How does He protect us from the effects of the energy of His being? God told Moses that "there shall no man see me, and live" (Exodus 33:20). As an old man John saw Jesus, "and his countenance was as the sun shineth in his strength" (Revelation 1:16). And when Jesus returns to take us to heaven, those people who have chosen to remain wicked will be destroyed "with the brightness of his coming" (2 Thessalonians 2:8).

It seems clear that the King of kings is an incredibly powerful force. That's what Saul found out on the road to Damascus. And Jesus speaks to us today also—perhaps not in a blinding flash, but through His Word, which is "a lamp unto [our] feet, and a light unto [our] path" (Psalm 119:105).

A WORD FROM OUR CREATOR

At midday, O king, I saw in the way a light from heaven, above the brightness of the sun, shining round about me and them which journeyed with me. Acts 26:13.

MAY 29

Fire and Ice

The sun beats down on the equator and the temperature soars to 100°F. The heat acts as a mighty pump evaporating billions of gallons of water from the ocean into the atmosphere. Meanwhile, some 6,000 miles away at one of the poles, the temperature may be almost 80°F below zero. Even though thousands of miles separate the two locations, we experience their effects on each other through the movement of air within earth's atmosphere, movement that we call wind. And according to our text for today, all of these forces are simply fulfilling God's word. How?

After the Flood, God promised Noah that "while the earth remaineth, seedtime and harvest, and cold and heat, and summer and winter, and day and night shall not cease" (Genesis 8:22). And one vehicle by which God has kept that promise of livability is the wind.

If the earth had no winds, the poles would freeze up and the equator would be scorching hot. As it is, tropical winds constantly carry heat northward and southward to meet the winds coming from the poles. This transfer of heat and cold creates all our weather. We hear the action described as cold fronts, warm fronts, low-pressure areas, and high-pressure areas. It's all very complicated in its detail, and meteorologists spend lifetimes studying the process. But it's really very simple in its overall effect. Something we call "the weather" keeps this planet that we call home reasonably warm and reasonably cool.

Weather is so common that we create our own methods of making it interesting. Every day we hear something about the weather, such as "Everybody talks about the weather, but nobody does anything about it" and "If you don't like the weather here, stick around a while and it will change." We pray for rain when there's not enough, then we pray that it will go away when we get too much. Often we joke about the weather and talk about whether or not the local weather forecaster is accurate. Even though we know that our talk isn't likely to change the weather, we still spend a lot of time talking about it.

Praise God for the weather that is constantly fulfilling His word.

A WORD FROM OUR CREATOR

Praise the Lord from the earth, ye dragons, and all deeps: fire, and hail; snow, and vapours; stormy wind fulfilling his word.
Psalm 148:7, 8.

May 30

A Very Special Tree

A Word From Our Creator

Who his own self bare our sins in his own body on the tree, that we, being dead to sins, should live unto righteousness: by whose stripes ye were healed. 1 Peter 2:24.

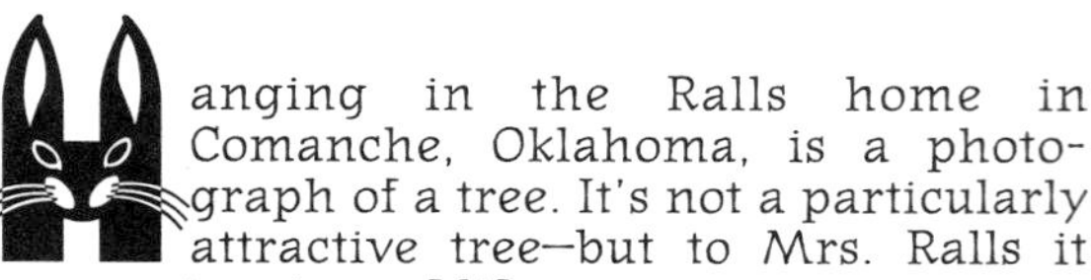

Hanging in the Ralls home in Comanche, Oklahoma, is a photograph of a tree. It's not a particularly attractive tree—but to Mrs. Ralls it represents a tree of life.

One day in May 1987 the Ralls family were camping a few miles from home beside Waurika Lake. In the middle of the night a severe thunderstorm hit and the lake water began to rise. Trying to get their boat to the trailer at the landing, Mr. Ralls broke off the key in the ignition, so Mrs. Ralls drove home for the spare key. The storm got worse, and on the way back, the truck that Mrs. Ralls was driving was suddenly washed into the lake.

Mrs. Ralls, who didn't know how to swim, pushed her way out of the truck and found herself in deep water with no idea where she was. She remembers crying out, "Lord, help me!" And then she felt a branch. Grabbing it, she pulled herself toward the tree. Getting to the trunk, and clinging to branches, Mrs. Ralls found herself wondering if God was listening. In a panic she fought to climb higher in the tree. And then she heard a voice. "Don't climb higher until morning." She obeyed.

In the morning she saw that the next limb above was dead. It would have broken under her weight. All that day the storm raged while she clung to the branches of the tree. No one could hear her calls above the sound of the wind and rain. The light began to fade into evening, and Mrs. Ralls became lonely.

And then she saw him—the largest man she had ever seen—and he was sitting on another branch in the same tree. Strangely, she was not afraid. The man's eyes were very kind. Suddenly Mrs. Ralls felt safe. Neither she nor the man said a word for several hours, but whenever she looked he was there, as though he was watching over her. He finally spoke, telling her that he was leaving but that she need not be afraid because help would arrive soon. Then he was gone.

It was close to dawn when she heard the voices. Two men in a boat rescued Mrs. Ralls from the tree that had saved her life. But she will never forget the fact that with her in that tree was a heavenly messenger assuring her that everything would be all right.

May 31

Multiple Stars

The sky is full of wonders. When you go out at night and look up into the starry sky, you see what appear to be single stars. It may surprise you to learn that about half the stars that you observe in the sky are either double stars or star systems with multiple stars.

All you need in order to see that some stars are double is a good pair of binoculars. A telescope is even better, of course. You might start by looking at Mizar, the middle star in the handle of the Big Dipper—the first star after the North Star. Mizar is a double-double star. With your naked eyes you may be able to tell that Mizar appears to be a double star, but if you look at it through binoculars, you can see that each of the two points of light is itself a double star.

Double stars are fun to look at through a telescope. Sometimes one of the stars is a great big star and the other is so small it looks like a moon orbiting a planet. Sometimes the two stars are of different colors. The head star in Cygnus, the swan (also called the Northern Cross—the star at the end of the longest end of the cross), is a double star. The brighter of the two stars is yellow, and the dimmer one is blue-white.

You can't see the movement of the stars by looking at them, but double stars rotate around each other. To get a feeling for how this happens, go out into the yard with a friend, face each other, grasp hands, and skip in circles. To make the illustration really authentic, while you're skipping in circles, move across the yard. Now you are a double star journeying through space. If you want to get really complicated, have two doubles skipping in circles across the yard, and have each of the doubles moving in circles around the other. Now you are a double-double star traveling across the sky.

The reason you won't see the stars circling each other is that it takes years—sometimes hundreds of years—for them to make one complete circle. The universe is God's estate—like a huge yard within which He watches over each star system with infinite care. Won't it be wonderful when Jesus takes us on a tour of His estate!

A Word From Our Creator

Thou, even thou, art Lord alone; thou hast made heaven, the heaven of heavens, with all their host, . . . and thou preservest them all.. Nehemiah 9:6.

June 1

Mantis Shrimp

A Word From Our Creator

Behold, I shew you a mystery; We shall not all sleep, but we shall all be changed, In a moment, . . . the dead shall be raised incorruptible, and we shall be changed. 1 Corinthians 15:51, 52.

n his letter to the Christians in Corinth, Paul uses dramatic language to describe how Jesus will change us when He comes. The apostle seems to want to emphasize that the transformation takes place in a very short time, so first he writes "in a moment." Then, as though a moment is too long, he makes sure that his readers know that it happens so fast that you can't see it: "in the twinkling of an eye." One of the best examples in nature of how fast that can be is the speed of one of earth's most unusual creatures.

The mantis shrimp looks like a cross between a praying mantis and a shrimp. It may be as short as half an inch or as long as 13 inches in length, and it lives throughout the world in holes in the ocean floor. When the mantis shrimp goes after prey, it illustrates today's text.

Mantis shrimp fall into two groups: the smashers and the spearers. In terms of brute strength, few things its size can match the power of the smasher type of mantis shrimp. It can break open clam shells with a single blow of its forelegs (the legs that develop into claws on a lobster). The force of that strike has been compared to that of a small-caliber bullet.

The spearer type of mantis shrimp swims at the speed of about 33 feet per second. (The fastest a human has swum has been about six feet per second.) When an unsuspecting fish or other small sea creature passes within range, the spearer's spine-covered forearms strike and grab with a speed that almost defies belief. For the unsuspecting victim, it's all over in one four thousandths of a second. Now *that's a twinkling of an eye*!

We have seen a demonstration of the spearer's speed in an aquarium. A swirl of sand in the water told us that something had happened, but we hadn't even seen the shrimp move!

For its size, the mantis shrimp is stronger and faster than a tiger. And it uses its power and speed to kill and consume. When Jesus comes, He will use His power and speed to give us eternal life and perfect bodies. People who are alive as well as those who arise from the sleep of death will be changed in the twinkling of an eye.

 salt flat is a patch of land left when a body of saltwater completely evaporates. If you think that a salt flat doesn't have much life on it, you're right. Comparatively speaking, a salt flat is one of the most arid forms of desert on earth and, as a result, it cannot support a great variety of life-forms. But it was to just such a barren spot that Dr. Lee Herman, an entomologist, went to study insects. Dr. Herman selected a salt flat that covers an area of about 43 square miles in northern Oklahoma. Although several kinds of creatures inhabit it, Dr. Herman was interested in only two types of burrowing insects.

First, Dr. Herman wanted to find out how many of the two kinds of insect species lived there. He marked off the same number of square feet in various parts of the salt flat, counted the number of burrows in each area, and computed the number of burrows per square foot.

He learned that every square foot of that Oklahoma salt flat supports an average of about 250 burrows—or 250 of the burrowing insects that he was studying. That may not seem to be many insects, but when you multiply 250 by the number of square feet on the entire salt flat, you learn that 300 billion of just those *two kinds* of insects inhabited that barren land! Think what the total number of insects would be if you also counted all the other forms present on that salt flat!

If that many insects live on an arid piece of land, the number in a lush tropical rain forest must be larger than we can even imagine. Another entomologist studied just the number of beetles living in the tops of the trees in a jungle and estimated that there are more than 30 million different kinds.

The Creator operates in big numbers. This is all easy math for Him, but it's impossible for us to calculate the numbers of many of God's simplest creatures. All we can do is to make estimates until we get to heaven, where we can learn from the Supreme Entomologist all about His six-legged friends.

Billions of Bugs

A WORD FROM OUR CREATOR

O the depth of the riches both of the wisdom and knowledge of God! how unsearchable are his judgments, and his ways past finding out! Romans 11:33.

JUNE 3

A Merry Heart

ore and more scientific research supports the healthy way of living described in the Bible. You undoubtedly already know about the value of eating the proper foods, drinking enough good water, getting an adequate amount of rest, breathing plenty of fresh air, and exercising regularly. But have you ever thought about the health-giving value of being merry? Having a merry heart is more than just being happy and content. Merriment also includes having a sense of humor and the ability to laugh.

Some sad souls have gone so far as to advise that "true" Christians should always be serious and never laugh. But that is *not* what the Bible teaches. In fact, according to our text for today, the bones of such a person may end up prematurely dry—as in dead.

Recent research has provided a direct link between merriment and health. It turns out that a merry heart actually makes you less likely to get sick because it improves the functioning of your immune system. Your body is then better able to prevent, as well as to fight, disease. For example, someone with a cheerful attitude toward life is less likely to have such stress-related health problems as ulcers and cold sores than is someone with a gloomy outlook on life. "Mirthful laughter" actually reduces the chemical factors associated with stress in the body. Your body is able to heal itself and make you feel better faster. Rather than adopt a happy attitude, however, some people feel more comfortable asking a pharmacist for a pill to treat their symptoms—when all they need is a good laugh.

By the way, when we talk about merriment here, we are not talking about silliness. Silly chatter and giggling often are associated with cruel or inappropriate jokes or gossip. Laughter that comes at the expense of other people does not create a merry heart—and it certainly is not health-producing.

A merry heart does you good—like a medicine. And unlike pills and syrups, you don't have to swallow it. It's natural, and it's free.

A WORD FROM OUR CREATOR

A merry heart doeth good like a medicine: but a broken spirit drieth the bones. Proverbs 17:22.

June 4

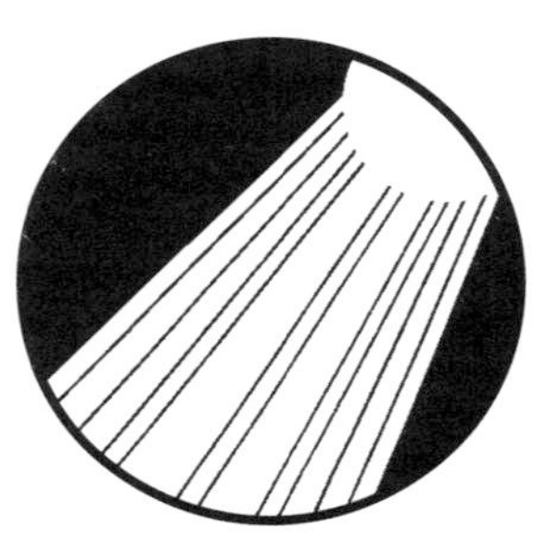

Quantum Leap

We often call a really major breakthrough in the world of science a "quantum leap." The term commonly means "big jump," but a real quantum leap is so tiny that no one has ever actually seen one occur.

A scientist named Niels Bohr was the first to propose the idea of a quantum leap. According to Dr. Bohr's theory, atoms shift back and forth between energy levels. And when they jump from a low-energy level to a high-energy level, they absorb light. But when they drop from a high-energy level to a low-energy level, they emit, or give off, light. Therefore, all light indicates that quantum leaps are occurring. For there to be one photon of light, a quantum leap has to take place. When an atom gets zapped with a high-energy source like a laser beam, some of the atom's electrons shift from a low-energy state to a high-energy state. In the process, the atoms absorb light and remain at the high-energy level. As long as the high-energy source remains present, the atoms maintain their high-energy level and continue to absorb the light energy.

But when you remove the high-energy source, the atoms lose their high-energy state. The electrons in those atoms drop back to the low-energy state, and emit light. Each electron that jumps back to a low-energy state emits one photon of light. And that amount of light is what Dr. Bohr called a quantum. The word "quantum" simply means "an amount." So, for every electron that jumps from high-energy state to low-energy state, *an amount*, or quantum, of light is emitted as a photon. It is that jump that's called a quantum leap.

There is no higher source of energy in the universe than God, and when He brought light to the first day of Creation Week, He provided sufficient energy for the production of a world. On occasion, Jesus proves that He is the most powerful energy source of all. This occurred when Peter healed a lame man in His name. When the disciple called on the energy from the throne of God, the world witnessed a quantum leap. The Light of the world was at work. Praise God for His power to save you and me!

A Word From Our Creator

Then Peter said, . . . In the name of Jesus Christ of Nazareth rise up and walk. . . . And he . . . entered with them into the temple, walking, and leaping, and praising God.
Acts 3:6-8.

June 5

Hidden Snow

We find a lot of meteorological information packed into this passage. Why were the brooks blackish? The text states that it was because of the ice where the snow is hidden. Can you think of a condition in which the snow hides in the ice?

All glaciers start out as snow. In order for a glacier to form, more snow has to fall during one winter than can melt during the following summer. The unmelted snow continues to accumulate over several years. As the falling snow continues to add to the snow pack, the tips of the delicate snowflakes break off as the weight from above increases. The result is a compact mass of tiny snowballs. The growing weight compresses the snow on the bottom. This increase in pressure causes the temperature to rise, and the snow momentarily melts and releases the air trapped inside. Then the melted snow freezes again and becomes a solid mass of ice.

By drilling holes into glaciers and pulling out plugs of ice, climatologists—scientists who study climate—can read the weather of past years just as botanists count the rings of a tree to determine its age. For example, if a huge volcanic eruption occurred in a given year, then the falling snow will contain volcanic ash, and the ash will be deposited in the glacier that year. The ash layer remains as long as the glacier lasts and is obvious in the ice plug pulled from the glacier.

Glaciers are slow-flowing rivers of solid ice. As they move along, they pulverize everything in their path, including the solid rocks they pass over. When the ice at the tip of the glacier melts, the types of minerals ground up and dissolved by the ice flow affects the color of the water.

It's quite possible that in our text Job is describing "blackish" water runoff from a glacier in a nearby mountain. Even today you find glaciers on mountains in the Near East, and at the time of Job, more than 3,000 years ago, we believe that region of the earth had many more active glaciers.

How do you think that such a stream is like deceitful men?

A Word From Our Creator

My brethren have dealt deceitfully as a brook, and as the stream of brooks they pass away; which are blackish by reason of the ice, and wherein the snow is hid.
Job 6:15, 16.

Nagyvary and Stradivari

For more than 150 years the one violin maker who stood out above all the rest was Antonio Stradivari (pronounced STRAH-duh-VAH-ree). For all those years other violin makers have been trying to duplicate the matchless tone of Stradivari's violins. Without success, they used all sorts of ways of drying and seasoning the very same wood that the Stradivari family made their violins from. The conclusion was always the same—that Stradivari had some secret method for creating his violins.

Now comes Dr. Joseph Nagyvary (pronounced NAH-gee-VAH-ree) of Texas A&M University, who decided that maybe there was no secret, just a mistake in the origin of the wood and how it got to Stradivari. In his analysis of the wood in the great violins, Nagyvary found traces of a fungus that didn't show up in any of the attempted copies. Identifying the species of fungus, the professor has discovered two surprising things:

The fungus is an *aquatic* variety. That means that the wood used by Stradivari would have had to come from the water at some point. In checking shipping records for the early 1700s, the time when Stradivari was making violins in Cremona, Italy, Nagyvary learned to his delight that shipments of logs were often floated downstream to Cremona from the Alps.

Nagyvary also discovered that the fungus spreads through the wood and eats a gummy substance found there. This leaves the wood lighter in weight and able to vibrate more.

To prove his theory, Nagyvary has built violins out of wood from logs containing this fungus, and professional violinists say they cannot tell the difference between a Nagyvary and a Stradivari. Apparently the mystery has been solved. Stradivari used "baptized" wood. To produce the heavenly music for which his violins are famous, the wood had to be submerged in water.

And by our submersion in baptism, we show the world that we have accepted God's promise to "put a new song in my mouth, even praise unto our God" (Psalm 40:3).

A WORD FROM OUR CREATOR

For as many of you as have been baptized into Christ have put on Christ. Galatians 3:27.

JUNE 7

A Little Star

Ever since I took a class in astronomy, I've been intrigued by the idea that the moon once may have been a tiny sun that lighted up our night sky. The author of the book of Genesis writes that "God made two great lights; the greater light to rule the day, and the lesser light to rule the night" (Genesis 1:16). We find direct evidence all over the moon that it was once a hot globe and that it cooled some time in history. Curiosity has led me to search for references to any stars that might be as small as our moon.

The first stop in my search led to a star chart that lists stars by relative size and classifies them by color and brightness. To begin with, you find the average-size suns like Sirius and Capella. The really big suns are called *giants* and *supergiants*. Betelgeuse is a supergiant, as is Canopus. Astronomers call the small suns dwarfs and divide them according to color. Color indicates their temperature: red dwarfs are the coolest and brightest, while blue dwarfs are the hottest and dimmest. In between fall orange, yellow, and white dwarfs. Our sun is on the small side of average between the giants and the dwarfs.

To find the really small stars, we must look among the dwarfs. One of them is the twin of Sirius—Sirius B. (Sirius is a double star.) Sirius A is a relatively hot sun of average size and temperature, but Sirius B is a cooler, very bright and tiny sun going in circles with Sirius A. About the size of the planet Uranus, Sirius B is a really small star to be sure.

But then there is Van Maanen's Star (named for its discoverer)—a sun only 6,000 miles in diameter, making it smaller than Earth! But the smallest star appears to be a white dwarf with a diameter of about 3,500 miles. That's close to the size of the moon! Our moon is not too small to have been a sun. But that doesn't mean that it *was* one. A sun consists of gases, while the moon is rock.

The Creator in His mercy provided exactly what our world needed, and He still does, because "His mercy endureth for ever"!

A Word From Our Creator

To him that made great lights: for his mercy endureth for ever: The sun to rule by day: for his mercy endureth for ever: The moon and stars to rule by night. Psalm 136:7-9.

ts name is pronounced pita-HOO-ey, which is supposed to be close to "pitooey!"—the sound you make when you spit out something in a hurry that tastes bad. And it was only a few years ago, in Papua New Guinea, that science discovered the pitohui's secret. It's a poisonous bird!

The poison is located in the feathers and the skin of the hooded pitohui, a strikingly black-and-orange dove-sized bird. The poison is not lethal to humans, but it is very irritating to the skin and causes numbness of the lips and mouth. So you should never hug and kiss a pitohui! However, low levels of the poison cause paralysis in mice and higher ones produce convulsions and death.

But it wasn't until biologists analyzed the poison that the really remarkable truth emerged. The poison was identical to that found in the arrow-poison frogs of Central and South America. And that poison is not known to exist anywhere else on earth. Explaining how animals from two different classes in two different parts of the world can have the same exclusive poison is going to require a lot of study and soul-searching about the way in which scientists thought the poison evolved in the frogs. Given the theory that evolution is the result of chance, the odds that exactly the same complex chemical formula can evolve in frogs in tropical America and in birds in tropical New Guinea—some 9,000 miles apart—are virtually zero.

So what purpose does the poison play in the life of the pitohui? Naturalists believe that the poisonous feathers protect the bird from predators like the little eagle, a bird that feeds on the smaller birds of the tropical forest. The eagle might take a pitohui once, but—pitooey!—it would quickly spit out the bird, and it would not be likely to nibble on one again.

Isn't that what Jesus did for us? As sinners, we are prey for Satan. But Jesus took our place and gave us a protective covering. Satan learned that he was no match for the Creator. And when we rely on the power of Jesus, the predator has no power over us. We are safe.

Pitohui

A WORD FROM OUR CREATOR

So Christ was once offered to bear the sins of many; and unto them that look for him shall he appear the second time without sin unto salvation. Hebrews 9:28.

Spider Silk

A Word From Our Creator

Behold, I come quickly: hold that fast which thou hast, that no man take thy crown. Revelation 3:11.

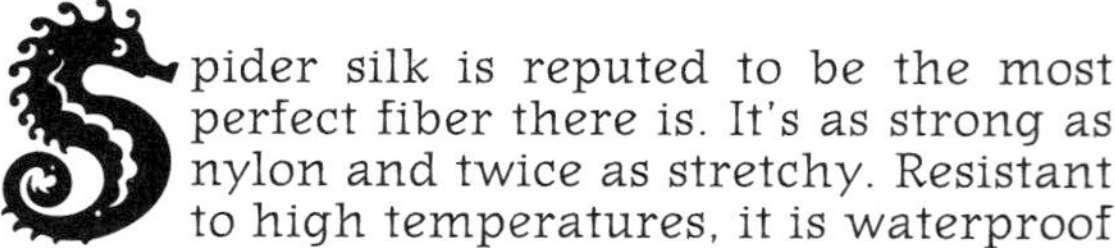

Spider silk is reputed to be the most perfect fiber there is. It's as strong as nylon and twice as stretchy. Resistant to high temperatures, it is waterproof and nonallergenic. But spider silk is too fine to use for manufacturing cloth. In fact, it's so fine that it would take all the silk produced by 5,000 spiders in their lifetime to provide enough fabric for one garment. One adult female can spin five or six feet of silk a minute, but a single strand long enough to stretch around the world would weigh only 15 ounces.

Researchers who have identified and studied the proteins that spiders use to produce silk compare the structure of one of these proteins to a chain made of alternating links of rubber and steel. This combination gives the silk elasticity and strength at the same time.

Different types of spiders produce different kinds of webs, and individual spiders can manufacture different types of silk. Each kind of silk comes from sets of glands called spinnerets, located on the end of the spider's abdomen. For example, one set of spinnerets produces sticky thread that holds prey in place until the spider arrives. Still other spinnerets make swathing strands, reinforcing threads, and cocoon silk. Each spider is like a factory with machines to manufacture various kinds of material as needed.

The most common type of spider silk is called dragline silk, the lifeline that spiders lay down as they move from place to place. A spider always remains connected to its dragline. When the spider falls, it just climbs back up its dragline, which is still attached to the place from which it fell. And what a powerful connection that dragline is—a single strand would have to be almost 50 miles long before it would break of its own weight.

God never asks us to do something without providing the power to do it. In today's text Jesus challenges us to hold on to the salvation that He paid for with His life. In the spider the Creator has given us an example of His ability to provide the power to hold fast. The same God who endowed the spider with a powerful natural fiber that scientists are only now learning to appreciate will give each of us the power to stay close to Him.

t is not surprising to learn that both Hitler and Stalin were devoted to the theory of evolution. What they attempted to do with the masses of German and Russian people under their control came from the idea that the strong are superior to the weak and that it is morally right for the strong to survive at the expense of the weak. That logic dictates that if you are more advanced along the evolutionary scale, then it is appropriate for you to squash the less advanced. One writer of evolutionary thought is the entomologist Vernon L. Kellogg, who states that "human growth which is in the most advanced evolutionary state . . . should win in the struggle for existence." I'm sure that you'll agree that such a philosophy provides no place for the power of God's love.

But you might be surprised to learn that people who say they believe in God and who preach what they claim to be the principles of heaven will sometimes express the same kind of idea. A good example were some of the Pharisees, who by a form of haughty superiority kept the Jews of Jesus' time in subjection to their religious views. Of them Jesus said: "Verily I say unto you, They have their reward" (Matthew 6:5).

We call the survival of the strong over the weak the "survival of the fittest." The spiritual realm also has such a struggle for survival. Early in the ministry of Jesus Satan took Him to a high mountain and offered Him the whole world if Jesus would just worship him. Here was a struggle for power—power of the strong over the weak. Satan was a powerful angel, while Jesus was by choice in a weakened human condition.

But the *real* struggle for human survival reached its pinnacle later on Calvary, where, by all appearances, it appeared that the strong had indeed overwhelmed the weak. But in His death Jesus vanquished Satan.

Now each of us has a choice to make. We are weak—Jesus is strong. Our choice is whether or not to accept His strength as our survival. "Let no man beguile you of your reward" (Colossians 2:18).

The End of Evolutionary Theory

A Word From Our Creator

For what shall it profit a man, if he shall gain the whole world, and lose his own soul? Mark 8:36.

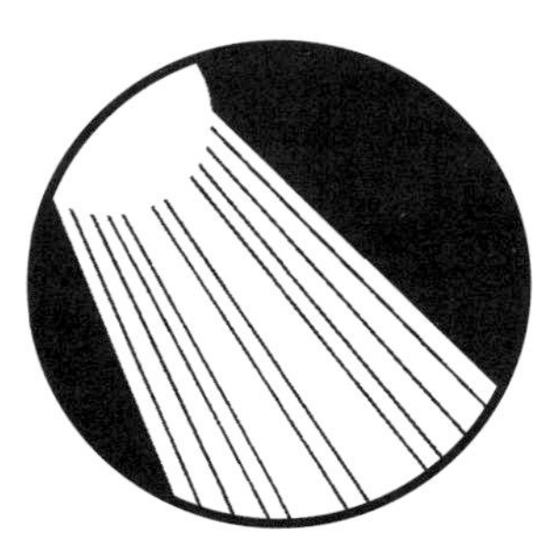

Irradiated Gems

For centuries gemologists (experts who appraise the value of gemstones) have been trying to improve the quality of jewels. They wanted to create gemstones of different colors and hues as well as to increase the intensity of the color in natural gemstones. So they tried dyes, bleaching, heating, and other processes. But nothing worked—until recently. The secret is a process that uses light, and the technique was fully developed by the 1970s.

Light rays improve the color of gemstones. But these are no ordinary light rays. If they were, you could leave stones out in the sun to improve their quality.

The light waves that are needed are the invisible ones—gamma rays, X-rays, and ultraviolet light. Color is produced by the effect of atomic particles called photons on the atomic makeup of different substances. When these energy waves bombard certain completely colorless or almost colorless crystals, they transform the gems into spectacular blues, golds, and reds. The process works for such gems as sapphires, topazes, and diamonds.

The radiation involved is not dangerous, because the beams of high-energy rays don't penetrate the atomic nuclei of the crystals. The light only stimulates a change in the organization of the electrons around the nuclei. The radiation causes the electrons to "bump" into different energy states within the already orderly state of the crystal. This causes the energy level of the mineral to change, giving off a different color than before.

Jesus tells us that a day is coming in which He will make up His jewels. You have a chance to be one of the jewels that form the treasure of the King of kings and Lord of lords. As you allow His light to shine on and through you, your gem quality continues to improve, and you will shine forth to His glory and honor. He has the power to transform you into a crown jewel in the kingdom of God.

A Word From Our Creator

And they shall be mine, saith the Lord of hosts, in that day when I make up my jewels; and I will spare them, as a man spareth his own son that serveth him. Malachi 3:17.

esus often quoted well-known sayings. He even recounted familiar stories as illustrations for His teachings. In today's text Jesus is speaking to the Pharisees and the Sadducees when He mentions the familiar saying about the color of the sky as it relates to the weather. We don't know how long the saying had been in use at the time of Christ, but we do know that it's been almost 2,000 years since Jesus quoted the saying, and we still hear it in one form or another today. A more current version of Jesus' admonition is "Red sky at night, sailor's delight; red sky in the morning, sailors take warning."

There's actual meteorological truth to the statement. The only time when the sky is red is when the sun is shining through the atmosphere near the horizon. At that angle the sunlight has to pass through a greater amount of air than it does when it's higher in the sky. The shorter wavelengths of visible light, including blue through orange, get deflected, so we don't see those colors. But the longer red wavelengths are more stable and persistent, and they color the sky crimson.

At our latitudes in the earth's temperate zone the prevailing winds move from west to east. Therefore, when we see the red sky in the west, it means that the rain clouds have moved on to the east, the sky is clearing, and tomorrow's weather will probably be clear: "Red sky at night, sailor's delight." By the same token, when we see a red sky in the east, it means that the rain clouds have just arrived from the west, bringing stormy weather with them: "Red sky in the morning, sailors take warning."

When Jesus used this saying to the Pharisees and Sadducees, they had just tried to trick Him into giving them a sign from heaven to prove that He was God. He condemned them for knowing how to predict the weather but not being able to recognize the Messiah by the nature of His message. Even today, Jesus' life and His teaching represent all of the evidence that we need to prove that He is God.

JUNE 12

When the Sky Is Red

A Word From Our Creator

He answered and said unto them, When it is evening, ye say, It will be fair weather: for the sky is red. And in the morning, It will be foul weather to day: for the sky is red and lowering. Matthew 16:2, 3.

Cork

Do you know where cork comes from? We asked a 10-year-old friend that question one time, and he said that cork is a mixture of wood and Styrofoam. While that's a good description of cork, it is not a correct answer.

Cork is the outer bark of the cork oak, a tree that grows in Portugal, Spain, and Algeria, a country in Africa. Cork oaks grow to heights of 30 to 40 feet and have diameters of three or four feet. Like all oak trees, they produce acorns.

But cork oaks are special. Cork oak bark grows to be very thick, and when a tree is about 20 years old, people can harvest its bark for the first time. They carefully strip the bark lengthwise from the tree's lower branches and trunk. Ten years after this first harvest, the bark has again grown thick enough to cut. Stripping the bark takes place about every 10 years until the tree dies at the age of 200 or 300 years.

The early Romans wore comfortable cork sandals as early as 400 B.C. The apostle Peter probably used cork floats for his fishing nets. More recently, we have used cork as bottle-stoppers, insulation, and gaskets, as well as in the manufacture of floor coverings, tires, and wadding for shotgun cartridges. Burned cork shavings will make Spanish black, a paint used by artists.

Cork is certainly useful, but one tiny feature provides the secret to its value. Cork oak bark consists of very thickly packed cells, and each cell contains a tiny air pocket. The air keeps the cork afloat in the water, retains heat, absorbs sound, allows the cork to compress easily and then spring back into its original shape when released, and does not readily absorb water. If cork oak bark had only a few cells, it would not be able to do everything described above. But since it has many cells working together for one purpose, it is very valuable.

Many people make up God's church. By working together with the common purpose of bringing glory to Him, we keep His church afloat.

A Word From Our Creator

A nation has invaded my land. . . . It has laid waste my vines and ruined my fig trees. It has stripped off their bark and thrown it away, leaving their branches white. Joel 1:6, 7, NIV.

y the standards of the universe the average person is almost blind. Of all the wavelengths that exist in the full spectrum, only visible light, infrared, ultraviolets, and radio waves pass through Earth's atmosphere. And we can see only the narrow band of the spectrum that is visible light. Our atmospheric canopy blocks out the dangerous high-energy rays.

Using radio telescopes, astronomers have found stars that give off no visible light—only radio waves. And radio telescopes can "see" right through the clouds of space dust that block visible light from getting through to us. If we could see the radio waves, it would add immeasurably to our view of the universe.

With the aid of telescopes placed on satellites outside of Earth's atmosphere, we can study those rays that it otherwise blocks. For example, X-rays come from points in the universe that emit no visible light. These rays have helped convince scientists of the existence of black holes, stars so dense and powerful that light cannot escape. If we could see X-rays, we would be able to see a number of objects in space that generate and emit only X-rays. And if we could see gamma rays, we would be able to watch, among other things, mysterious bursts of gamma radiation from strange objects in space.

By detecting ultraviolet light rays, astronomers have detected massive clouds of various gases that some stars have spewed into space. If we could see these clouds, we would view their different colors and densities as they make a continuous light show in the heavens—an "aurora celestialis."

Even if all that we knew about the universe were only what we can see with the naked eye, or through a telescope, we would still be in awe of what we observe out there. But imagine what it would be like to view the rest of the spectrum. We'd watch a universe teeming with images that defy our imagination.

The Invisible Universe

A WORD FROM OUR CREATOR

For by him were all things created, . . . visible and invisible, . . . all things were created by him and for him: And he is before all things, and by him all things consist. Colossians 1:16, 17.

JUNE 15

The Reed Warbler and the Cuckoo

The reed warbler is a drab, brownish marshbird that breeds in Europe and western Asia and winters in tropical Africa. A very small bird, it averages only five inches in length.

Each pair of reed warblers builds a nest suspended among the reeds of their marshy habitat. Then the female lays four or five greenish-white eggs splotched with olive-green. Normally, the female warbler sets on the eggs until they hatch and then works hard to provide enough food to sustain the hungry little warblers. But an ever-present problem lurking nearby can drastically alter this picture.

Living in the same region is a much larger bird, the cuckoo, which is a healthy 13 inches long. The cuckoo's name comes from its common "KOO-koo" call—the one that lends its chime to the cuckoo clock. Although the cuckoo's call may be attractive, the bird has another habit that is not at all admirable. Rather than build its own nest, the cuckoo lays its eggs in those of other birds and depends on them to do all the child-rearing chores. The large cuckoo lays its eggs in the nest of much smaller birds. Through amazing subterfuge, the cuckoo lays eggs that are similar in size, shape, and color to those of the birds whose nests it invades. And the cuckoo's egg hatches sooner than the other birds' eggs.

So, while Mrs. Warbler is out feeding, Mrs. Cuckoo sneaks in and adds one of her eggs to those already in the nest. When Mrs. Warbler returns, she doesn't notice anything unusual and incubates all the eggs. The cuckoo egg hatches before the others, and Mr. and Mrs. Warbler immediately begin to feed their new baby. The baby cuckoo needs as much food as five baby reed warblers, and it grows rapidly. To make sure that it will have no competition for food, the cuckoo chick uses its scoop-shaped back to get under each of the unhatched warbler eggs and push them up and over the side of the nest, where they fall into the water below. That leaves the young cuckoo as the sole object of affection of its tiny adoptive parents, who work very hard to raise their monster baby.

Does the behavior of the cuckoo remind you of someone?

A Word From Our Creator

That we henceforth be no more children, tossed to and fro, and carried about with every wind of doctrine, by the sleight of men, and cunning craftiness. Ephesians 4:14.

Cholesterol Is Good for You

Everywhere you look in the grocery store you see the label "no cholesterol," as if cholesterol were something that isn't good for you. The truth is that you can't live without it. So, if cholesterol is so valuable, why do doctors make such a fuss about it?

Our bodies need cholesterol to replace millions of worn-out or damaged cells. Produced in the liver, it travels by way of the bloodstream to all points of the body to do its work. The blood then carries unused cholesterol back to the liver.

A regulator in the liver determines the production level so that your body will make just the right amount for you. When you eat food that contains cholesterol, your body gets extra cholesterol that the bloodstream absorbs. There it joins your own cholesterol, and now you have more than enough. As your cholesterol filters through the liver, your body takes the extra cholesterol into account and instructs it to slow down the absorption and production process. That means that there is now an excess of cholesterol in the bloodstream—and here is where the danger comes in.

Since your body cannot use more than it needs, the excess cholesterol deposits as a hard, waxy substance on the walls of your blood vessels. If this process continues long enough, the walls get so thickened with wax that the blood cannot flow through the blood vessels. At this point you're in critical danger of having a stroke or heart attack.

Your body needs about 300 milligrams of cholesterol a day, and your liver will produce all that you need. You don't need to obtain any from your food. The cholesterol found in food appears in such animal products as eggs, cheese, and meat. Plant foods do not contain cholesterol.

As with most things, the right amount is good, but too much can be dangerous. That is certainly true with cholesterol. The very best diet is the one that God created for us—plant foods, which contain no cholesterol at all.

A Word From Our Creator

He causeth the grass to grow for the cattle, and herb for the service of man: that he may bring forth food out of the earth.
Psalm 104:14.

Woolly Bear of the Arctic

The rust-colored woolly bear is the caterpillar of a member of the tiger-moth family living in the arctic regions of North America. The moment it hatches from its egg this caterpillar begins to chomp on the buds and leaves of the arctic willow. Most tiger-moth caterpillars spend only two to four weeks eating and growing before they enter the pupa stage, the transformational stage from which the adult moths emerge a few weeks later—or, at the most, the following spring. But the rust-colored woolly bear spends at least 14 years *as a caterpillar*. In fact, no one knows exactly how long this little insect may remain in the larval stage. Nor does anyone know what triggers its entrance into the pupa stage. What we do know is this:

Toward the end of the arctic summer, something (probably a growing scarcity of food) tells this woolly bear that it is time to prepare for winter. The woolly bear then begins to produce glycerol—a natural antifreeze. It eventually quits eating, finds a place to hide, and stops moving.

As the temperature begins to drop and the snow starts to fall, the little ball of fluff slowly freezes—but not totally. First the caterpillar's stomach freezes, then its blood, then every other organ and bit of tissue—*except* the fluid inside some of its cells. From all appearances and measures of life, the caterpillar is dead. It doesn't breathe and it has no heartbeat. The rust-colored woolly bear rests through the winter tucked under a blanket of snow.

In late spring the warm June sun melts the last of the snow, and the woolly bear's delicate hairs act like tiny solar cells to soak up the sun's rays. Soon the caterpillar is ready for another summer.

The power of those rays streaming from the sun stimulate a return to life for the rust-colored woolly bear. And so it will be with each of us. Whether we are alive or dead, when the Sun of righteousness (Malachi 4:2) comes in the clouds to rescue us from this world, His life-giving power will reach us wherever we are, and we will be rejuvenated for an eternal summer.

A Word From Our Creator

And after that he saith unto them, Our friend Lazarus sleepeth; but I go, that I may awake him out of sleep. John 11:11, 12.

June 18

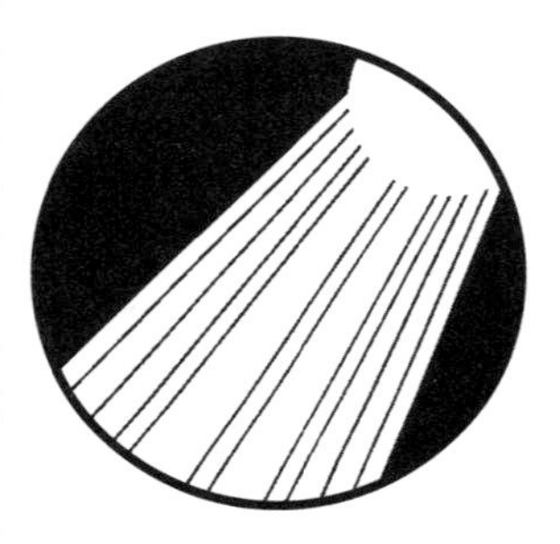

Refraction

Light doesn't really play tricks on you. But if you don't know the laws that affect the way light behaves, you may fool yourself. What if you're wading in a stream and see a silver dollar under the water in front of you? As you reach for the coin you're surprised to discover that it isn't where you saw it. Your hand appears almost to separate from your arm as you reach beneath the water. You eventually find the coin and retrieve it, but it was not where you thought it was. Depending on the angle of your vision against the surface of the water, the coin may have been anywhere from a fraction of an inch to several inches away from where you assumed it to be. If this has happened to you, you would be experiencing something called *refraction*.

Refraction is the change of direction that light takes when it passes from one kind of matter into another—in this case, from water into air. Light travels at the speed of 186,000 miles a second in a vacuum and only slightly slower than that in air. But it moves only about three quarters of that speed in water. This fact causes light rays to bend as they emerge from one kind of matter into another.

Refraction also causes mirages and rainbows. In both cases our eyes see images that aren't really there. Why does a rainbow keep moving away from you when you try to catch it? Why don't you ever reach that mirage in the highway ahead of you?

Refraction is a natural effect of light. Years of experience have trained our eyes to see things in a certain way, and it's difficult for us to adjust for the distortion caused by light refraction. Fishes and birds, on the other hand, have learned to compensate for the effects of refraction, a skill that allows birds to spear fish in water and fishes to grab insects from the air. They aren't deceived by the refraction.

Jesus tells us that some people will claim to be Him. In fact, Satan himself will appear as an angel of light (2 Corinthians 11:14). When someone tells us that Jesus has appeared here or there in the world, we know that it can't be true. Jesus, the Light of the world, told us what to expect: He is coming in the clouds, and "every eye shall see Him" (Revelation 1:7). Jesus won't trick you.

A Word From Our Creator

Then if any man shall say unto you, Lo, here is Christ, or there; believe it not.
Matthew 24:23.

JUNE 19

Air Plants

Most plants send their roots into the ground to absorb food and water. But an air plant is different. It uses its roots to anchor itself to a tree. However, it is not a parasitic plant that steals nutrients and moisture from its host plant. Instead, an air plant manufactures its own food, relying on its host to serve only as a base of operation. In fact, the many thousands of varieties of air plants—that include lichens, mosses, liverworts, Spanish moss, and some ferns, orchids, and cacti—may also grow on rocks, buildings, timbers, and telephone wires.

Bromeliads are also air plants. The largest and most colorful of the bromeliads grow in the rain forests and jungles of Central America and South America. The pineapple, probably the most familiar edible air plant, is a bromeliad that grows on the ground.

The leaves of the world's 2,000 kinds of bromeliads are typically long and narrow, providing lots of surface area for lots of specialized scales, called trichomes. Trichomes serve two important purposes. First, they absorb food and moisture from the rain and fog of tropical forests. Second, they reflect sunlight, preventing the bromeliads growing high in trees from getting sunburned.

The leaf-base of many bromeliads forms a cup that collects water, while the leaves make a protected nestlike structure. Mosquito larvae, tree frogs, and spiders have their homes in the miniature ponds of these plants. When rain is scarce, the bromeliad uses the stored water and food (the latter in the form of dead insects) to stay alive until the next rainfall.

In the plant kingdom God has left wonderful examples of His ability to sustain life with little more than moist air. As Christians, we survive in much the same way. That is what breath is—moist air. Prayer has been called the breath of the soul, and it is through prayer and the absorbing of God's Word that He sustains us.

A WORD FROM OUR CREATOR

And the Lord God formed man of the dust of the ground, and breathed into his nostrils the breath of life; and man became a living soul. *Genesis 2:7.*

hink about this question carefully before you answer it: What two things does a seed need in order to sprout? One thing is obvious, the other is not. One element is provided directly, the other indirectly. What's your answer?

Did you say water and light? You're wrong—even though that's the answer that most people give. Water is correct, but light is not. Did you say water and *sunlight*? You're partly right. But it's not the *light* in the sunlight that the seed needs. If it were, then why would we plant seeds *under* the ground, where it's dark?

Have you figured out the second requirement for a seed to sprout? It is *warmth*, which is why sunlight is a partially correct answer. The warmth that seeds use to sprout comes from the effect of the sunlight on the soil. The amount of energy bathing a square mile of the earth's surface at a given moment is equivalent to that released by an atomic bomb. The difference is that the energy in the bomb is concentrated in one tiny space, so it becomes destructive. But the energy from the sun spreads out evenly over the land and turns into a life-giving force—it warms the soil, thereby providing a warm bed for the seeds to start their growth.

All you have to do is add water, and the seeds swell up and burst open, sending down new little roots and poking up new little shoots that soon develop leaves. While the seed did not need light to sprout, the leaves do need it to grow. Together, the water, air, and light are the raw materials that the plants use to grow and to produce food for humanity and the hungry animals of the world.

Today's text says that the seed represents the word of God. The Word of God is Jesus (John 1:14). Just as the seed in the garden needs water and warmth, when we take Jesus into our hearts, we need the water of His Spirit and the warmth of heavenly sunshine to provide the conditions for a Christlike character to grow in us.

Seeds

A Word From Our Creator

Now the parable is this: The seed is the word of God. Luke 8:11.

JUNE 21

The Very Large Array

Astronomers now use our entire planet as a telescope. That makes a telescope thousands of miles in diameter—certainly larger than the 200-inch mirror on Mount Palomar, in California. How do they do that?

Initially, astronomers constructed an array of parabolic reflectors. These look like giant satellite dishes standing in a row, but they are really radio receivers picking up signals from deep space. They call the arrangement of receivers a *very large array*, or VLA. The one 50 miles west of Socorro, New Mexico, has 27 such receivers on tracks so that scientists can move them to focus on different objects in space.

While the VLA in New Mexico was being built, another VLA was under construction in Great Britain. When both of these VLAs were operating, scientists focused them on the same object in space. Together they act as a single receiver thousands of miles wide. That reveals details invisible through any optical telescope on earth. And what they reveal is mind-boggling.

Take NGC 6251, for example. Routine optical photographs showed NGC 6251 as an ordinary elliptical galaxy, which means that it was egg-shaped instead of round. Beyond that astronomers had no reason to assume that it was unusual in any way. But through the radio-sensitive eyes of the VLA, we discover an awesome river of energy spewing from the center of NGC 6251 into space for a distance of hundreds of thousands of light-years. Scientists have compared the stream of energy to the jet of water from a fire hose. Although they can now clearly see the energy emission, astronomers can only speculate about what is causing it.

And NGC 6251 is only one example—there are billions more. "The heavens declare the glory of God" (Psalm 19:1), and "the heavens declare his righteousness" (Psalm 97:6).

A WORD FROM OUR CREATOR

The heavens declare his righteousness, and all the people see his glory.
Psalm 97:6.

It is refreshing to be reminded that, even with all our intelligence and wisdom, we have much to learn about our world. Taking a unique approach, marine-mammal specialist Richard Ellis has written about what we do *not* know about sperm whales.

For example, although we know what sperm whales eat, no one knows how they feed. They have no teeth until they are 10 years old, when they get 20 to 25 on the lower jaw only. Then, after waiting so long to get them, they don't use their teeth to capture prey or to chew their food. So why do they have teeth at all?

Here's another oddity: Sperm whales are huge and are slow swimmers, so they can't chase and catch their prey. Yet their favorite food is squid, which are not only swift swimmers but live at depths where no light reaches. How can the whales catch something much faster than they are and that they can't even see?

Another mystery about the sperm whale is in its head. A male sperm whale can be 60 feet long and weigh 53 tons. Its head, with its huge snout, makes up about one third of its body mass, or about 21 tons. A special sac in the whale's head contains as much as a ton of clear or yellowish oil, but no one knows for sure what the oil is for. For centuries people have killed whales for this oil that they once used in lamps and still put in some cosmetics. But what purpose does the substance serve for the whale?

One theory about the oily fluid in the whale's head is that as the animal dives down into deep water—sometimes to a depth of more than 10,000 feet—the oil gets cold, hardens, and becomes heavier. With this added weight, it's easier for the whale to reach the depths, like a stone dropping to the bottom of a glass of water. As the animal returns to the surface, the blood pumping through its capillaries warms up the oil again and melts the solid mass, allowing the whale to float again. But as marvelous as this explanation is, no one *knows* if it's correct or not.

We know a great deal about the world that God gave us, but we are still full of questions about His creatures. Won't it be wonderful to get the *real* answers when we meet Him face-to-face?

Whale Mysteries

A Word From Our Creator

He hath made every thing beautiful in his time: also he hath set the world in their heart, so that no man can find out the work that God maketh from the beginning to the end. Ecclesiastes 3:11.

June 23

Beneficial Nematodes

A Word From Our Creator

So foolish was I, and ignorant: I was as a beast before thee. Psalm 73:22.

Farmers and gardeners often discuss the evils of nematodes, wormlike creatures that inhabit soil in large numbers. The mere mention of nematodes brings comments of how horrible the tiny creatures are because of how much damage they do to crops. Although many species of nematodes do attack roots and cause stunted plants, other kinds prey only on insects harmful to plants. These nematodes are actually helpful.

Beneficial nematodes search for their prey both below and on the surface of the soil. Above the surface they stand on their tails and wave their heads around in hopes of making contact with a passing insect. Underground they simply move along in search of prey. Once they make contact, the nematode enters the victim's body and within 48 hours releases a deadly bacteria that kills most insects.

The life cycle of these nematodes ranges from seven to ten days. Although they reproduce, not enough of them survive winter to be an effective control in the following season. Since only young nematodes can infect harmful insects and since it takes so many, gardeners should put nematodes—the beneficial kind, of course—into the soil each year. Introducing nematodes into the soil requires no special equipment. The creatures are so tiny that gardeners put them into water and spray them on the soil's surface with an ordinary sprinkler or watering can. And nematodes are inexpensive—just a few dollars buys a million of them.

If you look up nematodes in an encyclopedia, you will probably read about the harmful ones famous for the damage they do. As is often the case, you can't just say something is "good" or "bad." The beneficial nematodes are just as valuable to us as the harmful ones are damaging.

People are like nematodes: the fact that one member of a family does something wrong doesn't mean that all the members of that family behave in the same way. You can't judge a nematode by its name. "Ye shall know them by their fruits" (Matthew 7:16).

June 24

Without Wax

Another translation of this text could be as follows: "That ye may be without wax and without offence till the day of Christ." The English word "sincere" comes from the Latin word *sincerus*, made up of two root words: *sine* (without) and *cera* (wax).

The Romans most commonly used the word to describe pure honey without the wax of the honeycomb. Perhaps you know how much fun it is to get a good piece of honeycomb and chew it up, letting the honey squeeze into your mouth. It tastes sweet as you swallow it and spit out the wax. But when you want to use honey in cooking, or on your cereal, or to spread on a slice of bread, you don't want wax mixed in with it. It's then that you know how important it is to have honey that's "sincere"—without wax.

Second, the Romans employed the word to indicate the quality of sculpture work. In this situation it also meant "without wax." Sculptors would begin with a shapeless stone and sculpt a figure that they hoped would bring a good price. When the statue was finished, the sculptor or his assistant would take it to market to sell it. Some of the vendors would stand under awnings as they called out for passersby to buy their wares, whereas others would stand out in the full sun, calling, "Sincerus! Sincerus!"

Good sculptors worked carefully and made no mistakes. The less-talented or careless sculptors covered up their mistakes with wax. As long as they kept the poor quality statues out of the warm sun, no one could see the difference. If left in the sunlight, however, the wax would melt and reveal the defects.

When the apostle writes to the Philippian Christians, he first tells them, "He which hath begun a good work in you will perform it until the day of Jesus Christ" (Philippians 1:6). He then prays that they will be sincere, or as we might say, "without wax," until Jesus comes.

A Word From Our Creator

That ye may be sincere and without offense till the day of Christ. Philippians 1:10.

June 25

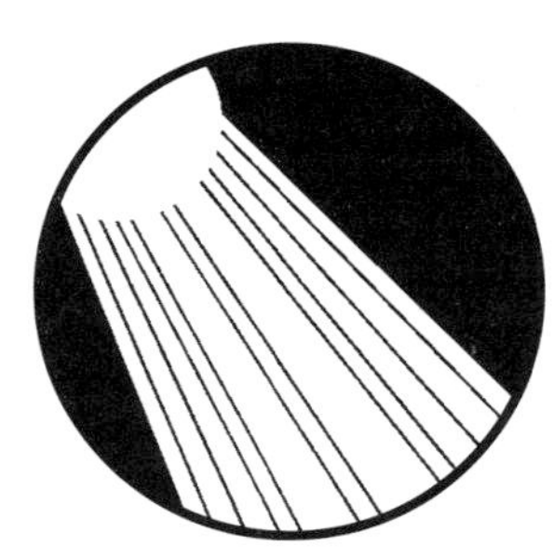

Why Does It Get Dark at Night?

Why *does* it get dark at night? You may think that that's a silly question, because anybody knows that it becomes dark when the sun goes down. But not so fast. It's not as simple as that. Certain physical laws of light and distance suggest that our night should be as bright as our day. Scientists call the problem Olbers' paradox, after Heinrich Olbers, who described it in 1826.

Every time an object's distance from light doubles, the brightness of the light divides by four. To picture this, think of the space around a lighted candle as the inside of a balloon. From the outside you "see" the balloon as a glowing bubble because of the candle inside. Now let the balloon expand so that the distance from the candle to the wall of the balloon doubles. The brightness of the glow of the candle on the wall of the balloon will be only 25 percent as bright.

Every time you double the distance, the amount of light from one of the candles will be cut to a fourth of what it was before.

Another rule says that with every time the distance from you to the wall of the balloon doubles, the amount of space in the balloon multiplies by eight. Now imagine that there is a candle for every cubic inch of space in the balloon. Every time you double the distance, you increase the number of candles eight times, but the amount of light coming from those candles is only one fourth of what it would have been at half the distance. So, if space is infinite—that is, if the balloon has no wall—then as you keep doubling the distance, you also keep multiplying the number of possible stars by eight and dividing by four the amount of light that reaches the earth from space.

Light does not diminish in brightness as it travels through space, so the light from trillions of stars, like the light of unnumbered candles, maintains all of its intensity as it streams out in all directions, including ours. So why isn't night as bright as day with the light from all of those star "candles" shining upon the Earth? No one really knows the complete answer to this riddle.

There are things that we just don't know. We have many things to learn throughout eternity.

A Word From Our Creator

Great is our Lord, and of great power: his understanding is infinite. Psalm 147:5.

onald Pinkerton, of Bath, New York, tells the story of the day that God used a hawk to save his life. When it happened he was hang gliding from a ridge on Mount Washington, near his home. He waited on the mountain for a thermal to use to soar into the heavens. A thermal is a bubble of warm air that forms on the ground and grows larger and larger until it breaks away and floats upward, sometimes quite rapidly.

Rustling leaves told Ronald that a thermal was approaching. He gripped the control bar of his hang glider and took several running steps to launch it into the updraft of air that now surrounded him. Then he maneuvered until he was soaring in wide circles, like a hawk on a summer day. Never had he risen so fast into the sky. In fact, he was more than 4,000 feet above the mountain before the lift let up. The ride had been fantastic. Now he would simply glide back to the mountaintop. Off in the distance he saw several red-tailed hawks seeming to enjoy the same exhilarating conditions as he did.

Then it hit—another thermal smashed into the hang glider before Ronald had adjusted his position to descend properly. The wind was blowing at least 40 miles per hour, but it was not lifting him. Instead, the angle of the glider caused it to plunge toward the ground, and he could do nothing about it. Totally at the mercy of the wind, Ronald struggled desperately to get control of the glider. And then he saw the hawk. It was right beside him, apparently dropping to the same unknown fate below. The man and the bird were about 300 feet above the trees and still falling.

Why doesn't that hawk save himself? Ronald wondered. Suddenly, the hawk banked and shot straight down. *Why is the hawk committing suicide?* the man's mind demanded. And then: *Follow the hawk!*

Side by side, the two fliers dived straight toward the ground, and just as suddenly, at about 100 feet above the ground, the wind stopped. The glider righted itself and began to gain altitude again. Breathing a prayer of thanks, Ronald looked for the hawk. It was nowhere to be seen.

At the Mercy of a Thermal

A Word From Our Creator

Doth the hawk fly by thy wisdom, and stretch her wings toward the south? Job 39:26.

The Botany of Love

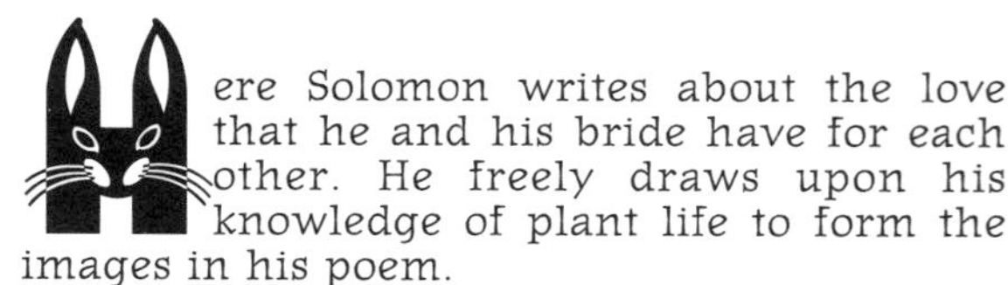

Here Solomon writes about the love that he and his bride have for each other. He freely draws upon his knowledge of plant life to form the images in his poem.

For example, spikenard (Song of Solomon 1:12) is a powerful perfume extracted from a plant that grows from 11,000 to 17,000 feet up in the Himalayas of India. People often kept it in a sealed alabaster box, to be opened only on special occasions. The spikenard that Mary Magdalene used to anoint the feet of Jesus was worth almost a year's wages. Myrrh (verse 13) is a perfume and incense that forms as a gum resin on the trunks of a type of small tree in eastern Africa and Arabia. Myrrh was one of the gifts that the wise men took to Jesus. Camphire (verse 14), or henna, is a very fragrant flowering shrub of southern Palestine. Even today the young women of that region consider a bouquet of henna flowers a generous token of love. Fir (verse 17), probably cypress, was one of the most valuable types of wood in the land. People used it for fine detail work in furniture and woodwork.

The rose of Sharon (Song of Solomon 2:1) is probably a variety of narcissus that grows in profusion on the Plain of Sharon in the spring. Scholars are still debating what flower is referred to here. And the exact identify of the lily of the valley is also unknown. Solomon may have meant either the lotus, tulip, anemone, autumn crocus, Turk's-cap lily, ranunculus, iris, or gladiolus. The fruit of the apple tree (verse 3) may be the apple that we know, or it may be an apricot, citron, or quince. The fig (verse 13), however, is the same fruit that we call a fig today. The fig tree was an important food plant, and the Bible uses it as a spiritual symbol. In fact, it is the first and one of the last plants mentioned in the Bible (Genesis 3:7; Revelation 6:13). Grapevines (verse 13) were commonly cultivated in Bible times. People ate the grapes and made wine from them.

Through the ages flowers and their perfume, trees, and other plants have played an important part in human love stories. Do you suppose that when Jesus gave us flowers He was saying "I love you"?

A WORD FROM OUR CREATOR

The flowers appear on the earth; the time of the singing of birds is come, and the voice of the turtle is heard in our land. Song of Solomon 2:12.

JUNE 28

The Lesser Light

Our moon is unique among all of the 50-plus moons of all of the planets of our solar system. First of all, it is the closest moon to the sun. Both Mercury (the planet closest to the sun) and Venus (the next planet) have no moons. So the moon revolving around Earth, the third planet, comes closer to the sun than does either of the two moons of Mars, the next planet in line. Why is this important?

Because of their great distance from the sun and their proximity to their host planets, all the other moons are more influenced by the planets that they orbit than they are by the sun. But that is not true for our moon.

The sun's gravitational pull on Earth's moon is twice as powerful as Earth's gravitational pull on the moon. The mystery, then, is why, when the sun pulls it so strongly, the moon continues to orbit around Earth. Actually, it doesn't orbit around the Earth as a true moon satellite does. A moon should orbit around the planet's equator. But our moon orbits the Earth on the plane that the Earth and all of the other planets circle the sun.

We are fortunate that the sun does not pull our moon away from Earth into orbit as an independent planet. If it did, it would drastically alter the conditions that support life on Earth. Those conditions are perfectly balanced and held in place by a power that humanity is only beginning to understand and appreciate.

Yet all of these strange facts about our moon lead astronomers to wonder if it was once a planet, or if the earth and its satellite were at one time linked together in a more intimate fashion—perhaps as a double planet. We don't know, of course, and God has not seen fit to tell us any more than that He created Earth's moon as "the lesser light to rule the night." Won't it be wonderful when we can ask the Creator directly to show us what the conditions were between Earth, the moon, and the sun at the time of Creation?

A WORD FROM OUR CREATOR

And God made two great lights; the greater light to rule the day, and the lesser light to rule the night. Genesis 1:16.

June 29

Tuna

What do you think of when you hear the word "tuna"? Do you think of a grocery-store shelf filled with small cans illustrated with mermaids, bumblebees, or well-dressed fish? Or do you think about the animals behind the advertising—the 13 species of a group of large, streamlined fishes that inhabit the world's oceans?

Tuna can zip through the water as fast as 45 miles an hour in pursuit of food such as squids, eels, and smaller fishes, including other tuna. They also eat crabs, shrimp, and other sea animals.

Tuna can also dive quickly to escape from predators such as seabirds and larger fish. The rare bigeye tuna is known for the depth and speed of its dives. One was observed to dive 750 feet in less than a minute. Scientists cannot explain how tuna can survive such rapid changes in water pressure, and no other animal—or man-made machine—can duplicate this feat.

Tuna species range in length from about two feet to more than six feet. They weigh as little as six pounds to as much as 3,000 pounds.

The tuna's sleek body becomes even more streamlined when the fish retracts its fins into its body. Unlike most fish species, the tuna has no muscles that pump water through the gills. As the tuna races through the ocean, seawater flowing over the gills provides needed oxygen. But if the tuna stops swimming, its gills are useless, and it suffocates.

Prayer has been called the breath of the soul. The tuna must continuously swim through the water to keep oxygen coming into its bloodstream. But the tuna doesn't have to think about it—it just does it. When we develop a relationship with Jesus, we don't need to think, *Today I have to remember to talk to Jesus.* That would be like saying, "Today I have to remember to talk to my best friend." Talking to your best friend is just natural—you don't have to remind yourself to do it. And because He is your Friend, you don't have to tell yourself to talk to Jesus—anymore than the tuna has to remind itself to keep swimming.

A Word From Our Creator

Rejoice evermore. Pray without ceasing. In every thing give thanks: for this is the will of God in Christ Jesus concerning you.
1 Thessalonians 5:16-18.

June 30

One Cunning Wolf

The arctic hare is one of the primary sources of food for North American timber wolves living in the Arctic. One morning a biologist, who had been studying wolves for 28 years, observed what he calls "a most memorable hare hunt."

A female of the wolf pack had been resting on the tundra when she suddenly spied an arctic hare on a hilltop about a quarter of a mile away. The wolf, that the scientist had nicknamed "Mom," got up and began to trot toward the hare. Naturally, the hare could see the wolf coming and had plenty of time to run away if Mom got dangerously close. When the wolf approached within 50 yards of the hare, she made a short dash at it. The hare ran. But Mom did not chase it—instead, she stopped to sniff the ground near the spot where the hare had been crouching.

What was wrong with Mom? First, she had tried to walk right up to an animal that she intended to eat. That was obviously not a good way to catch a hare. Then when the animal ran, she didn't bother to chase it. She just sniffed around where the hare had been, as if she could not believe that it had gone. Was the wolf just lazy? Crazy? Or was Mom tricking the hare?

She sniffed around on the ground until several young beige-colored hares seemed to erupt before her. Immediately Mom took after the young hare that headed straight downhill, catching it at the bottom.

It seems clear that Mom never intended to catch that adult hare, which had a good chance of outrunning her. By deceiving the adult hare into thinking that she was after it, Mom was almost assured of getting a meal easily and quickly.

The earth is full of deceit, both in nature and in the ways of human beings. But when God makes all things new, "they shall not hurt nor destroy in all my holy mountain, saith the Lord" (Isaiah 65:25). Won't that be wonderful?

A Word From Our Creator

For they speak not peace: but they devise deceitful matters against them that are quiet in the land. Psalm 35:20.

July 1

The Incessant Katydid

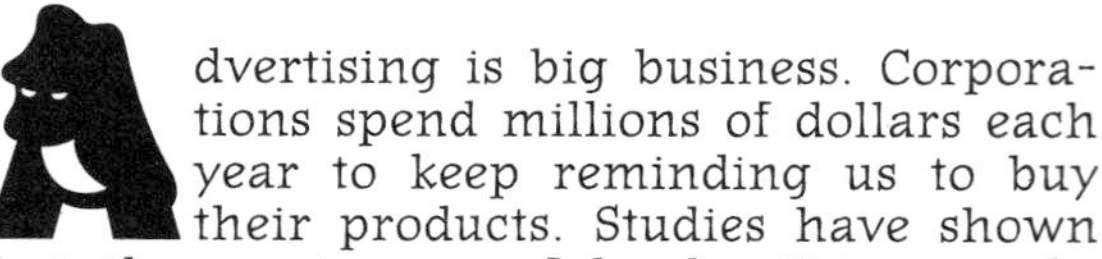

Advertising is big business. Corporations spend millions of dollars each year to keep reminding us to buy their products. Studies have shown that the most successful advertising works when you repeat it again and again. When through repetition we become used to an advertisement, its message goes straight to our subconscious mind—we don't even realize that we have heard or seen it.

Have you noticed that throughout a hot summer day the sound of cicadas and other insects goes on and on, and that on a warm summer evening the calls of crickets and katydids fill the air? Day and night the incessant sounds of insects drone in the background.

Thousands of species of katydids live in all parts of the world. Male katydids are the noisemakers. They attract mates by rubbing their wings together. One wing is equipped with a filelike apparatus with many tiny teeth, while the other has a scraper. When the katydid rubs the file on one wing along the scraper on the other, a grating sound results. Katydids in the eastern United States have a call that sounds like the insect is saying its name—*katydid*.

We get so used to the katydid's call that we don't hear it after a while. In fact, we're not even aware that we've tuned it out. Yet the katydid is always there, calling, and our subconscious does hear the sound. Unlike modern repetitive advertising, the katydid's incessant call is so soothing to our nerves that people sell recordings of nothing but crickets and katydids. The sounds can lull us to sleep.

People have invented repetitious advertising that irritates, but the Creator gave us repetitious messages of peace in the soothing sounds of nature. Fossilized katydids found today still have the soundmaking instruments preserved on their wings, so more than likely katydids were calling in the Garden of Eden.

A Word From Our Creator

And these words, which I command thee this day, shall be in thine heart: and thou shalt teach them diligently unto thy children.

Deuteronomy 6:6.

JULY 2

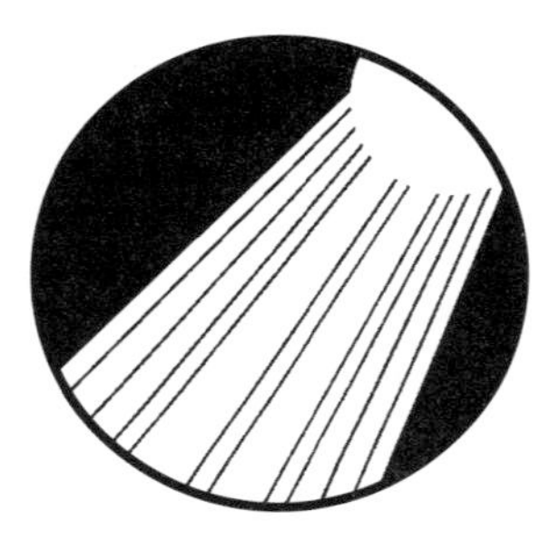

Biolumi-nescence

It's pronounced by-oh-loo-mih-NEHS-uns, and it refers to the ability of living things to give off light. While plants as well as animals exhibit bioluminescence, it's more commonly observed in animals. Some bacteria and fungi emit light, but you could live a lifetime without seeing them. Light-producing animals, on the other hand, are fairly common. Nearly everyone has watched fireflies, and you may have seen glowworms. If you live in the tropics, you will notice many other kinds of luminescent insects. But most of the bioluminescent animals live in the sea. In the deepest part of the ocean, where no sunlight ever reaches, lighted creatures flash and glow.

Scientists have been studying bioluminescence for a long time, and for many years they were unable to duplicate this natural light. But recently they have discovered the secrets of this process. In fireflies, for example, it involves a complex chemical process. To start with, a chemical messenger assembles five chemicals in the firefly's abdomen—adenosine triphosphate, luciferin, oxygen, magnesium, and luciferase. When the firefly wants to make light, it releases yet another chemical, pyrophosphate, that breaks the bond holding the five chemicals together, releasing energy and producing the light. After a very precise amount of time, the firefly injects still another chemical that eliminates the pyrophosphate, and that allows the five chemicals to bond again, and turns off the light.

Scientists have now learned how to mix these same chemicals and produce in a test tube what they call a "biolamp." Someday, we may have flashlights that use this process. But that idea isn't new. For many years people of the tropical areas of the world have collected fireflies and put them in perforated gourds to provide lanterns to light their path through the dark jungle. And, even more amazing in light of our text for today, people who travel through tropical forests at night have for centuries attached fireflies to their toes or the front of their shoes to light the path in front of their feet.

God is the light of the world (John 8:12) and the light that lighteth every man (John 1:9).

A WORD FROM OUR CREATOR

Thy word is a lamp unto my feet, and a light unto my path.
Psalm 119:105.

July 3

Making Haste in the Rain

In our text Isaiah is discussing the building of a strong foundation for life. He says that we should not do it in haste. It is so tempting to believe that if we get a job done faster, it is somehow better. Well, you remember the old saying "Haste makes waste."

Have you ever had to walk or run through the rain? You've forgotten your umbrella and have to get from one place to another in the downpour. Will you get wetter if you walk or if you run? The theory is that the faster you move forward, the more raindrops you'll hit. Even though you'll get to your destination quicker, you'll be wetter. The argument against this theory is that the slower you go, the more raindrops you'll have to contend with because it will take you longer to reach where you are heading. However, since you're moving more slowly, more drops will fall in front of you without hitting you. So how would you answer the question? Do you get wetter when you walk or when you run?

An Italian scientist has calculated the mathematical answer to that question. If two people start out at the same point in the rain and one of them runs at a sprinting speed of 22.4 miles per hour while the other walks at a brisk pace of 6.7 miles per hour, the walker will get wetter, but not by much—only 10 percent wetter. But running in the rain has dangers that outweigh getting a little less wet. For example, your chances of slipping and falling are much higher on a wet surface if you are running.

So the question for today is this: Is it better to run or to walk through life? According to our text, "he that believeth shall *not* make haste." We are building a foundation for our Christian life. Its "Precious Cornerstone" is Jesus, of course, and we need to take time to get acquainted with Him. Building a "sure foundation" requires quality time with the Cornerstone. You wouldn't think of rushing through an experience with your friends—you take time and savor every second of your time together. That's the way it should be with you and Jesus.

A Word From Our Creator

Therefore thus saith the Lord God, Behold, I lay in Zion for a foundation a stone, a tried stone, a precious corner stone, a sure foundation: he that believeth shall not make haste. Isaiah 28:16.

It's been said that because of selfish hearts human beings are the only form of life that live completely for themselves. All other forms of nature give as well as get. Consider plants, for example. They exist almost totally to give.

In order for a plant to produce, it has to have water. It needs water to transport minerals from the roots to the leaves, to use in combination with carbon dioxide in the leaves to produce food, and to transport food down to the roots to keep them healthy. Without water, the plant dies. But you might be surprised at what the plant does with most of the water it receives.

A large oak tree may drink 300 gallons of water each day. That's certainly a lot of water! But the amazing truth is that the oak tree uses only about one quart to sustain itself. It returns all the rest of the water to the air.

Have you ever noticed that the air temperature is cooler where a lot of plants grow together? It is always cooler in the woods than in open country, and if you walk through a healthy cornfield on a hot summer day, the air feels cooler among the cornstalks. A process called transpiration makes the air cooler. Plants require water to stay healthy, and they need water to produce flowers and fruit. But through transpiration plants put back into the air most of the water they drink.

The plants literally sweat, and the moisture escaping from their pores evaporates into the air around them. That moisture around the plants is what makes the air feel cooler there. A one-acre cornfield gives back about 300,000 gallons of water in a growing season. That's enough water to form a lake of water five feet deep.

Every plant is an example of how much more God gives to us than we can ever hope to return to Him. Each plant is also a living example of how our lives can reflect the character of the Creator, Jesus, who said, "It is more blessed to give than to receive."

JULY 4

Plants Live to Give

A Word From Our Creator

Ye ought to support the weak, and to remember the words of the Lord Jesus, how he said, It is more blessed to give than to receive. Acts 20:35.

JULY 5

Andromeda

Andromeda is more than 12 quintillion miles away, but you can see it with your naked eye. Tiny units of light, called photons, traveling steadily at 186,000 miles a second for 2 million years to get here, have carried its image to us.

The spiral galaxy nearest our own Milky Way, Andromeda is a majestic island universe of magnificent proportions. Located in the upper portions of the constellation Andromeda, it appears on a clear fall or winter night as a faint elongated area of hazy light. With the aid of a telescope, the speck of light emerges as a swirling mass of light measuring 35,000 light-years across and 8,700 light-years thick.

The amount of light projected by this tiny fuzzy spot in the sky is so massive that it would take more than 20 billion of our suns to shine as brightly from that distance. That fact leads astronomers to believe that Andromeda has more than 200 million stars. But our own Milky Way is estimated to have a thousand times that many stars, so Andromeda is not as large as our own home galaxy.

Andromeda is so interesting because it's the most visible neighboring galaxy. We cannot see all of our own galaxy because we're inside it. Since the Andromeda Galaxy is a spiral galaxy like ours, by looking at Andromeda we can see what our galactic system looks like from a distance.

As God looks out across the universe, we can imagine that His eyes hesitate with eternal love at each galaxy in the panorama. What does He call them? Each one has its special characteristics. When He comes to the Milky Way, He sees a well-proportioned system of stars spiraling out from the center of what appears to be a gigantic celestial storm system but is actually a perfectly ordered arrangement of stars and solar systems. His all-seeing eyes focus sharply as He searches for a small sun near the perimeter of the galaxy. There it is. Now He concentrates on the special planet. The great God of the universe is watching over us today and every day.

We can imagine how our galaxy looks to God, because we have seen Andromeda.

A WORD FROM OUR CREATOR

Before the mountains were brought forth, or ever thou hadst formed the earth and the world, even from everlasting to everlasting, thou art God. Psalm 90:2.

Nature is full of illustrations of the truth of today's text. For example, it is common for a parent bird to protect its young even in the face of certain death.

When I was a boy, I discovered the nest of a common nighthawk on the gravel roof of the factory in which my father worked. I wanted to photograph the nighthawk on its nest, so my father and I climbed up onto the roof and cautiously approached the setting bird. Our caution was unnecessary, however, because that bird gave no indication that it would leave its nest. As a result I photographed Dad touching the nighthawk. He could have picked it up, but he didn't, of course. The bird's fear of humans had been replaced by the even stronger sense of parental protection.

Northern mockingbirds often attack pet cats that get too close to their nests. Even though a stalking cat could turn on the adult bird and kill it, a nesting mockingbird seldom gives up its vigil.

A much more dedicated type of obedience unto death is illustrated by the egg-laying of a northern bobwhite, a type of quail, some years ago in Massachusetts. An ornithologist wanted to know just how long the bird would continue to lay eggs, so he began to take eggs from the female's nest one day. She laid new eggs day after day, and he continued to remove them. Finally she laid her fortieth egg—and died of exhaustion. The ornithologist never imagined that a bird would be so dedicated to its destiny.

Jesus has given us the ultimate example of being obedient unto death. As our protector, He fights our enemies and fulfills His destiny so that you and I might find salvation. "So by the obedience of one shall many be made righteous" (Romans 5:19).

JULY 6

Obedient Unto Death

A WORD FROM OUR CREATOR

He humbled himself, and became obedient unto death, even the death of the cross. Philippians 2:8.

JULY 7

Japanese Beetles

No one can accuse Japanese beetles of being finicky eaters. As grubs, they feed on the roots of flowers, grass, and vegetables in late summer and early fall. If large numbers of them attack turf that's already unhealthy from too much heat and lack of water, they can cut through so many roots that you can roll the grass back from the soil like a rug. Since each female beetle lays 20 to 100 eggs in midsummer, just one golf course can contain hundreds of thousands of grubs. The grubs burrow deep into the soil to spend an inactive winter. As spring returns, they move to the surface, feeding on roots again.

When the adults emerge, they're so hungry that they begin to eat every flower, leaf, fruit, and vegetable in sight. Japanese beetles prefer to feed in sunlight and in large groups. They start at the tops of plants, devouring roses and other garden flowers, as well as stripping leaves until nothing but lacy green skeletons remain. When they feed on corn, they eat the silks, preventing the kernels from developing properly.

You can control Japanese beetles by applying poison to foliage and flowers, but this method is dangerous to bees. You can also use scented traps that lure adults away from plants and milky disease spore (a bacterium that attacks only Japanese beetle grubs).

Japanese beetles were accidentally introduced into the United States about 1916. The first individuals were spotted in New Jersey, and their descendants have been moving southward and westward ever since. They can travel either by flying or by hitching rides on cars, trucks, and even airplanes. All it takes is one female carrying her cargo of eggs to establish a new infestation. It certainly doesn't take much of an "accident" to throw nature out of balance.

Since all of us have "sinned, and come short" (Romans 3:23), we are as powerless as a plant under attack from a mass of Japanese beetles. But just as under a mass of beetles there might be a rose, so under our sins there is a person who wants to spend eternity with Jesus. Jesus overcame the world and all its natural results. He is our source of survival in a world filled with sin and despair.

A WORD FROM OUR CREATOR

But your iniquities have separated between you and your God, and your sins have hid his face from you. Isaiah 59:2.

July 8

How Do You Sleep?

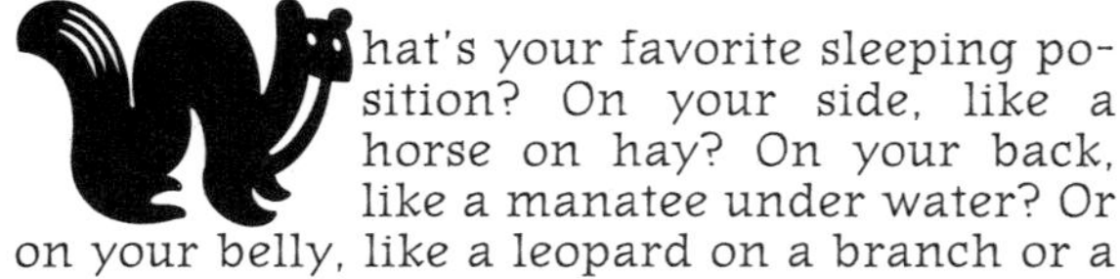

hat's your favorite sleeping position? On your side, like a horse on hay? On your back, like a manatee under water? Or on your belly, like a leopard on a branch or a polar bear on ice? You probably *don't* sleep hanging upside down like a bat, or standing on one leg like a duck.

Do you burrow under the covers, like a prairie dog does in its den? Do you pull the covers up to your chin, like a sea otter pulls a blanket of kelp over itself while it floats on more kelp? Or do you keep one leg out of the covers, like a sea lion holds one flipper up while it floats in the ocean? You probably *don't* sleep standing up with your toes curled around the bedframe, like a bird curls its toes around a branch.

How long do you sleep? For 19 hours at a time, like a bat? Or do you take lots of short naps, like a hare? You probably do get some sleep every day, unlike fish and amphibians—that never sleep but sort of "space out" for short periods of time. And you probably don't sleep for weeks at a time, like bears in winter or desert lizards and frogs in summer.

In general, large predatory animals, those that kill other animals for food, sleep longer and in less protected conditions than do the animals they hunt. Lions, for example, rest for hours on the open savanna. But the gazelles that they eat sleep for only one or two hours a day because they must stay alert. And polar bears nap alone out in the open while the seals that they hunt rest in gatherings of hundreds, even thousands, on rocky cliffs.

Scientists have never determined why we sleep. Perhaps the slowdown in our body functions during sleep means that our bodies won't wear out as fast and thus we will live longer. Without sleep, we lose energy, become cranky, and are unable to do simple tasks. We must sleep to renew energy, especially to the brain and nervous system.

Whatever the reason our bodies need sleep, our spirits need the sweet rest that sleep provides, when we aren't worried or afraid. The polar bear on ice isn't worried, but the seal is. In Jesus we can sleep in complete peace. He has overcome the enemy for us.

A Word From Our Creator

Come unto me, all ye that labour and are heavy laden, and I will give you rest. Matthew 11:28.

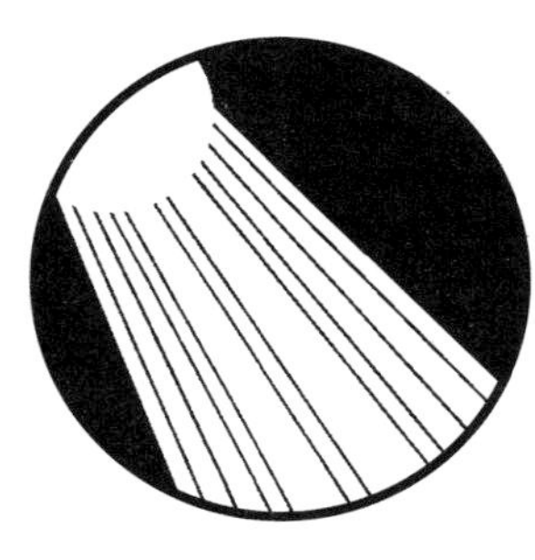

Fluorescence

Pronounced floor-EHS-ens, it's the light that some substances give off after they have absorbed energy. It works like this: photons of a particular wavelength of light strike a substance and excite, or add energy to, the atoms in that material. But that excitement doesn't last long—only for a hundred-millionth of a second, in fact. After that length of time the atoms release the energy as light again. But the light now has less energy—it lost some of its energy while producing the light. The light that now comes from the substance is a stream of photons with longer wavelengths, which means that the color of the light is different from the color of light absorbed in the first place. Here is an example:

Laundry starch made from corn is fluorescent. Let's say that you put on a shirt treated with this starch. Now you happen to walk into a dark room. As soon as you do, your shirt begins to glow with a blue-white light that's bright enough to allow you to see in the room. That could only happen if there were an ultraviolet lamp in the room. Since ultraviolet light rays are so short they're invisible to the human eye, you would have been unaware of the light except for the effect that it had on your shirt.

This is what happens. The photons of ultraviolet light reach you, and your shirt starts absorbing them immediately. Those invisible photons are bombarding your shirt at a rate of about 700 trillion a second, give or take a few trillion. The excitement that the starch molecules experience is something to behold. The atoms are busy absorbing photons, keeping them for a hundred-millionth of a second, and releasing them as photons of blue-white light.

Our text today tells us that, as Christians, we are fluorescent. "For, behold, the darkness shall cover the earth, and gross darkness the people: but the Lord shall arise upon thee, and his glory shall be seen upon thee. And the Gentiles shall come to thy light, and kings to the brightness of thy rising" (Isaiah 60:2, 3).

A Word From Our Creator

Arise, shine; for thy light is come, and the glory of the Lord is risen upon thee. Isaiah 60:1.

July 10

Waves of the Sea

When wind sweeps across the surface of open ocean, the resulting friction generates ripples on the water. Each ripple joins other ripples in rows called swells. Ocean swells, or waves, can travel thousands of miles before they die on a distant shore. Scientists tracked one wave from New Zealand to Alaska! As the swells move toward shore, they pick up speed until they reach shallow coastal water. Then they slow down before breaking against a sandy beach or rocky cliff. When a wave finally reaches the shoreline, it may have only enough strength left to stir up the sandy bottom, or it may have so much power that its spray can break the windows of a lighthouse.

Even though scientists can explain, mathematically, the form of waves, they cannot accurately predict when a really strong wave will hit. Wave watchers, especially surfers, try to guess which wave will be "the big one." They've contrived superstitious formulas, such as every seventh wave or every ninth wave—but waves just aren't predictable. Sometimes huge "killer waves" appear from a relatively calm sea and send unsuspecting swimmers to their deaths against the rocks. Along the coasts of Washington, Oregon, and northern California three or four such deaths will take place each year.

A tsunami (pronounced su-NAH-mee) is the strongest and most dangerous of the killer waves to strike the coast. Often mistakenly called "tidal waves," they have nothing to do with the tides. Whereas the gravitational pulls of the moon and sun control the tides, undersea earthquakes and landslides produce tsunamis, and the waves may travel long distances at speeds of up to 500 miles per hour.

But the amount of death and destruction caused by waves is slight compared to the massive amount of useful power that they generate. Ocean life depends on the movement of waves to provide shellfish with new supplies of microscopic plants and animals and with fresh oxygen.

Just as the largest wave begins as a small ripple, the righteousness of Jesus starts small in our lives and grows to a mighty surge of life-giving power.

A Word From Our Creator

O that thou hadst hearkened to my commandments! then had thy peace been as a river, and thy righteousness as the waves of the sea: Isaiah 48:18.

July 11

Milk Fever

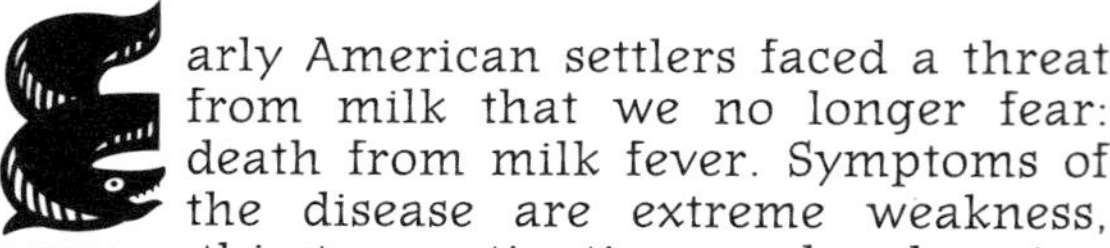

Early American settlers faced a threat from milk that we no longer fear: death from milk fever. Symptoms of the disease are extreme weakness, nausea, thirst, constipation, and a burning feeling in the stomach. Doctors often confused the symptoms with those of typhoid fever, malaria, and gastroenteritis. In 1810 doctors recognized milk sickness as a separate disease, but they still didn't know what caused it. During the 1700s and 1800s milk sickness claimed the lives of thousands of people. One of them was Nancy Hanks Lincoln, Abraham Lincoln's mother, who died of the disease when Abe was only 9 years old.

By observing when milk sickness struck, a pioneer midwife traced the cause of the disease to the leaves of white snakeroot, a wildflower that grows throughout the United States and much of Canada. In times of drought or in areas where the soil was too poor to support grassland, cattle wandered into the forests in search of food. White snakeroot grew abundantly in the moist, rich forest soil, and it stayed green all summer and most of fall. But the snakeroot plant produces a deadly chemical called tremetole, and when cattle fed on the plant's green leaves, they poisoned themselves.

Oddly, eating the snakeroot will not kill nursing cattle. Tremetole dissolves in the fat in the milk of nursing cattle and gets passed on to anything—or anyone—who drinks the milk. Mother cattle lived while their calves died, and people who drank the poisoned milk got sick, and many died.

Today, commercial dairies take precautions to eliminate the possibility of our getting milk fever. Only people who drink milk from their own cattle or from cattle from small, local dairy farms risk getting the disease.

From the beginning of time Satan has taken things that look, feel, smell, sound, and taste good and put in them his most subtle poisons. Sometimes sin comes to us in what appears to be a harmless—even a good—wrapping. We can be thankful for God's Word, which tells in advance what sin is so that we don't have to suffer its consequences.

A Word From Our Creator

And when the woman saw that the tree was good for food, and that it was pleasant to the eyes, and a tree to be desired to make one wise, she took of the fruit thereof, and did eat. Genesis 3:6.

The Bible is full of scientifically accurate statements. Solomon understood the relationship between the circuit of the sun and the cycles of weather in summer and winter. The winds are constantly blowing the atmosphere around over the surface of the earth, but they follow a very carefully designed pattern.

Earth's tilt causes the sun to shine more on the Northern Hemisphere for one half of the year and more on the Southern Hemisphere for the other half. And the amount of time that the sun shines on any part of the earth gradually changes with every day. In the Northern Hemisphere the days get longer and the amount of warming continues to increase through the year until it reaches a maximum about June 21 of every year. And then, as the days shorten, the amount of sunshine begins to decrease until it reaches its lowest level about December 21.

We easily might assume that the shortest day of the year would also be the coldest, because the earth receives less sunshine that day. But that isn't the case. In fact, the average daily temperature in the Northern Hemisphere doesn't drop to its lowest level until sometime in January or February. Can you figure out why that might be?

Think about your house. When you turn off the heat, it takes a while for the house to cool off. And when you put the heat on in a cold house, it needs some time to warm up again. That's the way it is with Planet Earth. Earth's land and water store up the heat of the longer days. It isn't until midwinter that we begin to feel the effects of reduced sunlight, and then the earth has to warm up again. But the warming effect of increased sunshine will not have its greatest impact until sometime in late February.

Heat from the sun causes air to heat up and rise, and the fact that the earth is spinning produces the major winds that circle the earth. The combination of those two forces creates the cycle of winds that Solomon mentions—the winds that move warm air north and cool air south to temper the climates.

Why Isn't the Shortest Day Also the Coldest?

A Word From Our Creator

The wind goeth toward the south, and turneth about unto the north; it whirleth about continually, and the wind returneth again according to his circuits. Ecclesiastes 1:6.

July 13

Amazing Wings

Have you ever wished that you could fly? At one time or another you have probably flapped your arms, pretending that they were wings that could lift you to wonderful heights. That was the wish of the psalmist when he wrote the words of our text.

Wings are amazing appendages. Although a few are able to glide, only one mammal, the bat, flies. Otherwise flight is an ability reserved primarily for birds and insects. Wingspans of birds range from two inches in the bee hummingbird to more than 11 feet in the wandering albatross. Flying insects include large moths and butterflies that have wingspreads of nearly one foot, yet the tiniest flying insect is probably the fairy fly, which scarcely can be seen by the unaided eye and can fly through the eye of the smallest needle.

Just as wingspreads vary, so does the speed of flight. For example, certain swifts have been clocked at speeds approaching 200 miles per hour. Careful measurements also have been made of the speeds of insects in flight. Suppose you staged a race between a bumblebee and a dragonfly—which insect would win? Data show that the dragonfly can outfly all other insects, attaining a speed of 55 miles per hour, while the bumblebee can reach 35 miles per hour.

Related to flight speed is the rate at which insects vibrate their wings. Some mosquitoes beat their wings more than 550 times per second, but this fact shrinks into insignificance in light of the fact that tiny insects called midges (less than a tenth of an inch long) beat their wings 2,200 times every second! Think about that for a minute. A midge can perform one complete up-and-down stroke of its tiny wings in less than a two-thousandth of a second. You try doing that! Flap your arms and have somebody count how many times your arms go up and down in one minute. To match the midge, you will have to flap 132,000 times! Can you do it?

When we get to heaven, we will be able to fly throughout the universe with the angels. Do you suppose that we will fly by flapping?

A Word From Our Creator

And I said, Oh that I had wings like a dove! for then would I fly away, and be at rest. Psalm 55:6.

July 14

Cats on Patrol

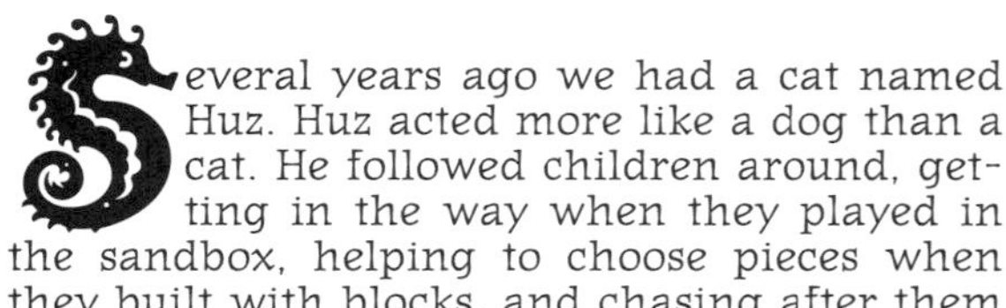

Several years ago we had a cat named Huz. Huz acted more like a dog than a cat. He followed children around, getting in the way when they played in the sandbox, helping to choose pieces when they built with blocks, and chasing after them when they rode their bikes. The cat would greet us when we came home, and he would ask to be petted by gently touching our noses with his paw. Huz was usually gentle and sweet.

But Huz had another side to his nature, one that we didn't like. The cat was a hunter—and a very good one, too. Once we saw him take a flying mockingbird right out of the air. Another time he figured out how to knock down a barn swallow nest from where the birds had built it over the light in the center of the porch ceiling (about nine feet up). To do that, he climbed up onto the transom over the front door and made many flying leaps and painful hard landings until he succeeded. And although we never saw how he managed it, Huz even caught hummingbirds. He also trapped mice, moles, gophers, and baby rabbits—animals that the local farmers would have been happy to be rid of.

Cats are well-known for helping to control pests. The Birmingham Zoo in Alabama uses cats to keep the animal cages free of rats and mice. The rodents were a problem because they not only got into the animals' food but also carried disease. Setting out poison might control the rats and mice but would also endanger the zoo animals. So zoo officials adopted four cats from an animal shelter and let them roam freely to hunt at will. The system benefits the zoo *and* the cats. The zoo has its animal cages kept rodent-free, and the cats have a good home where a veterinarian gives them regular checkups to make sure that they stay healthy.

Every time Huz killed a bird, we threatened to pack him off to Birmingham. But we were kidding, of course. Huz couldn't help doing what came naturally as a result of sin. In heaven rats and mice won't be pests and hazards to health. And cats won't want to kill anything!

A Word From Our Creator

And they shall no more be a prey to the heathen, neither shall the beast of the land devour them; but they shall dwell safely, and none shall make them afraid. Ezekiel 34:28.

July 15

Chuck-walla

The chuckwalla is a large rusty-brown lizard of the American Southwest. It grows to more than a foot long, and rough skin covers its bulky body and thick tail. Loose folds of skin on the creature's neck and sides give it a saggy, baggy appearance.

Unlike most other desert lizards that must find shelter in the shade during the hottest part of the day, the chuckwalla thrives in extreme heat. It stretches out on a rock in the morning and basks until its body temperature reaches 100°F. The chuckwalla won't forage for the fruits, flowers, and foliage that make up its diet until its body hits that 100-degree mark.

Once the chuckwalla was an important food for native tribes of the Southwest and Mexico, but now the lizard's primary enemies are hungry hawks. When a chuckwalla sees the shadow of a soaring predator, it scrambles into a crevice in the rocks, its sandpaper-textured skin making a rasping sound as it moves. Then it gulps air to inflate its lungs to enlarge its body. That loose skin now fills, wedging the chuckwalla so tightly into its rocky refuge that nothing can pull it out. To get one out, curious naturalists sometimes have to use a crowbar to pry the rocks away from the crevice.

The chuckwalla's habitat is desert rocks. It must have rocks for basking, for shelter during the night, and for refuge from its enemies. Without those desert rocks, this harmless lizard would quickly die from starvation, because it wouldn't have a place on which to absorb the sun's heat and become more active, have shelter from the chill of the night air, or from becoming another creature's dinner.

God has provided you and me with a Rock of safety, too. Like the chuckwalla on the rocks, we can depend upon the power of God to save us. "Be thou my strong habitation, whereunto I may continually resort: thou hast given commandment to save me; for thou art my rock and my fortress" (Psalm 71:3).

A Word From Our Creator

But the Lord is my defence; and my God is the rock of my refuge.
Psalm 94:22.

n today's text Job uses several examples of how much he longed for relief from his misery. Hirelings expect to be paid for their work, but indentured servants work to pay a debt that may not even be their own. Servants get no wage, so their only reward is easier working conditions.

What do you think is the shadow that the servant desires so much? Suppose you have a job mowing grass or pulling weeds in the hot sun. What kind of shadow do you hope for?

If you're like most people, you glance at the sky occasionally to see if any clouds are coming your way that might pass between you and the sun, giving you some momentary relief. And then one passes over, its shadow sweeping across the ground. It seems to approach too slowly and to pass too quickly. A coolness comes over you, and you revel in the brief moment of relief until the cloud continues on its way and the direct rays of the sun hit you once more.

You know that the heat is in the light. Photons of visible and invisible light, having traveled from the sun at a speed of 186,000 miles a second for more than eight minutes, slam into you. Much of the light gets reflected, but some of it your body absorbs, resulting in heat. And there is no letup. You can't reach out and turn off the sun just because you're too hot. So you wish for and wait for the relief of another passing cloud. But how does the cloud help? It can't turn off the sun's rays any more than you can.

A cloud consists of water droplets. When the cloud passes between the sun and you, many of the light rays strike the water droplets and get deflected from their original path toward you. So not so many photons hit you, and you don't feel as much heat. And the more water in the cloud, the more light it deflects and the cooler you feel.

Jesus is the Sun of righteousness (Malachi 4:2). If He appeared in His pure form as God, we would be unable to stand the intensity of His light. So He has given us His Spirit as water (Isaiah 44:3) and wind (John 3:8)—the two ingredients that bring the cooling shade of clouds—to support a comfortable relationship with our Lord.

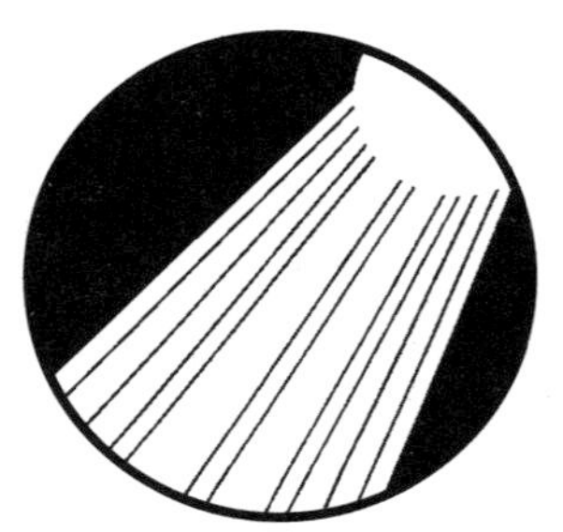

Shadows

A Word From Our Creator

As a servant earnestly desireth the shadow, and as an hireling looketh for the reward of his work: so am I made to possess months of vanity, and wearisome nights are appointed to me. Job 7:2.

Old Faithful

A geyser occurs when rainwater seeps down thousands of feet into an underground hot spot formed by molten rock. The water in this spot gets hot, but the surrounding rock and the weight of the column of water above it won't let it boil. The superheated water begins to rise and moves back toward the surface through cracks in the rock. As the water gets closer to the surface, where it has more room to expand, it begins to boil. The resulting sudden release of steam and boiling water is a geyser.

You may have heard that a geyser in Yellowstone National Park in Wyoming is so punctual that you can set your clock by it. The story is so pervasive that the geyser's name bears witness to it—Old Faithful. Faithful? Yes, and even somewhat predictable.

But Old Faithful is neither the most punctual nor the most powerful geyser in Yellowstone National Park. Other geysers in the park provide more spectacular demonstrations and send their plumes to a much greater height than Old Faithful.

Yet even an eruption of Old Faithful is nothing to miss. When it does erupt, this star of geysers blows thousands of gallons of steam and boiling water straight upward to a height of 150 feet. The show continues for two to five minutes before Old Faithful rests to regain its strength for the next show.

Old Faithful has been spouting off regularly for as long as anyone remembers, and, according to geologists, for thousands of years before that. But what is "regular" to the public relations agent is "unpredictable" to the geologist. As it turns out, the resting periods between Old Faithful's eruptions range from three minutes to two hours—hardly punctual.

There are any number of things on earth that you're told will never fail. The media is forever trying to seduce you into believing that you can really depend on this product or that item. To convince you further, companies even provide you guarantees. But Paul said it best: "Whether there be prophecies, they shall fail; whether there be tongues, they shall cease; whether there be knowledge, it shall vanish away" (1 Corinthians 13:8). Only the love of God is completely dependable and unchanging.

A Word From Our Creator

For I am the Lord, I change not.
Malachi 3:6.

JULY 18

Poppies

Sometimes the most beautiful things in life bring great distress. Consider the poppies.

Legend says that brilliant banks of golden poppies guided ships to the coast of California, serving as beacons that sailors could see 25 miles out at sea. This California state flower is only one of many beautiful varieties in the poppy family.

The most famous member of the family is the opium poppy. Opium, the substance made from the dried juice of the seed pods of this Mediterranean cousin of the golden poppy, is so potent that physicians used it in the 1500s to anesthetize patients before surgery. Because opium can produce hallucinations, many writers and painters of the 1600s and 1700s believed that the opium-induced visions inspired them to produce truly great works of prose and painting. Most of these would-be authors and artists simply became addicts, for no drug can provide you with a talent that you don't already have.

The even more potent and more dangerous drugs morphine and heroin also come from opium. Patients who received morphine as a pain killer during the past two centuries more often than not became addicted to the drug, and today heroin ruins minds and lives. Many countries in the world have now made such drugs illegal even for medicinal purposes.

Our contact with poppies can be safely limited to enjoying the beautiful fields of the wildflowers, to planting them in our gardens, or to eating the tiny black seeds sprinkled on bread and rolls (the seeds do not contain opium or other drugs).

Our lives are not unlike poppies. As we grow and develop naturally under the watchcare and guidance of our heavenly Father, we become beautiful representations of His character. But sometimes people are tempted to take some of the most beautiful elements of life and turn them into ugly and even dangerous pursuits. Can you think of some examples from life in which something beautiful has been transformed into something ugly?

A WORD FROM OUR CREATOR

The troubles of my heart are enlarged: O bring thou me out of my distresses. Psalm 25:17.

July 19

Mars

For centuries—perhaps for millenniums—people have gazed into the night sky and wondered about the red planet.

Traveling outward from the sun, you would pass through the orbits of Mercury, Venus, and Earth on your way to Mars. Moving at the speed of light, you would cover the 142 million miles in about 13 minutes. When you got to the red planet, you would find that:

1. The diameter of Mars is about 4,200 miles, slightly more than half the diameter of Earth. Only Mercury and Pluto are smaller.
2. Mars rotates from one sunset to the next in 24 hours and 37 minutes, Earth time. So a day on Mars is almost the same as it is on Earth. Your biological clock would feel pretty normal there.
3. At a speed of 48,000 miles per hour, Mars orbits the sun in 687 Earth days, which is almost two Earth years. If you were a Martian and counted years as we do, you would be about half your current age.
4. On Mars the gravity is 38 percent of what it is on Earth, so if you weigh 80 pounds on Earth, you would weigh about 30 pounds on Mars.
5. Two moons, that look more like giant potatoes, fairly streak around Mars. Deimos orbits Mars once every 30 hours, but Phobos zips around the planet once every eight hours.
6. One of the most striking facts about Mars is that it has polar ice caps. But the ice cap at one pole is frozen carbon dioxide (dry ice), and at the other pole it is frozen water.

On Mars you will need very warm clothes, food, oxygen, and probably water to drink. The average surface temperature is -85°F, so you would have to bundle up sufficiently to exist. But breathing would be another matter. Because the atmosphere on Mars is carbon dioxide, you also would have to provide your own oxygen. And while Mars has water, it is all frozen solid in the ground and locked up in the water ice cap. If you visited Mars, you would understand perfectly what God was pointing out to Job by the question in today's text: it takes a Creator to provide the environment perfect for life.

A Word From Our Creator

Canst thou lift up thy voice to the clouds, that abundance of waters may cover thee? Job 38:34.

ome species of birds build their nests in trees. Other species construct them on the ground. But a few species prefer soggy nests, so they make them on water.

The common loon assembles an untidy heap of reeds, grasses, and twigs anchored to cattails and other plants growing along the shoreline of a lake, but the horned grebe builds a floating nest and lines it with soft moss. Both species breed in northern North America. The limpkin, a large brown marshbird of the southeastern United States, interweaves reeds and grasses with growing plants.

The magpie goose does more than secure a pile of loose vegetation to rooted water plants. First, it builds a platform by using its bill to bend down tall reeds. Then it tramps down the reeds with its feet. The bird stands in one spot, turning in a circle to grasp the reeds within the range of its bill so that the resulting nest has a neat, circular shape.

Floating nests have several advantages. They protect nesting waterbirds from land animals. If something disturbs the birds, they can easily slip into the water and swim away—sometimes under water, as in the cases of the loon and grebe. Chicks also readily take to the water when they have hatched on an island. In addition, some scientists believe that the body heat from incubating birds heats the moisture in the nest and helps to warm the developing eggs. One more advantage to floating nests is the fact that they float. They never flood, for if the water level rises, the nests stay on top of it.

Floating nests are much like houseboats safely anchored to a mooring. Waterbirds enjoy the security of having their nests tied to well-rooted plants.

Floating Nests

A WORD FROM OUR CREATOR

And Jesus said unto him, Foxes have holes, and birds of the air have nests; but the Son of man hath not where to lay his head. Luke 9:58.

Heavenly Haystacks

A pika (pronounced PIE-ka) looks like an animal that sometime during its development changed its mind about what it wanted to be when it grew up. It is about the size of a hamster and almost resembles a tiny bunny—but it has short, round ears and no visible tail.

North American pikas live in rockslides in the West and Northwest, preferring places where few people ever even visit. If you're lucky, though, you might see pikas in one of the national parks located in their range.

You might think that a little brown animal living among the rocks wouldn't have much to do except nibble the plants in a nearby field and doze in the sun, but pikas are some of the busiest creatures in the animal kingdom. Although several pikas live together in a colony, each individual animal has its own territory and takes care of its own food needs. All summer and into autumn each pika builds a huge haystack of grasses, stems, and flowers. The haystack is so big compared to the size of its builder that the easiest way to find a pika is to locate its haystack first, then keep a close watch out for the little animal as it drags still another ingredient of its super salad to the growing pile.

In winter the pika wears a thick coat. A blanket of snow also helps keep its home under the rocks warm. Even though it tunnels through the snow in search of bits of fresh vegetation, it relies on its haystack harvest to keep it strong and healthy through the winter.

The pika doesn't wait until the last minute to think about what it will eat during winter. It spends months working in order to be sure that it harvests enough food. As Christians we can't wait until the last minute to tell others about Jesus and His love. Jesus talked about a harvest in which the laborers are few. We can become partners with Him as we share our love for Jesus and thereby help Him to prepare His heavenly harvest.

A Word From Our Creator

Pray ye therefore the Lord of the harvest, that he will send forth labourers into his harvest. Matthew 9:38.

One evening when we lived in Texas, we stepped outside into the moonlight for a few minutes to enjoy the night sights and sounds. We were walking across the grass when suddenly we heard the wild laughter of coyotes coming from what seemed like all sides. Actually we were listening to two packs calling from two directions. Each pack seemed to be trying to outyip the other. It was wild and wonderful. When the calls died away, we listened to the silence with the same wonder and appreciation that we had felt during the cacophony of sound. While there was nothing particularly unusual about this experience, still we were left with a sense of awe and reverence that only such a natural moment in the wilderness can invoke.

Returning to the house, we talked of the coyote music, and then we thought of another setting, one in which the grass is artificial, giant floodlights (instead of moonlight) bathe everything, and one hears, instead of the calls of wild animals, the shrieks of wild humans screaming at the tops of their lungs. It is the night of a championship football game, and all the people gathered around the artificial turf are cheering their team to victory as their heroes run, fall, push, and kick their way across the field with the ball. The game draws to a close. Only one play remains. The score is 14 to 13 in favor of the home team. The visitors have the ball. A hush falls over the stadium. No one notices the full moon overhead. The mighty floodlights make the arena as bright as daylight. The final play moves almost in slow motion. The visitors score. The game is over. The visiting team and fans whoop it up and head for celebration parties. The home team and fans stare through unbelieving and despondent eyes at the field on which their hopes so quickly ended. They silently file out of the stadium to wait for next year.

Which of those two night scenes do you suppose provides an experience more like the one that Jesus had when He went out into the night before dawn to pray?

The Reverence of a Wild Moment

A WORD FROM OUR CREATOR

And in the morning, rising up a great while before day, he went out, and departed into a solitary place, and there prayed. Mark 1:35.

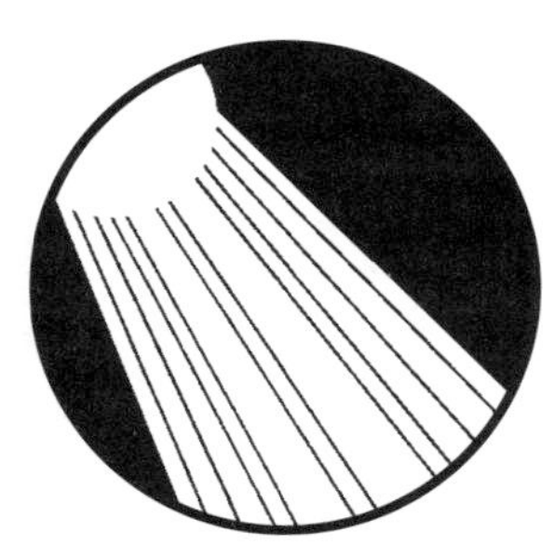

Laser Light Surgery

Today, with the use of light alone, surgeons are healing the blind. They use a laser, a concentrated beam of light in which all the photons vibrate at exactly the same frequency and move in an exact parallel path. Surgeons can use laser light to do some amazing things for people's eyes.

By using beams of laser light, physicians can treat diseases of the retina, the layer of tissue that forms the lining of the back of your eye. The laser beam can repair from the outside a leaking blood vessel inside the eye. It can clean away diseased tissue and can operate as a bloodless scalpel to make microscopic incisions in the eye to repair a small problem without affecting the rest of the eye.

The laser beam used in these operations is only four tenths of a millimeter in diameter. It's pure infrared light, so it's virtually invisible—making it even more amazing. Can you imagine a person who lived during the time of Jesus walking into a modern hospital and watching a physician using a computer to direct a laser beam at precisely the right spot in a patient's eye to restore that person's sight? What would someone like that think as he or she watched the operation? I am sure that person would tell everyone that a miracle had just occurred.

Jesus is the source of all power—even laser power, atomic power, and computer power. He has the ability to call on powers that we are only beginning to understand. When the Light of the world shines into your heart, He also has the power to clean away diseased character traits and to repair aching hearts in the same way that He can heal the eyes of the blind.

A Word From Our Creator

So Jesus had compassion on them, and touched their eyes: and immediately their eyes received sight, and they followed him. Matthew 20:34.

ou hear about it during the weather forecast, but do you know what the jet stream really is?

1. Is it a stream of water or of air?
2. Is it cold or warm? Or both?
3. Where would you go to find it?
4. Is there only one jet stream, or are there more than one?

The polar regions of earth consist of large low-pressure areas. The tropical regions have a wide band of high pressure that extends northward and southward to meet the polar areas of low pressure. A permanent flow of air occurs where the polar areas of low pressure meet the band of warm high-pressure air. It goes round and round the globe—never stopping—and it has been doing so for thousands of years. This is the jet stream.

The jet stream is a mighty wind that resembles a river in the sky. Flowing five to eight miles above sea level, the stream of air reaches speeds of up to 180 miles per hour. When airplanes head in the same direction, they often take advantage of the push of the jet stream to make better time and to use less fuel. An aeronautical weather reporter would describe such a tailwind by using the phrase "winds aloft."

The nature of the jet stream significantly affects the weather down on the earth's surface. Because of all the different meteorological forces operating on the planet, the jet stream doesn't just flow straight around the planet, but moves in an ever-changing crooked path. Sometimes it heads across the northern part of the United States and southern Canada. At other times it dips down into the central and southern U.S. Wherever it goes, it helps to shape the weather. And there is another jet stream that flows around the globe in the Southern Hemisphere.

It is easy to see how the ancients believed that God used clouds as His chariots as He rode the wind through the sky. But more important, God did employ the clouds as His chariot when, as His disciples watched, "He was taken up; and a cloud received him out of their sight" (Acts 1:9).

Jet Stream

A Word From Our Creator

Who layeth the beams of his chambers in the waters: who maketh the clouds his chariot: who walketh upon the wings of the wind. Psalm 104:3.

July 25

The Flower Is the Glory of a Plant

One spring we went to the flower show at the U.S. National Botanical Gardens in Washington, D.C. As we approached the entrance, the aroma of hyacinths was already in the air, and when we got inside the arena, the sights that met our eyes were beyond description. Never had we seen such natural beauty concentrated in one spot, and we took roll after roll of film in a feeble attempt to capture some of the magnificence of the blossoms that surrounded us.

Now suppose we had gone back a couple weeks later. Most of the flowers would have faded and died and been discarded. Even the glorious beauty of flowers lasts only a few days. Everyone admires them while they're in full bloom, but no one wants them when they shrivel up and turn brown.

Do you believe that students who get high grades are better people than other students? What about people who seem to have a lot of friends or who own expensive clothes, bikes, or sound equipment? Are they more worth knowing than people who don't have much money? What about people who are famous, know someone famous, or just see someone famous across a crowded restaurant? Are they more valuable as people than your teachers, parents, or friends?

On earth, glory seems to come from how much you know, how many things you have, or whom you know. Think about today's text. Is anything more glorious than flowers?

It is safe to say that your glory is in your character instead of in what you know or how strong you are or the things that you own. "Thus saith the Lord, Let not the wise man glory in his wisdom, neither let the mighty man glory in his might, let not the rich man glory in his riches: but let him that glorieth glory in this, that he understandeth and knoweth me, that I am the Lord which exercise lovingkindness, judgment, and righteousness, in the earth: for in these things I delight, saith the Lord" (Jeremiah 9:23, 24).

A Word From Our Creator

For all flesh is as grass, and all the glory of man as the flower of grass. The grass withereth, and the flower thereof falleth away. 1 Peter 1:24.

Wanderers

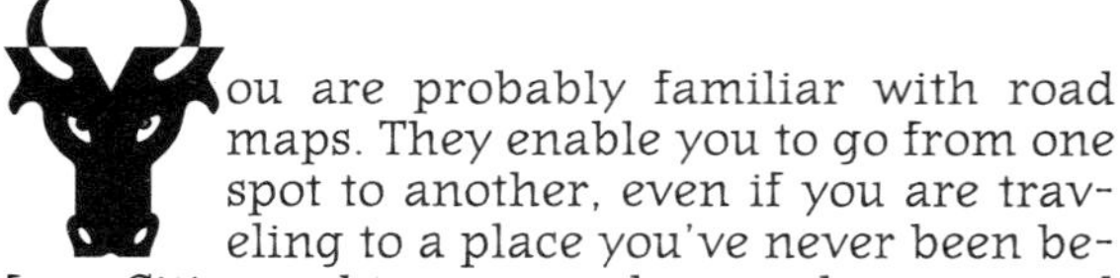

You are probably familiar with road maps. They enable you to go from one spot to another, even if you are traveling to a place you've never been before. Cities and towns are dots on the map, and lines that represent roads and highways connect the dots. The dots stay in the same place, because towns usually don't pick up and move. The lines may shift slightly when old roads get rerouted or new ones built. But generally the maps don't change much over time.

Star maps are very much like road maps. You can rely on the stars plotted on such maps, and you can create imaginary lines to connect them to form constellations. The stars are like cities and towns. Their positions in relation to each other never change, or they shift so slightly over thousands of years that we don't notice the difference in our lifetime.

As the earth moves in its yearly orbit, the stars rise about four minutes earlier each day. But they stay in formation at all times, so the stars that form the Big Dipper *always* form the Big Dipper. And Polaris, the star at the tip of the Little Dipper's handle, is *always* at the tip of the Little Dipper's handle.

When ancient astronomers noticed a few stars—five, to be exact—that did not remain in formation, they realized that they were observing a special phenomenon. By plotting the movements of these renegade stars, they discovered that they followed their own routes according to their own set schedules—independent of the rest of the stars. The astronomers named the five different "stars" planets, a name that means *wanderers*. They had discovered Mercury, Venus, Mars, Jupiter, and Saturn, but they did not know that planets were other worlds, like Earth, obeying the law of gravity and traveling in perfect orbits around the nearest star—the sun.

Not a star or planet in space defies the law of gravity. Every object in space obediently follows a precise path around the sun, the source of celestial light. And every Christian is on a path set by Jesus, the Light of the world.

A Word From Our Creator

They are of those that rebel against the light; they know not the ways thereof, nor abide in the paths thereof. Job 24:13.

JULY 27

Floaters

Have you ever had friends who spent a lot of time and money building a nice house, only to lose it because they couldn't make the house payments? Our world is full of heartache over the loss of property. The common Eurasian Starling provides a living example of how this happens in the bird world.

When a female starling cannot find a suitable place to build a nest, she has two ways to make sure that at least one or two of her eggs will hatch. She either lays them in the nest of another female starling, or she steals another bird's nest.

Ornithologists call nestless birds "floaters." When a nesting starling is away from the nest, a floater typically sneaks into the nest and lays an egg, adding to the ones already there. The nesting female then incubates all the eggs and raises all the chicks. Out of every three starling nests at least one holds a floater's egg.

But some floaters are not content to leave their offspring in the care of foster parents. A more aggressive nestless bird simply takes over an established nest. She begins by picking up each egg in her beak and dropping it several feet to the ground. (The eggs usually break, but occasionally they do not, and it is not uncommon to see the pale-blue starling eggs lying on the grass as though the mother bird had laid them there.) The former floater is now a nestowner and settles in to lay her own eggs. Unfortunately, the new nestowner can't count on keeping her stolen nest. Another starling may turn up to evict her from the nest that she's just stolen!

When they have no homes of their own, starlings use what seem to us to be extreme—and heartless—ways to get a place to lay their eggs and raise their young. That's also the way it often is among human beings, too. Perhaps having lost their home because they are jobless, a couple may become desperate and willing to do anything to find a place to live.

That's the way it is here on the earth. But we have God's promise that in the new earth we "shall not build, and another inhabit" (Isaiah 65:22). Our home in heaven is forever.

A WORD FROM OUR CREATOR

And they shall build houses, and inhabit them; and they shall plant vineyards, and eat the fruit of them. Isaiah 65:21.

o text can better describe God's care and concern over such a lowly creature as the earthworm, which lives most of its life in the underground darkness of the soil. There it discovers enough food to thrive, and in the process it fertilizes the soil.

The earthworm is an excellent example of economy of design. Its body essentially consists of two tubes, one inside the other. The inner tube contains the worm's simple brain, five hearts, and an intestine. The outer tube consists of two kinds of muscles covered by reddish-brown skin. One set of muscles extends along the earthworm's body and gives the creature the ability to become shorter and thicker. Another set of muscles encircles the body and allows the worm to become longer and thinner.

The earthworm has no bones, so its body is very flexible. To move forward, the worm lengthens the front part of its body to push through the soil. Then it pulls up the rear part to "catch up" with the front. The earthworm has no legs, but does have four pairs of tiny bristles called setae located on all but the first few and last few segments of its body. The setae give the earthworm traction as it moves. Mucus, the slimy substance secreted by the skin, helps the worm to slip easily through the soil. Some of the mucus rubs off the earthworm's body and hardens the walls of its tunnels.

During daylight hours the earthworm tunnels in warm dark earth. As it eats its way along under the ground, it churns air, water, and nutrients into the soil. In addition, it leaves behind its waste products, called castings, as a natural fertilizer. At night, when the hot sun has set, earthworms venture above ground to feed on vegetation.

An earthworm's body is not cluttered with eyes, ears, and a nose. It has neither lungs nor gills. Instead, it uses sensitive receptors in the skin to pick up sound vibrations and changes in light, temperature, and the chemicals in the soil. And it breathes through the pores in its skin, using the tiny pockets of air trapped between grains of sand. Only God's creative and sustaining genius could make something so perfectly simple as an earthworm.

The Earthworm: Efficiency in Design

A WORD FROM OUR CREATOR

And I will give thee the treasures of darkness, and hidden riches of secret places, that thou mayest know that I, the Lord, which call thee by thy name, am the God of Israel. Isaiah 45:3.

JULY 29

Slavery or Freedom

A WORD FROM OUR CREATOR

And it came to pass . . . that . . . the children of Israel sighed by reason of the bondage, and they cried, and their cry came up unto God by reason of the bondage. Exodus 2:23.

In the ancient world despotic kings used thousands of slaves to build magnificent tombs and temples. The slaves hated their work, and many lost their lives as their masters drove them unmercifully to complete tasks that the kings ordered done. But sometimes free people drive *themselves* to finish a difficult and dangerous job, as the following story demonstrates.

The people of Bangladesh had no money and no machinery, but they had to build a barricade across the mouth of the Feni River. A dam would control flooding and create a freshwater lake, making it possible to plant and harvest two crops of rice each year instead of just the one watered by the July rains. They built that dam using the only strength that they had—people.

First, they covered the river bottom at the barricade with huge mats to prevent erosion. Then they used trucks and barges to bring in tons of rock. Dividing into relay teams, they unloaded the rocks and passed them one by one from person to person to the river, where they dropped the rocks to hold down the mats.

The next step was to dig clay from nearby hills, truck it to the river's edge, and scoop it into jute bags. Then 15,000 laborers carried the dripping bags on their heads to 11 sites to build artificial islands. Each island was 13 feet high and consisted of 100,000 bags.

At low tide, a team of 1,000 workers assigned to each island shifted the top layers of bags to fill in the gaps between the islands. They had only seven hours in which to accomplish this task before the tide came in again—and they did it!

During the first year of its existence, the Feni River Dam withstood a tropical cyclone and provided the water for a second rice crop. As you can imagine, the people of Bangladesh are very proud of their accomplishment. God created men and women as free beings. Sin brought slavery. What do you suppose is the difference between the way the people of Bangladesh felt and the way the children of Israel felt about their accomplishments?

s Creator, Jesus started the whole creation process with light (Genesis 1:3). Since light is power, why haven't we learned how to use light as an energy source for the power plants that supply electricity for our daily use? As a matter of fact, scientists are conducting intensive research to do just that.

The most efficient energy generator known is a star, like our sun. At the center of the sun hydrogen atoms join together to become helium atoms, releasing energy as they do so. The sun produces all its power this way. Scientists believe that if they can make energy as the sun does, we will have an unlimited supply of inexpensive energy that is almost pollution-free.

According to the theory, tiny amounts of nuclear fuel containing the two atomic elements deuterium and tritium, which are two heavy forms of hydrogen, could be bombarded by concentrated light in the form of a laser beam. The speed of the photons hitting the fuel would provide enough initial energy to start the chain reaction of thermonuclear fusion, and once started, it would only be a matter of controlling it and harnessing it to operate electrical power plants that would supply us with electricity.

Scientists are preparing the world's most powerful laser for this purpose at the Lawrence Livermore National Laboratory near San Francisco. This huge laser operates as a unit consisting of 20 different chains, or "arms," of lasers. It is planned that the combination of 20 lasers will provide the 30 trillion watts of power needed to begin the chain reaction in the nuclear fuel. The scientists have named this many unit laser Shiva, after the Hindu god with many arms. Shiva is supposed to provide the earth with the ultimate source of power.

Why do you suppose that America's leading energy engineers are so quick to give glory to the Hindu god Shiva when the nation was founded on a belief in the Creator-God, Jehovah?

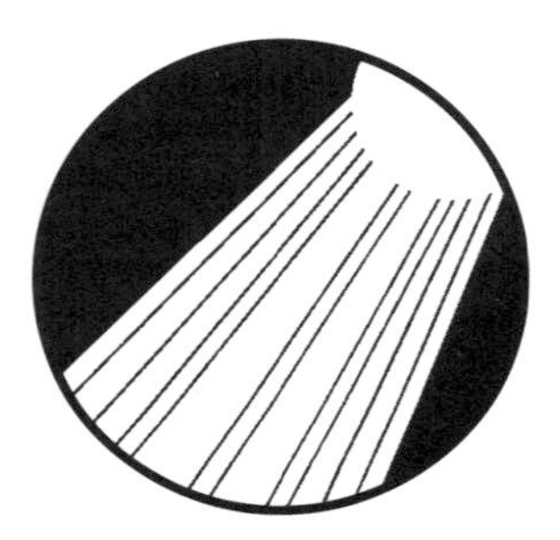

Shiva vs. Jehovah

A Word From Our Creator

And the city had no need of the sun, neither of the moon, to shine in it: for the glory of God did lighten it, and the Lamb is the light thereof. Revelation 21:23.

Ame-thyst

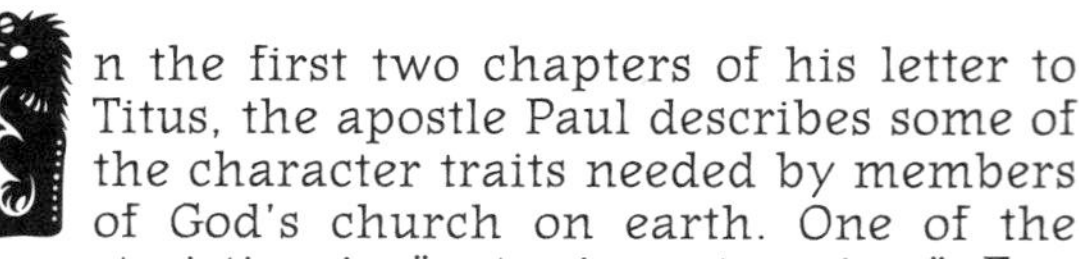

In the first two chapters of his letter to Titus, the apostle Paul describes some of the character traits needed by members of God's church on earth. One of the characteristics is "not given to wine." Few things are sadder than having to observe a friend or family member drunk. The intoxicating effects of alcoholic drinks were well known in Bible times, and many texts in the Bible advise against the use of wine and strong drink.

Amethyst is a variety of quartz. It comes in shades of purple ranging from the faintest tinge of violet to deepest purple. The deeper the shade, the more valuable the gem. Most of the deep-purple shades of amethyst originate in Brazil, Uruguay, and Russia. The word "amethyst" is a combination of two Greek words meaning "not" and "to intoxicate." The Greeks believed that wearing an amethyst would keep them sober. But the Romans attributed a different power to this jewel. Roman women used the amethyst to ensure their husband's love.

Precious stones had symbolic meaning in the Bible as well. For example, the high priest wore a breastplate with 12 precious stones, one for each tribe of Israel. Bible scholars are not absolutely sure that it is the correct translation, but an amethyst is given as the third stone in the third row of gems on the high priest's breastplate (Exodus 28:19).

John the revelator lists all the foundation stones when he describes the Holy City as a symbol of God's church on earth (Revelation 21:19, 20). The twelfth foundation stone is amethyst. Since John would have been aware of the meaning of the stones used in the description, it may have occurred to him that the final foundation stone symbolized a church membership made of people who were not given to intoxicating drinks and—most of all—people who represented the enduring love of the Creator for His bride, the church.

A WORD FROM OUR CREATOR

For a bishop must be blameless, as the steward of God; not self-willed, not soon angry, not given to wine, no striker, not given to filthy lucre.
Titus 1:7.

AUGUST 1

Much Ado About Dirt

In 1983 the state of Wisconsin passed a law declaring Antigo Silt Loam to be the official state soil. Legislators had presented many other types of soil as candidates, including Kewaunee loam, Waukesha clay, and Suamico muck. The debates were heated and long in the Wisconsin legislature as its members decided this heavy issue. After all, the citizens of Wisconsin didn't want just any old dirt to represent their state. We might be tempted to suggest that making such a fuss over dirt is much ado over nothing. But wait!

Based on the biblical account of the creation of the first human being, you would have to say that dirt is extremely important. All of humanity descended from a figure formed from dirt. So isn't dirt a valuable commodity, something worth a lot of our time in considering? How about that very dirt that Jesus used to form Adam? Of course, that patch of dirt, soil, dust, or clay is no longer there, but if it were, you can bet that the world would build a shrine over it and set it up as an object of worship. People would make pilgrimages from all over the world to touch that dirt, to run it through their fingers, to take dust baths in it, and to fashion images and other objects from it. That dirt would probably be one of the world's most revered elements of nature. Fortunately, the dirt is not available for us to treat so foolishly.

What made that dirt so valuable was the touch of the Master's hand as He fashioned Adam. But even then the dirt was no more than an image until the Creator breathed the breath of life into Adam's form. Only in that way could Adam become our original forefather.

After Adam sinned, it was God's plan that humanity should be dependent upon the dirt to grow food: "In the sweat of thy face shalt thou eat bread, till thou return unto the ground; for out of it wast thou taken: for dust thou art, and unto dust shalt thou return" (Genesis 3:19).

Jesus is the only being in the universe who can give life. In the presence of Jesus, death is nothing more than sleep until the Creator breathes new life into us, and takes us home with Him.

A WORD FROM OUR CREATOR

And the Lord God formed man of the dust of the ground, and breathed into his nostrils the breath of life; and man became a living soul. *Genesis 2:7.*

AUGUST 2

Jupiter

If you could grab onto a bunch of photons leaving the sun and heading toward Jupiter, the fifth-closest planet, you would travel 486 million miles in about 43 minutes. As you streaked past the orbits of Mercury, Venus, Earth, and Mars, you would notice that Jupiter is HUGE! Here are the facts:

1. Jupiter, the largest of the nine planets, is about 90,000 miles in diameter, compared to Earth's diameter of about 8,000 miles.

2. Jupiter is the fastest-spinning planet. Even as large as it is, the time it takes to go from one sunrise to the next is only 9 hours and 55 minutes. That means that Jupiter rotates on its axis 2.4 times in every Earth-day.

3. Jupiter moves along its orbital path around the sun at a speed of 29,000 miles per hour. It takes almost 12 Earth-years for Jupiter to orbit the sun once. That means that if you are 12 years old now and you had grown up on Jupiter, you would have just celebrated your first birthday!

4. The gravity on Jupiter is two and a half times greater than it is on Earth. If you weigh 80 pounds on Earth, you would weigh about 200 pounds on Jupiter.

5. At least 17 moons revolve around Jupiter. They range in size from tiny Leda, only 9 miles in diameter, to Ganymede, which is not only the largest of all of the moons in the solar system, but is also larger than Mercury or Pluto. In fact, Ganymede is almost as large as Mars.

6. A faint ring shimmers around Jupiter, which *Voyager* photographed, but it is too dim to see from Earth.

You won't be able to land on Jupiter. Jupiter's mantle consists of layers of gas hundreds of miles thick directly surrounding the molten metal core. The atmosphere is about 90 percent hydrogen. The gases making up the remaining 10 percent include helium, methane, and ammonia—not a healthy place for you and me.

Every new fact about the planets leaves us more thrilled than ever about the perfection of our home planet.

A WORD FROM OUR CREATOR

Praise ye the Lord. Praise ye the Lord from the heavens: praise him in the heights. Psalm 148:1.

ouble-crested cormorants are black waterbirds that live along the seacoast and along major rivers of North America. Excellent swimmers, they catch fish with the sharp hook on the end of their beak.

One day a baby double-crested cormorant sat in its nest waiting for its mother to bring it another fish. Instead, along came two boys who grabbed it, put it in a sack, and carried it to a boat. Then followed a bump-bump-bumpy truck ride to the home of one of the boys.

The boys made a cage for the bird and tried to keep it full of fish. But the cormorant ate more fish than the boys could catch, and they decided to give it to a summer camp. Luckily there was a naturalist who liked birds there. That's how I met Iktheater. We named him that because he ate fish, and the Greek word for fish is *ikthos*.

Food, food, food—as in fish, fish, fish—was all that the growing cormorant seemed to think about. Every time someone walked past him, Iktheater flapped his wings and opened his big mouth, begging for a fish. We had to catch fish *and* buy fish to keep him happy.

One day we decided to untie Iktheater. Free at last, he followed us around begging for food until he learned that the fish came from the refrigerator. From then on, he would just hang around waiting for someone to open the refrigerator door.

Iktheater soon discovered the campers, and he suddenly had lots of friends. He would line up with the campers and march with them to the dining hall or to the swimming pool. Needless to say, Iktheater was the top swimmer in camp that summer.

As his flight feathers matured Iktheater realized that he could fly. Now he didn't have to march with the campers. Instead, he could beat them to the swimming pool and get in a few laps before they got there. Eventually, Iktheater wandered farther and farther from camp. When he learned to fish for himself in the river, he wasn't interested in refrigerator fish anymore. One day Iktheater flew away. We never saw him again. but he taught us a lot about how wild creatures and human beings can enjoy life together.

August 3

Iktheater

A Word From Our Creator

But ask now the beasts, and they shall teach thee; and the fowls of the air, and they shall tell thee. Job 12:7.

Ant Scent

What mental image do people get when they hear your name? Maybe they "see" the way you look, like the color of your hair or how tall you are. Or maybe they "hear" the sound of your voice or the rhythm of your step on the sidewalk. But, unlike much of the animal world, humans don't usually recognize each other by smell. Wild creatures, on the other hand, use the sense of smell to identify friend or foe—someone who belongs from someone who doesn't.

How would you feel if your friends and family rejected you because you washed your hair with an herbal-scented shampoo instead of a floral-scented one? Or if you ate peppermint candy instead of spearmint? If people behaved as ants do, you would get kicked out of your school and locked out of your house if anything about you smelled slightly different from anyone else in your community.

Since an ant is blind or nearly so, it must rely on its sense of smell to recognize its nestmates. Each colony has its own odor called a pheromone (pronounced FAIR-a-mone). The ant queen daubs the eggs and workers with the distinctive pheromone of her colony—a scent that belongs to no other colony.

Workers keep the queen's scent fresh by licking the eggs and larvae. When two adult ants meet in a tunnel of the colony or on a trail above ground, they share a drop of saliva. Special scent receptors in the antennae tell each ant whether the other is a friend or an enemy. If both ants recognize the scent, they go about their business. But if they don't, the stranger is driven away or killed.

If you were an ant, the most important thing in your life would be how you smell. It would be your ticket to life or death. An ant's world has no individual names, only one name—the name of the colony—and that name is painted on in the form of a pheromone.

As a Christian you have such a family name—the name of Jesus, who writes your name in His family album. And, just as surely as with the ants and pheromones, it is a matter of life and death. "He that overcometh . . . I will not blot out his name out of the book of life" (Revelation 3:5).

A Word From Our Creator

And the Lord said unto Moses, I will do this thing also that thou hast spoken: for thou hast found grace in my sight, and I know thee by name. Exodus 33:17.

August 5

The Bembex Door

Before a female bembex wasp lays her eggs, she prepares a tunnel in the ground that will serve as the home for her young. First she carefully selects the location. Then she constructs the entrance with delicate care, making sure to note the exact features of the doorway to the chamber so that she will be able to find it when she returns.

Once she memorizes the location, the wasp mother sets about the task of stocking the tunnel with food for her offspring. Each trip back to the nest is preceded by a deliberate flight pattern to make sure the nest is hers. She will not enter the chamber unless it's hers, and she recognizes it by the familiar doorway. When she has stocked the nest with food, the bembex mother lays her eggs, then departs. She returns periodically to replenish the food supply and to check on the status of her young. But the door must be there, and it must be exactly as she remembers it. If anything disturbs the features of the doorway, Mrs. Bembex becomes confused and disoriented. She cannot even recognize her own eggs or young.

The famous French naturalist Jean Henri Fabre tells of finding a bembex nest where something had destroyed the entrance and left the young wasps exposed to the heat and bright light of the sun. The mother returned to the location and began looking for the doorway to her nest. Not even noticing the obvious movement of her young, she continued to return again and again to the spot where the door should have been. In her desperate attempts to find the door to her young, the mother wasp actually stepped on them without being aware of them. She had to find that door. As Fabre puts it, "she wanted her entrance door, the usual door, and nothing but that door."

Every person in this world needs a door—a doorway to life. There is only one door, and nothing but that door will do. That door is Jesus. It is a sad fact that sometimes people do not recognize the door. It is our job to point others to it. We are guides, as it were, and as faithful guides we are true representatives of the Door. Jesus is counting on you.

A Word From Our Creator

I am the door: by me if any man enter in, he shall be saved, and shall go in and out. John 10:9.

AUGUST 6

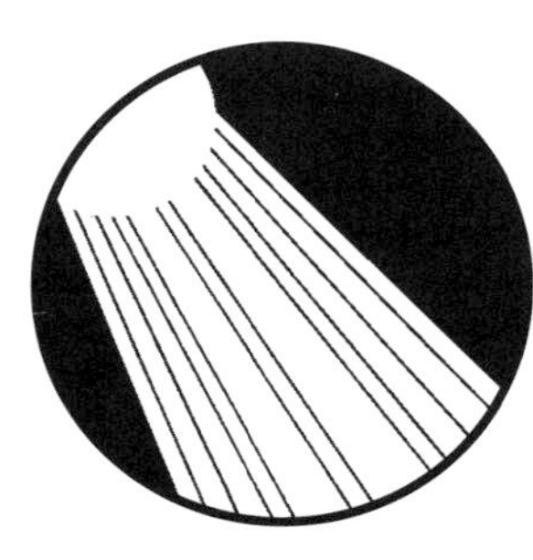

Micro-waves

If you could take visible violet light waves and start lengthening their wavelength, you would eventually run through the spectrum of colors. First the rays would change to blue light, then to green, yellow, orange, and, finally, red visible light. Now if you could continue to lengthen the wavelengths, you'd produce invisible infrared light and eventually radio waves—first short waves and then longer waves. Just beyond infrared and at the beginning of the shortwave radio waves, you have the very short wavelengths—the ones called microwaves. We use them for radar, to cook with, and to transmit television and FM radio signals.

Right now, as you are reading this, microwaves are transmitting information in hundreds of languages all over the world, and all those transmissions are racing through the air at the same time. To hear them, all you need is a tuner—a device that picks up the frequency of a transmission and directs it into another device called a speaker. A radio has both a tuner and speakers. You turn the dial and hear a message spoken in Russian that's being broadcast from Moscow. Adjust the dial a little more and you hear a message in Japanese originating in Tokyo. And so it goes.

Messages from all over the world flash all around us. It is impossible to get away from them unless we go deep into underground caverns. Microwaves pass through windows and most walls. They are all around you all the time. Every one of those waves is acting as a messenger—in a sense fulfilling today's text.

Humanity didn't invent microwaves. The Creator provided them as part of His complete plan, and they have been here from the beginning. People have only recently learned to use them to transmit messages. Such waves also come from heavenly bodies in deep space, bringing with them information about the wonders of the universe—declaring the glory of God.

A WORD FROM OUR CREATOR

The heavens declare the glory of God; and the firmament sheweth his handywork. Day unto day uttereth speech, and night unto night sheweth knowledge. There is no speech nor language, where their voice is not heard. Psalm 19:1-3.

August 7

Why Is the Sea Salty?

Ask someone why the sea is salty when all of the water running into it is fresh. The answer will probably go something like this: the sea is salty because every freshwater stream has a small amount of dissolved salt in it. In the sea that salt becomes concentrated because the sun evaporates the water, leaving the salt to accumulate.

That answer may make sense, but it's not correct. If it were, the amount of salt in the sea would be steadily increasing. In fact, the amount of salt in the sea hasn't changed since science began to test for it. Furthermore, the sea has more salt than could possibly have come from the land.

Every cubic mile of seawater has about 166 million tons of salt. If you could take the minerals out of the sea and spread them on land, all the continents would have a salty crust 500 feet thick. Eighty-five percent of it would be sodium chloride—common table salt. Where did it come from?

Nobody knows, but there is a theory that is consistent with biblical history. Some scientists believe that all that salt resulted from a period of intense volcanic activity that altered the mineral composition of the earth's surface. Remember the story of Sodom and Gomorrah and Lot's wife, who lagged behind instead of fleeing from Sodom? She became a pillar of salt. The Old Testament refers to the area as the Valley of Salt (Deuteronomy 29:23; 2 Samuel 8:13), and today it is the location of the Dead Sea, the saltiest body of water on earth. As long as 4,000 years ago people spoke of the Dead Sea as the "salt sea" (Genesis 14:3), and scientists tell us that the water is no saltier today than it was then. That Dead Sea Valley has abundant evidence of intense volcanic activity spanning the ages of human history.

We believe that the Flood had intense volcanic eruptions, and it's possible that the salt in the ocean resulted from that activity. But the truly amazing thing is that once the current amount of salt was established in the sea, a perfect unchanging balance has supported thousands of different kinds of sea creatures and saltwater plants. This fact offers evidence not only of a powerful God but also of a loving God.

A Word From Our Creator

. . . so can no fountain both yield salt water and fresh. James 3:12.

Corpse Flower

Looking like something more imaginary than real, this rare flower measures three feet in diameter, smells like rotten meat, and grows only on a certain type of woody vine on the islands of Sumatra and Borneo. The plant's bright-red blossom, often called "corpse flower" because of its odor, consists of a bowl-shaped center the size of a bucket and five huge white-speckled petals. The world's largest flower, its official name is *Rafflesia arnoldii* (pronounced Raf-LESS-ee-uh ar-NOLD-ee-eye), after explorer Thomas Raffles (the founder of Singapore) and naturalist Joseph Arnold. The two men were together when they discovered the corpse flower in 1818.

Rafflesias are parasites, getting all their nourishment from the tiny root hairs of the host vine. They do not have stems or green leaves. Someone has described the flower buds as "pale-orange cabbages wrapped in charred newspaper." When a bud bursts open, the stench attracts carrion flies—flies that eat dead meat—into the pollen-covered spikes inside the flower's center. As the flies move from flower to flower, they pollinate them.

Each pollinated flower can produce as many as 4 million seeds. But the seeds just drop in a heap under the flower. In order to sprout and grow, each tiny seed must become lodged in the bark of the woody stem of the *Testrastigma* vine, a relative of the grape. *Rafflesia arnoldii* must rely on small mammals, such as squirrels and tree shrews, to scatter the seeds. Out of the millions of seeds, only a few find their way to the vine that means life to them.

As sinners we are like the corpse flower. The apostle Paul said, "O wretched man that I am! who shall deliver me from the body of this death?" (Romans 7:24) Then he answers his own question by stating that the deliverer is "Jesus Christ our Lord" (verse 25).

Jesus is the vine. We are as dependent upon the Vine as is the rafflesia. But our case is very different. Instead of leaving our fate to chance, Jesus came to earth "to seek and to save that which was lost" (Luke 19:10).

A Word From Our Creator

I am the vine, ye are the branches: He that abideth in me, and I in him, the same bringeth forth much fruit: for without me ye can do nothing. John 15:5.

August 9

Ring Around the Galaxy

A galaxy is a somewhat flat, platter-shaped mass of swirling stars. At least that was the accepted description until 1980. In that year an astronomer with the Department of Terrestrial Magnetism at Carnegie Institute in Washington, D.C., found the first-known gyroscope-shaped galaxy. Another ring of stars perpendicular to the first crossed the usual island of stars. And neither ring is stationary—both spin, one within the other.

Since astronomers discovered the first gyroscope-shaped galaxy, they have spotted several more. What celestial occurrence made these galaxies different? What caused the hooplike band of stars? No one knows.

One theory for the gyroscope-shaped galaxies is that each one of them is the result of a collision between two galaxies. According to this theory, the larger galaxy prevailed and the ring is all that is left of the other galaxy. There is no way to prove or disprove the theory at this point, so it's not much more than a fantastic idea.

Scientists are observing the gyroscope-shaped galaxies carefully, however, because it is possible that these unique objects in space can explain another mystery. Astronomers estimate the mass of a galaxy by measuring the speed and angle of its rotation. But when they do this, they always calculate more mass than they can account for by what they see. Where is the rest of the mass that mathematically has to be there, but is not visible?

For some time a theory has suggested that the missing mass was in a dark invisible halo circling the galaxy. But science had no visible evidence of this "dark halo phenomenon" until the discovery of the gyroscope-shaped galaxies. In the words of Vera Rubin, one of the astronomers at the Carnegie Institute, "most galaxies would seem to consist of much more than what we see."

Isn't it thrilling that we keep seeing more and more proof of God's infinite power in the universe? The wonders never stop—and we'll never discover them all. Praise Him, all ye stars of light.

A Word From Our Creator

Praise ye the Lord from the heavens: praise him in the heights. Praise ye him, all his angels: praise ye him, all his hosts. Praise ye him, sun and moon: praise him, all ye stars of light. Psalm 148:1-3.

August 10

Siphonophores

Have you ever heard of a church group called the Siphonophores of the Sea? Of course you haven't, but when we finish telling you about these creatures, you will understand the question.

A siphonophore (pronounced cy-FAHN-ah-for) may look like a jellyfish, but it's not one. The many different kinds live in tropical oceans. Some of them, like the Portuguese man-of-war, drift on the surface, and others inhabit the waters several thousand feet below the surface. A siphonophore is actually an association of hollow-bodied translucent organisms that work together as a unit. In the case of deep-sea siphonophores, the colony resembles long strands of rope that in some species reach 100 feet in length.

Scientists refer to individual organisms that make up siphonophores as "persons," and they call the whole unit a "colony." Each siphonophore person has its own distinctive purpose. It is a specialized organism that joins with other person specialists to form a complete colony. Thus a siphonophore person may capture and eat food for the entire colony, defend the entire colony, or carry on the reproductive functions of the entire colony. A person may also form the sail for the colony or the swimming-bell that expands and contracts to propel the colony through the water.

Like the jellyfish, its relative, the siphonophore provides food and shelter for other deep-sea creatures. Tiny fish hide among the stringy persons of the colony, where, protected from predators, they feed on scraps dropped by the food-collecting persons. Other creatures hitch rides on the floating colony. Still others, like sea turtles, eat the colony itself.

What a perfect example of how we human persons are members of the church that the Bible calls the body of Christ. In 1 Corinthians 12 Paul has much to say about how even though each of us has different gifts and different responsibilities, we all work together to the glory of God.

A Word From Our Creator

For as we have many members in one body, and all members have not the same office: so we, being many, are one body in Christ, and every one members one of another. Romans 12:4, 5.

It seems that we are less likely to hurt or destroy things that we know about and appreciate. Most people think nothing of killing bees and wasps, for example, but as we become knowledgable about the remarkable talents of these tiny creatures, our appreciation for them grows as well.

An English naturalist studying insects in the Pyrenees Mountains of southwestern Europe claims to have made a pet of a wasp. Mr. Lubbock collected a female digger wasp, along with her nest, and put them into a container to take them back to England. On the trip home, Mr. Lubbock tried to get the wasp to feed on his finger. At first the wasp stood with her stinger always ready to defend herself. But as the wasp got used to the new arrangement, she relaxed, only stinging him ever so slightly a couple times when he had to hurry her back into her cage because the ticket agent had arrived. Over the coming months the wasp became tame, even allowing Mr. Lubbock to pet her without her showing her stinger at all.

When winter came, the wasp went into a sort of hibernation where she seemed to sleep most of the time. She would awaken occasionally and come out to be fed, only to return to her dark quarters to sleep again. In February the wasp apparently awakened for good, because she came out to feed and did not seem to want to go back to sleep. One day she just stopped eating, and after several days she died. Her tiny preserved body now occupies a place in the British Museum.

It's probably hard to imagine making a pet out of a creature that's so quick to sting. But think about it—the Creator provided the stinger to protect the wasp, not to give the world a mean-spirited creature. When the wasp felt safe, she was not inclined to use her weapon. In the complete safety of the new earth there will be no hurting stingers—or destroying of wasps.

A Pet Wasp

A Word From Our Creator

They shall not hurt nor destroy in all my holy mountain: for the earth shall be full of the knowledge of the Lord, as the waters cover the sea. Isaiah 11:9.

AUGUST 12

Ulm Pishkun

If you are ever near Great Falls, Montana, you should visit the Ulm Pishkun State Monument. *Ulm Pishkun* means "buffalo jump" in the language of the local Native Americans. Archaeologists tell us that the ancient inhabitants stampeded herds of buffalo over the cliff at Ulm Pishkun to obtain meat and skins.

Centuries ago the people of what is now Montana had no guns and horses, so they devised a way to drive large numbers of buffalo over the Ulm Pishkun to their deaths. It's believed that they preserved enough buffalo meat to use to trade for other goods with other tribes and villages throughout the country. Ulm Pishkun was the Montana meat market hundreds of years before there was even a Montana. Archaeological evidence suggests that this location provided buffalo products from as early as A.D. 500 until the 1700s.

You would think that those buffaloes would avoid Ulm Pishkun after a few years. But every year the herd came through, and every year the people stampeded many of them over the cliff. Wasn't there at least one brave buffalo who said, "Enough of this! I am going to take a different route next year"?

Evidently not, because for more than 1,000 years the buffalo continued to go over the cliff. Were the buffaloes just stupid, or were they somehow tricked into going over the Ulm Pishkun?

Early American cowboys and soldiers operating on the plains learned that no amount of pushing and chasing can get a *few* buffaloes to leap over a cliff. The animals knew better! You had to stampede a whole herd before they lost their common sense and rushed headlong over such a precipice.

And so it is with humans. People seem more likely to do stupid things in a crowd than in smaller groups. They don't seem to be able to sense that they are on a dangerous course when many others are on that same route with them. Young people must be especially careful when deciding to join a crowd. Remember the buffaloes of the Ulm Pishkun. Sometimes only the lone buffalo survives.

A WORD FROM OUR CREATOR

Enter ye in at the strait gate: for wide is the gate, and broad is the way, that leadeth to destruction, and many there be which go in thereat. Matthew 7:13.

AUGUST 13

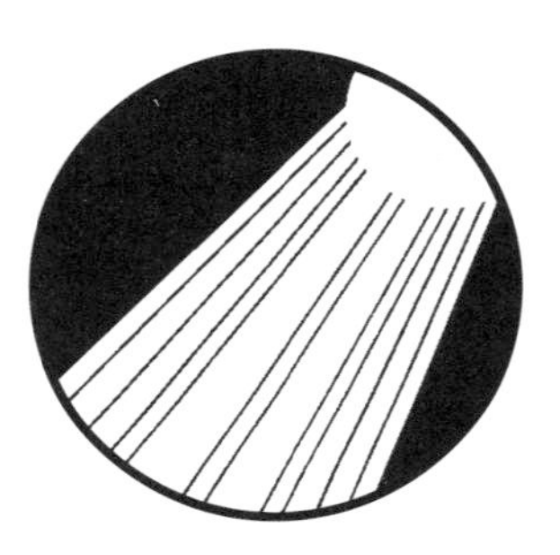

The Color Red

We often associate the color red with danger. A red octagon at an intersection tells you to stop to avoid getting hit by another vehicle. A red traffic light does the same thing. A red sky in the morning warns sailors that a storm is brewing. And the red phone on the president's desk rings only if there's an international emergency.

Red can also indicate embarrassment, as in being "red-faced." Being caught "red-handed" means that you've been discovered doing something you shouldn't have been doing.

Probably you've heard the phrase "seeing red." It comes from the bullfighting ring, in which the bullfighter waves his red cape at the bull. Actually the bull is color-blind. But when it responds to the waving cloth by charging the bullfighter, spectators get the impression that the red color is responsible for the animal's snorting and pawing the ground. Therefore, "seeing red" now means being extremely angry.

It really doesn't matter what the different interpretations of red are if you can't see the color. And to see red, you need light. For example, you see a red traffic signal only if there is a light source projecting the color red to your eyes. And the red stop sign is red only if sunlight, a streetlight, or a headlight is shining on it to be reflected back to your eyes.

Certain sea creatures prey on smaller sea animals that are quite capable of seeing red. But since the sun's red rays are the longest of the visible light rays, they often get blocked out before they reach the ocean depths. Only the shorter, blue light rays penetrate below 40 feet, so you don't have to go very deep before the reds and oranges disappear. Consequently, a predatory fish that's bright-red in shallow water has to swim down only a few feet to blend into the shadows. Its red color no longer warns smaller fish, and they become easy prey for the larger red but invisible one.

Without the presence of Jesus as our source of light, we cannot see danger and take appropriate action.

A WORD FROM OUR CREATOR

This then is the message which we have heard of him, and declare unto you, that God is light, and in him is no darkness at all. If we say that we have fellowship with him, and walk in darkness, we lie, and do not the truth.
1 John 1:5, 6.

August 14

Air Pollution

Our text refers to the time when the Lord used a wind to pile up the water so the Israelites could escape. Even today, God uses the winds to protect us from danger. By His wonderful design the circulating air currents of the earth purify the atmosphere.

Human inventions have brought us the problem of pollution. To make the things that we want—things like television sets and automobiles—we built factories. Factories require energy. And energy means burning something as fuel. Burning produces smoke containing harmful chemicals.

And then we want to be on the go, so we want more vehicles, each of which requires energy. That means burning gasoline as fuel. And burning gasoline creates exhaust containing chemicals that make the air even more harmful.

What about God's wonderful design for purifying the atmosphere? The natural circulation of the air works, but under certain conditions, our need for more energy has disrupted the natural purifying aspects of the firmament—especially in large cities surrounded by mountains.

Take Mexico City, for example. With more than 20 million people, it is one of the world's most populated cities. It has so much pollution that breathing the air does as much harm as smoking a pack of cigarettes a day. Why don't the natural winds of the world purify the air in Mexico City?

The cold air above the mountains acts like a lid over the enclosed basin where Mexico City lies. The polluted air within the basin cannot break through the lid. Some scientists have proposed building giant fans to blow the polluted air up through the lid of cold air and away from the city. Another proposal calls for digging a huge tunnel through the volcanic mountain south of the city so that the natural winds could suck the pollution out of the basin.

Remember the group of people long ago who thought they could outsmart God by building a tower to heaven? When, to satisfy our own greed, we polute a planet that God gave us to take care of, we can't very well expect to use His natural winds to fix that problem.

A Word From Our Creator

Then the channels of waters were seen, and the foundations of the world were discovered at thy rebuke, O Lord, at the blast of the breath of thy nostrils. Psalm 18:15.

AUGUST 15

Scarlet Gilia

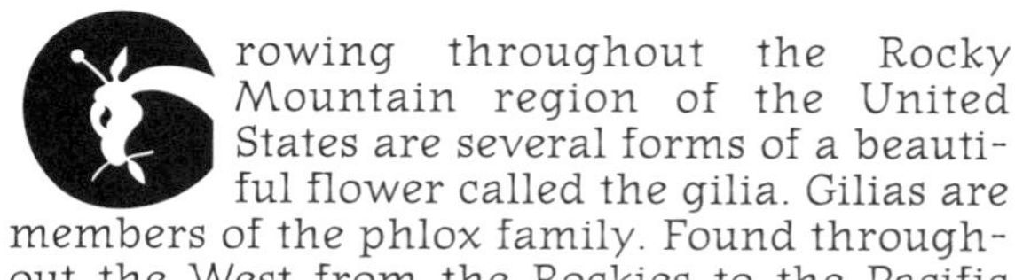

Growing throughout the Rocky Mountain region of the United States are several forms of a beautiful flower called the gilia. Gilias are members of the phlox family. Found throughout the West from the Rockies to the Pacific Ocean and from southern Canada to Mexico, they range in color from blue-violet and purple to red, pink, and white.

Perhaps the most beautiful member of this group is the scarlet gilia. Growing to a height of one to three feet, it blooms in profusion from May into August. They are a common wildflower from the lowest valleys up to the timberline in the Rockies, and they bloom as spectacular splashes of brilliant red amid the endless gray sage from Montana into British Columbia. The flowers form clusters of trumpet-shaped blossoms three fourths of an inch to one and a half inches long.

On Fern Mountain in northern Arizona, the scarlet gilia begins to bloom in July, just at the time that hummingbirds are nesting and looking for red flowers to provide enough nectar to feed themselves and their young. As they visit the gilias, the hummingbirds pollinate the plants. But the hummingbirds leave in August, returning southward toward their wintering grounds. The scarlet gilia now needs a new pollination service. That's where hawkmoths come in. The hawkmoths are members of the sphinx moth family. They fly at night and are attracted only to white flowers easily seen in the darkness. Scarlet gilia flowers are red and virtually invisible at night. If only they could change and produce white flowers!

Wonder of wonders—that is exactly what they do. In August, when the hummingbirds leave, the scarlet gilia begins to bear white blooms instead of bright-red ones. By changing color, the scarlet gilia supplies food for the hawkmoths and guarantees pollination for itself.

Thanks to the Creator's power to transform, your sins, which may be as red as the flowers of the scarlet gilia, shall be as white as those on Fern Mountain in August.

A WORD FROM OUR CREATOR

Come now, and let us reason together, saith the Lord: though your sins be as scarlet, they shall be as white as snow.
Isaiah 1:18.

August 16

Seven-teen Moons

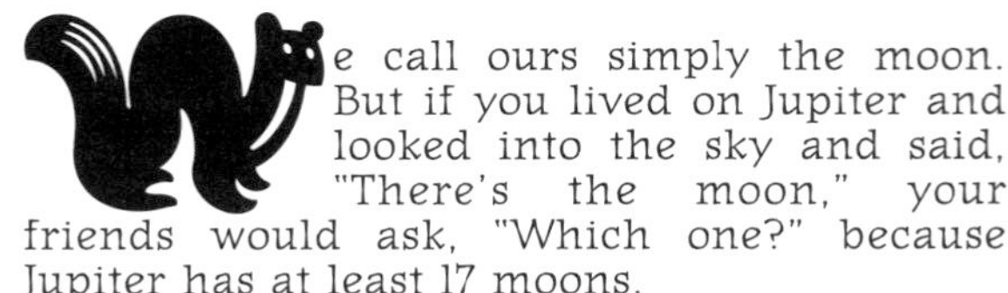

We call ours simply the moon. But if you lived on Jupiter and looked into the sky and said, "There's the moon," your friends would ask, "Which one?" because Jupiter has at least 17 moons.

The list of Jupiter's moons reads more like a collection of names for a large family of cats. Callisto, Europa, Ganymede, and Io are the four big moons that orbit the planet. Smaller moons include Adrastea, Amalthea, Ananke, Carme, Elara, Himalia, Leda, Lysithea, Metis, Pasiphae, Sinope, and Thebe. Some of Jupiter's moons take as long as two Earth-years to circle the planet, while others zip once around the globe every seven hours. So from Jupiter's surface, moonlight would take on a whole new meaning depending on how many moons are out on a given night and what phases they're in.

But wait. There's a serious problem. You couldn't stand on Jupiter even if you found a way to get there. Jupiter doesn't appear to have any solid land to walk on—only liquid and gases, all of them inhospitable to us humans.

Jupiter measures 90,000 miles in diameter—that's more than 11 times the diameter of Earth. This huge planet, the largest in the solar system, rotates once every 9 hours and 55 minutes. It's spinning like a top, which is one reason for the intense turbulence that exists on the planet. Can you imagine the winds that whip around the planet? If Jupiter had a solid surface like that of Earth, you still wouldn't be able to stand up on it, let alone look at any moons.

To make matters worse, the barometric pressure at the surface of Jupiter is thought to be millions of times greater than it is on Earth. Even if you could get to the planet with so many moons, and even if you could survive winds in excess of 10,000 miles per hour, you'd be compressed into a tiny blob in a split second. You wouldn't have the chance to see any moonlight at all.

When we consider the other planets and the conditions that exist on them, the fact that Earth is such a beautiful and hospitable place is further evidence of a loving Creator and Redeemer of the human race.

A Word From Our Creator

It shall be established for ever as the moon, and as a faithful witness in heaven. Psalm 89:37.

August 17

Uncompahgre Fritillary

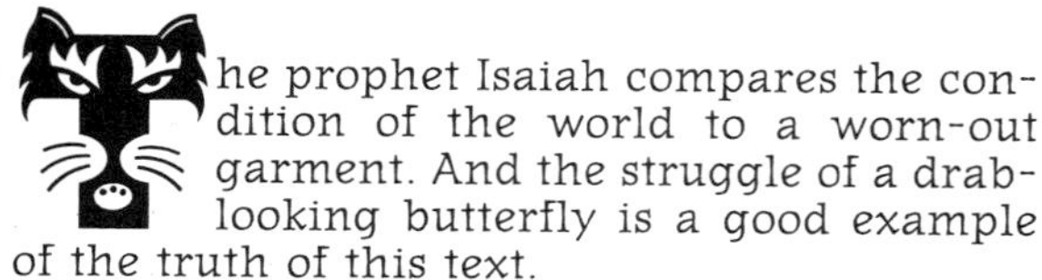

The prophet Isaiah compares the condition of the world to a worn-out garment. And the struggle of a drab-looking butterfly is a good example of the truth of this text.

In 1978 scientists discovered the Uncompahgre Fritillary (pronounced Un-com-PA-gray FRIT-ul-ary) living 13,000 feet above sea level on Uncompahgre Peak in the San Juan Mountains of Colorado. Shortly afterward they found them also at the same elevation on Redcloud Peak about 10 miles to the south. Both groups of butterflies were restricted to the cooler northern slopes of the two peaks.

When the U.S. Forest Service conducted a census of the fritillary in 1982, they estimated that only 2,000 of the insects existed. Over the next 10 years, the Uncompahgre Peak population disappeared altogether and the Redcloud group dropped to only 360 butterflies. By the time you read this, the Uncompahgre Fritillary may be extinct. All their relatives live in the Arctic, and this southernmost member of the species once found a suitable habitat only on the frigid north side of the highest peaks of the Rocky Mountains.

The world appears to be heating up slowly. Human activities on the Earth have produced what scientists call the "greenhouse effect," or "global warming." First, creatures that thrive in cold weather and can't adapt to warmer temperatures will die. If the warming process continues, the world will eventually be unable to support life of any kind. Earth will become a dead planet.

The sin-ravaged earth is like an old garment getting beyond repair. Change may come slowly, but eventually the planet won't be able to be mended—regardless of drastic conservation methods. But God has reminded us of another garment—a robe of righteousness—that He will give to each of us and that will cover an earth made new as well.

A Word From Our Creator

Lift up your eyes to the heavens, and look upon the earth beneath: for the heavens shall vanish away like smoke, and the earth shall wax old like a garment.

Isaiah 51:6.

Fear of the Tachina

Have you ever been afraid of something, like spiders, or dogs, or tight places? People have all sorts of phobias—irrational fears. The thing you fear is probably no real threat. In fact, you may not even know where the fear comes from, but you're afraid of it anyway. The female bembex wasp provides an interesting example. Even though she captures and destroys flies, she appears to fear one in particular: the tachina fly (pronounced ta-KEY-nah).

The tachina fly is so tiny that the bembex could easily overtake it and kill it. But instead of simply eliminating the tachina threat, the bembex appears to be terrified by the flyweight monster. She rushes away in a panic as soon as she sees one. The bembex female has good reason not to trust the female tachina, because the fly's goal is to parasitize the wasp's young.

With unblinking eyes the color of dried blood, a pack of tachina flies quietly waits and watches while the bembex wasp prepares her nest and hunts for prey to feed her young. The flies sit absolutely still through the whole process. When the wasp arrives at the nest with her prey, the tachinas attack. Rather than fighting back, the bembex, after several unsuccessful attempts to outmaneuver the little flies, alights with her cargo and accepts the inevitable. While the bembex stands by in apparent helplessness, the tachinas lay their eggs on her prey. Now the food intended for the wasp's babies will become food instead for the baby flies.

The tiny fly's eggs hatch before the wasp's eggs, and the wasp continues to bring fresh food for the interlopers. The baby flies not only consume all of the baby wasp's food, but will often consume the baby wasp as well.

You may be wondering how this story can illustrate a text that says "Be of good cheer!" We live in a world where Satan and his angels constantly wait to pounce on us and devour us spiritually, if not physically. But we have absolutely nothing to fear, because Jesus has eliminated the threat. As the text says, we will have problems, but as God's children our eternal life is secure.

A Word From Our Creator

These things I have spoken unto you, that in me ye might have peace. In the world ye shall have tribulation: but be of good cheer; I have overcome the world. John 16:33.

r. Douglas Pratt, an ornithologist with the Louisiana State University, calls it "the greatest avian disaster of the twentieth century." Beginning after World War II there has been a systematic extermination of the native forest birds on the island of Guam.

Ornithologists once called this tiny island an avian Eden because its forests fairly rang with the constant melodies of a chorus of birds. For thousands of years the island had remained isolated—a paradise for birds that existed nowhere else in the world.

By 1970, however, few native birds remained on Guam. When Dr. Pratt first visited the island in 1976, he reported that "the southern two thirds of Guam was just a desert. There were no birds left." What was happening? Scientists first suspected pesticides, for during World War II soldiers had sprayed large amounts of DDT on the island. But further research showed that theory to be incorrect. The next theory was that some deadly epidemic was responsible. Extensive studies, however, revealed no deadly disease.

They did find, though, that one creature was increasing throughout the island. Brown tree snakes were everywhere. In fact, they were a public nuisance. This formidable predator is not native to Guam and probably arrived accidentally with military shipments during or shortly after the war. Growing to a length of eight feet, the brown tree snake can kill and swallow most adult birds. Not only can it climb trees with ease; it is also slender enough and lightweight enough to slither out onto the smaller branches where birds had roosted in safety for centuries. When ornithologists began to collect systematic data, the results were clear. Within about 30 years the brown tree snakes had killed and eaten virtually all the native forest birds on Guam. The avian Eden is gone, and we cannot restore it. The results are forever.

"The serpent beguiled me, and I did eat," said Eve. The damage was done, and Eden was gone. But thanks to a loving Saviour, here the results do not have to be forever. Jesus has overcome the serpent and made a way for us to enjoy Eden restored.

Eden Despoiled

A WORD FROM OUR CREATOR

And the Lord God said unto the woman, What is this that thou hast done? And the woman said, The serpent beguiled me, and I did eat. Genesis 3:13.

AUGUST 20

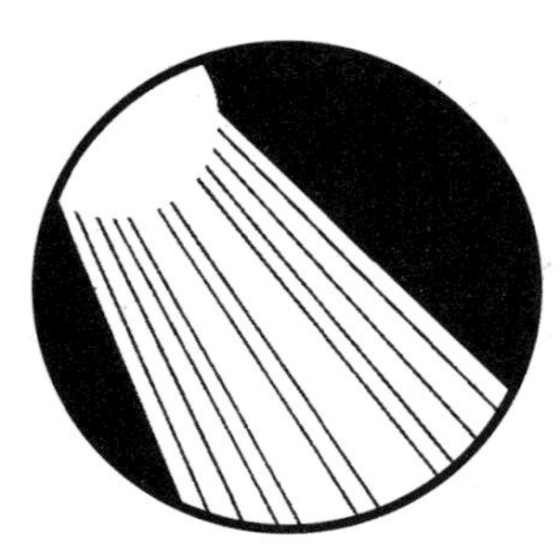

Fiber Optics

A WORD FROM OUR CREATOR

But I say, Have they not heard? Yes verily, their sound went into all the earth, and their words unto the ends of the world. Romans 10:18.

An application of laser technology has revolutionized the telephone industry. Whoever would have thought that one day light would transmit our conversations? Yet that is exactly what is happening through a process called fiber optics.

Bundles of fibers made of plastic or glass are replacing bundles of copper wires as telephone cables. A half-inch cable of fiber can contain 144 tiny hair-sized glass fibers. This cable, through which light impulses instead of electric currents send telephone signals, can carry more than 40,000 telephone conversations at the same time! To handle that many calls by copper-wire cable, you would need about 9,000 separate copper wires in four to five cables, each about two inches in diameter. On a more practical and smaller scale, just 12 plastic or glass fibers embedded in a strip of plastic can handle more than 4,000 calls. Because glass and plastic are so readily available compared to the depleting reserves of copper, fiber optics will eventually cost less than traditional telephone transmission.

Fiber optics use concentrated laser light. The laser beam moves through the tiny fibers like water does through a hose. The light bounces off the walls of the fiber, a property called "total internal reflection." The light goes wherever the fiber does, even if it bends or loops.

By a process called modulation, the laser light can have a coded message—like your voice talking on a telephone—attached to it. That modulation travels intact through the fiber and is decoded on the other end, where your friend will hear your voice. The process literally beams your voice from one place to another at the speed of light.

In our text for today, Paul is telling the Romans that the world has no excuse to claim ignorance about God's power and glory. The words of His prophets and messengers have circled the globe many times, and still new ways are being created every day to spread the gospel to every corner of the earth.

August 21

Rogue Waves

Rogue waves are the most feared and least understood natural phenomena of the sea. They have terrified sailors from the dawn of history. In fact, ancient mariners feared them as much as they did sea monsters and great white sharks because they come out of nowhere and rise to heights of 50, 60, and even 70 feet or higher. In 1933 the crew of the U.S. Navy oil tanker *Ramapo* measured the highest wave ever observed in the Pacific Ocean. From the peak of the crest to the depth of the trough, the wave measured 112 feet—higher than a 10-story building. The psalmist was probably thinking about just such waves when he wrote Psalm 93.

The fear of rogue waves comes not so much from the size of the wave—although that is certainly terrifying enough—as from the fact that they can't be predicted. We can detect and avoid giant waves resulting from earthquakes or hurricanes. But since scientists have no way of knowing when or where a rogue wave will occur, they can't study them. The only information available is from the few observers fortunate enough to see one and live to tell about it. At the moment, only God can predict when they will happen and what the result will be.

The danger comes not only from the great height of the wave but also from the steepness of the side of the wave going down to the trough. If the wave doesn't break, then small craft have a better chance of surviving than large ships because they ride the wave like corks in a stream. The danger to small boats is being struck broadside or pitched from one wave into the next and thus getting flipped end over end. Large ships caught by a single wave can get lifted so that both the bow and the stern rise out of the water. Few ships can survive the resulting structural strain without breaking apart.

Rogue waves are still one of the great unsolved mysteries of the sea. When Jesus rebuked the waves in the Sea of Galilee, His disciples said one to another, "What manner of man is this, that even the winds and the sea obey him!" (Matthew 8:27). What manner of Man indeed!

A Word From Our Creator

The Lord on high is mightier than the noise of many waters, yea, than the mighty waves of the sea.
Psalm 93:4.

August 22

Nature's Hydraulic Power Pump

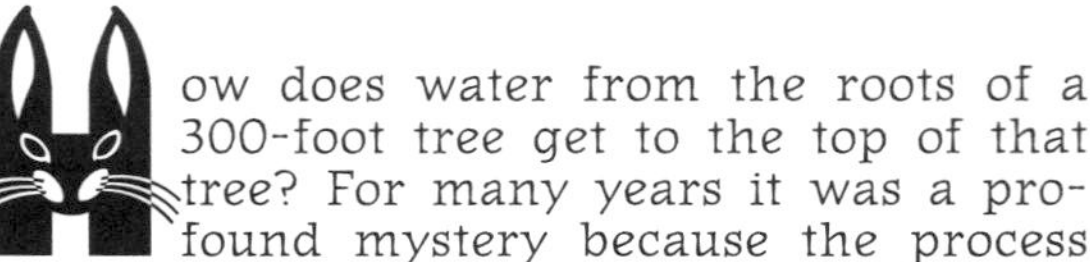

How does water from the roots of a 300-foot tree get to the top of that tree? For many years it was a profound mystery because the process defies gravity. Even now, when we know the answer, it still seems amazing.

Perhaps you already know that water goes both up and down in a tree trunk through special cells just inside the tree's bark. Tubelike cells carry nutrients dissolved in the water up from the roots to the branches. Other tubelike cells carry food produced in the leaves down to the roots. The cells that transport materials up from the roots botanists call xylem (pronounced ZY-lem) cells, and cells that carry materials down to the roots are labeled phloem (pronounced FLOW-um) cells. The law of gravity explains how water flows down to the roots. But how does it get up to the tops of the trees?

Water consists of two elements—hydrogen and oxygen. Each molecule of water contains two hydrogen atoms and one oxygen atom, hence H_2O. As a result of this arrangement, each water molecule has a small negative charge on one side and a small positive charge on the other. Since negative and positive charges attract each other, water molecules grab hold of each other if given only the slightest chance. And that's how water reaches the tops of trees.

As the water evaporates through the leaf surface, it leaves a shortage of water in the outer leaf cells. Inner leaf cells respond by providing water molecules to replace those lost. This starts a chain reaction, somewhat like a bucket brigade, that goes all the way down to the roots. When one water molecule is brought in from the next cell, its electrical charge pulls along the next molecule in line, and so on all the way to the roots, where the cells bring in water from the soil.

As Christians we are constantly sharing the water of life with others. This starts a chain reaction that draws more of that water through Jesus, who has promised us an unlimited supply.

A Word From Our Creator

And he shall be like a tree planted by the rivers of water, that bringeth forth his fruit in his season; his leaf also shall not wither; and whatsoever he doeth shall prosper. Psalm 1:3.

If you were to travel to Saturn from the sun at the speed of light, by the time you reached Saturn you would have traveled 893 million miles in one hour and 20 minutes.

1. Saturn is the second-largest planet in our solar system. It's 75,000 miles in diameter. But like Jupiter, it has no land surface, so you couldn't land on the planet. Layer upon layer of gases and liquids cover its core, and its upper atmosphere consists of clouds of ammonia that whip around the planet at supersonic speeds because of the high velocity of Saturn's rotation.

2. Saturn orbits the sun once every 29.46 Earth-years at a speed of about 22,000 miles per hour. If you were to grow up on Saturn and count years as we do—as the time it takes to orbit the sun—you'd be a lot younger. As a 10-year-old Earthling you'd have to live another 19.46 years before celebrating your first birthday.

3. On the other hand, it takes only 10 hours and 39 minutes in Earth time for Saturn to rotate from one sunrise to the next. So it takes two and a half Saturn-days to equal one Earth-day.

4. Saturn is most famous for its beautiful rings. What astronomers originally thought to be only one or two flat rings around the planet they now know to be thousands of rings organized into at least six bands. The rings consist of icy particles that reflect different colors and different amounts of light.

5. No fewer than 17 moons revolve around Saturn! There are so many that from a distance the planet looks like a miniature solar system all by itself. All but Phoebe, the outermost moon, travel in the same direction. Phoebe, 8 million miles from Saturn, revolves backward around the planet.

6. The gravity on Saturn is almost exactly what it is on Earth. In other words, you would weigh about the same on Saturn as you do on Earth. Even though the planet is much larger than Earth, its mass is much less concentrated, so the gravity is relatively low compared to its size. How does the Creator hold more than 17 moons and a band of solid particles thousands of miles wide in orbit around a huge ball of liquid and gas? Certainly we stand in awe of Him.

August 23

Saturn

A Word From Our Creator

Let all the earth fear the Lord: let all the inhabitants of the world stand in awe of him. Psalm 33:8.

AUGUST 24

Eels

The psalmist could have written this text specifically for the freshwater eels of both the Atlantic and Pacific oceans. They remain one of earth's major natural mysteries. Although they are the most abundant fish in some streams and rivers of North America and Europe, they are the least well-known.

A baby eel is a finless, leaf-shaped little creature swimming in the Sargasso Sea, a region in the North Atlantic Ocean south of Bermuda. The Sargasso Sea received its name for the sargassum, a seaweed, that grows there in profusion. After birth, the tiny eels begin to drift toward the edge of the Sargasso Sea and then into the currents that will carry them to their freshwater homes. The young American eels drift westward and northward, while the young European eels float northward and eastward.

As it grows, each eel becomes long and round, shaped more like a small snake than its trout and herring relatives. The adult eel keeps its snakelike form and may grow to be six feet long. Once in the freshwater rivers and streams of its ancestors, the eel may live to be 18 years old.

How does the baby eel know to make its way thousands of miles through open ocean to fresh inland waters? As adults, do they return to the same streams that their parents left? If they do, how do they find their way back to their birthplace to spawn and lay eggs—a place that they left up to 20 years earlier?

We do know that when eels are ready to migrate south, their eyes grow huge and round so that they can see better in the ocean's deep, dark depths, where scientists believe that they spawn. We also know that they change from their usual greenish color to silver, making them appear to overhead predators as a reflection of sunlight. Nothing stops them when they begin their long journey. They even travel short distances over land, using the thick mucus on their bodies and the dew on grass to help them on their way.

If the Creator and sustainer of life can guide the millions of eels as they journey to a place where they have never been, surely He will guide us through life to our heavenly home.

A WORD FROM OUR CREATOR

Thy way is in the sea, and thy path in the great waters, and thy footsteps are not known. Psalm 77:19.

AUGUST 25

The Praying Monster

Whom was the Pharisee praying with in this text? Himself! He certainly wasn't praying with other believers. The only person he believed in was himself. On other occasions Jesus described the hypocrisy of some of the Pharisees who sometimes led people into the very sins they themselves condemned.

The praying mantis behaves like some pharisees. Virtually nothing about the creature suggests a life of prayer. The praying mantis should be called the *preying* mantis because it's one of the most savage beasts of the insect world, but it certainly looks pious. The forelegs, which appear to be sanctimoniously folded in reverence, are really spike-lined lethal weapons. And the meditative pose helps the insect blend in with its surroundings so that potential prey suspect nothing.

When an insect, such as a grasshopper, inadvertently comes upon a mantis, the pious demeanor vanishes in a split second. The mantis rears up on its hind legs, hisses like a snake, and spreads its wings wide to appear larger than it is, paralyzing the grasshopper with fright just long enough for the monster to attack. One of the spiked legs falls on the grasshopper's midsection to hold it while the other leg strikes the head and pushes to turn the grasshopper over and expose the vulnerable underside. One bite, and the grasshopper hops no more. The feast begins, and about two hours later the mantis licks up the crumbs. Then it moves somewhere else to lie in wait again.

If a male mantis comes upon a female, she allows him to fertilize her eggs—then she bites off his head! Beginning at his neck, she works her way down his body, consuming him as eagerly as she would any other insect.

Some creatures in the natural world almost seem like perfect representations of the devil himself, and this insect is one of them. Satan tries to make you believe that he's an angel of light, and when you fall for his lies, he has you in his clutches. But—praise the Lord!—Jesus has done battle with the devil—and won. You can claim that victory as your own.

A WORD FROM OUR CREATOR

The Pharisee stood and prayed thus with himself, God, I thank thee, that I am not as other men are, extortioners, unjust, adulterers, or even as this publican. Luke 18:11.

August 26

Calling All Doodle-bugs

As an adult the long-bodied, cellophane-winged antlion does not eat ants. Instead, the insect gets its name from its habit of catching and eating ants when it's young. To further confuse the issue, when the creature is an ant-eating larva, it's not called an antlion—it is a "doodlebug."

You have undoubtedly seen doodlebugs. They are the funny-looking little insects that dig cone-shaped holes in sand. Sometimes their little pits riddle the ground. Each pit has its own doodlebug waiting at the bottom for an unsuspecting insect to stumble into the cone-shaped trap.

The doodlebug's excavating ability is an engineering marvel. When the tiny creature digs its pitfall trap, it may kick out as much as a cubic inch of sand—more than 100 times its own weight. To match this feat, you would have to shovel about eight tons of sand out of a hole in about a half hour.

But there is something even more interesting than its talent for digging. Mysteriously, the doodlebug comes when you call it. There are many versions of the doodlebug chant, but one from North Carolina goes like this: "Doodlebug, doodlebug, your house is on fire!" If you repeat that little ditty directly over the doodlebug's burrow, it will come out of hiding. In Arkansas a favorite chant says, "Oh, Johnny Doodlebug, come up and I'll give you a bushel of corn." People in Indiana have a less-complicated chant: "Doodlebug, doodlebug, doodle, doodle, doodle."

No one knows why the doodlebug leaves its pitfall trap when it hears one of these chants. But that mystery is no greater than the one that causes us to respond when our heavenly Father calls each of us out of the pit that we've dug for ourselves. Our actions only cause us to sink deeper, but when we respond to God's summons, Jesus reaches down and lifts us out of the pit of death and destruction to rejoice in eternal life.

A Word From Our Creator

[God] who hath saved us, and called us with an holy calling, not according to our works, but according to his own purpose and grace, which was given us in Christ Jesus. 2 Timothy 1:9.

ome people get depressed when they don't get enough light. According to some scientists, light has a profound effect on the immune system—that system in our bodies that helps us fight off disease. Such depression is a serious problem in the Far North, where during winter the sun doesn't rise above the horizon for long periods of time. We often call the resulting depression "cabin fever" because people once believed that it resulted from being confined inside during the cold weather. But now some scientists believe it is a symptom of light deprivation.

Our daily lives follow cycles that are slightly more than 24 hours long, and we have a clock in our brain that resets every day so that we don't get off schedule with the sun. Some people have greater difficulty adjusting to times of less light. They seem to need longer periods of bright light than other people. So doctors are beginning to experiment with using intense light as medicine—and it works.

Scientists aren't sure how light therapy operates. Light may have a positive effect on the light receptors in the brain. Your internal clock appears to be located in a tiny gland called the pineal body at the base of your brain. Strangely, it is not near the eyes or the optic nerve, yet light somehow seems to affect one or more different neural pathways other than the optic nerve. One of those pathways passes a gland called the hypothalamus and finally reaches the pineal body, where it tells your body's regulatory system that it's light or dark outside. Scientists want to know why the light passes through the hypothalamus on the way to the pineal body. The hypothalamus is an extremely important regulatory control center in your body, and light may play a part in that control. If that's true, it could explain why light deprivation causes negative side effects.

Could it be that depression and discouragement are the result not only of the lack of physical light but also a lack of spiritual light? Whenever you are feeling blue, let the rays of the Sun of righteousness, the Light of the world, into your spiritual control center.

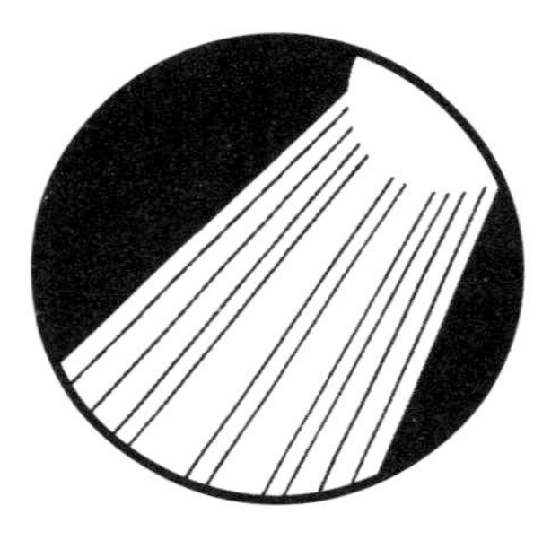

Light as a Prescription

A WORD FROM OUR CREATOR

But if thine eye be evil, thy whole body shall be full of darkness. If therefore the light that is in thee be darkness, how great is that darkness! Matthew 6:23.

August 28

The Point of a Diamond

A Word From Our Creator

The sin of Judah is written with a pen of iron, and with the point of a diamond: it is graven upon the table of their heart, and upon the horns of your altars. Jeremiah 17:1.

It is more likely that the gem translated as a diamond in this text actually was a very hard stone, such as flint. After filing the stone to a point, people used it to inscribe information on animal horns, metal, wood, and softer stones. Modern Bible translators wanted to emphasize the hardness of the stone, so they used the diamond to represent this quality.

The diamond is the hardest substance known. Nothing on earth in its natural state can scratch or scar a diamond except another diamond. Diamonds are also among the most valued of all gems, primarily because of the ways in which their crystals refract and reflect light. Surprisingly, diamonds are not all that rare. A group of companies own the best mines and can thus control the availability of the stones so as to keep the prices high. But all that may soon change.

John Angus of Case Western Reserve University in Cleveland, Ohio, has discovered how to make diamonds. While he was not the first to grow diamonds synthetically, his method is so much simpler than others that now we can manufacture diamonds more easily.

Angus uses an ordinary welder's torch, which combines oxygen and acetylene (pronounced ah-SET-ah-lin) gases to produce a flame. He directs the flame toward the surface of a metal called molybdenum (pronounced mo-LEB-den-um). A diamond is pure carbon, and the acetylene gas is carbon and hydrogen. The flame causes the hydrogen to break away from the carbon. Then the carbon atoms accumulate on the molybdenum. The atoms first form microscopic rings, then cross-links, and finally diamond crystals. It isn't as simple as it sounds, however. The gases have to be mixed just right and the flame has to be 6,300 °F while the molybdenum remains at a cool 1,600 °F.

We may eventually use diamonds as a coating on eyeglasses, knives, and car windows. And they will probably continue to serve as points to write on other hard surfaces. As suggested in today's text, something written by a diamond point cannot be erased. Satan would like for us to think that our sins are written down forever, but Jesus has decreed that He will blot them out—as only He can do.

AUGUST 29

A Spiny Shield

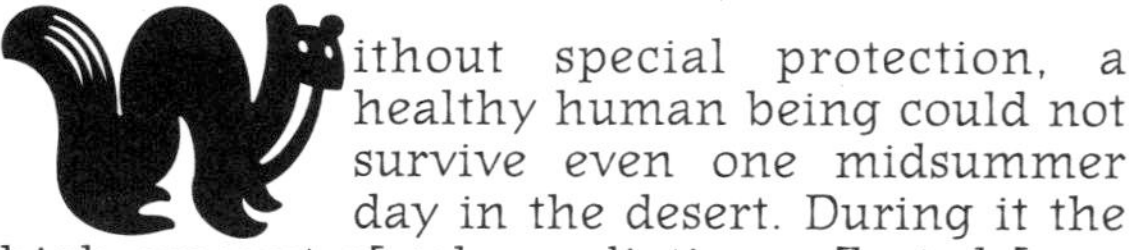

Without special protection, a healthy human being could not survive even one midsummer day in the desert. During it the high amount of solar radiation reflected from the desert floor can produce temperatures of up to 150°F (in sunlight). Nighttime temperatures that may be as much as 30 degrees lower follow the extreme heat. The desert soil doesn't absorb heat during the day, so it cannot return heat to the air at night. A person exposed to 15 hours of daytime heat would become dehydrated. Then the extreme temperature drop at night would bring on fatal shock.

Yet thousands of kinds of plants and animals are specially adapted to life in this hostile environment. Take the cactus, for example. The very aspect that makes it unfriendly—its spines—represents one of its primary means of survival.

Cactus spines may be smooth, curved, or barbed. Some are even hairy. Depending on the species of cactus, any number of spines may grow from the same spot. Some cacti have only one kind of spine, while others have as many as three kinds in various sorts and sizes.

Spines protect the cactus plant from the scalding sun by filtering the otherwise deadly rays. Acting together to form a screen, they can lower the temperature at the surface of the plant by 20 degrees or more. Since the spines can also retain heat, they help to keep the plant warm when the temperature drops at night.

Outer sheaths protect the spines themselves from the drying effects of the sun and wind, while an inner jellylike resin protects and preserves their hard cores.

Cactus spines are special. They shelter the plant from external harm while helping it to maintain a healthy, balanced life from within. Ever since sin entered the world in the Garden of Eden, earth has been a hostile environment for human beings. But just as God has provided protection for the cactus in the desert, so He has given us the cooling shade of His love and the life-giving water of His spirit. Jesus is our shield. He will protect us and provide for our every need.

A WORD FROM OUR CREATOR

They shall not hunger nor thirst; neither shall the heat nor sun smite them: for he that hath mercy on them shall lead them, even by the springs of water shall he guide them. Isaiah 49:10.

August 30

Life From Outer Space

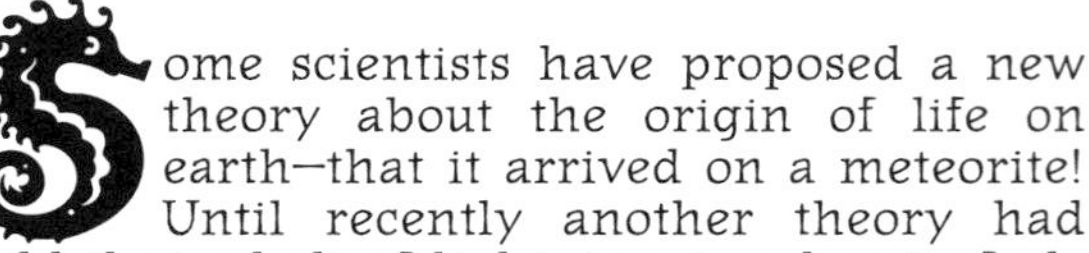

Some scientists have proposed a new theory about the origin of life on earth—that it arrived on a meteorite! Until recently another theory had held that a bolt of lightning or a burst of ultraviolet radiation bombarded simple molecules in the earth's atmosphere and converted them into the more complex organic molecules that became the basic building blocks for living organisms.

John Cronin and some of his associates, scientists at Arizona State University, have proposed that the first life on earth came from outer space aboard a space rock. As evidence for their idea, they point to a meteorite that fell in 1969 near the town of Murchison in Australia.

The Murchison meteorite contains amino acids, the organic molecules that form the building blocks of life. The molecules in the Murchison meteorite are different from any others that have ever landed on earth. Where in the universe did they come from? Is it possible that this piece of rock contains the remnants of living material from somewhere in space?

Writing in the science journal *Nature*, Cronin and his associates reported that the molecules contain deuterium (pronounced do-TEAR-ee-uhm) in similar proportions to those observed in interstellar dust clouds. From that observation, the scientists have decided that the molecules could be billions of years old—from a time when the galaxy was first forming.

Let's assume for a minute that they're correct. Where did the life in the space rock come from? Are we back to the lightning bolt again? Or is it possible that no matter how far back we go, we find ourselves forced to at least consider the possibility that life originated not by chance but by a creative act of God?

We believe that there is no sin elsewhere in the universe, and since death is the result of sin (Romans 6:23), there cannot be death in outer space. How, then, could dead molecules wind up in a space rock? But an amino acid molecule is not life. Only God can create a living thing.

A Word From Our Creator

For thus saith the Lord that created the heavens; God himself that formed the earth and made it; he hath established it, he created it not in vain, he formed it to be inhabited. Isaiah 45:18.

Have you ever felt that your problems were too big to handle? Have you ever bitten off more than you could chew, as the saying goes? A creature of the deep ocean reminds us of problems that we sometimes face. In this instance, however, we aren't sure whether it is the predator or the prey that is in worse trouble. See what you think.

Black gulpers are eels that live in the deepest parts of the ocean. They have slender bodies, huge jaws, and small eyes, and they can be more than six feet long. Gulpers can survive only at depths where the water pressure is so great that it would crush fish that live closer to the ocean's surface. If a gulper were to move up to a higher level, it would die.

The black gulper is a predator. In fact, it gets its name from its terrible table manners—it swallows its food whole. The fish's loosely attached jaws enable it to open its mouth as wide as the skin stretches. The gulper's body also expands to accommodate an oversized fish. After the eel has swallowed a meal, the food digests so slowly that the process may last several days. And therein lies a big problem for the gulper.

Once in a while the black gulper swallows a fish that fights to escape. For some reason, as the fish struggles inside the eel's rubbery stomach, it forces the gulper up out of its normal depth. Unfortunately, the unlucky fish inside the gulper does not escape, but it has its revenge in one way—that gulper will not live to eat again.

Have you ever found yourself trying to cope with a problem that was too big for you? Well, unlike the gulper, when you bite off more than you can chew, you have a Friend whom you can call on for help. On the other hand, maybe you feel more like the fish that the gulper swallowed. You struggle and struggle, but it doesn't seem to do any good. The problem won't go away. Well, here too, as Jonah found out, you have a friend in Jesus, and He is waiting for your call.

In this world of sin we can be either predator or prey—it doesn't matter which. Without Jesus, death is the only option. But He has given us life. All we have to do is ask for it.

August 31

The Black Gulper

A Word From Our Creator

When my soul fainted within me I remembered the Lord: and my prayer came in unto thee, into thine holy temple. Jonah 2:7.

September 1

The Tongue

Without your tongue you couldn't taste. Its taste buds allow you to distinguish salty, sour, sweet, and bitter flavors. And without your tongue you wouldn't be able to chew or swallow easily, because the muscles in the tongue direct your food to your teeth and down your throat.

Can you roll your tongue? The gecko not only rolls its tongue but also uses it to clean the transparent membrane that covers its eyeball. Can you touch your nose with your tongue? Dogs, cats, and other mammals wash their faces by sweeping their long tongues not only over their noses but also over the rest of their faces.

Some amphibians and reptiles have specialized tongues that help them to obtain food. For example, the extremely long tongues of frogs and chameleons have a coating of sticky saliva. When a frog spies a fly, it flicks its tongue outward, traps the insect, and flips the meal into its mouth.

The alligator snapping turtle uses a pink, wormlike projection on its tongue as a lure. This huge freshwater turtle lies in the mud at the bottom of a lake or river with its mouth open. Then it wiggles the projection and waits for a fish to take the bait. When the fish starts to nibble the "worm," the turtle snaps its mouth shut. To track a mouse, lizard, or bird, a snake uses its forked tongue to pick up scent particles from the air and ground. Then the snake inserts the tip of the tongue into two pits in the roof of its mouth that act as organs of smell. By continuing to take readings this way, the snake locates its prey.

Like other creatures, we use our tongues to obtain and process food. But we also employ them for speech. Our tongue helps us to form sounds. But that can be dangerous. James wrote, "The tongue can no man tame; it is an unruly evil" (James 3:8). Perhaps he was speaking from experience. Scripture calls one person named James and his brother John the "sons of thunder" because of their temper and sharp tongues. If this James was the same person as the writer of the epistle, Jesus gave him a new heart and helped him to control his tongue. When you sometimes speak before you think, He can do the same for you.

A Word From Our Creator

If any man among you seem to be religious, and bridleth not his tongue, but deceiveth his own heart, this man's religion is vain. James 1:26.

ama Raccoon and four little ones made up the family living under Harriett Weaver's cabin in the woods. For young raccoons, every waking moment is raccoon school.

One night Mama decided that it was time to introduce the youngsters to humans. Harriett had known that the family was living under the house because she could hear them chattering and banging against things as they rolled and tussled, but she had never seen them. Mama Raccoon had kept them carefully out of sight.

Deliberately, Mama now led the little guys up onto the porch and over to the kitchen door, where she lined them up so they could peer into Harriett's kitchen. All the while Mama quietly but constantly chattered to them. Of course Harriett couldn't understand what the mother raccoon was telling her children, but as she watched them sitting there in a row and looking into her kitchen, she was fascinated by the display of order and attention that the little raccoons displayed.

Suddenly one of the little ones misbehaved, and Mama turned to him. She gave him a mighty cuffing that set him crying. Then, nose-to-nose, Mama told the boy what was what and then ordered the whole family off the porch. At the corner of the house, she stopped the offender and gave him another talking-to. This time she apparently told him that he must learn his lesson the hard way: he would stay home alone tonight while she took his brothers and sisters to the creek for hunting class.

It was a sad but telling picture. Mama and three little raccoons ambled off into the dark woods, leaving one behind to think about his behavior. He spent the next two hours trudging around and around the house, crying at the top of his little lungs. But he didn't make the slightest attempt to run after his mother. Mama had said stay home, and he did.

Raccoon mothers mean what they say. For them it is a matter of life and death. Some of the little ones learn easily, and some have to discover things the hard way. How about you? Do you learn easily how to behave? Or are you someone who often has to find out the hard way?

Raccoon Discipline

A Word From Our Creator

Foolishness is bound in the heart of a child; but the rod of correction shall drive it far from him. Proverbs 22:15.

SEPTEMBER 3

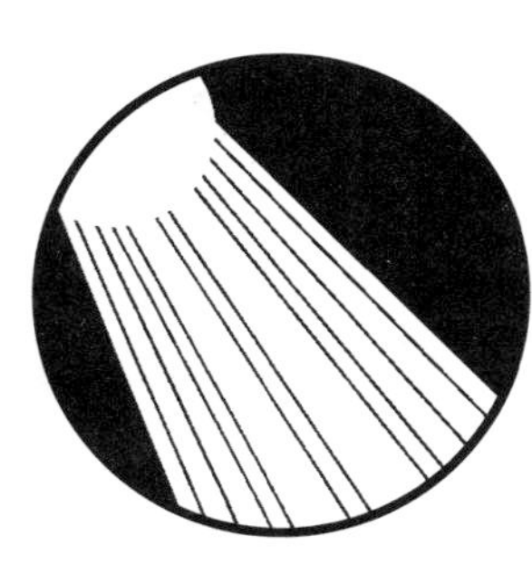

Zeitgeber

eitgeber (pronounced ZITE-gay-ber) is a German word meaning "giver of time" or "time cue." Scientists who study our body's natural rhythms often use it. We have a built-in clock that operates naturally on a daily schedule about 25 hours long. Since the world operates on a 24-hour schedule, we would soon get way out of whack if we didn't have a *zeitgeber* to reset our body clocks every day.

A *zeitgeber* is an outside signal that tells our body what time it is. As it turns out, the zeitgeber for our bodies is light, but it has to be a very bright light. Normally it is sunlight. The daily cycle of the sun produces enough light to reset our body clock every day.

You have probably heard about "jet lag," the condition that occurs when you travel quickly across several time zones and your body clock has not had time to catch up. It usually takes several days to get adjusted to the new time schedule.

One of the primary methods of correcting jet lag turns out to be very bright artificial light. To use this method, you begin in advance of your trip to create a new schedule of daylight. If you're going to travel west, you should place yourself in the presence of an unusually bright light later into the evening each day and sleep in a darkened room later each morning. But if you're going east, you should place yourself under a very bright light earlier and earlier each morning and retire earlier in the evening to a darkened room. In this way the artificial light becomes the *zeitgeber*, resetting you to the new daily rhythm of the sun's light at the place where you're going. Interestingly, bright light in the middle of the day has virtually no effect on your internal clock.

This world is also on a schedule. The *Zeitgeber*—the Giver of time—will reset the history of our world. "At the time appointed the end shall be" (Daniel 8:19). Jesus will return. "His glory covered the heavens. . . . And his brightness was as the light" (Habakkuk 3:3, 4). "And then shall that Wicked be revealed, whom the Lord shall . . . destroy with the brightness of his coming" (2 Thessalonians 2:8). Is Jesus the *Zeitgeber* of *your* life?

A WORD FROM OUR CREATOR

Watch therefore, for ye know neither the day nor the hour wherein the Son of man cometh. Matthew 25:13.

September 4

Scintil-lation

Did you ever wonder why the stars twinkle? Did you know that the twinkling is stronger in the winter than at other times of the year? The technical name for the twinkling of stars is scintillation (pronounced SIN-till-A-shun). "Scintillating" is another form of the word.

The temperatures of different layers of air between you and a point of light in the sky causes the scintillation, or twinkling. Since the light has to pass through air, stars low on the horizon tend to twinkle more than those higher in the sky. If you pay attention on a dark night to stars near the horizon, you may be lucky to see several other exhibitions of how the air plays tricks on us. You also may see stars do more than twinkle—you may see them change colors and appear to jump from place to place. Again, such things happen because the starlight has to travel through more air.

Scintillation occurs when light rays pass through the earth's atmosphere on their way to your eyes. Layers of air with different temperatures surround the earth. The atmosphere is like a giant sandwich of many such layers. Not only that, but the layers of air move in different directions. They undulate like a flock of birds in flight. Starlight coming to you through such layers scintillates. But why?

Air of a certain temperature also has a corresponding density—that is, it has a certain proportion of molecules to the amount of space available. Each density causes light rays to bend at an angle specific to that density. So the light coming through several layers of air with different temperatures will constantly get bent back and forth. Consequently, the light appears to dance before your eyes. It is really quite scintillating!

Our society idolizes movie stars, rock stars, Broadway stars, and sports stars. The news media often refer to them as "scintillating," meaning that they have characteristics that cause them to shine on the world's stage. But our text makes it clear what characteristics scintillate on God's stage. What are they?

A Word From Our Creator

And they that be wise shall shine as the brightness of the firmament; and they that turn many to righteousness as the stars for ever and ever. Daniel 12:3.

September 5

Passion Vines

We see God's original diet for living things in this text. Most of the creatures on earth still exist on a vegetarian diet, and the fascinating interrelationships between plants and animals illustrate how plants produce food for wild creatures.

Of the 400 or so species of passion vines, each one has a specialized flower. The flower attracts a particular pollinating agent, like a hummingbird or a bee, and at the same time protects its nectar from other insects and birds that might also want to collect it.

Only hummingbirds can polinate one kind of passion vine, *Passiflora vitifolia*. It produces its nectar deep in the throat of a tube-shaped blossom. *Vitifolia*'s nectar also attracts insects who would enter the flower and drink the sugary substance without pollinating it. So, to protect its nectar supply for the pollinating hummingbirds, *vitifolia* has a trumpetlike corona that prevents any probe except the hummingbird's long bill from getting to the nectar.

But stingless bees aren't so easily discouraged. Although they want *vitifolia*'s nectar, they are the wrong size and shape to pollinate the flower. Because of the corona the bees can't get to the nectar from the front. So the resourceful stingless bee goes to the back of the flower and chews holes directly into the pool of nectar. That is, it does so if it can get past the flower's guards.

To defend itself from the determined bees, *vitifolia* pays ants and wasps to act as guards. The ants and wasps sip nectar that the plant has stored in tiny cups in its leaves. In return, the insects defend the plant by driving off invaders, including the stingless bees, and by removing the eggs and larvae of other insects as well.

Passiflora vitifolia not only illustrates several ways that animal life forms use plant food; it also shows several ways that the Creator has provided for plant and animal adaptation so that they can cope with the results of sin. Jesus has also provided for our livelihood, even though sin's effects surround us on every side.

A Word From Our Creator

And to every beast of the earth, and to every fowl of the air, and to every thing that creepeth upon the earth, wherein there is life, I have given every green herb for meat. Genesis 1:30.

September 6

Titan

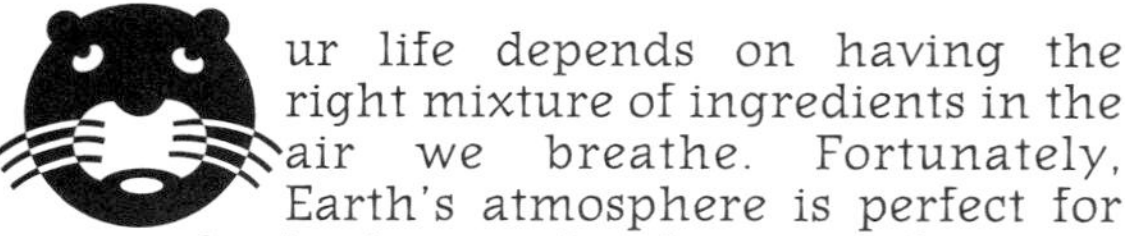

Our life depends on having the right mixture of ingredients in the air we breathe. Fortunately, Earth's atmosphere is perfect for our needs. As they study planetary objects in space, scientists stay on the lookout for another atmosphere that would allow us to breathe without wearing a space suit. Perhaps the closest that we've come to date is the discovery that Titan, one of Saturn's moons, actually has an atmosphere that might support an Earthling. Here are the facts.

Titan, the biggest of Saturn's moons, is much larger than Earth's moon. In fact, Titan is bigger than either Mercury or Pluto. But what sets Titan apart isn't its size but the fact that it's the only one of the over 50 moons in the solar system that has much of an atmosphere.

According to data transmitted back to Earth from the space probe *Voyager*, Titan's atmosphere consists mostly of nitrogen, as ours does. And closer to the surface we find significant amounts of other gases, like argon and methane, that are also present in Earth's atmosphere. Titan is wrapped in a permanent blanket of clouds that scientists say is methane smog. Perhaps it's not that different from the air over Los Angeles.

Voyager wasn't able to "see" through the fog to the surface, so we don't know what's there. Some astronomers believe that the surface is an ocean of liquid methane gas. Others are just as sure that it's a hard surface with methane rain and methane snow. But just about everyone agrees that the surface of Titan is a dark and gloomy ice-covered place. Whatever light reaches the surface has to pass through reddish clouds.

But don't pack your bags yet. Even if you could breathe on Titan, you might want to consider the temperature there. Scientists estimated that the atmosphere at the surface of Titan is colder than -200°F.

Titan is like a planet in a deep freeze. Could it be that the planets and their moons are raw materials just waiting for the Creator's touch?

A Word From Our Creator

God that made the world and all things therein, seeing that he is Lord of heaven and earth, dwelleth not in temples made with hands.
Acts 17:24.

September 7

Weed Milk

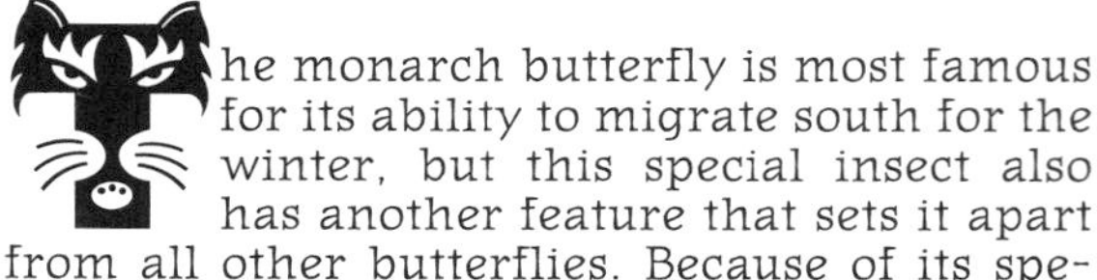

The monarch butterfly is most famous for its ability to migrate south for the winter, but this special insect also has another feature that sets it apart from all other butterflies. Because of its specific diet both as a caterpillar and as an adult butterfly, the monarch is one of the most protected of all creatures.

Monarch caterpillars eat only the leaves of milkweeds and nightshades. Both types of plants contain milky, foul-tasting, poisonous juices. As the caterpillars feed on these juices, they store the toxic substances from the plants in their bodies. The toxins continue to accumulate throughout the different stages of development from caterpillar to chrysalis to the adult monarch. It is at the adult stage that the Creator has provided the monarch with double protection.

The adult monarch no longer feeds on plant juices from the leaves. Instead it now sips the nectar of flowers. And by so doing, the butterfly adds other poisons, called alkaloids, to the already-stored toxins from the milkweed and nightshade plants. Thus, the monarch uses two completely different chemical protections at different stages of its life, a practice extremely rare in nature.

A butterfly's primary predators are birds, but when a bird tries to eat a monarch, either as a caterpillar, a chrysalis, or as an adult, the bird suffers from severe, painful indigestion. Studies with captive birds show that after it has eaten a single distasteful monarch, you can't tempt even the hungriest bird to eat another one. One dedicated and curious scientist who decided to sample a monarch for taste reported that it had the flavor of dry toast.

The monarch provides a wonderful example of the protection that God has given to His creatures. When the butterfly follows the instincts that the Creator gave it, it finds itself guarded for life. The monarch sincerely feeds on the milk of the weed. As followers of the same God, you and I receive protection from the earth's primary predator, the devil, by sincerely feeding on what the Bible calls "the sincere milk of the word."

A Word From Our Creator

As newborn babes, desire the sincere milk of the word, that ye may grow thereby. 1 Peter 2:2.

In ant colonies, industrious worker ants put out the trash, carrying decayed vegetation and discarded seed husks to the surface. Having trash duty also includes being responsible for removing the bodies of dead ants. Ants don't live forever, and if they weren't taken out, they would begin to accumulate in the halls and in the various rooms of the colony—that would be a mess. But the ants have the problem covered.

Ants communicate almost entirely by scent, and they use an intricate language of scent messages. All the activities in an ant colony, including all the assigned chores that ants carry out so faithfully, originate as a chemical message that workers of the colony receive through the sense of smell. Each different scent message is a particular chemical compound called a pheromone (pronounced FAIR-a-mone). Ants transfer pheromones to each other. For example, the queen ant gives an identification pheromone to every member of the colony so that it can recognize other members of the colony. If you are an ant and you don't smell right, the colony will drive you out.

One of the most interesting scent-messages is the special pheromone that an ant gives off when it dies. This message tells the other ants to dispose of the body. Scientists discovered this pheromone not long ago, and to prove its function, they performed an experiment. First they isolated the dead-ant pheromone and smeared it on a living ant. Then they watched as the workers assigned to trash duty promptly picked up the live ant and carried it out to the trash heap. As far as they were concerned, it was a dead ant because it smelled like one. Of course, the ant was very much alive and promptly returned to work, whereupon the trash detail grabbed it again and returned it to the Ant Town dump. Naturally it returned to the colony. This went on until the dead-ant pheromone evaporated from the living ant.

The ants provide us with a living example of cleanliness, cooperation, and dedication to duty. The ant's house has no untidy rooms.

Trash Duty

A Word From Our Creator

Go to the ant, thou sluggard; consider her ways, and be wise: which having no guide, overseer, or ruler, provideth her meat in the summer, and gathereth her food in the harvest. Proverbs 6:6-8.

SEPTEMBER 9

A Blue Grouse Experience

It happened one morning on the Pacific Crest Trail in the Mount Hood wilderness area of northwestern Oregon. My friend Monty Church had a special place that he wanted me to see.

"Jim," he said as we hiked up the trail, "you're going to see something you'll never forget." Even Monty didn't know how true that was going to be.

The virgin forest surrounded us like a misty shroud. Songs of varied thrushes and hermit thrushes echoed through the forest, winter wrens scolded us, and a hermit warbler sang overhead. It was one of those mornings where the air tingled with anticipation.

Suddenly we emerged from the forest onto a steep alpine meadow carpeted with flowers. And there, looming before us in all its majestic splendor, was Mount Hood, the highest peak in Oregon (11,239 feet). I gazed in awe at the sight. In the foreground spread a myriad of wildflowers in yellows and blues accented profusely with the red of Indian paintbrush. And behind that frame was a sea of green forest supporting the towering snow-laden peak with its multiple shades of purple, blue, and white. Mists rose from the streams below to evaporate in the still, pure air that surrounded us.

Then it happened. Monty spotted a blue grouse chick. As if on cue, two chicks began calling softly to an unseen parent. Then the adult male materialized right before our eyes. He had been there all the time—just 30 feet from us—but by remaining motionless he was virtually invisible. The chicks flew a short distance, and the adult marched slowly and deliberately up the mountainside. Surrounded by the sky blue of lupine in a perfectly framed picture of mountain tranquillity, he stopped to study us.

I started to whistle softly in the language of the blue grouse chicks. With a start the adult grouse came quickly toward me, clucking loudly, and then took wing and flew past my head and up into a fir tree nearby. Did he think that I was a lost chick needing his protection? From the fir tree he studied me and continued to cluck his messages of reassurance. I'll always wonder what I said in grouse that day.

A WORD FROM OUR CREATOR

O Lord, thou preservest man and beast. How excellent is thy loving-kindness, O God! therefore the children of men put their trust under the shadow of thy wings.
Psalm 36:6, 7.

What if that text were to read "He maketh me to lie down in purple pastures"? How would you feel about purple grass?

Why is the grass green? We know that plants have been green from the beginning, because at Creation, Jesus said, "I have given every green herb for meat" (Genesis 1:30). You may wonder why anyone would question that fact. But evolutionary theory has a problem with green plants.

Visible sunlight arrives on earth in an array of different energy levels that we see as different colors ranging from red through orange, yellow, and green to blue. Different kinds of jobs require different energy levels. And God gave the plants the task of producing food, which is stored energy. The color you see on leaves is the color of the energy level that they don't use—the plants just reflect it back.

Living plants look green because of a substance called chlorophyll, the energy-producing part of plants. By a process called photosynthesis, the chlorophyll uses sunlight to produce food. But the plants don't use all the available sunlight in this process. If they did, plants would appear *black* because they would absorb all light energy. As it turns out, the process of photosynthesis uses both red, yellow, and blue light waves of sunlight, but it doesn't absorb the green energy level of light. The green gets reflected—making grassy pastures look green.

Since the color green appears in the center of the spectrum of visible light (between blue and yellow), it would have been a lot easier for plants to evolve the ability to use that color and to reflect the red and blue. For that reason, Andrew Goldsworthy of Imperial College, in London, has proposed that plants were originally purple. According to Dr. Goldsworthy the green in plants is a recent development in evolution. Imagine, if you can, tropical islands of purple palm trees. Instead of evergreens, we would have everpurples.

From the beginning the plants have provided the cooling and refreshing color green to soothe the nerves and quiet the soul. To make it so, the Creator had to provide the plants with a more complex physiology from the start.

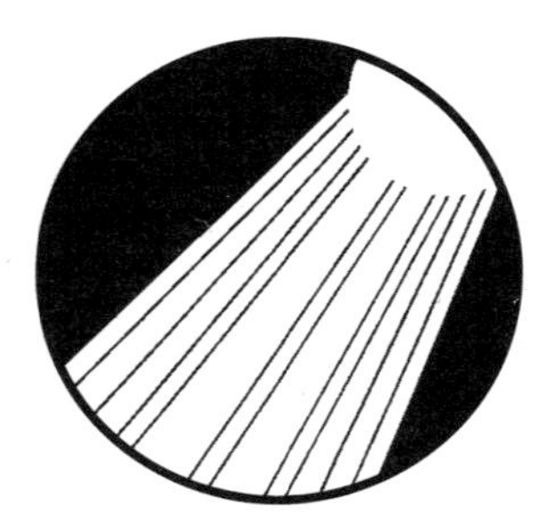

Green Light

A Word From Our Creator

He maketh me to lie down in green pastures: he leadeth me beside the still waters.
Psalm 23:2.

The Dew

God is wonderful in the way He teaches us about Himself. Some people would like to hit you over the head with what they call "The Truth." They want to cram it down your throat because "it's good for you." Have you known people like that? Well, God's way is different. His instruction comes like the dew.

When you wake up in the morning, there it is. You didn't hear or see it happen. Without your even realizing it was going on, the dew formed. Even on the driest day in the desert, the morning dew collects on plants. It fills the flower cups of desert plants, and birds come to drink its life-giving substance. Small creatures lick the dewdrops from the leaves, the only moisture that some will ever drink. Where does that water come from in the middle of the desert?

Air holds water. The clear air that you breathe has water in it—pure H_2O. The amount varies. The weather forecaster reports the amount of water in the air as a "relative humidity" measure. When the relative humidity is 100 percent, the air has as much water as it can hold without its turning into rain. A relative humidity of 50 percent means that the air has half the water that it can hold. And so forth.

Cool air can't hold as much moisture as warm air can. When the air cools down to a point where it can no longer retain all the water that it contains, it must release some of it. Sometimes it comes out in the form of a cloud in the sky or fog close to the ground. But more often it appears as dew.

At the point during the night that the air cools down to what the weather forecaster calls the "dew point," water begins to collect on solid objects. The water continues to form droplets until the sun comes up and warms up the air so that it can absorb the dew again through evaporation. The process is a gentle one that waters plants and gives creatures a morning drink.

That is the way God teaches you. As you read His Word and listen to His Spirit, God instructs you quietly and gently. Before you know it, you realize the way you should go and how you should act.

A Word From Our Creator

My doctrine shall drop as the rain, my speech shall distil as the dew, as the small rain upon the tender herb, and as the showers upon the grass. Deuteronomy 32:2.

Sunflowers

If ever a flower illustrated the wisdom described in this text, it is the sunflower. The approximately 70 kinds of sunflowers range in size from the small wood sunflower, with its one-inch-diameter blossom, to the giant sunflower, which measures more than a foot across. The flowers grow on stalks 12 feet tall or more, and no matter what the size of the blossom, one can easily identify them by their seed-laden flower heads surrounded by rays of yellow, orange, or red petals.

American Indians valued the sunflower as a food and medicinal plant. They ate the meaty seed kernels and rubbed them between smooth stones to make a flour to bake into cakes. Also they made medicine from the plant to cure rattlesnake bites and to ease chest pains. Some tribes used the juice from freshly crushed sunflower stems to cover wounds. The sticky juice hardened to form a bandage. The Indians pounded the seeds and boiled the resulting paste to separate the oil, then used the oil to season food, groom their hair, and serve as a base for the skin paint they wore during special ceremonies. They even extracted yellow dye from the petals and purple dye from the seeds, dyes used to color their baskets and decorate their bodies.

Today the sunflower is still an important crop. The oil is a healthy substitute for animal fats, and the seeds provide a high-protein snack and medicine for coughs, colds, and other chest problems. In addition, various parts of the plant serve in the manufacture of ethyl alcohol, fuel, and building materials, and as a coffee substitute.

Perhaps the most remarkable trait of the sunflower has nothing to do with its commercial use but with its habit of following the sun. You can almost see the hundreds of thousands of blossoms in a field of sunflower plants slowly pivot to keep the sun's light shining full on their upturned faces.

We are like sunflowers in God's harvest field. As long as we are constantly looking to Jesus, "the Sun of righteousness" (Malachi 4:2), God imparts His wisdom to us in His service.

A WORD FROM OUR CREATOR

Wisdom is good with an inheritance: and by it there is profit to them that see the sun. Ecclesiastes 7:11.

September 13

Uranus

Sir William Herschel at first thought that he had located a comet. What he actually discovered in 1781 turned out to be a new planet—the first in recorded history. What do we know about this mysterious planet?

1. Uranus is the seventh planet from the sun. It takes sunlight about 2.7 hours to travel the almost two billion miles to get there.

2. Uranus is about 32,000 miles in diameter, making it the third-largest planet in our solar system. Currently we have discovered at least five rings and 15 moons circling it.

3. Uranus takes 84 Earth-years to orbit the sun, traveling at about 15,000 miles per hour. If you were to grow up on Uranus and count years as we do, you would have to live 840 Earth-years to be 10 years old.

4. Uranus moves through space on its side like a ball rolling along on an axis almost pointing toward the sun. Because the poles are sideways compared to the rest of the planets, it has no year-round day-night sequence as we know it on Earth. For a quarter of its year, one half the planet has daylight all the time, and for another quarter of the year, the other half of the planet has daylight all the time. During the two other quarters, day and night alternate somewhat as they do on Earth.

5. The surface gravity of Uranus is 90 percent of what it is on Earth. If you weigh 100 pounds on Earth, you would weigh about 90 pounds on Uranus. (That happens to be the same as it is on Venus, by the way.)

6. The upper atmosphere of the planet consists of methane gas along with hydrogen and helium. At the highest altitudes, winds blow around the planet at about 440 miles per hour. The atmosphere is about 5,000 miles thick. If you could survive a trip through that "air," you would probably splash down into a sea of boiling water and ammonia. Uranus would not be a great place for a vacation.

Uranus certainly cannot support life as we know it, but remember that Earth was not habitable before Creation. It was "without form, and void" (Genesis 1:2). God can turn even the most toxic and inhospitable planet into a paradise, just as He can take the most wicked sinners and mold them into His image.

A Word From Our Creator

Can any hide himself in secret places that I shall not see him? saith the Lord. Do not I fill heaven and earth? saith the Lord.
Jeremiah 23:24.

We take it for granted that boys grow up to be men and girls mature to be women. That's the way it has been from the beginning, but that's not the way it is with all of God's creatures.

The males and females of many tropical fish look nothing like each other. In fact, the differences are so dramatic that confused marine biologists originally classified the males and females of several parrot fishes, wrasses, angelfishes, gobies, damselfishes, and anemone fishes as separate species.

Eventually, though, scientists were able to sort males and females into the correct pairs. For example, they discovered that while the female bluehead wrasse is yellow, the male is royal blue, with black and white bands circling the front part of its body. They noted that the stoplight parrot fish female has a blue-green head, white body scales outlined in black, and a red belly, tail, and fins. The male, however, is bright aqua. And they found that the male and female of the Mexican hogfish differ not only in color, but also in body shape. Silver-blue scales outlined in black cover the body of the female. Lengthwise black lines stripe her body, and she is shaped much like a trout. The male is blue-gray, and he has a bump on his forehead and long, wispy fins.

Even more remarkable than the color differences in these tropical fish is that every one of them is born female. As they change color, they also change gender. Biologists suggest that certain fish do not become males until they are large enough to compete for females and father offspring. While awaiting the right time to be a male, the fish carries out the role of the female—that is, it lays eggs.

Other fish change from male to female. In these species males become females when they can produce a large number of eggs. The larger the fish, the more eggs she lays. A few species change back and forth—from male to female to male—to be whatever best serves the population. Some switch gender several times a day!

Aren't you glad that you're not a fish?

It's a Boy! No, It's a Girl! No, Wait . . . !

A WORD FROM OUR CREATOR

And the rib, which the Lord God had taken from man, made he a woman, and brought her unto the man. Genesis 2:22.

SEPTEMBER 15

Profitable Pinnipeds

Pinnipeds are the finlike flippered creatures that we know by the general names of seals, sea lions, and walruses. True seals (those with no visible ears) hunch along the ground as caterpillars do and use only their rear flippers for swimming. Eared seals (those with visible ears) use all four limbs—front and rear flippers—to walk on land and ice, but they use only their front flippers for swimming. (Sea lions belong to this family.) Walruses have visible ears and walk like eared seals, but they swim like true seals.

Humans have relied on seals as a food source since ancient times, but it wasn't until the eighteenth and nineteenth centuries that human greed posed a threat to them. Unfortunately, the characteristics that allow the pinniped to survive in the cold oceans almost led to the complete extinction of several of the world's 34 seal species.

Like whales, seals are insulated with a layer of blubber to keep their internal organs warm when the animals swim in frigid water. For added warmth, seals also have fur—thus wearing a sort of overcoat over their blubbery "long underwear."

Hunters killed the animals for their pelts, which provided fur and leather, and for their protective blubber, which human beings processed into oil for lamps. Walruses added their ivory tusks to the merchandising, and sea lions provided 16-inch-long whiskers, ideal for cleaning opium pipes. By the mid-1800s many populations of pinnipeds had become "economically extinct"—that is, it was no longer financially profitable to hunt seals. Luckily, the slaughter stopped just in time to save the endangered seals from extinction, and now government regulations protect them.

Human greed can lead to the elimination of God's creatures. In fact, greed can lead to the loss of the very reward that people are seeking! By killing off the seals, nineteenth-century hunters were eliminating the source of their wealth. When are we going to learn that the wealth we *really* need is the wisdom and knowledge that God alone can give us? When we do, we will be rich with His love, wealthy with His grace, and honorable in His presence.

A WORD FROM OUR CREATOR

Wisdom and knowledge is granted unto thee; and I will give thee riches, and wealth, and honour, such as none of the kings have had that have been before thee, neither shall there any after thee have the like.
2 Chronicles 1:12.

A direct relationship exists between our mood and how we hold our head. Have you ever noticed how when people are sad or discouraged they go around with their heads down and their shoulders stooped? By that posture they send a message that says, "I'm so miserable! Things are bad. All I have are troubles."

David wrote about that feeling in Psalm 40:12. "For innumerable evils have compassed me about: mine iniquities have taken hold upon me, so that I am not able to look up; they are more than the hairs of mine head: therefore my heart faileth me." He felt so bad that it left him *unable to look up*. But David knew how to get over that feeling, because in the very next verse he says, "Be pleased, O Lord, to deliver me: O Lord, make haste to help me" (verse 13).

One day friends took a discouraged and miserable blind man to Jesus. The Saviour laid His hands on the man's eyes. "After that he put his hands again upon his eyes, and made him look up: and he was restored, and saw every man clearly" (Mark 8:25). It says that Jesus "made him look up."

Why do you think our language uses the word "down" to indicate discouragement and misery? Do you suppose that even our words tell us something about our natural inclinations? It's really hard to be discouraged when you look up to the sky, the mountains, the trees, the sunshine. But when you stare at the ground, all you see is the dirt, the trash that has fallen, your feet trudging along in life.

Science has found evidence of an actual connection between your mood and the angle of inclination of your head. Just the mere act of looking up will sometimes improve your attitude. Of course, it isn't a magic cure, and it won't necessarily make an angry person happy, but it's worth a try. When you're feeling down, try looking up. But don't go around stoop-shouldered and try to look up. Throw your shoulders back, take a deep breath, and praise the Lord.

Christians, of all the people on earth, have a reason to look up and be glad. First we look up to the cross and accept the sacrifice that Jesus made for us. Then we look up in hope, waiting for His return. So keep looking up!

Lift Up Your Head

A Word From Our Creator

And when these things begin to come to pass, then look up, and lift up your heads; for your redemption draweth nigh. Luke 21:28.

September 17

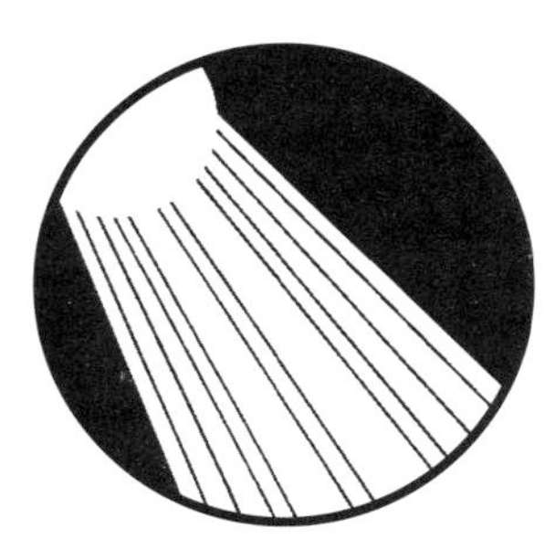

The Marfa Lights

Along Highway 67 east of the West Texas town of Marfa is a spot where during many nights of the year you can see what people have called the "Marfa lights." As you look southwest toward the Chinati Mountains, you may see small flickering balls of light flash across the sky. They move so fast that attempts to determine how far away they are have failed. And like a rainbow, if you try to approach them, they always seem to be in the distance until they disappear.

The first record of the Marfa lights dates from 1883 when a cowboy driving cattle through Paisano Pass saw a flickering light and thought that it might be an Apache Indian campfire. Through the years the mystery grew. Some thought that the lights were the ghosts of conquistadores who roamed the deserted plains, still searching for gold. Others suggested that the lights were moonlight reflecting off veins of mica—or even some yet-to-be discovered phosphorescent jackrabbits! The mysterious Marfa lights baffled scientists for more than a hundred years before someone finally explained them.

The West Texas plains are high—almost a mile above sea level—and dry. Consequently, at night the ground cools quickly, forming a layer of cool air close to the surface. A sharply defined boundary occurs between the cool air and the warmer air above. That boundary acts like a mirror to reflect the rays of far-distant lights back to the ground. The Marfa lights can be the reflection of stars at or just above the horizon, car headlights many miles away, or lights from a distant ranch house. The lights shift about for either of two reasons. The objects emitting the lights may be moving, as in the case of cars. But more likely, the air masses are constantly moving, and that means the level of the mirror effect shifts as well.

Bible prophecies may seem mysterious or even frightening to many people, but they are steady dependable lights in the darkness, pointing the way to Jesus, the Light of the world, who "cometh down from the Father of lights, with whom is no variableness" (James 1:17).

A Word From Our Creator

We have also a more sure word of prophecy; whereunto ye do well that ye take heed, as unto a light that shineth in a dark place, until the day dawn.
2 Peter 1:19.

If you get high above the earth and look down on it, you'll see clouds over part of the planet. Why is it that you can't see through a cloud, when everything in it is colorless? All the gases in the air are colorless, and the tiny droplets that make up the cloud are water, which is also colorless. So you should be able to see through the cloud, right?

When seen from space, the earth appears as a beautiful sphere of blues, greens, and whites. As you get closer to the planet, other colors begin to appear, except where there are clouds—there the areas are still white, and the thicker the clouds, the whiter they appear to the space traveler.

The reason for all of this is water and its effect on incoming light from the sun. More and more water accumulates in the air until the atmosphere finally cannot hold it all. Then the water molecules get together in such numbers that they form tiny droplets visible as clouds. As more and more droplets gather, the clouds become thicker and thicker.

But that still doesn't explain why you can't see through the clouds, when water is a clear liquid. After all, you can see through water in a clear stream or in the ocean, and such bodies have far more of it than do any cloud. But in a cloud each tiny droplet of water acts as a lens and a mirror at the same time. The droplets scatter the light before it hits the ground, thus obliterating what we normally would be able to see. In fact, when sunlight hits a cloud, about 25 percent of it gets reflected back into space. So when a perfectly clear substance like water hangs suspended between the space traveler and the ground, it blots out the view of the ground, and we can see only white light.

That is what God does for each of us. Jesus is the Water of life (John 4:10), and He clothes us with His righteousness so that it blots our sins out, leaving only the Light of the world visible any longer (John 8:12).

Thick Clouds

A Word From Our Creator

I have blotted out, as a thick cloud, thy transgressions, and, as a cloud, thy sins: return unto me; for I have redeemed thee. Isaiah 44:22.

Cranberry Judgment

Because the stems of the fruit curve like the neck of a crane, the name cranberry comes from "craneberry." And because a bog has so much plant material, its soil is highly acidic—the perfect soil for growing cranberries. In the United States the top cranberry-growing states are Massachusetts and Wisconsin, but New Jersey and Washington also have commercial cranberry bogs.

Growers flood cranberry bogs during much of the year to protect the vines from drying out, from insects, and from the freezing and thawing of early winter. Harvesting begins in late September and continues through autumn. Some pickers use special wooden scoops with rakelike tines to comb the ripe cranberries out of the vines while others use motor-driven picking machines. They put the berries into boxes and take them to the packing houses to be judged for quality.

The "sound berries" get packed in boxes or bags for sale as whole berries or to use to make juice, jelly, sauce, relish, and to string as garlands for the Christmas tree. The packing house discards the berries of lesser quality. To be a "sound berry," a cranberry has to pass the bounce test. The packing house drops every berry from a height of six inches onto an angled board, from which it bounces toward a barrier about three inches high. The firm and fresh berries pass over the barrier while the bruised or rotten ones do not. Machines at the packing plants drop more than 90 tons of cranberries each hour.

Every cranberry gets dropped seven times. After seven chances, if a berry doesn't make it over the barrier it's discarded. How would you like to be a cranberry and know that you had seven chances to pass a test? If you miss the seventh chance, you don't get another one.

Aren't you glad Jesus doesn't treat us as we do cranberries? How many times do we fail in life? Certainly, more than seven. Yet Jesus continues to love us and tell us, "Neither do I condemn thee: go, and sin no more" (John 8:11).

A Word From Our Creator

Then came Peter to him, and said, Lord, how oft shall my brother sin against me, and I forgive him? till seven times? Matthew 18:21.

September 20

Neptune

Astronomers discovered Neptune by using mathematics. Two different scientists—John C. Adams, in England, and Urbain Leverrier, in France—independently noticed that as it circled the sun, Uranus would speed up, then slow down. The two astronomers wondered why the planet didn't maintain a constant speed, and each concluded that the gravity of another planet—a more distant one—would have that effect on Uranus. So they each calculated the spot in the sky where the phantom planet should appear.

In September 1846 astronomers trained their telescopes on the point in space where Adams and Leverrier said the new planet would be. And there it was!

1. Neptune is 2.8 billion miles from the sun. It takes sunlight about four hours and 10 minutes to get there.

2. Even at a speed of 12,150 miles per hour, Neptune requires 165 Earth-years to orbit the sun. To be 12 years old on Neptune, you would have to live 1,980 Earth-years. When Methuselah died at the age of 969, he was less than 6 Neptune years old.

3. One day on Neptune equals almost 16 Earth-hours.

4. Neptune has eight moons, but they don't act like the moons of any of the other planets. Nereid is only 200 miles in diameter and follows an egg-shaped orbit more like that of a comet or an asteroid than a moon. It takes Nereid an entire Earth-year to complete its orbit. Triton, believed to be more than 2,000 miles in diameter and one of the largest moons in the solar system, circles Neptune once every six Earth-days. But its orbit is backward—in the opposite direction of which its planet spins.

5. Astronomers call Jupiter, Saturn, Uranus, and Neptune the gas giants, with Neptune being the smallest. It has no surface on which to land—just hydrogen, helium, and methane gases in an atmosphere above a continuous ocean of water and ammonia—much like Uranus.

One of the wonders of the universe is that we can predict the exact location of an object in space by mathematics. Only God could create such order.

A Word From Our Creator

Jesus Christ the same yesterday, and to day, and for ever.
Hebrews 13:8.

The Kiss of Death

Electricity is a wonderful thing when harnessed to give us light, to toast bread, to keep us cool, to wash our dishes, and to do a myriad of other things that we take for granted. But if we break the rules of safety when we use electricity, we can destroy things or even cause our own deaths. To get caught between a strong electrical current and the ground, for instance, means almost certain death.

We have an amazing photograph that shows four dead birds—two blue jays and two blackbirds. The cause of death is certain, but the reason the birds behaved as they did isn't clear. A flock of birds of several kinds, mostly blackbirds, landed on some electrical wires on a damp evening. As long as the birds remained on one wire at a time and didn't touch any of the birds on the other adjacent wires, everything was fine. But it appears that the birds began to squabble, and when they poked each other with their beaks they completed the circuit between the wire carrying live electricity and the ground wire, killing them instantly.

The accident electrocuted more than 400 birds. Most of them fell to the ground below, but some were fused to the wires with their beaks welded together. In the photo you can see the results. It isn't hard to imagine that the two blue jays got into a tiff over which would occupy that particular perch. They apparently started to peck at each other, and their beaks touched in a kiss of death.

When those jays got into an argument, they broke the natural safety rules. They didn't think about what they were doing. You could say that those blue jays sinned by breaking a law of nature and that they died as a result of their sin.

The laws of nature are unbending—unmerciful. And the law of God is just as sure. In the Garden of Eden, when the knowledge of good met the knowledge of evil, the circuit was complete and death was the result. But—praise the Lord!—Jesus in His fathomless mercy intervened and made a way for us to live and not die.

A Word From Our Creator

The sting of death is sin; and the strength of sin is the law. But thanks be to God, which giveth us the victory through our Lord Jesus Christ. 1 Corinthians 15:56, 57.

Too Many or Too Few Elk

In the early 1800s a half million tule elk munched grass on the plains of California. During the gold rush years, beginning in 1849, however, prospectors killed so many of these small elk for meat and hides that by 1873 only one small herd remained. Then the government declared killing the animals illegal. There were not enough elk anymore.

Conservationists attempted to reestablish the tule elk in several locations in California, with the most successful herd in Owens Valley. Most of Owens Valley belongs to local and federal agencies, all of which made it a policy to lease the land to ranchers for growing cattle feed. The elk easily adapted to their new diet of desert plants. In fact, they adjusted so well that the large herds are now a problem for the ranchers. The elk can live on desert plants, but they much prefer the cultivated alfalfa, and they break down fences to spend the night grazing in the ranchers' fields. So now there are too many elk.

In order to appease the ranchers, while providing a home for the elk, the U.S. Congress has limited the herd in Owens Valley to 490. Concerned preservationists think that is not enough elk. They would like to see 2,000 tule elk in California before declaring that the survival of the species is sure. So Congress also ordered the U.S. Department of the Interior to move extra elk from Owens Valley to other suitable spots in the state until they reach the goal of 2,000 animals.

Tule elk once roamed wild and free. Then people moved in, taking over their grazing land and killing them almost to the point of extinction. Now government agencies are attempting to reach a balance between wildlife and human beings. Is transplanting the elk a solution to the problem? What will happen when California has its 2,000 tule elk? Will that be enough—or too many? Would you like to be elk number 2,001?

Our world was perfectly created, with everything in balance. Sin tipped the scales, but only temporarily. In the new earth all creatures will again live in harmony and peace—and in perfect balance once again. There will be just the right number of everything.

A Word From Our Creator

And they found fat pasture and good, and the land was wide, and quiet, and peaceable. 1 Chronicles 4:40.

SEPTEMBER 23

Singing Caterpillars

Naturalists often call aphids "ant cows" because the ants tend to the aphids as a rancher takes care of his cattle. They protect them from predators, and they herd them to shelter in threatening weather. The ants milk their cows by stroking them with their antennae, and in turn the aphids secrete droplets of a sweet liquid, called honeydew, that the ants love to eat.

In the case of beetle larvae, the ants are not so well-behaved. The presence of the beetle usually means the end of the ant colony. The female beetle lays her eggs in the ants' nest. When the eggs hatch, the larvae produce droplets of a sweet-tasting liquid to which the ants become addicted. The ants gradually leave the duties of housekeeping and tend only to the beetle larvae.

Ants also tend to the larvae of some butterfly species in two families, the blues and the metalmarks. In the case of the blues, a family found throughout the world, the ants carry the caterpillars into their nest and care for them as they do beetle larvae. But ants tend the metalmarks, which live in the American tropics, as they do aphids.

For example, with the irenea (pronounced eye-REN-ee-a) metalmark of Panama, the relationship between the two insects is complicated. The caterpillar needs protection from a predatory wasp. The ants defend the caterpillars against the wasp and, in turn, receive the sweet-tasting droplets.

The irenea caterpillars are specially equipped to communicate with their hosts. Projections on the caterpillar's head are like tiny musical instruments. These projections move in and out across microscopic bumps on the insect's head to produce vibrating tones that attract the ants. Then four tentacles on the caterpillar's body go into action. Two produce the liquid that the ants crave. The other two make chemicals that signal the ants to come to the caterpillar's aid—like calling 911.

The Creator's power to protect and preserve extends even to the interrelationship between creatures as seemingly insignificant as ants, aphids, beetles, butterflies, and wasps.

A WORD FROM OUR CREATOR

And call upon me in the day of trouble: I will deliver thee, and thou shalt glorify me. Psalm 50:15.

SEPTEMBER 24

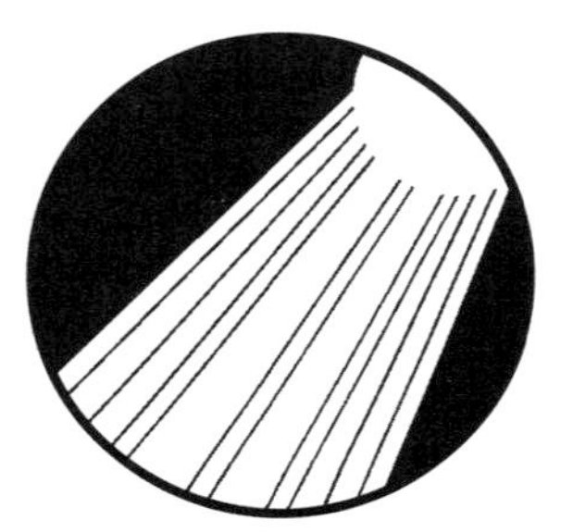

A Little Light Goes a Long Way

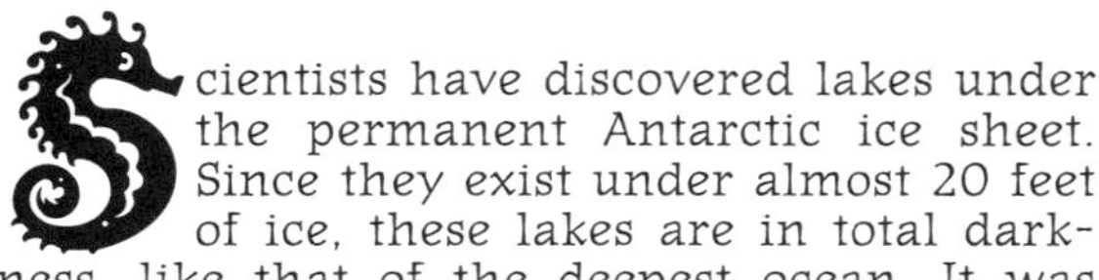

Scientists have discovered lakes under the permanent Antarctic ice sheet. Since they exist under almost 20 feet of ice, these lakes are in total darkness, like that of the deepest ocean. It was quite a surprise, then, when the scientists also discovered light-dependent plants growing on the floor of these lakes.

Using a special steam generator, researchers penetrated the thick layer of ice to explore the waters of one of the lakes, Lake Fryxell. They found tons of a pinkish-orange algae growing in mats three to four inches thick on the bottom of the lake. Also they discovered microscopic animals named rotifers living off the algae and thriving in the darkness.

At first scientists believed that they had discovered something new on earth—a place where light, through photosynthesis, is not the basic life support for plants and animals. Instead, however, they learned that photosynthesis exists even in the apparent darkness of Lake Fryxell.

For eight months of the year the sun shines over the ice of Antarctica. During that time the algae plants at the bottom of the lake receive a tiny bit of light—about one-tenth of one percent of the light available just a few feet above them on the surface. With that little bit of light the plants flourish and produce enough oxygen and food for themselves and for the rotifers.

The scientists discovered the bottom-growing pink algae during the four months of Antarctic winter darkness. As it turns out, during the eight-month period of light near the South Pole the algae plants pull away from the lake bottom and form columns, which the scientists say "look like pink stalagmites two or more feet in height." The algae gets as close to the light as it can to receive as much of its life-giving rays as possible.

What a magnificent illustration of faith! Remember the thief on the cross? He saw Jesus, the Light of the world, for only a few minutes, but that was enough. Jesus, the Light of life (John 8:12) drew the man to Himself.

A WORD FROM OUR CREATOR

Well done, thou good and faithful servant: thou hast been faithful over a few things, I will make thee ruler over many things: enter thou into the joy of thy lord. Matthew 25:21.

SEPTEMBER 25

It's Raining, It's Pouring

Y ou remember the story. Three and a half years earlier Elijah had prayed that it wouldn't rain. Now he reversed the prayer, and there came "a *great* rain." The storm was so fierce that Elijah sent a warning to King Ahab: "Prepare thy chariot, and get thee down, that the rain stop thee not" (1 Kings 18:44). Because of the storm, Ahab's chariot driver couldn't see to drive, so Elijah "girded up his loins, and ran before Ahab to the entrance of Jezreel" (verse 45).

To qualify as rain and not just as a drizzle, each drop must be at least two one hundredths of an inch in diameter. That's not very big, but when enough raindrops get together, they can really cause trouble.

The village of Cilaos, on Reunion Island, in the Indian Ocean, holds the record for the most rainfall—74 inches—in a 24-hour period. That's more than three inches an hour! It's hard to imagine that kind of a rainfall for even a few minutes, let alone for an entire day. But it doesn't rain like that all year there, so Reunion Island does not hold the record for being the rainiest place on earth.

The place where rain falls *most often* is on the island of Kauai in the state of Hawaii. There on Mount Waialeale it rains virtually every day of the year, so the annual rainfall averages 486 inches! If you like rain, that's the place to be. But that's still not the spot on earth where the *heaviest* rain falls. For that, you have to go to India. During one monsoon season some years ago 1,042 inches of rain drenched the Cherrapunji area of India—that's over 86 *feet* of rain! You could float an aircraft carrier in water that deep, and it's the record for the total amount of rain to fall in one place in one year.

Elijah sent his servant up seven times to look toward the sea. On the seventh trip, the servant said, "Behold, there ariseth a little cloud out of the sea, like a man's hand." That was the signal. The rain was coming. At that point Elijah's message went forth: "Get ready; a great storm is coming!" Elijah's message is still valid. Only next time when people see the small cloud, it will be Jesus returning in the clouds of heaven. Are you ready for Jesus to come?

A WORD FROM OUR CREATOR

And it came to pass in the mean while, that the heaven was black with clouds and wind, and there was a great rain. 1 Kings 18:45.

o you like blueberries? Have you ever picked and eaten ripe blueberries? How would you feel if blueberries vanished from the face of the earth? A disease is threatening the existence of blueberries, huckleberries, and even cranberries.

Mummy-berry disease is a fungus that first infects the leaves of berry plants. In the case of blueberry bushes, when the leaves become infected, they wilt in a way that causes them to resemble a blueberry flower. Then they produce a nectarlike substance that oozes from cracks in the leaves and emits the smell of fermented tea. Furthermore, they reflect ultraviolet light. To the eye of a scout bee looking for a source of food for its nest, all of these characteristics add up to a flower.

When bees and other insects try to feed at what they think is a flower, they quickly get seduced by the sticky, sugary goo oozing from the diseased leaves. As they lap up the sugar, spores of the mummy-berry fungus stick to their bodies. The insects then carry it to healthy blueberry blossoms. The spores infect that plant's reproductive system, causing it to produce whitish, seedless, fungus-filled mummy-berries.

The mummy-berries provide a home for the fungus through the winter. In spring new spores emerge from the mummy-berries and infect the budding blueberry leaves, starting the whole process again. The only way to control the spread of the disease is to destroy all the white mummy-berries during the winter. Once insects become carriers of the fungus spores, it is probably too late to save the crop.

By using deceit, Satan lured Eve to eat of the tree of the knowledge of good and evil. And when she ate the fruit of that tree and gave some to Adam, "and he did eat" (Genesis 3:6), it was too late to save humanity from the wages of sin—death (Romans 6:23). But, thanks to a just and loving God, we have a way of escape. "For as by one man's disobedience many were made sinners, so by the obedience of one shall many be made righteous" (Romans 5:19).

The Bush of Good and Evil

A Word From Our Creator

And the Lord God commanded the man, saying, Of every tree of the garden thou mayest freely eat: But of the tree of the knowledge of good and evil, thou shalt not eat of it. Genesis 2:16, 17.

September 27

Pluto: The Double Planet

Pluto is so far from the sun and so small in relation to the other planets that it's a wonder anyone ever discovered it at all. But so exact are the physical laws of the universe that astronomers predicted the existence of the planet long before they found it.

Basing his calculations on the irregularities in the orbit of Uranus, Percival Lowell predicted the orbit of a ninth planet. It was the beginning of the twentieth century, and Lowell couldn't wait for the wheels of science to get around to testing his theory, so he built his own observatory in Arizona. Sadly, Lowell died before he found his planet. But by using Lowell's data another astronomer, named Clyde Tombaugh, picked up the search and first saw Pluto on a crisp clear night in 1930—right where Lowell said it would be.

1. Pluto averages 3.7 billion miles from the sun. It takes sunlight about five and a half hours to get there.

2. Pluto travels through space at about 10,600 miles per hour on a lonely voyage around the sun that requires 248 Earth-years to complete. At that rate, it was only one Plutonian year ago that George Washington was a boy living in colonial America.

3. It takes 6 days, 19 hours, 18 minutes in Earth time for Pluto to rotate from one sunrise to the next. That means that a Plutonian year consists of about 13,300 Plutonian days.

4. Pluto is a frozen ball of ice about the size of our own moon, which makes it the smallest planet in the solar system.

5. Pluto has a huge moon named Charon (pronounced KAIR-on), which is so big and so close to the planet that some astronomers believe Pluto is actually a double planet instead of a planet with one moon. Other scientists conclude that Pluto is not a planet at all, but an escaped moon from Neptune's orbit.

No Earth scientist knows exactly what Pluto is, but the Creator and Sustainer of all things knows exactly what the solar system's biggest snowball is and why it's there. Pluto is a long way from the sun, but the sun's gravity holds it in place, and as our text says, the sun's heat—in the form of light—reaches even to the ninth planet in our solar system.

A Word From Our Creator

His going forth is from the end of the heaven, and his circuit unto the ends of it: and there is nothing hid from the heat thereof. Psalm 19:6.

September 28

Lying Mandibles

We often refer to a person who tells lies as having lying lips. So what would you call a bird that uttered an untruth? The bird equivalents to lips are the mandibles—the upper and lower portions of the beak. So we'll refer to a deceitful bird as having "lying mandibles."

The blue jay sometimes utters the call of one of several different kinds of hawks. No one is certain why the blue jay does this, but ornithologists believe that the behavior causes unsuspecting parent birds to try to chase away the imaginary hawk. In the process they leave their nests unguarded. Blue jays like to dine on eggs and baby birds. They watch an adult bird depart, and then they locate the nest and have raw eggs or fresh baby bird for lunch.

Mixed flocks of birds forage in the lower branches of the tropical rain forest in South America. In one part of Peru the bluish-slate antshrike appears to be the leader of the flock. Every morning the antshrike utters a special call to gather the flock, and throughout the day the antshrike sits on a lookout perch and guards the flock by watching for any one of several species of bird-eating hawks that come sneaking through the forest, seeking prey. When the antshrike spots a hawk, it utters another special call, and the flock disappears into hiding.

But about half the time when the antshrike cries "hawk" there is no hawk. And while the other birds are hiding, the antshrike swoops down and fills up on insects that the flock has discovered. Other birds flush out 85 percent of the antshrike's food. The other members of the flock may see the antshrike take their food, but they can't do anything about it—they have to rely on the antshrike to protect them.

The natural world has many illustrations of creatures that use deception to get what they want. That's the natural result of sin. Human nature also makes people's hearts "deceitful above all things, and desperately wicked" (Jeremiah 17:9). But in Jesus we can overcome our natural inclinations and replace them with honesty and integrity.

A Word From Our Creator

Lying lips are abomination to the Lord: but they that deal truly are his delight. Proverbs 12:22.

The Ant Colony as a Body

As hard as it may be to accept the idea, scientists have suggested that an ant colony is not many separate organisms but is, instead, one single superorganism consisting of many parts—at least one queen, a few males, and thousands of female workers.

An ant colony may have one queen or many—each with a section of the colony to care for and support. Each queen produces thousands of workers, and all of them are identical siblings. They all share similar genes because a single male fertilized all of the ant queen's eggs.

According to the superorganism theory of Dr. Edward Wilson of Harvard University, a single colony of ants begins as one ant—the fertilized queen, just as a human body begins as a single fertilized egg. And just as our bodies grow specialized organs that do different things for the body, so the ant colony develops specialized ants to do different things for it. Some ants tend the queen, some carry food, some clean the colony, and some protect it. As the colony grows, more and more different types of tasks need to be done, and the colony produces more and more different kinds of specialized ants to perform them.

The number of ants in a colony is really quite amazing. For example, an average colony of African driver ants may contain as many as 20 million workers. But the largest ant colony on record was one in Japan that consisted of 306 million workers supported by more than one million queens. How would you like to have been the scientists who had to count all those ants? That colony consisted of 45,000 interconnected underground nests in an area of about one square mile.

Writing to the Corinthians, the apostle Paul described the body of Christ: "And there are diversities of operation, but it is the same God which worketh all in all. . . . For as the body is one, and hath many members, and all the members of that one body, being many, are one body: so also is Christ. . . . And whether one member suffer, all the members suffer with it; or one member be honoured, all the members rejoice with it" (1 Corinthians 12:6-26).

A Word From Our Creator

For the body is not one member, but many. . . . Now ye are the body of Christ, and members in particular.
1 Corinthians 12:14-27.

September 30

How Much Are You Worth?

What are you worth? The most common answer to that question is the value of the raw materials in your body. Even if you allow for inflation, the water, carbon, iron, calcium, fat, and other substances that make up your physical self do not add up to $50. Do you think you're worth less than 50 bucks?

One author discusses our value in terms of the number of atoms in your body. We're made up of about eight octillion atoms—that's an 8 with 27 zeros after it. To help us comprehend that number, Dr. Donald Andrews of Johns Hopkins University uses the following illustration.

Imagine a snowstorm of peas falling from the sky. When the entire state of Pennsylvania is four feet deep in peas, we have about 1 quintillion peas—but we are still nine zeros short. So we need more peas. Let's bury all of the land areas on earth with peas to a depth of four feet. Now we have about 1 sextillion peas—still six zeros short of the total that we need. So let's surface the entire earth—even the ocean—with four feet of peas. And let's go out into space and get 250 more planets the same size as earth and smother them with four feet of peas. Now we have 1 septillion peas—but we are still three zeros short of an octillion. To finish the picture, we will have to go into deep space and get 250,000 more planets the size of earth and dump four feet of peas on them. Now you have an octillion peas—the same as the number of atoms in your body.

How does that translate into worth? A Dupont report analyzed the potential energy in the atoms of your body. It was a staggering 11 million kilowatt hours per pound! On our last electric bill we paid 7 cents per kilowatt hour. So if you weigh 100 pounds, your potential worth in electrical power would be $77 million. Of course, you would lose your life when you collected the money. Are you willing to die for $77 million?

Actually, you're worth much more than that. And you don't have to die to collect, because Jesus, the King of the universe, died instead, so that you can live. How much are you worth? God paid an infinite price for you. All He asks for in return is your love.

A Word From Our Creator

For ye are bought with a price: therefore glorify God in your body, and in your spirit, which are God's.
1 Corinthians 6:20.

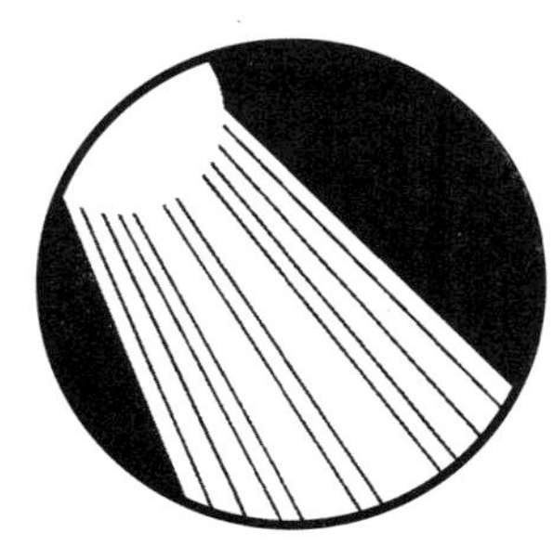

The Great Annihi- lator

No one has ever seen a black hole. In fact, you can't see one because it's so powerful that it sucks up everything nearby. The black hole's attraction is so strong that not even X-rays and gamma rays can escape its grasp. According to theory, black holes consume everything in their neighborhood. We don't know for sure, of course, but black holes may represent the Creator's conservation-of-energy system. Perhaps He compresses used materials in a black hole and uses them to build another island universe somewhere else.

But wait! What makes us think that such a thing as a black hole even exists if we can't see it and if we can't even detect any radiation from it? Good question! And one asked by many skeptics. But there doesn't appear to be any other explanation for some incredibly powerful sources of radiation that we do see. The explanation is that just before materials such as space dust or clouds of gas get sucked into a black hole, the process excites their atoms to a point where they emit powerful surges of radiation. Between surges occur periods of quiet when the black hole has no material to consume. Each time new material gets close enough to vanish into the black hole, that material issues a massive display of fireworks just before being "recycled" in the black hole.

A French satellite has focused its gamma radiation sensor on one suspected black hole called 1E 1740.7-2942. Most of the time only a slight amount of radiation comes from the area. But not long ago scientists measured gamma radiation at the awesome energy level of 511,000 electron volts. (The amount of energy released by visible light is only two electron volts!) This information led one astronomer to nickname 1E 1740.7-2942 the Great Annihilator. Apparently the black hole had sucked in a cloud of gaseous material that emitted the gamma radiation as it disappeared.

The question that God asked Job thousands of years ago is still a good one. Where does darkness dwell, and how does it get there?

A WORD FROM OUR CREATOR

Where is the way where light dwelleth? and as for darkness, where is the place thereof, that thou shouldest take it to the bound thereof, and that thou shouldest know the paths to the house thereof? Job 38:19, 20.

id you know that many of the vegetables that you eat were produced, in part, by lightning? It's true! This is how it works. The basic building blocks of all animal life, including humans, are proteins that come either directly or indirectly from plants. One of the essential elements of proteins is nitrogen, and since nitrogen makes up most of the air we breathe, we have no shortage of this necessary raw material.

But you can't use the nitrogen—and neither can plants—in its natural atmospheric, or gaseous, form. All the nitrogen in the air is locked up tight in molecules, each consisting of two nitrogen atoms held together by an almost unbreakable *triple* chemical bond. It takes a mighty blast of energy to break the bond—and that's where lightning comes into the picture.

When a streak of lightning rips through the air, it literally blasts the nitrogen molecules apart, leaving the single nitrogen atoms free to join with the oxygen in the air and the hydrogen in the raindrops to form a new compound called nitric acid. Nitric acid falls with the rain to the ground, where it mixes with minerals in the soil to produce nitrates, or fertilizer. The plants absorb the nitrates through their roots and use them in producing complex proteins. We consume those proteins as part of our food from plants. So, the next time you're enjoying carrots or green beans—or maybe even brussels sprouts or spinach—remember to thank the Lord for the lightning.

And while you're thanking God for your vegetables, make sure to thank Him for the moisture ("vapours" in today's text) that rises from the earth to make the clouds that provide the rain that brings the lightning. And thank Him for the winds that blow the rain clouds with the lightning to the garden that grows the vegetables on your table. It all works wonderfully, and you get to eat. Praise the Lord!

Lightning Produces Food

A Word From Our Creator

He causeth the vapours to ascend from the ends of the earth; he maketh lightnings for the rain; he bringeth the wind out of his treasuries. Psalm 135:7.

OCTOBER 3

Fruit Flags

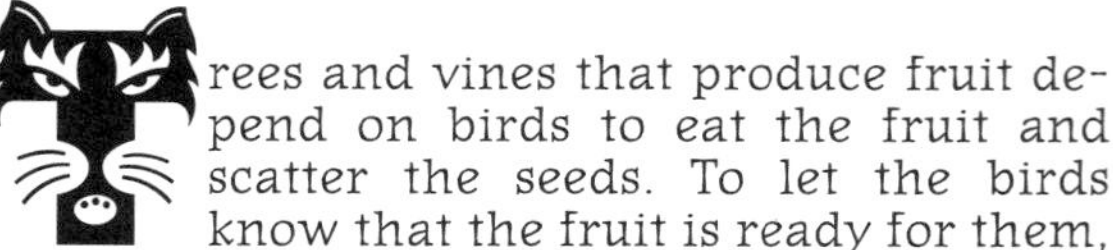

Trees and vines that produce fruit depend on birds to eat the fruit and scatter the seeds. To let the birds know that the fruit is ready for them, God has given many of the fruit-bearing plants brightly colored "flags" to advertise that their fruit stand has opened. Fruit flags come in two kinds—those of spring and summer and those of autumn.

The spring and summer flags, which botanists call preripening fruit flags, are the color changes in the fruits as they ripen. For example, blackberries, strawberries, blueberries, mulberries, and black cherries turn from white or green to shades of red and then, for most, blue or purple or black as they mature. Thus the showy fruits themselves serve as the flags, and birds spot them easily.

However, many fall fruits require a different kind of flag. Some trees and vines produce small inconspicuous fruits, so they need more-obvious flags. For sassafras, black gum, sumac, poison ivy, and Virginia creeper, leaves serve as the flags.

One October on our Texas farm we noticed a lot of commotion in one of the oak trees in our front yard. A flock of birds were fluttering in and around the top of the tree. The birds appeared to be feeding on something, but all we could see was the beauty of the birds as they fed in and around the brilliant red leaves of the Virginia creeper, a common vine in central and eastern North America. At first we thought the birds were eating a swarm of insects. But when we looked with binoculars, we discovered that they were feasting on the berries of the Virginia creeper itself.

Virginia creeper berries are no larger than a quarter of an inch in diameter. They are also blue, so they blend in with the blue-green color of the oak leaves. Obviously such tiny blue berries will not attract much attention. But the brilliant red leaves of the vine are a most effective sign inviting the birds to a banquet.

It's not the flag that makes the banquet—that's only the invitation. It's the presence of real fruit that gives the flag its meaning. As Christians we invite others to Jesus, but it is His fruit in our lives—the fruit of the Spirit—that causes them to listen.

A WORD FROM OUR CREATOR

Wherefore by their fruits ye shall know them. Matthew 7:20.

ncient peoples called Pleiades the Seven Sisters, for seven stars in the cluster were probably visible at that time. Today we can clearly see only six stars, but the name Seven Sisters remains.

The Japanese word for Pleiades is Subaru, and the star cluster is the trademark on the Japanese car of that name. The automaker chose the design because originally six companies merged to form the supercompany that produces the Subaru automobile. Contracts and corporate relationships now bind the six companies, so they must act as a unit. And that is exactly the relationship that the stars in Pleiades have with one another. They are united together as a unit.

Pleiades is one of the most studied groups of stars in the sky. It is 490 light-years away, and no fewer than 25,000 individual measurements indicate that all of the stars in the cluster are moving together like a flock of birds flying through the night.

The six visible stars in the cluster are six huge suns. Each is at least 800 times larger than our own sun. But Pleiades contains a lot more than six stars. Using telescopes, astronomers have counted more than 250 stars in the cluster. And the amazing thing is that all of them are traveling together in the same direction and at the same speed. They are a unit—a corporate entity in the heavens. How did the author of the book of Job know that? People had no powerful telescopes when he lived. That knowledge offers further proof that the Bible is as up-to-date as tomorrow in terms of its scientific accuracy.

A better rendering of the Hebrew word translated as "influences" in today's text would be "chains" or "fastenings," and in fact, in the Revised Version of the Bible the text reads "Canst thou *bind* the *cluster* of the Pleiades?" What is it that binds these stars together?

Look at the Pleiades tonight. You will be seeing light that left those stars almost 500 years ago to remind you that the God who spoke to Job more than 3,000 years ago was and is the Creator of the universe.

The Pleiades

A Word From Our Creator

Canst thou bind the sweet influences of Pleiades? Job 38:31.

October 5

Whale Songfest

Whales sing. And whale songs are so hauntingly beautiful that recordings of them are popular. But whale songs are not just idle sounds created by the huge creatures because they have nothing better to do. Their songs are their primary means of communicating with each other. Carried through the water, low-pitched whale songs travel farther than the higher-pitched ones. In fact, the very-low-pitched sounds of fin whales can be heard hundreds of miles away.

Whale songs are actually many different vocalizations that represent a complex language about such things as food, danger, courtship, and the conditions of the sea. Apparently whales talk about many of the same kinds of things that humans discuss.

Each pod, or group, of whales has its own distinct language. A young whale in a pod begins to learn its song soon after birth and modifies the song throughout its lifetime. Each whale adds to its song and constantly improves it through practice. The typical song of an adult whale lasts for up to 20 minutes and contains as many as eight identifiable themes. Each song has certain passages that the whale repeats. The themes are so specific that human listeners with undersea microphones can recognize individual whales by their songs. By recording the sounds of whales, scientists can track the migrations of specific family groups and even individual members of the group.

During the mating season, humpback whales gather in groups for an all-day songfest. At that time the family group appear to be celebrating in some way. Since scientists assume all the sounds represent different messages, it would be wonderful if we could interpret all their communications on such a day.

When we're born again, like the whales we begin learning a song—the Song of Moses and the Lamb (Revelation 15:3). And we constantly improve our song by living in harmony with Jesus.

A Word From Our Creator

And he hath put a new song in my mouth, even praise unto our God: many shall see it, and fear, and shall trust in the Lord. Psalm 40:3.

October 6

Frosty

Frosty, a raccoon, was orphaned at birth and raised by one of the rangers at California's Big Basin Redwood Park. The animal lived in the cabin of the ranger who had rescued him, and he was learning, as raccoons do, by watching his teacher—in this case, the ranger. Since the raccoon had no mother, the ranger set about to teach Frosty how to be successful in the wild. It was a tough job, but it was progressing nicely—until there was a setback. What the ranger didn't know was that Frosty also had watched when they weren't having raccoon school, and he had learned some human tricks in the process. For example, the animal had learned how to flush the toilet.

One day one of the park's picnickers came to headquarters to report that no water was coming out of the faucets. The chief ranger had just checked the water supply himself, so he knew that the tank was full and the water system was in good order. He politely told the angry man that there must be some mistake but that he would check it out.

Sure enough, only a trickle of water dribbled from the faucets. He and other rangers went back up the hill to check the water tank. It was almost out of water, but plenty of water was going into it. That meant only one thing—a leak somewhere—and they were going to have to find it and patch it. So the search began. They traced every pipe from its source to its end—but found no leaks! The rangers were getting desperate. The water needs of 2,500 people depended on their solving the problem.

Two of the rangers happened to stop outside Frosty's house. They heard the toilet flush, and then it flushed again, and again. That was strange. Frosty's owner was out on the trail, so who could be flushing the toilet? Quickly entering the cabin, they rushed into the bathroom just in time to see Frosty pull the lever and jump into the commode. The raccoon had learned to make his own swirling water to play in, and he was enjoying himself to the fullest. Never mind that he had drained the park's water supply.

Is it possible that in even a harmless pursuit of fun we can sometimes make trouble for other people?

A Word From Our Creator

Even a child is known by his doings, whether his work be pure, and whether it be right. Proverbs 20:11.

OCTOBER 7

The Good News Dance

Working in Austria many years ago, Dr. Karl von Frisch spent thousands of hours carefully observing honey bees to try to break the code that the scouts use to tell the bees back at the hive about the location of a fresh source of nectar.

Dr. von Frisch placed saucers of honey at different distances and in different directions from the hive. When a scout discovered a particular saucer, the scientist painted a special design on that bee. That way he knew how far each scout traveled and which direction it came from. Finally, Dr. von Frisch put a red light in the hive to allow him to watch the bees without disturbing them.

Dr. von Frisch learned that when they discovered a new source of honey, the scout bees returned to the hive and performed a "dance." By moving at different speeds and in different directions in a complicated series of circles and figure-eights, the scouts told the other bees the exact direction and the distance of the saucers as well as the quality of the honey. For example, they showed the direction by moving in a certain direction on the honeycomb in the hive. As it turned out, that direction was exactly the angle of the source of the honey relative to the position of the sun.

Every scout that arrives with information about a new source of food brings good news to the hive. The scout's dance is welcomed, eagerly watched, and brings a quick response. As the scout starts the dance, the other bees gather around to watch. When the information becomes clear, those bees also begin to get excited, and soon they are streaming toward the entrance of the hive and flying away in droves toward the source.

In many ways the human population of the world is like a population of bees. The swarms of people want nothing more than good news. But they've been disappointed so often that they want to *see* the good news performed in the daily lives of people who have experienced it firsthand. We are all Christian scouts commissioned by Jesus to let the human hive know the best news of all time—the gospel of Jesus Christ.

A WORD FROM OUR CREATOR

Come, see a man, which told me all things that ever I did: is not this the Christ? John 4:29.

October 8

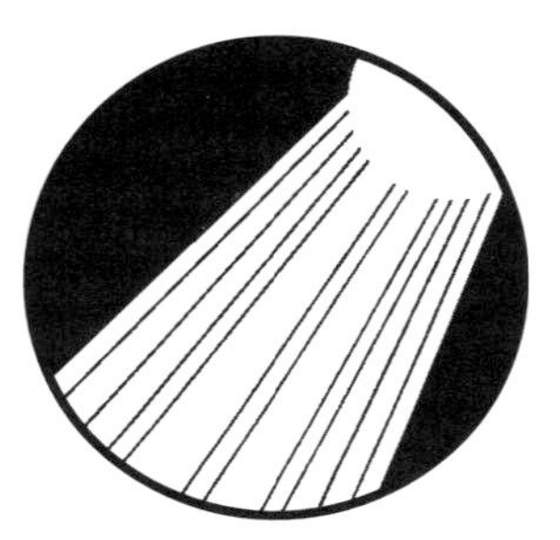

Light Bait

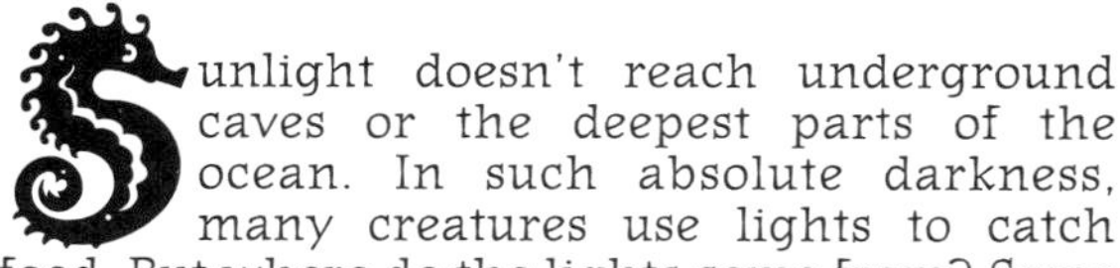

Sunlight doesn't reach underground caves or the deepest parts of the ocean. In such absolute darkness, many creatures use lights to catch food. But where do the lights come from? Some deep-sea fish carry the lights like we do flashlights. They have pockets in their bodies in which they collect and store luminescent bacteria—tiny one-celled organisms that glow in the dark. Other fish produce light through an elaborate process that mixes different chemicals in special light cups on their bodies.

The trapmouth wonderfish, which lives in the blackness of the deepest ocean, uses a light inside its mouth to lure its prey. When a passing fish investigates the light, its curiosity leads it directly into the jaws of the wonderfish's huge froglike mouth.

Some deep-sea anglerfishes have a fishing rod with lighted bait on the end. The rodlike appendages project from the fish's head, just in front of its mouth. The fish jerks the rod so that it looks like a wiggling, glowing something that is good to eat. An unsuspecting fish comes to check it out, and gets trapped by a huge gaping mouth with long razor-sharp teeth that act like bars on a prison cell. One gulp later, the passing fish is dinner.

Cave creatures also go fishing. Clinging to the ceilings of a cave in New Zealand are the now-famous cave-dwelling glowworms. Each glowworm is an insect larva spending its first stage of life in the darkness, "fishing" for food. To get food in this difficult environment, each glowworm drops a line with a light on the end of it. When a tiny moth or gnat flies over to investigate, it gets stuck to the line, and the glowworm quickly reels in its prey, eats it, and lowers its line once more.

We're all born into a world of spiritual darkness, and we are also born with natural God-given curiosity. Satan knows how to entice us, and he's not above disguising himself as an angel of light to entrap us. Thus we must be very careful to discern the false light of Lucifer from the True Light of the world—Jesus.

A Word From Our Creator

Satan himself is transformed into an angel of light. 2 Corinthians 11:14.

October 9

Graupel

For the more than 200 years since Ben Franklin flew his kite in a thunderstorm, scientists have been trying to figure out what causes lightning. We know that lightning is a streak of free electrons zooming through the air, but we don't know what causes the accumulation of free electrons in the first place.

On a small scale, you can create lightning by scuffing your shoes across a carpet and then touching a doorknob—or even another person! The friction of your shoes against the carpet produces the small sparks you see. But what kind of friction exists in the sky? With no shoes or carpet up there, how does the charge build up?

John Hallett, a scientist at the University of Nevada, has created a refrigerated chamber that duplicates the conditions necessary for lightning. His results provide at least a theory about how the gigantic electron charges occur in the clouds. By taking many dangerous airplane rides into the middle of thunderheads, where lightning originates, Dr. Hallett learned that lightning occurs only when the temperature is between 14°F and -4°F—a common temperature at high altitudes. Within that temperature range, electrons separate easily from the atoms that normally hold them, but they need friction to do so. Where does it come from? What exists in the clouds at that temperature that provides friction? *Graupel*, of course!

Dr. Hallett's data suggests that supercooled water that forms into pea-sized ice particles called *graupel*, a German word that means "soft hail," creates the necessary friction. Inside the thundercloud violent winds blow the frozen water particles against one another. As ice crystals bounce off the *graupel*, the friction rapidly builds up electrical charges. The result? Lightning.

We try so hard to understand what is so easy for God.

A Word From Our Creator

God thundereth marvellously with his voice; great things doeth he, which we cannot comprehend. Job 37:5.

Scarlet Leaves

It's October, and the display of fall colors in many parts of North America is glorious to behold. Everywhere we see shades of yellow, orange, and red—all perfectly accented by shades of green. The colors aren't just simple colors from a paint set, however. The Creator has provided us with a constantly changing painting that contains every imaginable hue and shade. Not only do the colors alter from day to day, but they also shift through the day as the sunlight becomes more intense or as the clouds shade the sun's rays.

Notice that maple tree in the foreground beside the road. It's been changing from green to brilliant red over the past week. In a day or two every leaf will be scarlet. Each translucent leaf is becoming a jewel as the light shines through it. Together the leaves glow iridescently in the sunlight. When seen from a distance, the tree is an explosion of color that defies description.

What a lesson this tree teaches! As the life-giving chlorophyll disappears from the leaves in autumn, the substances left can produce any number of colors, depending on their chemical composition. The colors were there all along but were invisible because of the overpowering influence of the chlorophyll. When the inner colors do come forth, they are short-lived. Soon the brightly colored leaves will fall and turn brown. Then comes winter.

It is interesting that really brilliant fall colors occur only where winters are snowy. Our sins, like the leaves of the maple tree, are scarlet. But they can fall away and be replaced by the pure covering of Christ's righteousness. "Come now, and let us reason together, saith the Lord: though your sins be as scarlet, they shall be as white as snow" (Isaiah 1:18).

A Word From Our Creator

Purge me with hyssop, and I shall be clean: wash me, and I shall be whiter than snow. Psalm 51:7.

OCTOBER 11

Why Siberia?

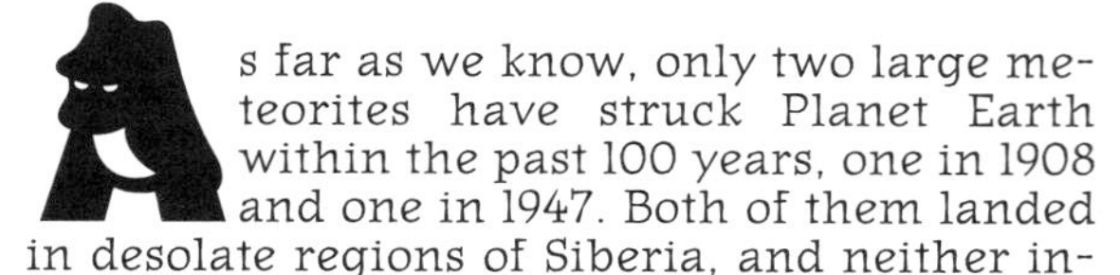

As far as we know, only two large meteorites have struck Planet Earth within the past 100 years, one in 1908 and one in 1947. Both of them landed in desolate regions of Siberia, and neither instance caused any loss of human life.

Yet if the 1908 meteorite had arrived just five hours later and on the same path, it would have made a direct hit on St. Petersburg, then the capital of the Russian Empire. Only five hours difference!

In the stream of eternity, can we even imagine how much difference five hours can make? Yet if that meteorite had struck St. Petersburg, it would have not only wiped out the entire city and most of its inhabitants, but it also would have profoundly altered history. As it was, the meteorite, weighing no more than a few hundred tons, gouged out 150-foot-wide craters and knocked down virtually all of the trees within 30 miles of the point of impact.

It's tempting to ask what-if questions. What if the meteorite had hit someplace else—almost anyplace else—on land? Few places are as uninhabited as Siberia. What if it had landed in the ocean near a coastline? The damage and loss of life from the resulting tidal wave would have been astounding. To date, nothing like that has ever been recorded. Yet the chances of a meteorite falling into the ocean are three times greater than its striking land. Why did both of the major earth-striking meteorites in recent history land in Siberia? Why indeed!

Isaac Asimov answered the question this way: "Mankind has clearly had an unusual run of luck." Do you think it was luck?

"Before the mountains were brought forth, or ever thou hadst formed the earth and the world, even from everlasting to everlasting, thou art God" (Psalm 90:2). And, as God's children, we don't have to fear such things as meteorites, because Jesus has promised that "thou shalt not be afraid for the terror by night; nor for the arrow that flieth by day; nor for the pestilence that walketh in darkness; nor for the destruction that wasteth at noonday" (Psalm 91:5, 6).

A WORD FROM OUR CREATOR

Knowest thou the ordinances of heaven? canst thou set the dominion thereof in the earth? Job 38:33.

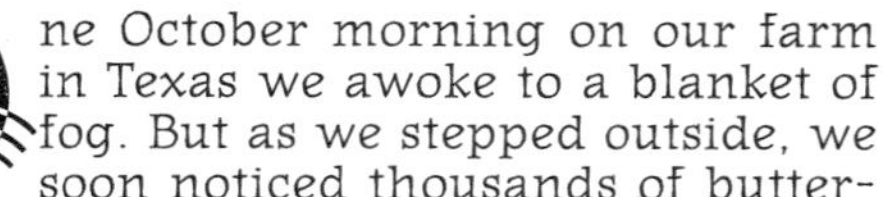

ne October morning on our farm in Texas we awoke to a blanket of fog. But as we stepped outside, we soon noticed thousands of butterflies flitting through the thick haze. All of them were going unerringly southward. We marveled as the tiny creatures flew so silently yet so exactly through the fog. The butterflies showed that they knew exactly where the sun was even in the densest fog, and that they could use that knowledge to orient themselves on their journey.

We know that bees can see polarized light, an ability that enables them to locate the sun even on the cloudiest days. Monarch butterflies also probably detect polarized light. God blessed the handsome orange-and-black butterflies with the innate ability to fly south for the winter and back north again for the summer. While most butterflies die when the cold winter blasts arrive, the migratory monarchs fly south by the millions—probably by the hundreds of millions. At first their flight is only a trickle, but soon groups from all over the United States and Canada join together along the way and travel through Texas in mid-October.

It's amazing that something as simple as a butterfly, which certainly has no brain as we think of one, can make all the necessary calculations and decisions that enable it to navigate to its winter home. Most monarchs winter in specific locations, roosting each night in the same trees. The most famous winter location for monarchs is in Pacific Grove, California, where the butterflies cling to the branches and bark in such great numbers that they appear to cover the trees.

If God can direct the path of the simple butterfly through fog so that it can live through winter, surely He can direct us in life. When we know Jesus, we're never lost. We always know the way—even through the fog of spiritual confusion that we face every day.

Monarchs Know the Way

A Word From Our Creator

For the Lord knoweth the way of the righteous: but the way of the ungodly shall perish. Psalm 1:6.

Three-score and Ten

A WORD FROM OUR CREATOR

The days of our years are threescore years and ten; and if by reason of strength they be fourscore years, yet is their strength labour and sorrow; for it is soon cut off. Psalm 90:10.

A score is 20, so threescore is 60, and threescore plus 10 equals 70. Our text clearly indicates that the life span of a human being is usually no more than 70, although a few people reach fourscore, or 80. Isn't it interesting that the length of the average potential life span hasn't changed much in more than 3,000 years?

But it's even more interesting to note that in terms of number of heartbeats, people outlive all other creatures on earth. Dr. Warren Thomas, the director of the Los Angeles Zoo, writes that, with the exception of humans, all the mammals on earth have approximately the same number of heartbeats to expend in their lifetimes. According to Dr. Thomas, that number is 800 million.

At a pulse rate of 30 times a minute, the elephant, earth's largest land mammal, takes about 50 years to use up its quota. On the other hand, the smallest mammal on earth, the pygmy shrew, goes through its allotment of heartbeats in only a year and a half because its heart beats 900 to 1,400 times per minute.

The average human heart beats about 75 times per minute. If the same rule governed us, we'd use up our quota of heartbeats by the time we turned 20! Dr. Thomas has this to say about that: "Somehow, human beings are exempted from the rule." Don't you wonder why?

God created humans in His image. That sets us apart from all of the animals. Yes, we share many similarities with many of the creatures that God made. But God brought us into being for a special purpose.

The human life span has changed at least twice: once when Adam and Eve sinned, and again after the Flood. We may live longer than the average for mammals, but as our text tells us, the sorrow and labor that are the result of sin still fill our lives. And eventually, no matter how long we live, we will "fly away"—we will die. But there is good news! "For if we believe that Jesus died and rose again, even so them also which sleep in Jesus will God bring with him" (1 Thessalonians 4:14).

We often call a dog "man's best friend." In no situation is this axiom more true than when a dog finds someone who is lost. Doing the work of 30 people, a dog can search an avalanche site as large as two football fields in 30 minutes. It can find a victim buried under 16 feet of snow or trapped under brush, under water, or under rubble. A dog's keen sense of smell makes it a better tracker than any human. When no other evidence is visible, a dog just sniffs the air to pick up the scent of someone.

Several organizations—some of them made up of volunteers—train search-and-rescue dogs by setting up regular teaching sessions and practice rescues so that the dogs and their handlers will know exactly what to do to find people lost in deep woods, mud slides, avalanches, and floods, and in the aftermath of tornadoes and earthquakes. A rescue dog must learn to climb ladders and cliffs and to walk narrow planks. It has to practice digging out victims and learn to uncover the heads of buried persons before the rest of their bodies. Also, it must be comfortable riding on ski lifts and in helicopters.

Being a rescue dog is hard work, but the animal doesn't seem to mind because people make the training fun. During practice sessions they bury the "victim" with one of the dog's favorite toys on his or her head to teach the animal to uncover that part of the body first. When freed, the victim uses the toy to play with the dog. The animal's reward is to get praise and to play with its trainer.

When a real emergency takes place, the dog responds instantly to such simple commands as "Find!" The animal doesn't hesitate—to delay could endanger the life of the dog, its handler, or most critical of all, the person who must be found.

Rescue dogs learn something that we also need to know. Obedience without hesitation provides safety for ourselves as well as for those around us. But it is even more wonderful to realize that when we get into trouble, we can trust our heavenly Best Friend to find us and lead us back to the right path.

Dogs to the Rescue

A WORD FROM OUR CREATOR

When thou art in tribulation, and all these things are come upon thee, . . . if thou turn to the Lord thy God, and shalt be obedient unto his voice; . . . he will not forsake thee. Deuteronomy 4:30, 31.

October 15

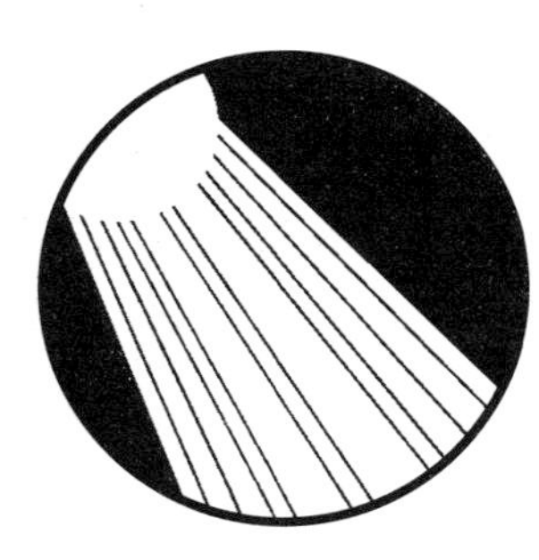

Do You Have a Single Eye?

When Eve approached the forbidden tree and listened to the deceitful words of the serpent, and "*saw* that the tree was good for food, and that it was pleasant to the *eyes*, . . . she took of the fruit thereof, and did eat" (Genesis 3:6).

The eye is one of God's most amazing creations. We use our eyes almost constantly, yet science still does not understand many things about how they work. To his dying day, Charles Darwin could not explain how the eye could have evolved.

Ten trillion photons, or light particles, enter the eye every second. These particles pass through the cornea (the transparent outside covering of the middle of the eye), the pupil (the dark circle in the center of your eye that is surrounded by the iris, the colored part of your eye), the lens, and the vitreous humor (the clear jelly-like substance that fills your eyeball), to reach the retina, at the back of your eyeball.

The retina works somewhat like the film of a camera. But a camera can take only one picture at a time. The retina is more like a video camera. The retina has more than 100 million receiver cells called rods and cones. Each cell attaches to a nerve, and each of the 100 million receptor nerves connects through a nerve cable to a part of the brain that translates sight into pictures and thoughts. And all this takes only a fraction of a second. We are truly "fearfully and wonderfully made" (Psalm 139:14).

How the eye works is wonderful. But what is even more amazing is how the things we see influence us—the color of things, the shape of things, the movement of things. Everything that we watch affects us for good or for evil.

In our text for today, the word "single" is a translation of the Greek word *haplous*, which means singleness of purpose. When our eyes come under the control of a brain focused on Jesus, they will search for sights that glorify Jesus, and will reject those that degrade and debase our Christian character.

A Word From Our Creator

The light of the body is the eye: therefore when thine eye is single, thy whole body also is full of light; but when thine eye is evil, thy body also is full of darkness. Luke 11:34.

ob's friend recognized that our view of God is always limited. We are like the farmer who, frightened by the thought of flying in an airplane, said, "I don't ever want to get any higher than picking corn or lower than digging potatoes."

Some people believe that hell is an underground place where wicked people burn forever. The Bible tells of a time to come when fire will destroy this earth and when all the wicked who prefer their sins to the salvation that Jesus Christ offers will perish in that fire. But the Bible does not teach that God tortures people.

Generally when the Bible uses the word "hell," it means the place of the dead, or the grave. Just about all those who have lived on earth have died and been buried. And those people are all in biblical hell, because hell is the place of all the dead—good *and* bad.

The Bible further teaches that God will raise everyone from the dead—some to everlasting life and some to everlasting death (see Daniel 12:2). So, for some, hell happens twice. The second time results from their choice of evil instead of good. It's the second hell that many Christians describe as "hellfire." The text of an early American sermon describes it in this way: "Like red-hot lumps of lead, the wicked will fall into the open mouth of hell, belching out flames of fire and brimstone." It makes hell sound like a volcano spewing out lava. In fact, some primitive societies used to appease their gods by hurling human sacrifices down into a volcano. But the Bible does not describe or discuss such a place.

Geologists tell us that red-hot liquid metals lie under the earth's mantle—a mantle 1,800 miles thick. But that doesn't mean that God sentenced the wicked to spend the rest of eternity in the center of the earth, boiling in all of that hot metal. Our God is a loving God, "not willing that any should perish, but that all should come to repentance" (2 Peter 3:9).

How Deep Is Hell?

A WORD FROM OUR CREATOR

Canst thou by searching find out God? canst thou find out the Almighty unto perfection? It is as high as heaven; what canst thou do? deeper than hell; what canst thou know?
Job 11:7, 8.

OCTOBER 17

Peanuts Grow in the Dark

A Word From Our Creator

He hath set me in dark places, as they that be dead of old. Lamentations 3:6.

As Jeremiah wrote the words of today's text, the world looked pretty bleak for God's chosen people. He said that their condition was as bad as the grave. But in God's plan, life springs forth from the grave. A special plant—the peanut—illustrates this truth.

Whether boiled, roasted, salted, or ground into a paste, the peanut is one of the world's most popular and most nutritious foods. Pound for pound, peanuts contain more vitamins, carbohydrate, and protein than beef does.

The peanut is native to South America. Early explorers took peanuts back to Europe, and from there traders carried them to Africa to exchange for spices, ivory, and other goods. European settlers also brought them to North America, where farmers used them for pig feed.

Peanuts did not become an important commercial crop until the early 1900s, when George Washington Carver found more than 300 uses for them, including the production of milk, flour, ink, and soap. Today we use peanut oil in machinery lubricants, shaving cream, shampoo, paint, and explosives, and industry grinds the shells into powder to make plastics, abrasives, and building materials.

Peanuts have a strange way of growing. They're not nuts, so they don't develop on trees. While they're beans, they don't form on vines—at least not in the usual way. First, small flowers open at sunrise, get fertilized during the morning, and wither and die usually by noon. A few days later the stems of the future pods begin to grow, but they head downward—away from the sun—until they're about seven inches long and have pushed into the soil. There the seeds—the peanuts—begin to develop in thin-shelled pods at the tips of the stems. Almost all other fruits grow out in the warming rays or heat of the sun. But even underground, the fruit of this plant needs the heat of the sun to develop. Peanuts require a long four- to five-month growing season to get the warmth that they need to ripen.

Later in Lamentations 3, Jeremiah concluded that "it is good that a man should both hope and quietly wait for the salvation of the Lord" (verse 26). The peanut does just that.

OCTOBER 18

Escape Velocity

id you know that it would be possible to pull the Earth out of its orbit? In fact, under the right conditions a powerful enough force could lure the Earth away from its path around the sun.

Astronomers have observed what appear to have been collisions of star systems in deep space. The stars themselves don't collide, but the systems merge. In the process, some of the stars probably assume new orbits around new centers of gravity. When this occurs, what do you think could happen to the planets and their moons orbiting those stars? Before you answer that question, here's a clue: Some astronomers believe that the planet Pluto may once have been one of Neptune's moons.

It could have happened like this: Suppose that sometime in the distant past a large star passed within a few billion miles of our solar system, and suppose that star was so big that its gravitational pull yanked one of Neptune's moons out of orbit. But suppose also that that star—as strong as it was—was still too far away to hang on to the moon. For a while a tug-of-war would have taken place between our sun and the other star—with our sun eventually winning.

Since the used-to-be moon is now far beyond all the other planets but is still being held by our sun, it begins a new orbit around the sun. So Neptune's former moon could have become a new planet—Pluto.

Now back to the original question. Could Earth be pulled out of orbit? Probably not. If the passing star came close enough, it's gravitational force might pull one or more planets out of our solar system. In order to capture Earth, the passing star would have to pull so hard that it would pull Earth away from the sun at a speed of at least 95,000 miles per hour. That speed astronomers call the planet's *escape velocity*.

Jesus is our Sun of Righteousness (Malachi 4:2), and His force is more than strong enough to hold us in His system. An alien star is attempting to attract us into orbit around himself, but Jesus has overcome the devil and his forces. So long as we remain faithful to Jesus, He will hold us close to Himself.

A WORD FROM OUR CREATOR

Behold, I come quickly: hold that fast which thou hast, that no man take thy crown. Revelation 3:11.

OCTOBER 19

Mallee Fowl

Unlike most birds, the mallee fowl does not sit on its nest to incubate its eggs. Instead, this chicken-like species of Australia spends 11 months building and maintaining a nest to precise specifications that guarantee that the chicks will hatch without benefit of the direct warmth of the parent birds.

During Australia's autumn season the male and female mallee fowl use their feet to dig a three-foot-deep pit in the sand. During winter the birds pile leaves, twigs, and other debris into the pit, then cover the vegetation with sand after each rainfall. The sand helps to keep the vegetation moist so that it will decay. As it decays it releases heat to warm the nest.

When the huge pile of sand and vegetable matter is deep enough, the male mallee fowl scoops out an egg chamber in the center, fills it with more leaves and sand, and tops off the whole structure with still more sand. Once he has the nest complete, he uses his beak as a thermometer, poking it into the mound to check the temperature. He keeps the female away until the temperature reaches 92°F. Then he allows her to lay an egg a week over the following months. She may lay as few as 6 eggs or as many as 30. After the female has laid each egg, the male covers it with sand.

While the eggs are developing, the male keeps the temperature of the nest constant. If the temperature gets too high, he opens up the nest to expose the eggs. But if it drops too low, he piles on wet leaves to raise the temperature.

About every seven weeks a hatchling emerges. Fully feathered and able to take care of itself, it struggles up through the sand and scampers off—never to know the father that cared for it so devotedly. Aren't you glad that it won't be that way with us and the home that our heavenly Father is preparing for us? He's making a perfect place, and when we emerge from the darkness of this world into the light of heaven, He will be there to welcome us home.

A WORD FROM OUR CREATOR

In my Father's house are many mansions: if it were not so, I would have told you. I go to prepare a place for you. . . . that where I am, there ye may be also. John 14:2, 3.

October 20

Tough Skin

Perhaps you never thought of your skin being an organ like your liver, your heart, your stomach, and your brain, but it has special features and properties that give it that status. In fact, your skin is your largest organ. It helps to hold you together and regulates your body temperature.

The average person's skin covers about 18 square feet and weighs about 9 pounds. A square-inch section of your skin contains about a yard of blood vessels, more than three yards of nerves, and about 3 million cells. When you cut or puncture your skin, you feel pain because so many nerves signal the brain that an injury needs attention.

Your skin varies in thickness from less than one sixteenth of an inch on your eyelids to up to one eighth of an inch on your back. Compared to most animals, you are relatively thin-skinned. For example, an elephant's skin is so thick that the animal can walk through a forest of trees covered with thorns and full of broken limbs and never feel any discomfort.

Shark skin is another example of thick, tough skin. Specialized scales called dermal denticles, or "skin teeth," cover its body. Unlike typical scales, the dermal denticles are embedded in the skin and are tiny and most easily seen through a magnifying glass. If you were to pet a shark (imagine that!) from the nose to the tail, you'd think that it's skin was smooth. However, if you were to run your hand back the other way, you might decide that you were rubbing sandpaper. With these razor-sharp, close-set denticles, a shark can flay large fish with a single sideways swipe of its body.

Having thick skin might be an advantage if you are an elephant or a shark, but God has given us skin that is just right for our health and for keeping us sensitive to the world in which we live. Have you ever heard someone described as being "thick-skinned"? That means that it is hard to hurt that person's feelings. Such a person may also be insensitive to the feelings of others. In fact, he or she might even hurt others without feeling responsibility for his or her actions. Do you think that Jesus wants us to be thick-skinned?

A Word From Our Creator

Thou hast clothed me with skin and flesh, and hast fenced me with bones and sinews. Job 10:11.

A Pearl of Great Price

Large, perfectly shaped pearls equal the value of the most precious gemstones. But pearls are different from other gems. Most gems are minerals mined from the earth. Gem-quality pearls, however, form inside the shells of one type of oyster, the sea pearl oysters that grow in the tropical waters of earth's Eastern Hemisphere.

If the oyster is to produce a pearl, a piece of sand or other foreign substance has to find its way into it's shell. The oyster immediately begins to coat the irritating grain with a type of lime. As it adds layer after layer of the pearly covering, the pearl keeps growing.

Divers must open thousands of wild oyster shells to find even a few pearls, and then most of them are flawed. It may take 20 years to collect a perfectly matched set of pearls. The cultured pearl industry began because of the scarcity of perfect pearls from wild oysters. Most of the pearls that you see in a jewelry store are cultured pearls grown in pearl farms where "farmers" insert mother-of-pearl beads into the shells of living pearl oysters, then put them into cages or baskets and keep them in quiet waters for one or more years. Pearls grown in this way are less valuable than those grown naturally, but they satisfy the demand for this gem.

Manufacturers produce imitation pearls by dipping glass beads into a fish scale solution to coat the glass with what appears to be a pearl coating. But the imitation pearls do not stand the test of time and do not exhibit the soft wonderful glow of a real pearl.

In Revelation, John describes the New Jerusalem with walls and foundations composed of gems. "And the twelve gates were twelve pearls: every several gate was of one pearl" (Revelation 21:21). It is impossible to imagine the size or the beauty of such pearls, but it is easy to understand what those gates of pearl mean. Jesus is the pearl of great price. He said, "I am the door" (John 10:9). Every one of those pearly gates represents Jesus. He is the only way in. Taking upon Himself a foreign substance—sin—He coated it with eternal love for us.

A WORD FROM OUR CREATOR

Again, the kingdom of heaven is like unto a merchant man, seeking goodly pearls: who, when he had found one pearl of great price, went and sold all that he had, and bought it. Matthew 13:45, 46.

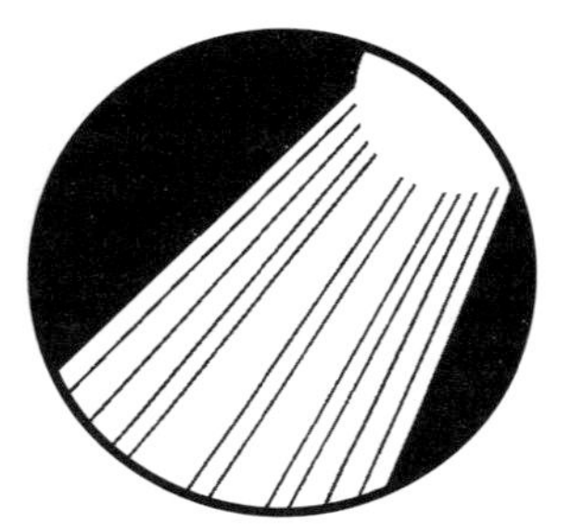

Enlightenment

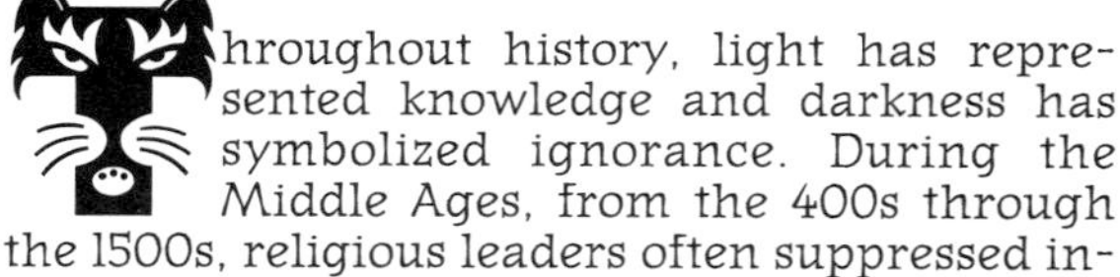

Throughout history, light has represented knowledge and darkness has symbolized ignorance. During the Middle Ages, from the 400s through the 1500s, religious leaders often suppressed information while tribunals squelched attempts to break out of the intellectual darkness.

Two movements brought the Dark Ages to an end: one called the Reformation, in the 1500s, based on freedom *of* religion, and another called the Enlightenment, in the 1600s and 1700s, based on freedom *from* religion. While Jesus, the Light of the world, inspired the Reformation, Lucifer, the prince of darkness, warped the Enlightenment and twisted it to his own purposes.

People held church leaders responsible for keeping them in the dark about such things as the nature of the universe and human intelligence. Religious leaders had distorted the concept of God so much that many people rejected Him. Instead of exploring the possibility that there might be a problem with the church's view of God, people threw out the idea of God altogether. Even if there was a God, they reasoned, He certainly didn't care about people and He didn't concern Himself with what was happening on earth.

In Paris people paraded a veiled woman through the streets and declared her to be the new deity—the Goddess of Reason. With mock adoration they took the goddess to the cathedral of Notre Dame and proclaimed her the object of all future worship. People believed that all they needed was the ability to reason, and since they were born with that, they didn't need God. Then they burned Bibles at public ceremonies. Scientific discovery became the means of enlightenment.

What people didn't know was that their enlightenment was a fulfillment of Bible prophecy: "But thou, O Daniel, shut up the words, and seal the book, even to the time of the end: many shall run to and fro, and knowledge shall be increased" (Daniel 12:4).

Satan's enlightenment brought an increase in knowledge, but it was the gospel of Jesus Christ that ended spiritual darkness.

A WORD FROM OUR CREATOR

That the God of our Lord Jesus Christ, the Father of glory, may give unto you the spirit of wisdom and revelation in the knowledge of him. Ephesians 1:17, 18.

October 23

Pinnacles in the Desert

On an isolated section of coastline about 150 miles north of Perth in Western Australia lies the Pinnacles Desert—a desert that's different from any other in the world. Because of the golden-orange color of the sand, the undulating dunes give the landscape a strange and eerie appearance. But the pinnacles punctuating the dunes are what really create the desert's extraterrestrial look.

Columns of limestone ranging in height from a few inches to more than six feet emerge from the golden sands as though they're growing from some subterranean root system. Persistent winds constantly change the dunes, so the columns grow and shrink, depending on the nature and intensity of the wind. The pinnacles vary in color. Most are yellow streaked with white, others show pink highlights, and still others have tinges of purple and brown. The texture of the columns ranges from marble-smooth to sandpaper-coarse. The first question that comes to mind when you see this desert is "Where did those pinnacles come from?" The answer illustrates today's text.

Hundreds of years ago, the Pinnacles Desert area was covered with sand, but a period of rainy years caused a hard calcified cap to form between the surface sand and deep sand. Plants started to grow on the surface of the sand and sent down roots that penetrated the cap rock, making channels for dissolved minerals to flow through the hard cap into the soft sand below. Carried in the water, those minerals drifted down into the sand and began to build the equivalent of stalagmites *in the sand*. The columns were growing under the sand, and no one knew that they were there.

Eventually the cap became so weakened by all the root channels that it broke down completely. The rainy period ended, and winds blew new sand in and suffocated the plants so that there was nothing to hold the dunes in place. The winds that had blown the sand in now began to sweep it away, exposing the pinnacles *for the first time ever*.

You never know when actions that you think are well covered will be exposed for the whole world to see. It's important to live in such a way that you have nothing to hide.

A Word From Our Creator

But if ye will not do so, behold, ye have sinned against the Lord: and be sure your sin will find you out. Numbers 32:23.

October 24

Fruitful

Everything in nature is interrelated. You cannot find a single plant or animal that does not depend on another plant or animal or both. For example, because of their diet, fruit-eating bats, birds, mammals, and even reptiles are directly responsible for the lush growth of fruit trees in tropical forests. Without the help of such frugivorous animals—fruit-eating creatures—fruit trees would eventually disappear from earth.

Fruits such as oranges, apples, figs, guavas, kiwis, mangoes, grapes—is your mouth watering yet?—bananas, strawberries, peaches, watermelons, and many others are delicious because nature meant them to be eaten. Not only are fruits good to eat, but it is also good for them to get eaten.

Generally speaking, the fleshy part of the fruit protects the seeds inside. When an animal eats a fruit, it usually eats it whole, including the seeds. The animal digests the pulp, but the seeds pass through the digestive tract and are eliminated. Biologists who study seed propagation and how it affects plant variety in a forest have discovered that seeds processed by fruit-eating bats sprout virtually 100 percent of the time. But the fruit seeds that just drop to the ground without passing through the bats sprout only 10 percent of the time. Frugivorous creatures also serve another important purpose in the propagation of plants: they scatter the seeds, so fruit trees literally crop up in new places. Bats, for example, have been known to drop seeds as far as 23 miles from the place where they ate the fruit.

God created plants with the ability to produce fruit that would be attractive to animals. The animals spread the seeds, thereby playing a vital part in helping more fruit grow. That's what it means to be fruitful, and multiply.

Fruit represents the indicators of a Christian character. "The fruit of the Spirit is love, joy, peace, longsuffering, gentleness, goodness, faith, meekness, temperance" (Galatians 5:22, 23). The best way to get more of the fruit of the Spirit is to enjoy its blessings and scatter the seed far and wide so that others can enjoy the fruit as well. "The seed is the word of God" (Luke 8:11). So, enjoy the fruit and spread the Word!

A Word From Our Creator

For the fruit of the Spirit is in all goodness and righteousness and truth; proving what is acceptable unto the Lord. Ephesians 5:9, 10.

October 25

Planet X

This text is one of the most tender and powerful promises in all of Scripture. Just think of what the children of Abraham had done to God. They had turned against Him again and again and again. Yet God tells them through the prophet Jeremiah that He will not forget them. He remembers the promise that He made to Jacob. In this text God finds a basis for certainty. Even when people become so knowledgeable that they think they can calculate and measure everything, God says that they'll still be dumbfounded by the mysteries of the universe. And God declares, "If this is not so, then you can believe that I will forget you."

It has become obvious that humans cannot measure the extent of the universe. Many of the world's leading astronomers admit that space may be infinite. And besides, if it isn't, what's on the other side of the end of it? So, heaven can't be measured, and God won't forget His promises.

A number of relatively simple measures have defied explanation so far. The existence of Planet X is one of them. For years astronomers have worked out the precise mathematical calculations to predict the location, approximate size, and orbital speed of a planet they have called Planet X. All the mathematical rules indicate that the planet has to be there, but it isn't. At least no one has found it yet.

It might be easier to understand why scientists haven't found Planet X when you realize that it would be more than 7 billion miles from the sun. That's 77 times farther than the distance from Earth to the sun and more than twice as far as the distance from Earth to Neptune. At that distance Planet X's movement would be hardly discernible even through powerful telescopes. One orbit would take it 680 Earth-years. From Planet X the sun would look like a bright star in a perpetually dark sky.

Planet X may or may not exist, but God's promises are sure.

A Word From Our Creator

If heaven above can be measured, and the foundations of the earth searched out beneath, I will also cast off all the seed of Israel for all that they have done, saith the Lord. Jeremiah 31:37.

ome people are born without the ability to taste. How would you like that? Of course, you wouldn't have to worry about eating food that you didn't like, but how would you know what you *did* like?

What kind of animal life do you suppose has the most highly developed sense of taste? It's not humans. As for birds, they may have fewer than 500 taste buds (compared to our 9,000 taste buds). A pig, on the other hand, has about 15,000 taste buds. So you would think that it would be a very discerning eater instead of one of the world's prime examples of a creature that will consume just about anything as long as there is enough of it.

Herbivores (animals that eat only plants) have highly developed taste functions. A rabbit has 17,000 taste buds, but a cow has 35,000! Perhaps if we ate nothing but grass, we'd need more taste buds so we could enjoy the subtle differences between the grass in this field and the grass in that field over there.

But the world's taste champions are fish. A catfish, for example, has 100,000 taste buds. Not only do fish have an abundance of taste buds, but some of them have taste buds on the *outside* of their bodies! Imagine that! Fish can literally taste the water they are swimming in. If they taste some favorite food nearby, like we get the scent of something, fish can home in on it and find it. If you were a fish and you saw something good to eat, you could truthfully say, "It looks so good I can taste it!"

How do you think it would be to have taste buds on your skin? It doesn't sound very appetizing, does it? God gave the fish what it needs, and He provided us with what we need. We can always trust Him to supply what's good for us. As is implied in our text for today, there is a spiritual taste also. And just as we can trust the Lord to provide food that tastes good, so we can trust Him to make His spiritual truth appetizing.

A Fishy Taste

A Word From Our Creator

O taste and see that the Lord is good: blessed is the man that trusteth in him. Psalm 34:8.

October 27

Essence of Skunk

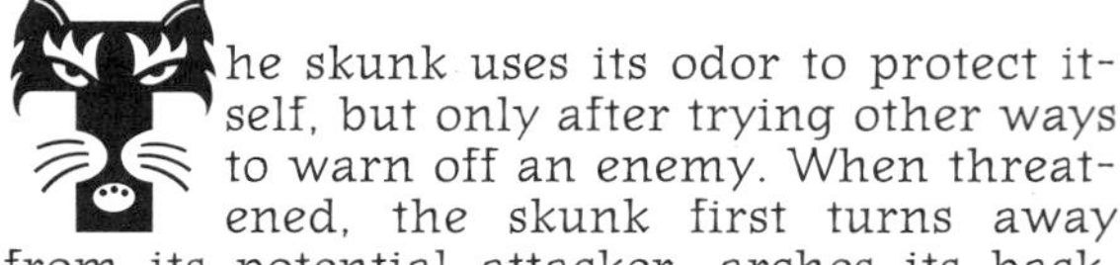

The skunk uses its odor to protect itself, but only after trying other ways to warn off an enemy. When threatened, the skunk first turns away from its potential attacker, arches its back, raises its tail, and stomps its feet. If those actions don't work, the skunk projects an amber-colored liquid with the familiar skunk smell. The effective range of its weapon is about 12 feet, and it can hit a target—usually the face of the enemy—at nine feet.

You probably hold your nose when you smell a skunk, but one scientist says that as many as 50 percent of us cannot smell it at all. Perhaps more amazing is the fact that some people actually find the odor so pleasant that they carry bottles of skunk-oil perfume to sniff (no, they don't wear it!) whenever they want to. In fact, one such person has formed what she calls the Whiffy's Club, complete with T-shirt and newsletter, for those who like the aroma.

Even people who don't like skunk odor have found its pungent fragrance useful. Cave explorers mark trails with it, Christmas tree farmers spray it on their trees to discourage theft, and a businessman once suggested that it be packaged in aerosol cans to repel muggers. It's hard to explain and even harder to imagine, but an extract of the skunk's spray has served for many years as the base for some of the world's finest perfumes. In order to do this, the perfume maker has to eliminate the offensive odor but keep the long-lasting essence and then attach new aromas to it.

Perhaps in the Garden of Eden the skunk was a source of incredibly wonderful fragrance—a walking aerosol "flower." Can you imagine a beautiful black-and-white animal strolling up to Adam and Eve to be petted, and then expressing its appreciation by providing the most wonderful aroma known in all of Eden—essence of skunk?

Our text for today compares God's love to a sweet-smelling savor. That love has filled the whole universe with an essence that cannot be explained. But perhaps the skunk helps us to understand that God takes us just as we are—like skunks in different ways—and through Jesus fills us with His love.

A Word From Our Creator

And walk in love, as Christ also hath loved us, and hath given himself for us an offering and a sacrifice to God for a sweet-smelling savour. Ephesians 5:2.

Of Kiwis and Dogs

No matter how large or how small it is, the human nose contains about 5 million olfactory sense cells, the cells that enable us to smell things. But our olfactory sense is only a shadow of what it could be or perhaps once was. We seem to use our sense of smell for enjoyment and to avoid some things like skunks. But other creatures in the world employ their sense of smell as a vital part of their daily life.

The champion smeller among birds is the kiwi—a New Zealand native that feeds partly on earthworms and uses its keen sense of smell to follow and capture its food. Scientists tested the kiwi's worm-tracking ability by allowing a worm to crawl away from the bird for a few yards. When they released the kiwi, which has very poorly developed eyesight, it went straight to the trail of the worm. By continuously tapping the ground along the trail, the bird followed the worm's path as accurately as any bloodhound tracks a person.

Kiwis are good trackers, but dogs are the champions. Most dogs have about 100 million olfactory cells in their noses. A barefoot human leaves fourteen hundred billionths of an ounce of sweat on the ground with each footprint—more than enough scent for any dog to follow. After centuries of breeding as a tracker, the bloodhound has more than 500 million olfactory sense cells in the membranes of its nose. The bloodhound's sense of smell is so accurate that the courts of the United States accept its "testimony" as evidence. No other animal has achieved that status. The lives of many boys and girls have been saved by the tracking ability of bloodhounds and other dogs.

The Creator has endowed His creatures with senses that we're only beginning to understand. Can you imagine how the sense of smell may be enhanced in heaven? But here on earth it's probably a blessing that we cannot smell all of the scents that are out there.

Nevertheless, just as God has given creatures like dogs and kiwis such incredible tracking powers, so He has taken upon Himself the task of seeking each of us to save us. But the decision about whether we will let Him find us is up to us.

A Word From Our Creator

For the Son of man is come to seek and to save that which was lost.
Luke 19:10.

October 29

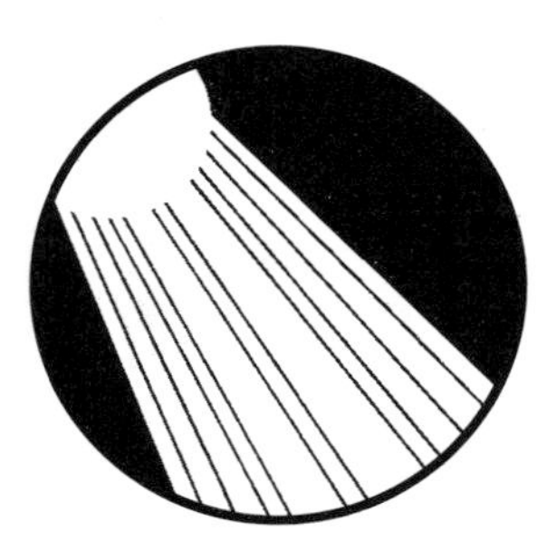

Irides-cence

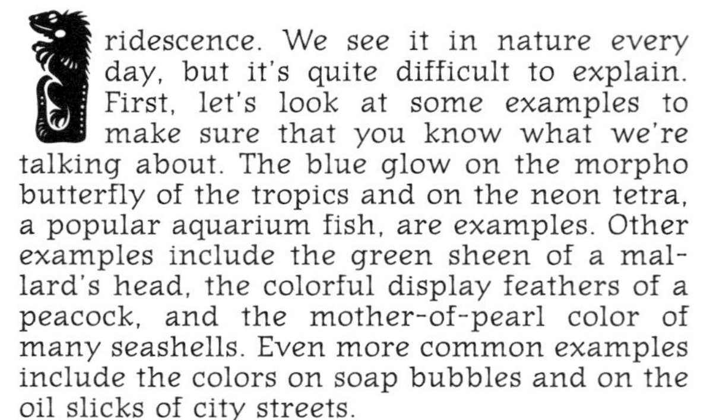

ridescence. We see it in nature every day, but it's quite difficult to explain. First, let's look at some examples to make sure that you know what we're talking about. The blue glow on the morpho butterfly of the tropics and on the neon tetra, a popular aquarium fish, are examples. Other examples include the green sheen of a mallard's head, the colorful display feathers of a peacock, and the mother-of-pearl color of many seashells. Even more common examples include the colors on soap bubbles and on the oil slicks of city streets.

Iridescence causes something to change colors right before your eyes. From one direction a grackle's head looks black, but as the bird turns its head, it is first green and then purple and then maybe back to black or green again.

Iridescence results when light rays reflect off two or more surfaces that are very close together and have different thicknesses. A soap bubble is a good example. The "skin" of a soap bubble is thicker in some places than it is in others. When light hits the bubble, some of it bounces back from the outer surface and some of it goes through the skin and reflects back from the inner surface. The light rays that shine off the inner surface may return to your eye at a different angle and therefore show a different color from the light rays coming back from the surface.

As the two different wavelengths reach your eyes simultaneously, they compete for prominence. Because of the different thicknesses of the film, you see different colors. What you see is a sheen that seems to change color depending on the direction and movement of the light source. That's why the same object can appear to be all of the colors of the rainbow either as you move or as it does.

God has given us beauty so many ways in the things that He made. He created everything with its own special splendor. No two things are exactly alike because God knows that we also find beauty in difference and in change.

A Word From Our Creator

He hath made every thing beautiful in his time. Ecclesiastes 3:11.

October 30

Fog to Smog

Fog is nothing but a cloud on the ground. Clouds form in the sky when warm air rises and cools to a point—the saturation point—at which the invisible water in the air becomes visible as tiny suspended water droplets. Fog forms when air near the ground cools to the saturation point. In mountainous areas, cool air from higher elevations drains downhill during the evening and into the night and collects in the valleys to become fog. Then during the day the air rises again and the fog disappears.

Fog is a hazard for drivers because even in broad daylight the water droplets diffuse the light rays, making it impossible to see very far ahead. Automobile accidents involving scores of cars in single crashes have occurred along roadways where fog is common.

However, fog itself is not harmful—it's just moist air—and perhaps even healthy to breathe. But when fog gets mixed with smoke and forms smog, it can be lethal. The smoke adds chemicals to the mixture—chemicals like sulphur that combine with the water in the fog to make sulphur dioxide, a poison.

People in the cities used to burn coal for heat in the winter, and the results were often terrible. During one five-day period in London during the winter of 1952, about 4,000 people died from chest and lung diseases caused by the poisons in the smog.

But the coal-caused smog of the past is now being replaced by the even more dangerous photochemical smog produced by automobile traffic. On hot, clear days sunlight converts car exhaust fumes into dangerous chemical compounds. Cities like Los Angeles and Mexico City suffer from periods when the photochemical smog is so bad that a smog alert tells people to stay indoors—if possible in an air-conditioned home or office with the windows closed.

Fog, which is safe to breathe, gets transformed by the addition of smoke into something that causes death. And so it is with our lives. We were created good, but because of evil we became subject to the death that results from the smog of sin. But Jesus has overcome the effects of that smog and has given us eternal life.

A Word From Our Creator

For the wages of sin is death; but the gift of God is eternal life through Jesus Christ our Lord.
Romans 6:23.

OCTOBER 31

Popcorn

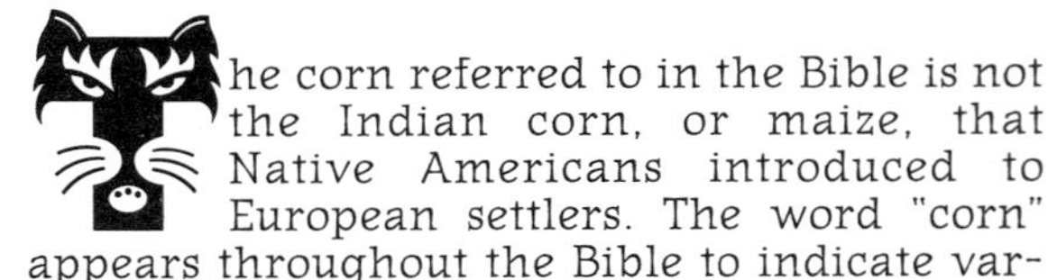

The corn referred to in the Bible is not the Indian corn, or maize, that Native Americans introduced to European settlers. The word "corn" appears throughout the Bible to indicate various kinds of grain, and a number of translations refer to the grain heads as ears.

Throughout North America the Indians planted and ate what we now call corn long before European immigrants arrived.

What makes popcorn pop? Do you have any idea? Would you be surprised if we told you that it is water? Every healthy kernel of popcorn has a small bit of water trapped in it. When you heat the popcorn, the water turns to steam, which builds up intense pressure and causes the corn to explode.

The first corn known was popcorn, and it grew on what appeared to be large stalks of grass. Each "ear" was no larger than a small strawberry and held only very small kernels. Native Americans experimented with the original versions of corn to produce better and better varieties over the centuries. When explorers from Europe arrived, the Native Americans were growing fields of popcorn with ears that were about four inches long.

To pop the corn, the original Americans would oil the ears with the husks on. Then they placed each ear on a stick and held the corn over a fire. The kernels popped inside the husks and provided the world's first bags of popcorn. The Europeans ate popcorn with milk and sugar, thereby creating the world's first puffed cereal.

Popcorn is one of the truly American foods. Virtually all the world's popcorn grows in the United States, with Nebraska and Indiana leading in its production. But it is a healthy natural food enjoyed around the world.

When we plant a kernel of popcorn, it sprouts and sends up a shoot while at the same time thrusting down a root. With good soil and the right amount of water the shoot will produce a strong, healthy full-grown corn plant with ears of corn. The plant is complete at every stage from the kernel to the adult plant, and that is the way it is with Christian growth.

A WORD FROM OUR CREATOR

For the earth bringeth forth fruit of herself; first the blade, then the ear, after that the full corn in the ear. Mark 4:28.

s today's text says, the brightness of stars differs. And those differences can be immense! The only evidence of the variations are the forms of radiation that they emit.

We can see only *visible* light with the unaided eye. Most star maps show you the differences in the amount of visible light from stars by describing them as having different magnitudes of brightness. But stars also transmit *invisible* rays, such as X-rays and gamma rays, and astronomers have developed star maps showing the stars in terms of the intensity of their X-ray and gamma ray magnitude.

The most powerful rays produced by stars are the gamma rays. A map of the sky depicting the various magnitudes of gamma ray emission reveals a sky packed with stars emitting gamma rays at various levels of intensity. The strongest gamma ray emission ever measured is from a galaxy called Markarian 421, only about 400 million light-years away from us. The gamma rays from Markarian 421 have *trillions* of electron volts of energy. Compare that to the amount of energy released by visible light—only *two* electron volts!

One type of gamma ray emission has scientists perplexed. Sensors have picked up superpowerful bursts of gamma rays from all over the universe, bursts that last from less than a thousandth of a second to a couple minutes. These bursts follow no particular pattern. They appear from every point in the heavens and at random times. And since they don't occur at specific intervals, astronomers have no way of anticipating where the next one will show up. These super rays are so powerful that, in terms of gamma radiation, when they appear they're momentarily the brightest spot in the entire sky.

Astronomers call whatever is producing these flares of gamma radiation "gamma ray bursters." Like gamma ray fireflies in the grand night of space, they never appear in the same place twice, and there seems to be no pattern to the location of the flashes. But they are certainly glorious.

Gamma Ray Bursters

A WORD FROM OUR CREATOR

There is one glory of the sun, and another glory of the moon, and another glory of the stars: for one star differeth from another star in glory. 1 Corinthians 15:41.

NOVEMBER 2

Making Gulls Fly—Try It!

Sometimes, in order to identify the species of an individual gull or of a flock of gulls standing at a distance, a birder must make them fly to see their wing patterns. When the gulls are so far away that they don't see or feel any need for alarm, they make no attempt to take to the air. They stay put only until hunger or fear makes them move.

But if you want those faraway gulls to take flight, all you have to do is go where they can see you, stand up straight, and face the gulls. Then, holding your arms straight out to your sides, begin to raise and lower them in slow, "stiff-winged" beats. How far away the gulls are doesn't seem to matter. It usually takes only a short time to see the results of your action. First one gull, then another, and finally the whole flock takes off.

You may be tempted to think that motion or noise would disturb the birds. Well, you can check that out too. Jump up and down, clap your hands, and yell—and the gulls just sit. Honk a car horn and slam car doors, and they ignore the noise. But pump your arms up and down like a bird taking flight, and watch the gulls respond by flying away.

Those gulls seem to be "running scared," always wary. When they see what their brain tells them is a bird taking off down the beach, they read the action as a danger signal, and their instinct tells them to fly. None of the other sounds and motions mean a thing to them.

When we spend years covering up the things that we're ashamed of having done, we usually develop a fear that someone will discover our past. Never able to relax, we're always "running scared" and act guilty even when we're behaving. We know that our sins eventually will find us out (Numbers 32:23).

Long ago our Saviour gave us the cure for such feelings: "If we confess our sins, he is faithful and just to forgive us our sins, and to cleanse us from all unrighteousness" (1 John 1:9). Our world has real danger, and it's important that we recognize it. But as forgiven Christians, we never have any need to be "running scared."

A WORD FROM OUR CREATOR

The wicked flee when no man pursueth. Proverbs 28:1.

he ability to smell is a wonderful sense, and human beings often associate it with love, affection, and beauty. The fragrance of flowers fills the air in a flower garden, and we collect those flowers into bouquets that bring the smell of the garden indoors. The scents of flowers and aromatic woods enhance the quality of our surroundings, and the burnt gums, resins, and sap of other plants become incense, perfuming the air.

The Bible frequently mentions incense as a part of the rituals of worship. The tabernacle of the Israelites had an altar upon which the priests burned only incense. The fragrance of burning incense represents the love of Jesus for His bride the church.

Men and women use colognes and perfumes to make themselves more attractive. We give various scents as gifts to those we love. But humans are not alone in using the sense of smell to be attractive to a mate. Insects respond to the allure of various scents. For example, to attract a female, the male monarch butterfly uses "cologne." He has a patch of scent-producing scales on each hind wing. To activate the scent, he uses a hairlike wand on his abdomen to rub the scent scales. This "scratch-and-sniff" method releases an aroma that attracts the female, who "smells" it through special receptors in her antennae.

With the 5 million scent-sensitive cells that we have in our nose, we can catch a whiff of a sweet-smelling aroma from a good distance away, and the brain cells that receive this sense from the cells in our nose tell us what the aroma is.

Our text describes the offering of Jesus on the cross as a sweet-smelling aroma before God—an indication of His love for humanity. Just as a person gives perfume to the one he or she loves, so Jesus gave His own life, and He offered it in a way that says, "Father, this perfume is to You from ______________________ (your name)."

The Scent of Love

A Word From Our Creator

And walk in love, as Christ also hath loved us, and hath given himself for us an offering and a sacrifice to God for a sweet-smelling savour. Ephesians 5:2.

Frosty and Tuffy

Frosty was a pet raccoon. Tuffy was a pet Scottie dog. When the two first met, it took a while for them to accept each other. But once they became friends, they became inseparable and it seemed that each tried to outdo the other in pranks. Whether they were inside or outside, they rolled and romped until exhausted. Then they would curl up to sleep, usually with Frosty's head resting on Tuffy.

But Frosty had one prank he loved to pull on Tuffy, and as many times as it happened, the dog just couldn't seem to learn that the raccoon was pulling his leg. Perhaps it was Frosty's way of getting some relief from the ever-present Tuffy. In any case, it never failed to work.

Pretending to discover something in the yard, the raccoon would start to dig as though unearthing a hidden treasure. Tuffy, who probably thought that Frosty had discovered a buried bone, would come to the bait every time, bumping his friend out of the way as if to say, "That's my bone. I buried it, and you can't have it!" And so Tuffy would take up the digging.

With Tuffy thus occupied, Frosty could go take a nap if he wanted to, or he could go exploring on his own. Forgetting everything else but that bone, Tuffy continued to dig, sometimes for an hour or more, grunting and yipping and panting while the dirt flew out of the hole into which he had now disappeared.

The funny thing was that when Tuffy finally gave up in apparent disgust, Frosty could take him back to that same hole and paw around in the loose soil at the bottom and start Tuffy digging all over again. The dog never found anything in those holes, and he never learned that his friend was playing him for a fool.

It's like that with people sometimes. So often it seems that we never learn, even though we suffer the consequences of the same folly again and again. Prudence is a form of wisdom whereby we learn from our mistakes so that we don't make them again. How prudent are you?

A WORD FROM OUR CREATOR

The simple believeth every word: but the prudent man looketh well to his going. Proverbs 14:15.

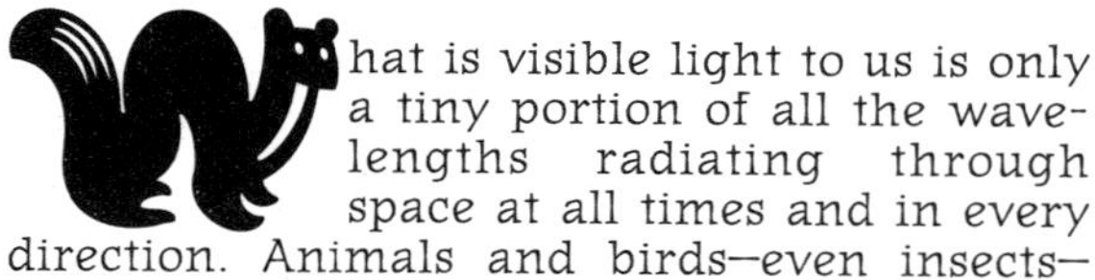

What is visible light to us is only a tiny portion of all the wavelengths radiating through space at all times and in every direction. Animals and birds—even insects—can see things that are invisible to us.

Our powers of sight are extremely limited, so we often think of darkness as being empty. But God can perceive everything: even what we call darkness is lighted up for Him. For God, there is no darkness. Imagine being able to see the full electromagnetic spectrum—gamma rays, X-rays, ultraviolet rays, infrared rays, radio waves, and microwaves. What would the universe look like? How would the world around us appear?

If our eyes could take in and process the full electromagnetic spectrum, we would be able to examine things with X-ray vision. Gamma ray vision would allow us to see through mountains and planets. Ultraviolet vision would enable us to view the flowers as the bees do—in different colors from those of visible light. We could detect the heat radiating from all living things if we had infrared vision, and our eyes could become a radio dial to tune in to the radio signals. Furthermore, we could watch TV broadcasts without a TV set. All we would have to do is to tune our minds into the channel, and our eyes would act as receivers.

As it is, we use such a small portion of the available spectrum that we can hardly imagine what life would be if our eyes were opened completely. What appears to us to be darkness is crammed full of rays and waves—particles of energy rushing about in our atmosphere and throughout space.

The perfect powers of vision that God endowed humanity with in Eden have been severely limited. When Jesus comes, we will be given glorified bodies. We think we can see a lot now, but just wait! Do you remember the story of Elisha's servant: "And the Lord opened the eyes of the young man; and he saw: and, behold, the mountain was full of horses and chariots of fire round about Elisha" (2 Kings 6:17)?

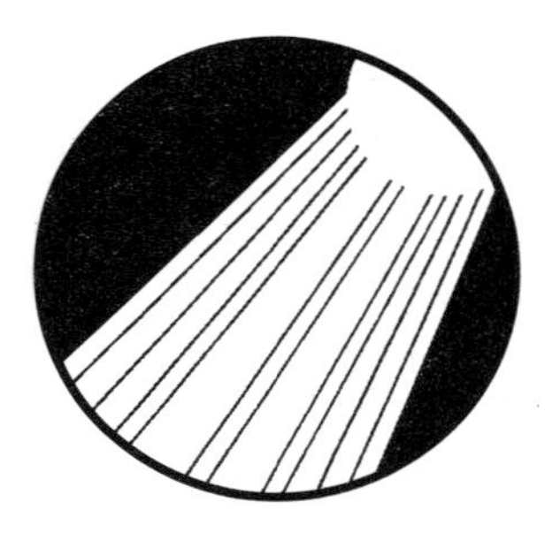

For God There Is No Darkness!

A WORD FROM OUR CREATOR

Yea, the darkness hideth not from thee; but the night shineth as the day: the darkness and the light are both alike to thee. Psalm 139:12.

November 6

Many Raindrops Make One Rainbow

A rainbow is certainly one of the most beautiful and spectacular events in the atmosphere. Its delicate beauty is unsurpassed. People stop and admire it, point it out to others, and talk about it. What is there about a rainbow that makes us wonder about it so much?

Perhaps it is because the rainbow is so elusive. Have you ever tried to touch one? You can't, of course. Do you know why you can't? What if we told you that the rainbow is really not anyplace at all? That's almost true. A rainbow exists, but only where your eyes are. It looks like it's right there in front of you, but it's actually only an image in your eye. When you move, so does the rainbow.

Maybe we're attracted to rainbows *because* they're elusive and amazing. Every rainbow forms because of the action of millions of tiny drops of rain. Each droplet acts like a lens both to reflect and refract sunlight to your eyes. As the light enters the raindrop, it's just white light. But the spherical shape of the droplet bends the light rays and splits them into colors. If there were only one raindrop, the amount of light reflected would be so small that you wouldn't see a thing, but since so many of them work together, you see the rainbow.

Perhaps there is another reason we're fascinated by rainbows. If you got a letter from the president or the king of your country promising you a special gift, wouldn't you cherish that letter and show it to everyone you knew? Every rainbow is exactly that—a solemn promise that God made not just to us, but to every creature on earth. He said, "I will remember my covenant, which is between me and you and every living creature of all flesh; and the waters shall no more become a flood to destroy all flesh" (Genesis 9:15).

The rainbow teaches us a wonderful lesson: when the light of the Sun of righteousness shines through a lot of God's people as His church, it creates a spiritual rainbow of promise to a hopeless world.

A Word From Our Creator

I do set my bow in the cloud, and it shall be for a token of a covenant between me and the earth. . . . I will look upon it, that I may remember the everlasting covenant between God and every living creature.
Genesis 9:13-16.

Enmity Between Tree and the Worm

We often call this war the great controversy between Christ and Satan. And it continues today. But it isn't in heaven anymore. It's right here on earth. The results of sin still cause strife and contention between the forces of heaven and those of hell. The prize each side seeks to gain in the war is your soul and mine.

Everything in nature provides evidence of the battle. Take the biochemical battle that goes on between plants and insects, for example. Natural substances in the leaves of many evergreen trees are toxic to insects. So those trees have protection from the voracious appetites of most caterpillars.

But in the ongoing battle, some insects have developed defenses against the evergreen toxins. One is the caterpillar of the aptly named southern armyworm that uses counterattack enzymes to convert the tree's poisons into harmless substances. When the caterpillar drinks, it washes the substances out of its system. So does that mean that the armyworm is going to win the war against the trees? Not at all!

The trees are beginning to strike back. Scientists have noted that some of the trees are changing the chemical makeup of their original toxins. Now when the insects convert them into water-soluble substances, instead of becoming harmless the toxins become time bombs. The transformed substance starts out as a harmless chemical but changes—in the caterpillar—into a poison. So far, the worm has no effective defense against it.

And the battle goes on throughout all nature. This is the way it had to be after sin entered the world. Until God makes the earth new, life will continue to be a struggle against the wages of sin. The Creator made it this way for our benefit. "And I will put enmity between thee and the woman, and between thy seed and her seed; it shall bruise thy head, and thou shalt bruise his heel" (Genesis 3:15). According to the promise God gave to Adam and Eve, Satan will lose and we will be saved through Jesus.

A Word From Our Creator

And there was war in heaven: Michael and his angels fought against the dragon; and the dragon fought and his angels, and prevailed not; neither was their place found any more in heaven. Revelation 12:7, 8.

November 8

Whence Come Comets?

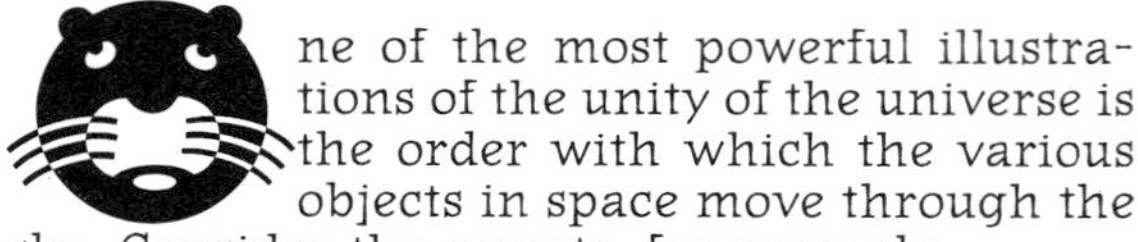

One of the most powerful illustrations of the unity of the universe is the order with which the various objects in space move through the sky. Consider the comets, for example.

Even though most of us hear about only a few famous comets—like Halley's, which returns in its orbit every 76 years—actually many, many comets zoom through space. And all the comets travel at very high speeds in orbits interconnected with the orbits of the planets around the sun. Comets all follow oval, or elliptical, orbits, with the sun at one end of the orbit instead of at the middle. But where do the comets come from?

Scientists are still debating about their origin, but they all agree that comets seem to originate from a distant section of our solar system called the Oort Cloud. The Oort Cloud, named after the Dutch astronomer Jan H. Oort, is a vast region of cosmic dust particles. It orbits the sun trillions of miles away. Astronomers believe that billions of comets drift together in cold storage in that part of the universe.

According to current theory, the gravity of a passing star pulls one or more of the comets out of their traditional orbits in the Oort Cloud, and they then begin to fall toward the star. But because the star and the comet are moving so fast, they usually don't crash into each other. The comets whip around the star in such a way that their own momentum takes them back into space until they run out of power and begin to fall back toward the star again. Comets orbiting around our sun range in size from the smaller ones like the Comet Encke, which revolves once every 3.3 years, to larger ones like Kohoutek, which takes more than a million years to orbit the sun.

By this huge illustration, the Creator shows us that every individual can be different and yet get along. Every person can be on a different path, so to speak, and yet be walking in harmony with everyone else.

A Word From Our Creator

Behold, how good and how pleasant it is for brethren to dwell together in unity! Psalm 133:1.

he normal life span of most adult monarch butterflies is only four or five weeks. But the final brood of monarchs each summer live much longer because they have a special mission to complete. Most butterflies die with the onset of winter, but the final generation gathers in great swarms and moves south in a long flight that takes them to their wintering grounds in the Caribbean, Mexico, and California. Let's follow the ones that winter in Mexico.

By the time the monarchs reach Texas, so many of them have assembled that it takes hours for them to pass overhead. It's difficult to believe that any one of these butterflies may have already traveled more than 1,000 miles and still has 1,000 miles to go. If the breezes are favorable, the butterflies sometimes continue flying all night. Pilots have reported migrating swarms of monarchs sailing along on wind currents at elevations from 1,500 to 7,000 feet. By conserving energy in this way and by eating along the way, the monarchs arrive in Mexico fatter than when they began their flight southward.

More than 100 million monarchs make the two-month trip to Mexico each year. How do they know where to go? They've never flown south before, so they aren't relying on memory. In fact, these navigating monarchs are four generations removed from those butterflies that had the knowledge of where their wintering area in the Mexican mountains is located. How do they know how to find that precise spot? The phenomenon is one of the most mysterious events of nature. Scientists still have no clue about how the monarchs are able to perform a feat unparalleled in the natural world.

The signs all seem to tell us that the end of the world is near. The spiritual equivalent of winter is approaching. Our text speaks of a final generation of God's people who will be saved. Do you have any doubt that the same God who guides the monarch will provide for the safety of the final generation in this world?

The Last Monarchs

A Word From Our Creator

And the dragon was wroth with the woman, and went to make war with the remnant of her seed. Revelation 12:17.

November 10

Tuatara

t looks like a prehistoric lizard, but the tuatara is in a class by itself. In fact, it's the last remaining representative of a group of reptiles that were more closely related to dinosaurs than to creatures now living. Its name means "sting-bearer," after the line of bony spines that march down the center of its head and back.

However, the tuatara is not only harmless; it also lives peacefully in a burrow with a bird. The pigs and cats that Europeans took to New Zealand once hunted it almost to extinction. Today the tuatara lives only on a few small, rocky, inaccessible islets between the two large islands of that country.

Most reptiles must avoid the hottest hours of sunlight because the temperature of the air largely regulates their body temperatures. The tuatara's normal body temperature is only about 55°F, more than 20 degrees lower than that of the toad, the creature with the next-lowest temperature. Because of its low body temperature, the tuatara's metabolism is extremely sluggish, so the animal has only to capture a few crickets or other insects each day to survive. The tuatara hunts at night to avoid the heat. If it wants to bask on what seems like a cool day, thermoreceptors in its eyes pick up infrared light and tell it about the outside temperature.

During daylight hours the tuatara stays in the shelter of a burrow dug by a nesting seabird called a shearwater. The shearwater spends most of its life at sea. But when the breeding season arrives, the bird digs a burrow on a remote island, lays its one egg in the burrow, and incubates it there. The adult shearwater goes out to fish during the day while the tuatara occupies the burrow. Then the shearwater stays in the burrow during the night while the tuatara hunts. But even if their schedules overlap, the two creatures get along just fine.

The tuatara relies on the shearwater to provide it with a home, and the shearwater is equally dependent on its reptile roommate to house-sit while she is at sea. Together, the tough tuatara and the delicate shearwater demonstrate how the meek can inherit the earth.

A Word From Our Creator

Blessed are the meek: for they shall inherit the earth. Matthew 5:5.

November 11

Deceitful Animals

A classic experiment with chimpanzees demonstrated what appears to be a conscious intent to deceive. Scientists showed only one member of a group of laboratory chimps where they had hidden a banana. When they let the animals out of their cages, that chimp got the banana. But the others quickly learned to watch that animal. If he started toward the food, they quickly ran past him and grabbed it.

Not to be outdone, the chimp with the inside information quickly learned an alternate plan. Instead of immediately heading for the food, he faked a move in a wrong direction. All the chimps would then rush off in that direction, and the chimp would retrieve the banana without competition. The chimps thus displayed deception, greed, and selfishness.

We have a springer spaniel named Daisy. A wonderful dog, she learns fast and almost always comes bounding to greet us when we come home. But Daisy has one bad trait that she just won't give up. She digs where she is not supposed to. We don't mind her digging in some places, but we don't want her rooting up the flowers and shrubs.

Daisy knows where we don't want her tearing up the ground, and she never does it when we're around. But as soon as we're out of sight, into the flower bed or under the shrubs she goes to excavate a new and deeper hole. When we happen to catch her digging in the wrong place, she immediately stops and slinks into the garage to hide. Knowing that she has done something that we don't want her to do, she doesn't come bounding up to us to welcome us home.

The hallmark of sin is deceit. First Satan lied to Eve, deceiving her into eating the fruit of the forbidden tree. Then when God came to the Garden of Eden, Adam and Eve hid in shame. Adam lied to God about whose fault it was that he had eaten the fruit. With the entrance of sin, the rule of all nature changed from open honesty and sharing to one of lying, cheating, and stealing. Selfishness replaced generosity, and fear replaced love.

There is only one cure for the natural and deceitful heart. Jesus.

A Word From Our Creator

The heart is deceitful above all things, and desperately wicked: who can know it? Jeremiah 17:9.

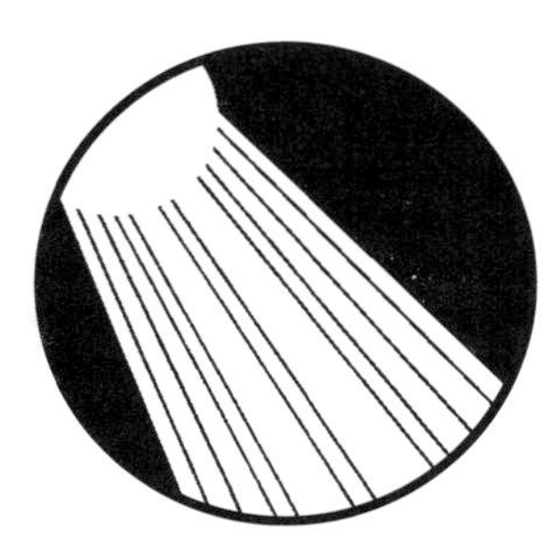

What Colors Make You Feel Better?

Did you ever wonder why the grass is green and the sky is blue? The different chemical makeups of the grass and sky causes them to absorb the photons of all other colors and reflect the photons of either only green or blue. But I believe there's another reason.

God shows His love in the way He designed the world so that every aspect supports all others—down to the smallest detail. Take color, for instance. God created everything in full color *before* He made humanity. As Adam and Eve came forth from the Creator's hand, they beheld a wondrous world. God had perfectly designed all the colors to keep the human pair healthy.

The human eye can distinguish millions of different colors. Each hue is a combination of different wavelengths of light striking the rods and cones on the retina of the eye. And now we are discovering that each of those colors has a different effect on the brain. Scientists are only beginning to learn about the emotional and intellectual effects of color, but we have known about the physical effects for some time.

When we look at various shades of red, orange, and yellow, our blood pressure rises, our brain waves become more active, our breathing speeds up, and our perspiration increases. Did you know that you sweat more when you look at the color red?

Dentists in Canada found that shades of blue ease the fears of their patients. Scientists also discovered that hues of peach, yellow, and blue relaxed patients in a clinic in Connecticut. And the peach color found on the walls of so many fast-food outlets stimulates you to eat more.

Other studies have shown that a person's intelligence increases under the influence of certain colors, and we've also learned that some shades of pink have such a calming influence that the only treatment needed for some mental patients is to sit in a room painted a certain shade of pink. They require no medication.

Perhaps it is no wonder that God made many roses pink.

A WORD FROM OUR CREATOR

And out of the ground made the Lord God to grow every tree that is pleasant to the sight. Genesis 2:9.

NOVEMBER 13

God Is Surrounded by Dark Clouds

A WORD FROM OUR CREATOR

Clouds and darkness are round about him: righteousness and judgment are the habitation of his throne.
Psalm 97:2.

Why would dark clouds surround God's throne? We often refer to misfortune as a dark cloud and refer to people to whom bad things seem to happen a lot as "living under a dark cloud." Such folk wisdom would have us believe that dark clouds are bad omens. But at times we really would welcome a dark cloud—the darker the better. And if we understand how dark clouds can be useful and even desirable, then perhaps we can understand today's text.

From our vantage point on earth, clouds blot out the sky. In fact, the thicker the cloud, the darker it is—until it looks almost black. When you're working hard on a hot summer day and the sky is clear and the sunshine is blazing down on you, you long for a cloud to shield you from the sun and give you relief from the heat. If you've ever been out in the desert in the middle of the day, you know just how hot it can get. The rays of the sun are unrelenting in their force, but when a cloud floats by, you immediately feel cooler. Why?

To say that you feel cooler because the cloud makes shade—the darker the cloud, the deeper the shade—is true, but how? Water makes the clouds dark. The water in the cloud reflects much of the light from the sun back into space. The more water contained in a cloud, the less light can get through it and the darker it will look to us on the ground. It turns back the light rays containing the energy that makes heat. You feel the result as cooling shade, and on a hot summer day the cooling effect of a dark cloud is remarkable.

To sinful humanity, God is a consuming fire. As He told Moses on Mount Sinai, "there shall no man see me, and live" (Exodus 33:20). We need the cooling protection of Jesus to come between us and God's judgment. The next time you feel the heat of the sun and long for the shade of a cloud, remember that Jesus is the Water of Life. He provides eternal shade for each of us so that we can live in safety in the presence of the omnipotent power of God.

NOVEMBER 14

Giant Fruits and Vegetables

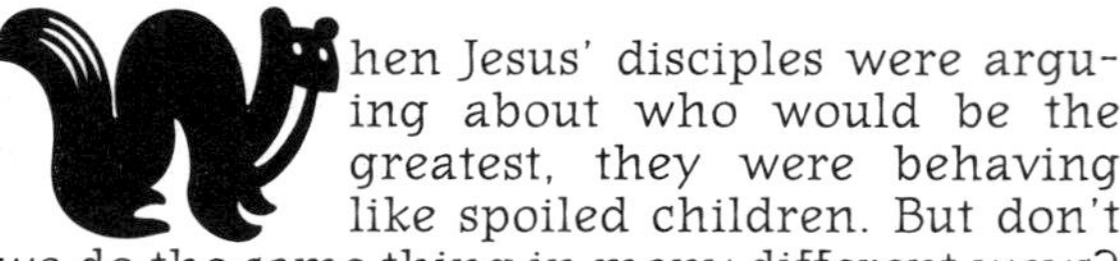

When Jesus' disciples were arguing about who would be the greatest, they were behaving like spoiled children. But don't we do the same thing in many different ways? For instance, how about the records that people are forever trying to break so they can get listed in the *Guinness Book of Records*?

You might not think that anyone would become very excited about growing the world's biggest pumpkin, but getting their names printed in the record book has become a prize that some people take most seriously. Some scientifically breed fruits and vegetables to produce larger and larger specimens just to shatter the previous record.

How about a 7-pound potato or a 10-pound 14-ounce onion? People grew these record holders in Great Britain. But those are small potatoes compared to the really big vegetables—again all British: a 28-pound radish, a 48-pound turnip, and a 124-pound cabbage. That's a lot of cabbage!

How about fruits? The world's largest strawberry—British again—weighed 8 ounces. The largest pineapple grew in the Philippines. It weighed 17 pounds 8 ounces. The world's largest watermelon appeared in 1990 in Tennessee and weighed 262 pounds! And the record-holding pumpkin turned up in New Jersey and weighed in at an incredible 816 pounds! That pumpkin was large enough to have been Cinderella's coach. A previous record holder only half that size was large enough for the grower's wife to fit easily inside. Remember the fable about Peter Pumpkin-eater and his wife?

As amazing as these records are, the lengths to which people go to produce such record-breaking items is even more startling. They build tents to protect the plants. Some potential record breakers camp out for weeks beside their fruit or vegetables to keep vandals and thieves from destroying or stealing their prize.

The disciples wanted to be important, and they thought that being the greatest would make them more important. But Jesus answered the question about who is the greatest: "And whosoever will be chief among you, let him be your servant" (Matthew 20:27).

A Word From Our Creator

And there was also a strife among them, which of them should be accounted the greatest. Luke 22:24.

November 15

Hop a Comet and Visit the Stars

People are constantly trying to figure out how to escape from the earth. But Jesus made us a promise that He will keep: He is coming back to get us. He will take us off this planet. That is the easy way. But human beings insist on imagining hard ways that will get us into space without God. Do you suppose there's another being stuck on this planet who wants to get away? Could it be that Satan is looking for a means to escape from the doom that he's chosen for himself and his angels? Is the devil hoping that humanity will save *him* somehow? But here's a new theory about how we could make our way to other galaxies.

Naturally, if you want to survive in space you'll need air and water. Wouldn't it be nice if we could find ready-made spaceships that already had a built-in supply of water that we could use for drinking and also for producing oxygen to breathe? Well, such space barges may exist. Comets consist largely of ice—frozen water. So some dreamers have suggested that if we could just hop onto a passing comet, we wouldn't even need energy for propulsion—at least not for a while. We could ride on the comet, using its momentum to take us deeper into space. And perhaps we could even transfer to another comet going in the direction that we wanted to go. Who knows—eventually we might reach an undiscovered planet or moon. Of course, it would take us thousands—maybe millions—of years, even at the speed of a comet. But we would be achieving the goal of getting off Planet Earth. God, who created the comets, has an easier way, though. "For the Lord himself shall descend from heaven with a shout, with the voice of the archangel, and with the trump of God: and the dead in Christ shall rise first: then we which are alive and remain shall be caught up together with them in the clouds, to meet the Lord in the air: and so shall we ever be with the Lord. Wherefore comfort one another with these words" (1 Thessalonians 4:16-18).

Are you ready to go?

A Word From Our Creator

And if I go and prepare a place for you, I will come again, and receive you unto myself; that where I am, there ye may be also.
John 14:3.

November 16

Crinoids

There is a group of sea creatures that look like plants but act like animals. They belong to the class of sea life called Crinoidea (pronounced krin-OY-dee-a). Biologists consider the crinoids to be animals, but each of these animals has a stem and what look like flowers with feathery petals at the tip.

Crinoids are far more common as fossils than they are as living creatures. Fossil records indicate that many more kinds of crinoids lived before the Flood. However, those crinoids that do survive today represent some of the most beautiful creatures of the sea.

A crinoid spends the daylight hours hidden in the crevices of rocks and coral reefs. At night it crawls and swims to a high perch, where it waves its 200 or so feathery arms, or tendrils, in all directions, reaching for tiny microscopic plants and animals to eat. Because of their flowerlike appearance, people call some of them sea lilies.

With their brilliantly colored feathery tendrils, sea lilies form a fantastic underwater garden. They come in all colors, and they provide ideal homes for some of the ocean's colorful creatures. Bright-yellow clingfish, only an inch long, live among the tendrils of bright-yellow sea lilies. Black-and-white-striped clingfish dwell among the tendrils of black-and-white sea lilies. And orange clingfish make their homes among the tendrils of orange sea lilies. Tiny shrimp and crabs also hide in the crinoid's tendrils. These little crustaceans depend completely upon the sea lilies for their food and safety.

Another group of crinoids, the feather stars, are many-rayed circular structures. They form a permanent, never-fading, underwater fireworks display—like starbursts suspended in time.

We often think of camouflage colors as mottled browns and greens. But protective coloration comes in many hues. The colors fit the situation. A number of small sea creatures are thankful for the protective arms of crinoids.

A Word From Our Creator

And God created great whales, and every living creature that moveth, which the waters brought forth abundantly, after their kind.
Genesis 1:21.

It has suction-cup pads on the ends of its long fingers and toes to help it to cling to upright tree branches—but it isn't a tree frog. It sleeps during the day, hunts at night, and can turn its head to look directly behind it with its huge round eyes—but it isn't an owl. And it has a furry six-inch body and naked 10-inch tail—but it isn't a rat. What is it?

If you deduced from its furry aspect that the animal is a mammal, you're right about that. But unless you're very well acquainted with the wildlife of the East Indies and the Philippines, you're probably still stumped about the creature's identity. The little animal is a tarsier.

A tarsier is a primate, so it's distantly related to monkeys and apes. Nocturnal, it dozes during the day but is wide awake all night as it looks for the insects, snails, and small lizards that it feeds on. Its keen eyesight gives it the ability not only to catch prey in the dark but also to stay clear of predators. When it senses the presence of an owl or other enemy behind it, it dilates its pupils and snaps its head around to check out the situation. And if it needs to get away in a hurry, it escapes by jumping away from the danger. And what an amazing jumper it is!

The tarsier doesn't just hop from branch to branch. It leaps as much as six feet—or about 12 times its body length (not counting the tail)—from one tree to another. Then when it lands on a new tree, it clings to the trunk with the adhesive discs on the bottoms of its hands, feet, fingers, and toes.

If the tarsier reaches the ground, it can hop like a frog. But even on the ground the little primate can cover five feet in a single bound. If humans could jump like the tarsier, a six-foot person could leap more than 70 feet from tree to tree and more than 60 feet in a standing broad jump. As a jumper, the tarsier is in a class by itself.

The same Creator who gave the tarsier such abilities in escaping danger is the Lord who has promised to deliver us, too.

Champion Jumper

A Word From Our Creator

And the Lord shall help them, and deliver them: he shall deliver them from the wicked, and save them, because they trust in him. Psalm 37:40.

November 18

The Unknown Spider

A Word From Our Creator

Remembering without ceasing your work of faith, and labour of love, and patience of hope in our Lord Jesus Christ, in the sight of God and our Father.
1 Thessalonians 1:3.

Mrs. Nien Cheng was a widow who lived with her daughter in Shanghai during the Chinese Communist Cultural Revolution. One day in 1966 soldiers of the Red Guard came and took Mrs. Cheng in for questioning. She never came home and she never saw her daughter again. The men who questioned her spit on her, called her "Dirty spy!" and demanded that she confess to being an enemy agent. All the while Mrs. Cheng kept repeating the twenty-third psalm silently to herself. She had done nothing wrong.

"Confess!" her tormenters screamed at her.

Mrs. Cheng lifted her head and said in a loud and steady voice, "I'm not guilty! I have nothing to confess."

Realizing that she would not give in, the men handcuffed Mrs. Cheng, took her to be photographed and fingerprinted, and then placed her in a prison called the Number 1 Detention House. She had never imagined that any place could be so filthy. Cobwebs hung from the ceiling, the guards rarely turned off the single light suspended on a cord from the ceiling, and the bed was crusty with greasy dirt. Yet it would be her home for the next six and a half years.

Days merged into weeks. It seemed that the world had forgotten her. She wanted to see her daughter or to hear some word from her, but she received no news of any kind. Desperately she longed for some evidence that God still cared for her.

Then she saw it. The spider had been there all the time, but she hadn't noticed it until that day. The small creature was living in the same horrible conditions that she was enduring. But that spider patiently laid down strand after strand of silk to construct its web. The creature had a job to do, and it carried out its assigned task with steady confidence.

Mrs. Cheng believed that God had sent the spider to encourage her. In her words, "a miracle of life had been shown me." Beginning to take heart, she never again lost her resolve, and in 1973 the government released her. Her daughter had died in the revolution, but thanks to God's gift of a spider Mrs. Cheng had never lost faith.

A beacon is usually located on a high structure so its bright light can guide ships and airplanes on a safe course. But wait. Is the beacon the structure itself, or is it the stream of light that comes from the structure? Can you have one without the other? In John 8:12 Jesus declared, "*I am* the light of the world." But in Matthew 5:14 Jesus said "*Ye are* the light of the world." Which is it? Is Jesus the light of the world, or are you?

Here we see two different ideas about the light. In Matthew 5:14, where Jesus says you are the light, He goes on to compare you to a city on a hill and to a candle on a candlestick that "giveth light unto all that are in the house" (verse 15).

What happens when you turn on the lights in a dark house? When you flip the switch, electricity provides the light bulbs with the energy to produce light. When Jesus lived on earth, people used tiny oil lamps to light their homes after dark. When travelers looked for lodging after dark, they were pleased to see the flicker of the light of a distant city. But the oil lamp, the torch, and the light bulb are only instruments that provide light. The light itself is something very different—something ultimately powerful and mysterious.

In John 8:12 Jesus is talking about the light itself when He says that He is the light of the world. Earlier in his Gospel, John mentions John the Baptist: "There was a man sent from God, whose name was John. The same came for a witness, to bear witness of the Light, that all men through him might believe. He was not that Light, but was sent to bear witness of that Light. That was the true Light, which lighteth every man that cometh into the world" (John 1:6-9). John the Baptist was the instrument—the lamp or light bulb—not the light itself.

Jesus needs beacons that will serve as vessels for His light. But as the song says: "You can't be a beacon if your light [doesn't] shine." You are the light because Jesus shines through you.

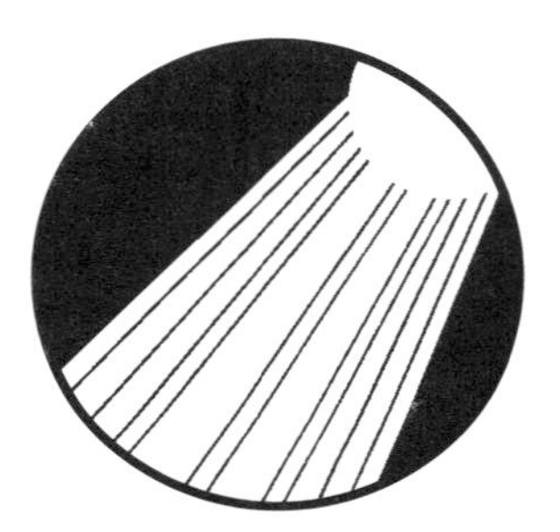

Be a Beacon

A Word From Our Creator

That ye may be blameless and harmless, the sons of God, without rebuke, in the midst of a crooked and perverse nation, among whom ye shine as lights in the world. Philippians 2:15.

November 20

Mirages

American explorer Robert E. Peary almost discovered the North Pole. He was only a short distance away when he saw a range of "snow-clad summits above the ice horizon" ahead. Knowing that it was too late in the season to make it over a mountain range and back again before winter, Peary turned back. He had not been able to achieve his goal because of the mountains he saw in the distance.

Donald MacMillan, another American explorer, made the same journey, hoping to succeed where Peary had failed. As he approached the mountain range, he could see them clearly. MacMillan wrote: "There could be no doubt about it . . . what a land! Hills, valleys, snowcapped peaks . . ." The party eagerly moved forward to explore the range. Thirty miles later, however, they found no mountains at all—only endless arctic ice. The entire mountain range had been a mirage.

A mirage is a trick that light plays because of weather conditions. The image of something far away gets projected as though it is just ahead of you. You may have seen what appeared to be a shimmering lake on the desert or highway ahead, only to have it disappear as you approached. Actually, what you saw was a patch of blue sky, but the light rays from the sky were bouncing off the hot air at the surface of the ground to your eyes. The dividing line between the hot air below and the cooler air above acts like a mirror.

What you see in a mirage is real—it's just not where you see it. For example, the first sighting of the rising sun and the last visible image of the setting sun are mirages. The sun is not where it appears to be. Because the earth's atmosphere bends the rays of the sun, we spot the sun in the sky before it has yet actually risen, and we still see it after it has already set.

Our goal as followers of Jesus is to achieve a character more and more like Christ's. Satan loves to play tricks on us as we move ahead. He plants mirages in our path—false hopes and false fears. Taking the true light, he bends it to give us inaccurate views that we must test by the Word of God. Only by keeping Jesus in our sights can we move steadily toward that prize.

A Word From Our Creator

I press toward the mark for the prize of the high calling of God in Christ Jesus. Philippians 3:14.

The manchineel (pronounced man-chih-NEAL) is a medium-size tree that grows in tropical America as far north as the beaches of southern Florida. It belongs to the spurges, a family that includes the rubber tree and the castor bean plant. Trees and plants in the spurge family produce a milky sap that's sometimes valuable, like the rubber trees, and sometimes poisonous, like the castor beans.

From its appearance, the manchineel seems ordinary. Large ones grow to 50 feet. The three- to four-inch leaves are oval with toothed margins, the bark is tan and smooth, and the yellowish green fruit looks like a crabapple.

But the manchineel is anything but ordinary. Although it appears harmless, it hides a secret—its sap is highly toxic. Natives of Caribbean islands passed down legends of the tree's poisonous powers, claiming that even the tree's odor was deadly. Those legends weren't too far off the mark, and fortunately they were successful in warning people to stay away from the tree. But some of the early American explorers were not impressed by legends.

Around 1850, British ship carpenters were temporarily blinded after cutting down a manchineel for lumber. When the ship's captain investigated the cause of the affliction, he picked up a few leaves and fruit and also lost his eyesight for a short time.

We now know that the sap and fruit of the manchineel are extremely poisonous to people and animals. Contact with the tree causes skin inflammation and temporary blindness. Even rainwater dripping from the leaves produces blisters on the skin, and smoke from the burning wood creates short-term blindness. This is a tree to stay away from regardless of how harmless it may look.

Life is full of things like the manchineel—things that look harmless enough but are deadly when we get involved with them. God's power to save includes giving us fair warning about dangerous pursuits. He then leaves it up to us to demonstrate the wisdom of following His direction.

Manchineel

A Word From Our Creator

And the serpent said unto the woman, Ye shall not surely die: for God doth know that in the day ye eat thereof, then your eyes shall be opened, and ye shall be as gods. Genesis 3:4, 5.

NOVEMBER 22

Neutron Stars

Neutron stars are also called pulsars because of the pulsating radio waves that they emit in all directions. Imagine that space is a pond and that the neutron star is a pebble that you toss into the water. The circular ripples that spread endlessly outward represent the radio waves projected into the far reaches of space from the star in the center. Scientists first detected their radio waves in 1967 when radio telescopes picked up the intermittent bursts.

At first, astronomers believed that the radio signals might be messages from outer space and called them LGM, for "little green men." And while scientists now know that the waves aren't messages from space beings, they still have many questions about the nature of pulsars. For example, what is the source of the radio waves? Are they coming from some spot on the star's surface, or from above one of the star's magnetic poles?

Scientists call pulsars neutron stars because the astronomical bodies consist entirely of subatomic particles called neutrons. Unlike protons, which repel each other, neutrons don't have an electrical charge, so they pack together very tightly. Consequently, a neutron star can be many times denser than our more gaseous and much larger sun. A teaspoonful of matter from a neutron star would weigh billions of tons on earth.

In addition to the radio waves, some pulsars also emit X-rays as well as visible light. One of the most familiar pulsars is the bright star at the center of the Crab Nebula. When the Crab Nebula exploded in 1054, it left behind a very tightly packed neutron star surrounded by a cloud of gas.

The heavens and the intelligent beings of other worlds do rejoice. We are sure of that. But so far the only messages sent for us to decipher have been those from God through His appointed natural agents. His primary Agent, of course, is His own Son, Jesus.

A WORD FROM OUR CREATOR

Let the heavens rejoice, and let the earth be glad; let the sea roar, and the fullness thereof. Psalm 96:11.

November 23

Tadpole Shrimp

People have described the Mojave Desert in southeastern California as a vast wasteland. The plants and animals that live in the Mojave have had to adapt to the hot, dry conditions of their habitat. Spines protect cacti from the intense heat of the sun by deflecting some of its rays, and animals hunt at night when the temperature drops. One creature, though, shows an incredible amount of patience as it waits for rain.

Lying in the hardened mud, the eggs of tiny tadpole shrimp stay buried for decades, hatching as soon as a rainstorm creates a temporary pond. Although in other deserts heavy rain occurs yearly, in the Mojave rain may not fall for 25 years or *even longer*. When it finally does rain, the eggs hatch almost immediately. After waiting so long, hundreds of thousands of little shrimp are impatient to grow up and lay eggs of their own so that their species will survive. Therefore, within weeks of hatching, the little larvae mature into adult shrimp and lay eggs in the soft mud. They have no time to lose, for when the pond water evaporates—as it surely will—they will die, just as their parents did so many years earlier. But the next generation of eggs is safe in its underground incubator, waiting.

The tadpole shrimp that are now isolated in the Mojave sand are probably the descendants of shrimp that originally lived in the waters of the Pacific Ocean. As the sea receded, the shrimp adapted to a habitat that became drier and drier. And in order to survive, the shrimp had to outlast the long droughts, so the eggs became accustomed to lying dormant for years. In fact, evidence suggests that tadpole shrimp eggs can survive being buried in the mud for a century as they wait for the rain to fall.

As Christians we are waiting patiently for a final outpouring of the Holy Spirit—the Bible refers to this as the "latter rain." "Ask ye of the Lord rain in the time of the latter rain; so the Lord shall make bright clouds, and give them showers of rain" (Zechariah 10:1). In the meantime, like tadpole shrimp we wait patiently for the rain.

A Word From Our Creator

Rest in the Lord, and wait patiently for him.
Psalm 37:7.

Outfoxed and Unbearable

Have you ever had a day when everything seemed to go wrong? Fred Bruemmer, a Canadian author and photographer, had a day like that one winter on the Arctic ice. He was planning to photograph the arctic fox, that mischievous little dog of the Far North, and he had no trouble finding a group of them. The only things he had to worry about were the temperature and the polar bears.

During winter the arctic day is very short and extremely cold. The temperature often drops to -50°F or -60°F, and any exposed skin gets frostbitten in a very short time, so Fred had dressed in his warmest parka and had covered his hands with heavy leather mittens.

The arctic fox is an adorable little creature. It's about two feet long and in winter has long and very thick snow-white fur. During the winter months the fox's primary food consists of the leftovers of polar bear kills. So when you find the foxes, a polar bear is often nearby, and the bear's keen sense of smell alerts it to the presence of an intruder.

Fred took the mitten off his right hand and tucked it under his left arm in order to make just one final adjustment to his camera. As he raised the camera, the mitten fell to the ice. In less time than it takes to tell about it, one of the foxes dashed in and made off with the mitten, probably thinking it was food. Realizing that he couldn't catch the animal, Fred ignored the fox—he pretended he didn't notice the animal. The fox buried the mitten in a snowbank and left it there.

Fred arrived at the snowbank and was starting to bend down to retrieve the mitten when he suddenly became aware of another snow-white creature—this one huge—bearing down upon him from out of nowhere. Fred reached the safety of his vehicle just in time to look back and see the bear dig up his mitten and swallow it whole. That was the end of Fred's day. Although he would not get his mitten back, he at least was safe from the bear.

That's what Jesus is saying in today's text. We will have trouble—we can't escape that in a sinful world—and we may not always get what we want. But in Jesus we are safe from the bear.

A Word From Our Creator

In the world ye shall have tribulation: but be of good cheer; I have overcome the world. John 16:33.

Armadillos

Armadillo is Spanish for "little armored one" and describes the most obvious trait shared by all the world's 20 species. Small overlapping bony plates cover the head, body, and tail of every armadillo. All armadillos have short, sturdy legs and strong claws, which they use to dig their burrows.

All armadillos live in the tropical or warmer areas of South America and North America. One species, the nine-banded armadillo, ranges as far north as the Gulf Coast of the United States. These armored mammals use their snouts to root in leaf-litter and soil for insects, spiders, earthworms, snails, slugs, and other small invertebrates. Then they lick them up with their long, slender tongues. To search for food above ground, an armadillo stands on its hind legs, using its stout tail for balance. The four-foot-long 100-pound giant armadillo of South America sometimes walks on its hind legs, but all the other members of the family scramble along on all four.

An armadillo doesn't fight to protect itself. Its small teeth are useless for biting, and it employs its claws only for digging, not for striking. So its primary defense is its armor. Some species have flexible armor that allows them to curl up into a ball, tucking head and feet safely inside. Others have rigid armor and must scurry into their burrows to escape their enemies. But the six-inch fairy armadillo uses still another method to protect itself. When the fairy armadillo finds itself far from the safety of its underground home, it quickly digs a shallow depression in the soil and scrunches down. Once the little creature is snug in its shallow hole, belly side down, its armor acts as a tight-fitting door that no enemy can break through.

The Creator has provided His creatures with the ability to defend themselves. And the defense is always equal to the power and cunning of the predator. Our God has provided us with the perfect defense against our most wily foe. He has given us armor, complete with helmet, breastplate, belt, boots, and shield (Ephesians 6:13-17).

A WORD FROM OUR CREATOR

Put on the whole armour of God, that ye may be able to stand against the wiles of the devil. Ephesians 6:11.

NOVEMBER 26

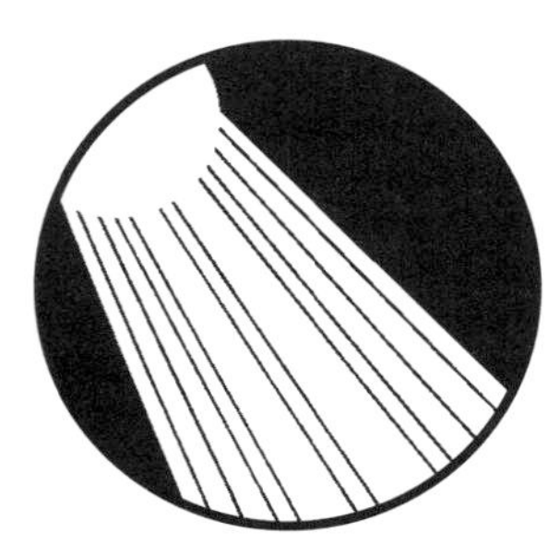

The Aurora

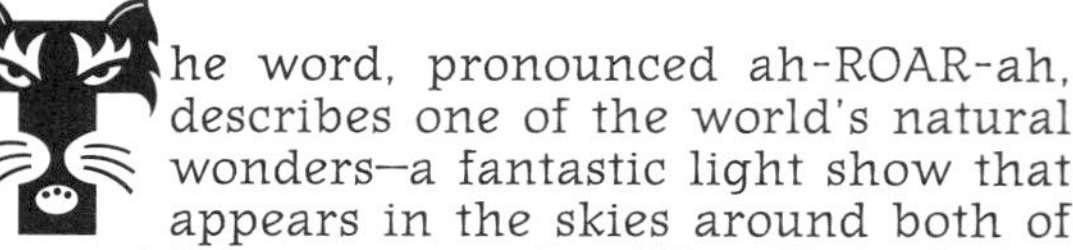

The word, pronounced ah-ROAR-ah, describes one of the world's natural wonders—a fantastic light show that appears in the skies around both of the earth's magnetic poles. We call the lights around the North Pole the aurora borealis (pronounced bor-ee-AL-iss) and refer to the display around the South Pole as the aurora australis (pronounced aus-TRAL-iss).

Theories to explain the lights have ranged from the reflection of lamps on the wings of angels to the flash of moonlight on the polar ice caps. Modern science believes that charged atomic particles from the sun cause gases in space to glow.

Anywhere around the Arctic Circle or the Antarctic Circle on a given night, the sky may suddenly light up with what appear to be shimmering curtains in shades of bright green, crimson red, and white. The bottom of the curtain is about 65 miles above the earth, but the top may reach as high as 600 miles. The colors shimmer and sweep across the sky at hundreds of miles per hour.

There is a wind, but it's a *solar* wind, not the kind of wind that ruffles the curtains at our windows. A solar wind consists of subatomic particles streaming out in all directions from the sun. Scientists tell us that the earth's magnetic poles attract the particles as they pass them. When they encounter earth's upper atmosphere, they excite the atoms in the high thin air and cause them to light up, sort of like a celestial fluorescent or neon bulb.

Some years ago, to study whether or not our atmosphere has anything to do with the aurora, a rocket carried a water bomb into the upper atmosphere above Manitoba, Canada, and released it 200 miles above the earth's surface. As the bomb burst, water vapor spewed out throughout the sky in the region of the aurora borealis. Presto! Just like a dimmer-switch, it turned down the aurora. Apparently the water had broken the electrical current causing the lights. But how? No one is completely sure.

We live in a spiritually dark world. But with the Light of the world as our Lord, we are changed. Jesus excites our spiritual atoms, and our characters shine as lights in the darkness.

A WORD FROM OUR CREATOR

That ye may be blameless and harmless, the sons of God, without rebuke, in the midst of a crooked and perverse nation, among whom ye shine as lights in the world. Philippians 2:15.

The text describes the promise that God made to Noah. The earth will always have seasons because God said so. The tilt of the earth causes a varying amount of sunlight to reach each part of the planet during the year. That difference in hours of sunlight causes the seasonal changes in weather.

In some places on earth the changes are slight, but in other places they're severe. For example, on the island of Fernando de Noronha, off the coast of Brazil, the weather varies only by a few degrees throughout the year. The hottest day in history on the island was during a heat wave when the temperatures actually reached nearly 90°F. And the worst cold snap ever caused the temperature to drop all the way down to 65.5°F.

On the other hand, the severest extremes of weather change show up in different ways in other places. Back in 1916 in Browning, Montana, for instance, the temperature dropped 100 degrees in 24 hours from 44°F to -56°F. In Spearfish, South Dakota, the temperature once rose 49 degrees (from -4°F to 45°F) in two minutes. How would you dress for weather like that?

Worldwide, the extremes are much greater, of course. The hottest day on record was in Libya, when the temperature reached 136.4°F in the shade. At the other extreme, the coldest day ever recorded was in Antarctica, where the temperature plunged to -128.6°F. That means that the maximum fluctuation of recorded temperature on the surface of the earth has been 265 degrees. But that's not much compared to the tremendous fluctuations on other planets in our solar system.

For the coldest average temperatures in winter, you would need to go to a place sometimes called the "Cold Pole" in northeastern Siberia. There the average January temperature is -59°F.

Even with these extremes in the world's weather we can still be thankful for a Creator that established the right conditions to maintain life on earth. And we have the promise of God Himself that as long as the world remains, this will continue to be true.

A Change in the Weather

A Word From Our Creator

While the earth remaineth, seedtime and harvest, and cold and heat, and summer and winter, and day and night shall not cease.
Genesis 8:22.

NOVEMBER 28

Roots in the Treetops

Just when we think we have nature's rules figured out, newly discovered facts will modify our understanding of them. Every science textbook tells you that roots push into the ground and that branches grow up into the air. So it was quite a shock when a young scientist from the University of Washington discovered tree roots sprouting from branches up in the treetops.

Several trees develop roots from their branches—trees like mangroves and banyans, for example. But their roots push downward and into the ground to provide additional support for the tree. Other kinds of trees, like cypresses, send roots up into the air from underground and underwater in the swamp.

But until Nalini Nadkarni began climbing into the canopy of the Olympic rain forest on the coast of Washington State, no botanist had even surmised, let alone observed, any evidence that tree roots can grow out of the limbs in the tops of trees. In the rain forest a group of plants called epiphytes inhabit the treetops. People also call these plants air plants because they seem to draw all their nutrients from the air and rain and not from the tree that gives them a place to live. Unlike parasites, epiphytes use the tree only for support, not for food. In a rain forest the epiphytes grow so thickly that they form heavy mats on the limbs of trees in the forest canopy. As a result, high above the forest floor we actually find gardens of ferns and mosses.

As the epiphytes flourish they build up a layer of decaying plant material on the tree limbs. And it is into this soil-like material that the tree limbs begin to send roots. The scientist found roots that ranged from tiny root hairs to large woody roots three inches in diameter. And these roots draw nutrients from the decaying vegetation to feed the tree just like those growing underground.

And so it is with us as we grow in grace toward the Sun of righteousness. He will provide us with whatever it takes to establish the roots of our faith.

A WORD FROM OUR CREATOR

As ye have therefore received Christ Jesus the Lord, so walk ye in him: rooted and built up in him, and stablished in the faith, as ye have been taught, abounding therein with thanksgiving. Colossians 2:6, 7.

ave you noticed that the moon seems to look larger some nights than it does others? Two things make this happen.

Your eyes carry visual perceptions to your brain, and your brain analyzes them. When the moon is close to the horizon, you see it beside such earthbound things as nearby trees and faraway mountains, and it looks huge compared to the size of those things. Thus when a moon appears in the sky between two trees or over your neighbor's house, your brain says, "That moon is *enormous*." But when the same moon floats high in the sky all by itself, your brain perceives it as being smaller than it was near the horizon.

Some nights the moon appears larger because it *is* larger! As you know, the moon revolves around the earth. But you may not know that the moon's orbit is elliptical, or oval. That means that sometimes the moon is closer to the earth than at others. When it approaches closest to the earth, the moon naturally looks larger. Six months later, when it's farthest away, the moon appears to be about 12 percent smaller. That's enough of a difference for you to notice, but since it is so gradual a change from month to month, you don't notice the change as it happens.

A possible third reason for perceived differences in the moon's size has to do with brightness. For example, the moon seems larger in winter than in summer. The humidity of summer produces a haze through which the moon's light must pass. In addition, the moon's path is lower in the sky in the summer, which causes it to shine through more of the hazy atmosphere and gives it an amber cast. (The term *honeymoon* may be derived from this common color of the moon in the summer, when many marriages traditionally occur.) In winter, however, when the moon shines through drier air and follows a higher path in the sky, it appears brighter and therefore larger.

The moon has no light of its own. Moonlight is reflected sunlight, but that doesn't make it any less valuable. God, who created both the sun and the moon, has often used them in His Word as examples of His character."

Moon Perception

A WORD FROM OUR CREATOR

My covenant will I not break . . . It shall be established for ever as the moon, and as a faithful witness in heaven. Psalm 89:34-37.

The Horse That's a Fish

Despite the shape of its head and the curve of its neck, the sea horse is a fish. In fact, when a baby sea horse first hatches and its head extends forward from its long, slender body, it looks like one of its relatives, the pipefish. But as the little sea colt matures, its body curves into a question mark that causes many of us to ask, "Is it a fish, or isn't it?"

The sea horse uses its long snout to probe into crevices and suck up tiny particles of plants and animals. The creature has no scales. Instead, hard plates and rings and bristly spines cover its body, so few sea creatures seek it as prey. It propels itself through the water in an upright position, beating the transparent fins on its chest and back to go forward and backward. To rest, it locks its tail around a plant. Sometimes two sea horses hook their tails together and play tug-of-war. At other times a sea horse wraps its tail around a plant stalk and executes a series of somersaults and other acrobatics.

But even the sea horse's talent as a gymnast doesn't surpass its skill at camouflage. Most sea horses are dark-gray, brown, or black, and they blend in with the rocks on the ocean floor. Even the brightly colored ones—those patterned with pink, red, yellow, white, or blue—can turn brown in the presence of danger. And one species is orange with ribbonlike appendages dangling from its snout, head, and body. With its ribbons trailing in the water, it looks like a floating piece of orange kelp that grows in the area of the Pacific in which it lives. All this sea horse has to do is anchor its tail to some seaweed to hide out in the open.

Every sea horse in the world is perfectly adapted to the environment in which it lives. A combination of colors and features that allow it to blend in with the rocks, coral, or plants all protect it from what few enemies it has. The sea horse is a wonderful example of the power of our Saviour to protect us in a dark and dangerous world.

A Word From Our Creator

He only is my rock and my salvation: he is my defense; I shall not be moved. Psalm 62:6.

id you know that your heart has a life of its own? In many ways your heart is independent of the rest of your body. It has its own time clock and its own regulator.

No one knows what triggers the electrical current that starts your heart beating, but it works something like this: The heart's pacemaker is a group of cells collectively called the S-A node. The cells look like muscle fibers, but they behave more like nerves. Sodium and potassium ions (from the food you eat) move through the cell walls and create an electrical charge between the inside and outside of the cells—a positive charge inside and a negative charge outside. The cells contract when they leak their positive ions. That's the "lub." When the cells stop leaking, the heart muscles relax—producing the "dup." A lub and a dup make one heartbeat.

That process happens about 70 to 80 times per minute, and more than 2.5 billion times in a lifetime. How can a muscle work that hard without a rest? It can't! The heart muscle rests for a fraction of a second between each dup and the next lub.

The alternating lubs and dups begin on their own in a baby's body long before its birth. The pattern starts without any signal either from the mother's body or the baby's developing brain. By some unknown miracle, the baby's heart starts beating, and it beats steadily for the rest of its life.

Your heart is sensitive to stress. When you're frightened, your heart speeds up to supply oxygen to the muscles in case they need to act quickly. But your heart can't tell the difference between appropriate stress, like when a bear chases you, and the stress that you feel when you're worried about something. The heart responds to all stress in the same way. If the stress doesn't stop, then the heart doesn't get enough rest between the dup and the lub, and it wears out too soon.

Jesus can help us cope with stress. If you believe and trust in Him, your heart won't wear out from worry.

"Lub-Dup"

A Word From Our Creator

Let not your heart be troubled: ye believe in God, believe also in me. John 14:1.

DECEMBER 2

Paddy

In 1936 Beryl Markham became the first person to fly an airplane solo across the Atlantic from east to west. But she had an even more exciting experience when she was a girl in Africa.

The Elkingtons were her neighbors, and they had a pet lion named Paddy. Since Beryl had seen Paddy many times and had watched Mrs. Elkington petting him, she wasn't afraid of the animal. Nevertheless, the Elkingtons warned Beryl to stay away from Paddy and never to run near the lion. But what does "near" mean to a little girl?

One day as Beryl ran through the Elkingtons' yard toward the open country, she didn't notice the lion until she came upon him sunning in the field. She stopped, as she should have, and looked at the lion. Paddy lifted his head, stood up, and stared back at her, but he did nothing more. Still unafraid, Beryl began to sing as she walked resolutely past the lion. Once past and thinking that she was no longer near the lion, she picked up her speed to a trot, and then began running full speed again. It never occurred to her to look behind her, so she didn't notice that the instinctual urge to chase had apparently overcome Paddy.

The Elkingtons' hired man had seen Beryl running into the field, and he knew that Paddy was out there. So he called Mr. Elkington, and both of them made a dash for the field.

The lion struck Beryl, knocking her down. She could feel the sting where the lion's paws had ripped five bloody grooves in her leg. And she could feel his hot breath on her back.

At that instant Mr. Elkington appeared, racing headlong toward the scene and screaming at the lion. Lifting his head to meet the challenger, Paddy roared. Beryl long remembered the deafening sound of that roar. Her whole body vibrated. Mr. Elkington charged the lion and ran past it, drawing Paddy's attention to him instead of the girl. The lion left Beryl to chase away the new intruder. Mr. Elkington quickly escaped up a nearby tree while the hired man scooped up the little girl and rushed her back to the house.

That's what Jesus did for you and me. He met the lion head-on, but He didn't escape. He died on the tree.

A WORD FROM OUR CREATOR

Notwithstanding the Lord stood with me, and strengthened me . . . and I was delivered out of the mouth of the lion. 2 Timothy 4:17.

December 3

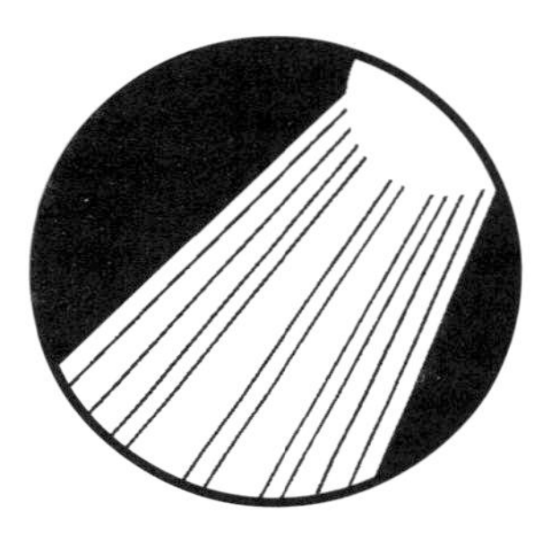

The Incredible Squid

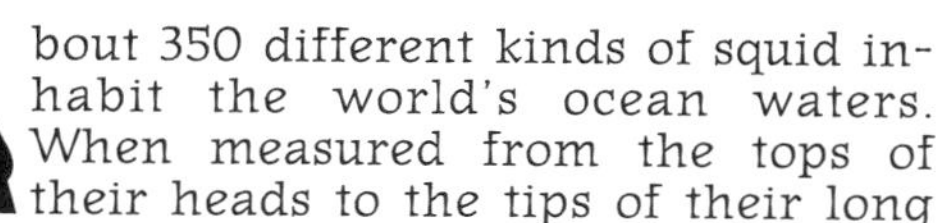

About 350 different kinds of squid inhabit the world's ocean waters. When measured from the tops of their heads to the tips of their long tentacles, they range from tiny species scarcely more than a half inch long to monsters approaching 40 feet. Scientists have classified squids with the shellfish. When you look at a squid, you'll note that it resembles an octopus more than any other animal.

Squids have an unusual way of protecting themselves from their enemies. When danger threatens, a squid squirts large quantities of inky-black liquid into the surrounding water. The squid's enemy can't find it in the dark water, and by the time the water clears, the squid is long gone.

By using a form of jet propulsion, squids are among the fastest swimmers in the sea. In fact, a squid sometimes reaches the surface with such force that it shoots 30 to 40 feet into the air. Yet no one knows exactly how fast a squid can travel because it darts back and forth so quickly that measuring its speed over a given course is impossible.

What is perhaps most remarkable about most if not all squids is their ability to change colors and to produce light of different colors. The entire squid can shimmer with one or more colors that seem to change with the mood of the animal. For example, one type of squid is flesh-colored when resting, covered with a blue glow when running with the school, and red when provoked. Another species, the fire squid, can choose from several colors—blue, white, pink, or yellow—and can even blink its lights on and off.

In the darkness of the sea the Creator has given the squids a way of not only seeing where they are going, but also of recognizing and communicating with one another by using lights. In our dark world the Creator has provided us His Word as a light to show the way and to use to communicate with others about His love.

A Word From Our Creator

The entrance of thy words giveth light; it giveth understanding unto the simple.
Psalm 119:130.

December 4

Manna From the Dew

What would you think if you went outdoors one morning after the dew had evaporated and found tiny white bits of sweet-tasting cookies? Of course, you wouldn't know what it was at first, and you would be curious. Probably you would say something like "What's all that white stuff?"

Bible scholars generally agree that the Hebrew word *manna* means "What is it?" because no one knew what the substance was. Moses told the people that it was food. Although people have speculated a lot about that special food, we still don't know exactly what it was. But it was very nutritious—a complete food for God's people in a hostile environment.

Let's look at the way in which the manna appeared. First, it came with the dew. As such, it was a product of God's creative power and served as a direct illustration that God can make something visible and useful out of something invisible.

The morning dew begins as moisture in the air. As the air cools during the night, the moisture leaves the air and accumulates on any available solid material, like leaves, rocks, and the ground. In the wilderness the Israelites were hungry and their faith had dimmed to a spiritual darkness. But in the morning, as the sunshine evaporated the dew, Jesus renewed their faith by perhaps turning water and air into food.

Actually, God works that same miracle every day in almost every living plant on earth. Through photosynthesis, plants absorb air and water, then use the power of sunlight to produce food—even the food in wheat, which we make into bread.

Manna. What is it? It is God showing us that He cares, that He loves us. He is the Dew (Hosea 14:5), the Living Water (John 4:14), and the Bread of Life (John 6:33).

A Word From Our Creator

And when the dew that lay was gone up, behold, upon the face of the wilderness there lay a small round thing, as small as the hoar frost on the ground. Exodus 16:14.

DECEMBER 5

A Weed 200 Feet Tall

Can you name a plant that grows up to 200 feet tall and lives in large tracts called forests—but is not a tree? This plant is abundant, but you may never see anything but the top of it. The plant is the giant kelp, a seaweed that grows in the cool waters along the Pacific coast of North America.

Giant kelp grows very fast—up to two feet a day. Gas-filled sacs called bladders at the base of its leaves keep it afloat. The plant doesn't have a trunk or main stem. Instead, several tall stalks grow from a base called a holdfast on the ocean floor. The huge plant is completely dependent on its holdfast. By clinging to the ocean floor, the kelp stays in the cool water that provides the necessary ingredients for its life.

A kelp forest is home to millions of sea creatures. One giant kelp plant may harbor a half million fish, mollusks, sea urchins, and sea anemones, as well as myriads of other marine animals. All of these creatures depend in some way on the kelp, and the forest is a carefully balanced environment.

Some years ago, when human beings had hunted sea otters to near extinction, the kelp forests were threatened as well. No one realized that the kelp depended upon the otters, because the otter doesn't eat kelp. The otter only uses the kelp to hide in and to wrap itself in to keep from drifting when it's asleep. But the otter eats sea urchins, and sea urchins feed on the kelp's holdfast. The sea urchins eventually munch through the holdfast, cutting the plant loose from its base. When this happens, the kelp plant dies. Without otters to control them, the urchins were literally cutting down the kelp forests. The return of the sea otter saved the giant kelp.

We too are anchored to a solid foundation—the spiritual Rock that is Jesus Christ (1 Corinthians 10:5). The Creator has provided a balanced environment for our spiritual growth. Many little urchins seek to destroy our base, but the Creator's power protects us. In Jesus we can stand tall without fear of losing the stronghold of our faith.

A WORD FROM OUR CREATOR

Let us hold fast the profession of our faith without wavering; (for he is faithful that promised). Hebrews 10:23.

DECEMBER 6

What Size Is the Moon?

Did you know that the moon rotates on its axis? But if that's true, why do we see the same side all the time? Why don't we see different sides as it turns? Think about it. If the moon *didn't* rotate, we would get to see all parts of it as it revolved around the earth. The only way that the moon can keep the same face toward us at all times is if its speed of rotation exactly matches that of its revolution around earth. The moon takes 27.3 days to orbit the earth and 27.3 days to rotate one time.

Here's another question for you. Which of the following items, when held at arm's length, comes the closest to blotting out the moon: a tennis ball, a golf ball, a quarter, a penny, or a pea? You'll have to try it for yourself, because we aren't going to tell you the answer. But here are some hints.

1. The moon is about 240,000 miles away from the earth.
2. It's about 2,170 miles in diameter. That means that you would have to line up 111 moons side by side to reach the spot where the moon hangs in the sky. So the answer to the question above is going to be whichever item you could line up 111 of to reach from your eye to your fingertips. Make your estimate and then test it.

This experiment is a good way to prove that the moon is not really larger when it is just above the horizon—it only looks larger there because of the "moon illusion" mentioned in a previous reading last month. It appears larger because of the relative size of other things in the foreground, such as trees and houses. But by doing your own experiment, you'll be able to prove that the moon is actually the same size no matter where it is in the sky.

Isn't it amazing how a small object can blot out something as big as the moon? That's the way it often is in life: it takes only a little folly to blot out the appearance of wisdom and honor.

A WORD FROM OUR CREATOR

Dead flies cause the ointment of the apothecary to send forth a stinking savour: so doth a little folly him that is in reputation for wisdom and honour. Ecclesiastes 10:1.

December 7

The Walleyed Pike

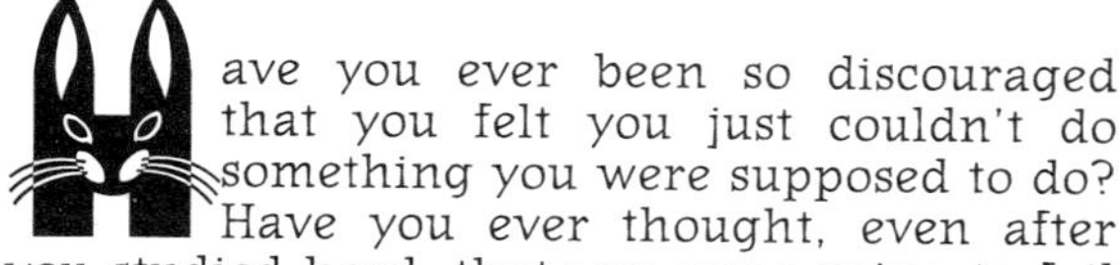

ave you ever been so discouraged that you felt you just couldn't do something you were supposed to do? Have you ever thought, even after you studied hard, that you were going to fail a test? Have you ever felt like just giving up instead of trying again?

Some years ago a scientist conducted a study about motivation using an unusual subject, an aggressive fish of the lakes and streams of the northern United States called the walleyed pike. The scientist first put the fish into a tank with several minnows. The pike snapped up the minnows one after the other. It was a normal, healthy, and hungry walleyed pike!

To begin the experiment, the scientist placed a clear glass panel into the aquarium to divide it into two chambers and confine the pike on one side. Then the scientist added more minnows to the other chamber.

Seeing the minnows, the hungry pike quickly went after one of them. *Blam*! It hit the glass wall that separated it from the minnows. Again it circled the chamber, and again it lunged for the minnows—with the same results. Over and over the pike tried for those little fish. But each time it hit the glass partition with a little less force. Finally the pike quit.

At that point the scientist took the glass partition out of the aquarium, making it all one chamber again. Now the pike was free to go after the minnows again, but it never did. The pike could see the minnows, but in its brain the message was clear: "Those are minnows. They're good to eat, and I'm hungry. But I've learned that I can't get those minnows." The walleyed pike died of starvation in that aquarium—with minnows swimming all around.

Sometimes we convince ourselves—or other people convince us—that we can't accomplish a goal. Maybe the challenge is getting a good grade in math. Or learning a piano piece. Or breaking a habit. It's very difficult for us to believe that we *can* when part of our brain is telling us that we *can't*. This is where Jesus comes in. We can always count on His help.

A Word From Our Creator

I can do all things through Christ which strengtheneth me. Philippians 4:13.

DECEMBER 8

A Mighty Fortress

A beaver is well equipped for life in a watery world. Its hind feet are webbed so broadly that when spread to their full seven inches, the resulting paddles easily propel the yard-long animal through the water. If the beaver wants to swim underwater, it can hold enough air in its lungs to go a half mile. And a transparent membrane covers each of its eyes, allowing the animal to see underwater.

The beaver's tail is not only a rudder and a warning device—it's also a pantry. As a beaver eats and eats during the summer and fall, its tail swells with stored fat. In winter and spring, as the fat gets used up, the tail shrinks by as much as half.

But it's the beaver's ability to build that provides us with truly remarkable monuments to the Creator's attention to the care of His creatures. Even beavers raised in captivity without ever having seen a pond or a forest know how to gnaw down trees and build lodges and dams. Using teeth designed to cut through a two-inch tree trunk in only 30 seconds, a family of beavers builds a dome-shaped lodge that looks like a hill of branches and twigs standing four or five feet above the water. All the entrances to the lodge are underwater, but a living area is contained above the water. The beaver family keeps a pile of branches and small logs—usually aspen, poplar, birch, maple, willow, and alder—underwater near the lodge as a food supply.

Inside their lodge the beavers are safe from all their aboveground enemies. And the design of the lodge, which includes insulated walls, easy-entry passages, and a spacious living room, keeps the animals cozy and comfortable even in the middle of winter, when the weather outside is cold and icy. Not only is the beaver's lodge built solid, but the layer of snow on top of it acts as further insulation against the weather.

God has provided the beaver with a veritable fortress. If God takes such care to provide for the needs of His creatures of the forest, we can be sure that He will take care of us, too.

A WORD FROM OUR CREATOR

The Lord is my rock, and my fortress. 2 Samuel 22:2.

In February 1985 thousands of beluga whales were wintering in Senyavina Strait in the Bering Sea off the coast of the Soviet Union. The whales had arrived in December, and normal conditions would have allowed them to exist relatively unnoticed. But something unusual happened. Pack ice drifted into the strait, trapping the whales underneath. The belugas took turns breathing at the holes in the ice, but each had to wait its turn. Because there were so many of them, the wait was too long, and they became exhausted. Since the whales couldn't escape from the strait, they quickly consumed all the available food and began to starve to death. The situation was grave. What could be done?

People stood by in helpless admiration of the determination as well as the incredible politeness of the whales. But the belugas were going to die if they didn't get help fast. They couldn't live until the spring thaw. Someone had to rescue them. But how do you free whales trapped in pack ice?

The captain of a Russian icebreaker, the *Moskva*, heard about the problem and responded. He headed his ship into the pack ice, and by the mighty power of the ship the captain plowed an escape path for the belugas. But the whales didn't take the path to freedom. They were so weak that they didn't understand that they could now reach the open sea and freedom.

According to the Russian report of the incident, someone remembered that whales respond to music. So, in an attempt to lure the whales into the channel, the Russian sailors began to broadcast jazz and popular music over the ship's loudspeakers, hoping that the whales would swim toward the source of the music and out to sea. But the whales still didn't respond. In desperation, the sailors switched to classical music. It worked! The whales swam toward the sound of the music and followed the *Moskva* to freedom.

On the cross 2,000 years ago Jesus made a way of escape for us. But in our weakened condition we sometimes don't recognize freedom when we see it. So Jesus surrounds us with songs of deliverance—the invitation of the Spirit and the bride who say "Come" (Revelation 22:17). Are you responding to the call?

December 9

Trapped Under the Ice

A Word From Our Creator

Thou art my hiding place; thou shalt preserve me from trouble; thou shalt compass me about with songs of deliverance. Psalm 32:7.

December 10

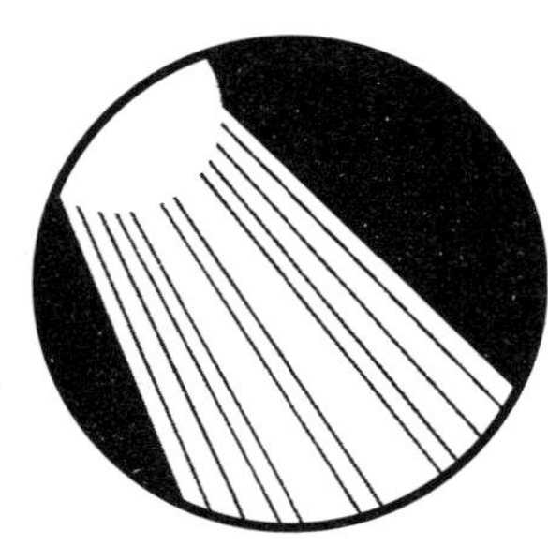

No Light? Eat Garbage

Almost all life on earth depends upon light for survival. With the exception of some recently discovered creatures that live deep in the sea near volcanic vents, all living things obtain life from sunlight. Either directly or indirectly, living creatures consume plants that use the power of sunlight to convert chemicals into food.

Coral is abundant in the tropical oceans of the world. Although scientists classify it as an animal, coral maintains a close association with a type of simple plant life called algae. By living together, coral and algae form a balanced community in which each supplies the nutrients needed by the other. Algae, like all plants, requires carbon dioxide and nitrogen. The coral provides both as waste products. Coral, on the other hand, must have oxygen. The algae gives off oxygen as a waste product—but only if there is light. Most of the world's corals live in shallow water, where plenty of light can reach them. But in some places, as in the Red Sea, corals live all the way down to a depth of more than 200 feet.

Light does not penetrate below about 200 feet into the ocean water. Divers exploring the coral growths of the Red Sea found that at the deeper depths the corals spread out in flat horizontal forms, allowing for maximum absorption of the ever-decreasing amount of light above. As long as there was even a precious little bit of light, the coral community included the algae in the production of food. But deep-sea corals growing below 200 feet didn't have the algae living in their bodies to assist them in food production. So how could they survive? They were living off the garbage that rained down from the living creatures and plants above. This garbage has a fancy name—detritus (pronounced de-TRY-tus).

Without Jesus, the Light of the world, we exist in a spiritual darkness very much like deep-sea creatures. People who live in such darkness love to feed on the sins of other people—the garbage of a sinful world. But Jesus says that He will cast all our sins into "the depths of the sea" (Micah 7:19). I can just imagine a host of demons living there who love to feed on the detritus of spiritual renewal.

A Word From Our Creator

And this is the condemnation, that light is come into the world, and men loved darkness rather than light, because their deeds were evil. John 3:19.

DECEMBER 11

Snow Rollers

Snow rollers exist as a rare phenomenon on a winter snowscape. They look somewhat like flat rolls of cotton batting. Cylinder-shaped with the ends hollowed in a funnel shape, they sometimes have a hole clear through them. People have described them as resembling old-fashioned ladies' muffs, and they can range in size from a few inches to nearly two feet in diameter.

Few people are fortunate enough to witness snow rollers, and even fewer photographs exist of the phenomenon. The only photograph that we've seen was in the January/ March 1985 issue of *Nature Canada*. The magazine listed all the known occurrences of snow rollers in Canada—10 examples.

There's only one known instance in which a person actually saw a snow roller being formed, and if it hadn't been for her careful notes, we might only imagine how they happen. Ione Jillson wrote the following of her observation in New York during the winter of 1895: "The wind seemed to sweep downward and get under a slightly projecting mass of snow and set it in motion. As the roll grew in size, the speed, at first very rapid, slackened until the mass became too compact and heavy to be moved farther." She went on to describe the start of the snow roller as looking "very much like the corner of a piece of paper as it rises and falls with the wind just before it is blown away."

The conditions have to be just right for snow rollers to develop: a thin soft new layer of snow on top of a hard smooth crust of old snow. Then the temperature must rise one or two degrees above freezing to allow for the snow to stick together.

Snow rollers have been observed to roll on flat surfaces and even uphill if the wind is strong enough, but they form easiest when wind and gravity work together to get them traveling downhill. They leave an ever-widening track as they gather snow. One left behind a track as long as a football field.

If you see snow rollers, get your camera and photograph the event as soon as possible, because they're very fragile and don't last long.

Can you imagine God's pleasure in designing the snow for snow rolling?

A WORD FROM OUR CREATOR

Hast thou entered into the treasures of the snow? Job 38:22.

December 12

Christmas Trees

A Word From Our Creator

And now also the axe is laid unto the root of the trees: every tree therefore which bringeth not forth good fruit is hewn down, and cast into the fire. Luke 3:9.

The Christmas tree is a carryover from when people worshiped nature and evergreens symbolized life in the winter. Today the Christmas tree has lost most of its traditional meaning. We now associate it with the family fun of decorating it for the Christmas season and for the toys and other gifts that rest under it until Christmas Day.

No one knows exactly where people used the first Christmas trees, but references to them go back at least 500 years ago in northern Europe. In the 1600s the Germans became the first large group of people to adopt the Christmas tree, and by the late 1700s Christmas trees had become widespread throughout Europe.

In early America the Christmas tree was unpopular because of its pagan origin. Many people believed that to put up a Christmas tree was at best sacreligious, and at worst devil worship.

A tree doesn't make Christmas either pagan or Christian. Christmas *was* originally a pagan holiday, but it has become so interwoven into modern living that this fact has been lost. Now Christmas is so closely tied to money, toys, gifts, and vacations that it's difficult to find spiritual significance—either good or evil—in the holiday.

As various forms of Christianity replaced the traditional pagan religions of Europe, legends tracing the Christmas tree to the Christ child began to develop. But the tree ritual had nothing to do with Jesus or Christianity. If there had been a tree associated with the life of Jesus, it would probably have been the fig tree or the olive tree. Jesus was interested in trees that bore fruit. (You remember the story of how He found a fig tree that had nothing but leaves, and cursed it because it bore no fruit.)

At Christmastime, above all other times of the year, if there is any truth to the idea of a "Christmas spirit," people should be more generous and more inclined to help others. Our text for today bases the value of a tree on the fruit that it bears. If it bears none, then we should cut it down.

December 13

Time Shall Be No More

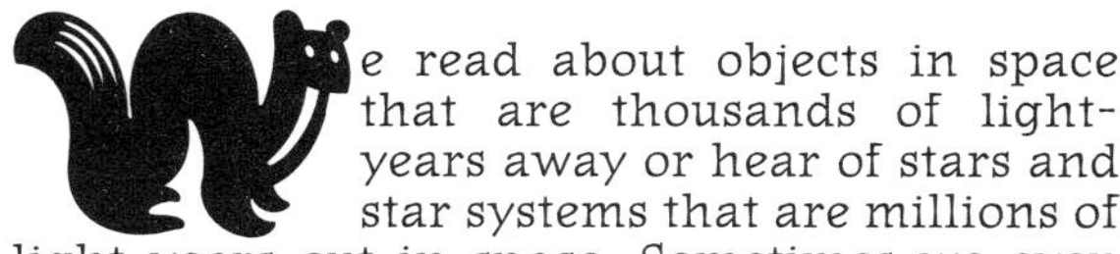

We read about objects in space that are thousands of light-years away or hear of stars and star systems that are millions of light-years out in space. Sometimes we even read of objects that are billions of light-years deep in space. But what does a billion light-years mean?

Light, traveling at 186,000 miles a second, covers about 6 trillion miles in a year—that's one light-year. You simply start with distance defined by the number of light-years and multiply that figure by 6 trillion to find out how many miles light has traveled to reach us from those distant points in the universe. By observing what those light messengers tell us, we see pictures of deep space. Those pictures have been quietly journeying through space at nearly 700 million miles an hour for millions of years. Actually, we are looking back in time.

But wait! If those pictures of outer space originated that long ago, how do we know if the universe still looks like that today? We don't. What we're seeing is the light that left those points in space millions of years ago. That light can tell us only what that part of the universe looked like then. We have no idea how that part of space appears today, because it will take millions of years longer for today's light to get from there to here. And by that time, what it shows will be millions of years out-of-date again. The problem that we have is a concept of time that's earthbound.

Life on earth has existed for only about 6,000 years. That seems like a long time, but it's not even a drop in the stream of eternity. In fact, if you think about it, unless it has a beginning and an ending, time is a meaningless idea.

When Jesus comes and gives us glorified bodies that will never die, time, at least as we know it, will cease to exist. We will no longer need it. That's what today's text says.

From a new earth that God has promised to create just for us, we will be able to visit those distant galaxies anytime we want. And it really won't matter how long it takes. What's a few billion years when we're going to live forever?

A Word From Our Creator

And the angel which I saw stand upon the sea and upon the earth lifted up his hand to heaven, and sware by him that liveth for ever and ever . . . that there should be time no longer. Revelation 10:5, 6.

December 14

The Takahe Survives

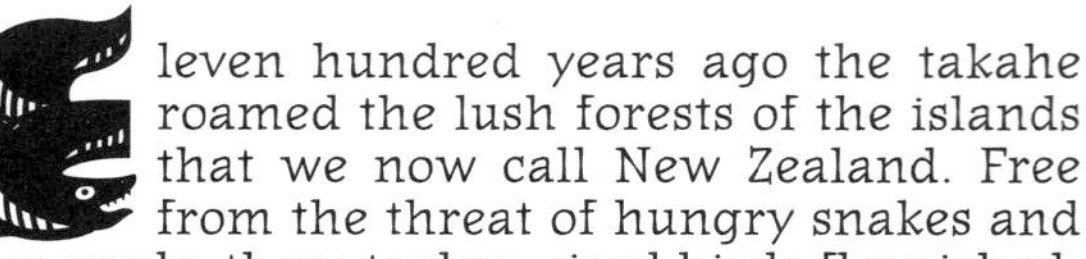

Eleven hundred years ago the takahe roamed the lush forests of the islands that we now call New Zealand. Free from the threat of hungry snakes and mammals, these turkey-sized birds flourished, using their large red beaks to snap off pieces of snow tussock, a type of tall grass that's the takahe's only food. The takahe and the tussock depended on each other, a fact that people would not discover until the late 1900s.

One thousand years ago the arrival of New Zealand's first human inhabitants, a Polynesian people called the Maori, threatened the existence of the takahe. The Maori easily captured the large, flightless birds. They used their blue and green feathers as adornments and ate the tasty flesh. The dogs and rats that arrived with the Maori also preyed on the takahe.

But the greatest threat to the takahe came with the European settlers, who by 1900 had burned grasslands, cut down forests, drained wetlands, and introduced tussock-eating deer. They also imported weasels to control the rabbit population, but the weasels also preyed on the takahe.

No one saw a single takahe for a half century. Then in 1948 a curious deer hunter decided to investigate reports of mysterious bird tracks and unrecognized bird calls high in the mountains. He followed a set of the tracks to the edge of a lake, where he came face-to-face with a takahe!

Since that sighting, the bird has been making a comeback. People almost eliminated the takahe, and now people are bringing it back. By raising takahe chicks in nurseries and then releasing them into the wild, ornithologists are helping the bird to rebuild its population.

Restoring the takahe's habitat is more difficult, and that's how naturalists discovered the interdependence of the takahe and the snow tussock. Recent studies showed that by tugging on the tussock's stems, the takahe stimulates the plant's growth. The bird actually contributes to the development of its own food. The natural world is full of such examples of how all creation works together for mutual support.

A Word From Our Creator

And we know that all things work together for good to them that love God, to them who are called according to his purpose.
Romans 8:28.

Who's in Charge Here?

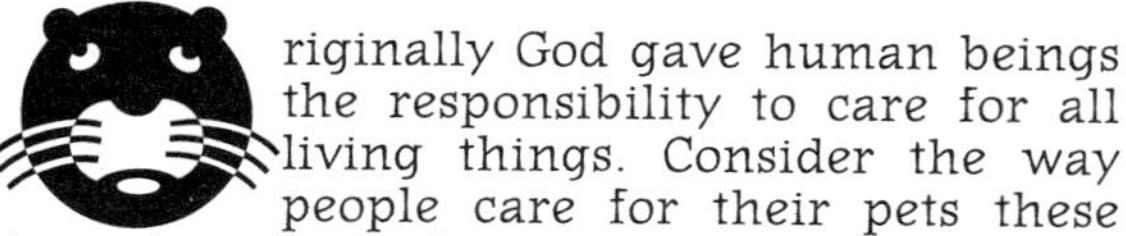

riginally God gave human beings the responsibility to care for all living things. Consider the way people care for their pets these days, then think about whether this was what the Creator had in mind as expressed in today's text. Dogs and cats have been pets for almost as far back as we have historical records. We can perhaps best illustrate the way people regard these animals today by a look through an issue of the *Pet Catalog*.

The catalog consists of 39 full-color, glossy pages of merchandise for dogs and cats. Let's describe what might be a typical day in your dog's life if you have shopped for him through the *Pet Catalog*.

Your pooch wakes up, stretches, and eats his breakfast out of a silver-plated dog dish ($29.95). After eating, you brush his teeth with a special plaque-removing toothpaste ($6.95) and give him his own brand of food supplement ($13.95/16 ounces).

Every dog needs exercise, so you take him for a walk—but check the weather first. During winter a matching sweater and hat set of 100 percent virgin wool will keep him warm ($41.90). If it looks like rain, he should wear his red slicker-style, hooded raincoat ($18.95) and his red vinyl boots with adjustable ankle straps for a snug fit ($9.95). As added protection, make sure that you attach his doggy umbrella ($14.95) to his collar. If the dog would prefer to ride, a specially designed pet tote with built-in screened windows ($34.95) makes it easier for you to carry him while *you* do the walking.

Once your dog is back home, he is probably worn out, so he needs a nap. He can snuggle into his sleeping bag ($39.95) or cuddle up on his own warming pad ($69.95). After his nap, you might want to give your dog a treat. Well, you can chose from cheese/garlic tidbits ($16.95), dog cookies ($9.50), and pet pizza ($8.50)—but only if you're too lazy to bake homemade biscuits for him ($6.95 for recipes and three biscuit cutters).

Keeping pets healthy and happy is the responsibility of anyone who owns them. But did Jesus have this in mind when He placed humanity in charge of the earth?

A Word From Our Creator

And God said, Let us make man in our image, after our likeness: and let them have dominion over . . . all the earth.
Genesis 1:26.

December 16

Exotic Apples

In a place aptly named Paradise Valley in northern California is an apple farm called the Living Tree Center. A modern Johnny Appleseed named Jesse Swartz operates the center.

Swartz became concerned because some of the old standby apple varieties were being lost to the commercialization of the apple industry. One hundred years ago more than 850 varieties of apples grew in America, but today it's hard to find more than five or six kinds for sale at the supermarket. So in 1980 Swartz began to search out and save the last remaining plants of the old apples. He grafted cuttings of the old varieties onto the healthy young rootstocks of apple trees. Now the Living Tree Center distributes many of the traditional kinds of apples that had become only memories for old-timers and never even tasted by young people.

One reintroduced apple is the Skinner, named for Judge H. C. Skinner, of San Jose, California. It's a large, deep-yellow apple with a faint red stripe, and it tastes like it's flavored with nutmeg, honey, licorice, and lemon. The last time anyone had remembered seeing a Skinner was in 1910, but Swartz was able to find a barely surviving tree in Mendocino, California. Through his careful propagation he rejuvenated the Skinner, and you can now order Skinner apples from the center.

Swartz has searched the world for special varieties of apples. He has fruit from Scotland, New Zealand, Holland, and Russia, as well as from the bygone years of America. One variety the center is now propagating is the Court Pendu Plat, which dates back to Roman times. Its color and texture resembles antique Italian marble. And then there is the famous Calville, a French apple with the aroma of a banana and said to be richer in vitamin C than an orange.

The quality of each variety of apple is unique, and when all apples began to look and taste alike, the world almost lost contact with a principle that dates back to the Garden of Eden. We are all different. Every member of the family of God is unique. Each of us is a special fruit in the tree of life.

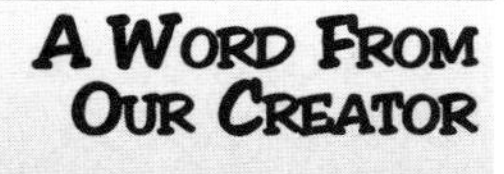

The fruit of the righteous is a tree of life; and he that winneth souls is wise. Proverbs 11:30.

eople originally decorated Christmas trees with fruit, nuts, cookies, and candy. Later they added beads and other shiny objects. The demand for more-elaborate ornaments eventually contributed to the development of the glassblowing industry in Germany in the fifteenth century. The manufacture of glass Christmas tree ornaments continues to be an important industry.

Early attempts to place actual lights on Christmas trees had disastrous results. When people attached candles to the tree, they didn't seem to remember that evergreen sap is highly flammable. The fires that resulted from this popular trend caused a number of deaths before electric lights replaced flaming candles.

Thomas Edison invented the electric light in 1879. It didn't take long for someone to see the electric light as a unique Christmas tree decoration. In fact, only three years later, in 1882, Edward Johnson, vice president of Edison's own electric company, demonstrated a tree that had lights in three different colors, and also an electrically powered stand that rotated the tree. The idea was an immediate hit.

In 1895 President Cleveland added lights to the White House Christmas tree. And in 1945 the NOMA Electric Company marketed a type of light that simulated a candle with glass tubes within which bubbles were constantly rising. Those lights were the rage during the 1950s. In the latter half of the twentieth century people began to string Christmas lights on their houses and in the trees of their yards to create dazzling displays to delight the townsfolk. But in all of this dazzle, which we can trace back for hundreds of years, where is the glory of the Lord?

Today's text follows one that perfectly describes the Christmas "spirit." "Is it not to deal thy bread to the hungry, and that thou bring the poor that are cast out to thy house?" (verse 7) If we follow such a spirit, then we have the promise of God that our light shall break forth. The radiance of the Christian character that comes from helping others is the glory of the Lord—a light unequaled by any artificial means.

December 17

Christmas Lights

A Word From Our Creator

Then shall thy light break forth as the morning, and thine health shall spring forth speedily: and thy righteousness shall go before thee; the glory of the Lord shall be thy rereward. Isaiah 58:8.

DECEMBER 18

Master of the Wind

A WORD FROM OUR CREATOR

The wind goeth toward the south, and turneth about unto the north; it whirleth about continually, and the wind returneth again according to his circuits. Ecclesiastes 1:6.

The Bible is scientifically correct. The words of today's text were written long before Christ, and yet they describe perfectly the global circulation of the atmosphere. A combination of the effects of the earth's rotation and the sun's thermal heating creates the winds. And one of the jobs of earth's winds is to distribute the cold polar air south and the hot tropical air north. At the point on the globe where Solomon lived when he wrote the words of our text, the prevailing wind at the surface generally flows south. And by a path that Solomon could not possibly have observed, the winds cycle upward near the equator, then return northward as "winds aloft." As they flow northward, they cool and fall to the surface to begin the southward journey again.

Scientists have only recently understood the global circulation of air. There was no way to see which way the winds were blowing because at different altitudes they go in different directions. It took meteorologists years of constant monitoring using high-altitude instruments in airplanes and weather balloons to get just a general idea of the wind's circulation. Now, with many weather satellites taking constant readings throughout all levels of the atmosphere, scientists know for a fact what the Bible writer expressed.

Throughout Old Testament times God used the elements of the atmosphere to demonstrate His great power. He could call on the wind to dry up the Red Sea, to deliver a massive flock of quails, to bring a plague of locusts—and to blow the locusts away. The wind was one of God's usual methods of showing that He was God.

But the event that was to take place in Bethlehem was not marked by any atmospheric phenomena. People experienced no great wind. No lightning. No thunder. Jesus came into the world quietly. The only announcement was made by angels to a few shepherds. The Master of the wind came in the still of the night without even creating so much as a breeze to herald His arrival. He would not use His power over the wind unless it was to bring glory to the Father and not to Himself.

It's hard to imagine what it must have been like in heaven. All the angels were preparing for the incarnation of Jesus. The King of the universe would soon be a helpless baby in a stable. Yet He was the King of kings. Their Eternal Master. Their Creator. He was going to earth, of all places—a totally rebellious little planet that was under the control of His archenemy, Lucifer. Why?

Because He loved the people that were rebelling.

Jesus had created the entire planet—the rocks, the drops of water, the blades of grass, and the trees. He had spoken into existence birds, fish, butterflies, and microbes. With His very hands He had formed the first man from the dust and breathed into him the breath of life. Now He was placing Himself at the mercy of Adam's descendants, all of whom had rebelled. How could this be?

And the Creator was to become a carpenter! The God who had originated the living tree was now going to help support His family on earth by making things out of deadwood. The angels might well have wondered what would happen when the King touched His first piece of wood. Would it immediately come to life? Would it sprout leaves and blossom as Aaron's walking stick had done 1,500 years earlier? The angels would have understood that. If all of the trees in every forest on Earth had clapped their hands at the birth of their Creator, the angels could have accepted that, too.

Jesus had created living trees hundreds of feet tall. How could He bear to work with the death of those trees? For the Creator, wood was alive and growing. For the Carpenter, it was dead and meant to be cut into smaller pieces and planed and sanded. How could the angels possibly realize that even in choosing a vocation, the Creator demonstrated His purpose: to turn deadwood into living service. In order for a tree to provide serviceable wood, it has to die.

The central act in the drama of salvation was to be the death of Jesus on a dead tree—a tree that His word had created and sustained. How could the angels ever have understood? How can we ever understand? What matchless love!

Deadwood

A Word From Our Creator

For ye shall go out with joy, and be led forth with peace: the mountains and the hills shall break forth before you into singing, and all the trees of the field shall clap their hands. Isaiah 55:12.

DECEMBER 20

Halley's Comet and the Birth of Jesus

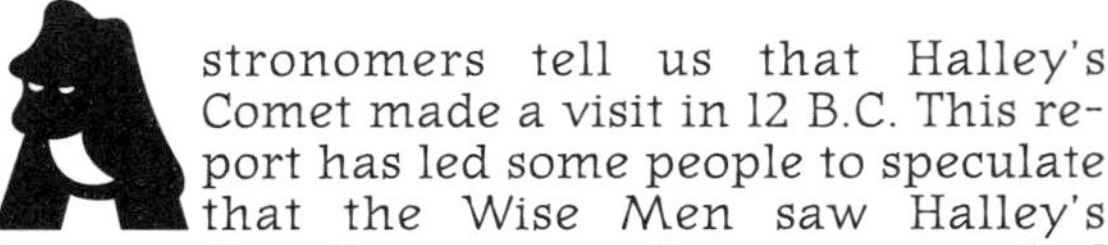

Astronomers tell us that Halley's Comet made a visit in 12 B.C. This report has led some people to speculate that the Wise Men saw Halley's Comet rather than a special star composed of angels. Jim Fleming, a biblical scholar from Israel, believes in the comet theory. He also believes that Jesus was not born in winter, as tradition holds, but sometime in the summer or early autumn 12 B.C. According to Fleming, shepherds didn't graze their flocks on the fields of Palestine during the winter months, because farmers plowed the fields in October and November to allow the winter rains to soak the dry ground. The sheep not only grazed earlier in the year; they were encouraged to do so to harvest the stubble of the earlier crops and to fertilize the fields.

There have been other theories about the "true" occurrences surrounding Jesus' birth, but the one thing that's certain about December 25 is the fact that the date was originally a pagan holiday celebrating the return of the sun. It had nothing to do with the birth of Christ. Several centuries after Christ lived and died, Roman emperors and church leaders combined the pagan festivals with Christian traditions to make Christianity more acceptable to the still largely pagan citizens of the realm.

Scholars who first dated the calendar from Jesus' birth made an error in calculating the year of that event. Scholars now believe that the more likely date was 4 B.C., but we cannot prove even that date. The exact season of His birth, the exact year of His birth, and the nature of the star that the Wise Men saw are all interesting topics for speculation, but we don't build our faith in eternal salvation on them.

What we know and believe about Jesus revolves around His death. So much focus on His birth may cause some of us to forget the absolute importance of *that* event.

A WORD FROM OUR CREATOR

Behold, there came wise men from the east to Jerusalem, saying, Where is he that is born King of the Jews? for we have seen his star in the east, and are come to worship him. Matthew 2:1, 2.

hen a normally busy woman named Pat suddenly found herself confined to her home for a year because of illness, she decided that she needed a pet to keep her company. Because she couldn't physically handle either a dog or a cat, she decided on a bird—a bird that would talk to her. With the help of her daughter, Pat visited a breeder of African gray parrots. Pat picked out a featherless chick, and three months later, when the bird was delivered to her home, she named him Casey.

Casey quickly picked up words and phrases. He also seemed to use them appropriately. When a guest stayed too late, Casey called out "Night-night." Or when his owner sprinkled him with water to stop him from trying to remove the washer from a faucet, Casey demanded, "What's the matter with you?" And when Pat opened and closed drawers as if looking for something, Casey asked, "Where are my glasses? Where is my purse?"

Sometimes Casey's words were a warning. Whenever Pat heard Casey say "Oh, you bad bird!" she knew that the parrot was using his sharp beak to peck at upholstery or wallpaper, something that she had scolded him for doing. At other times Casey's "words" caused confusion, such as when he learned to duplicate exactly the ringing of the phone. But the real payoff came on a day after Pat had returned from a three-week vacation: Casey snuggled against her and said, "I love you, Pat."

Did Casey know what he was saying? The African gray parrot is one of the world's most intelligent birds, and Casey certainly was no exception. But is it possible that a bird can feel affection for a person? We think so. Of course we don't know for sure, but can you imagine Jesus creating something as intelligent and beautiful as the original parrot in the Garden of Eden must have been and then not caring whether the bird felt any closeness to Adam and Eve? Somehow that doesn't seem right.

God created all things to illustrate His love for us. He gave His only Son to die for us. And with that gift God said, "I love you!"

Casey

A Word From Our Creator

And out of the ground the Lord God formed every beast of the field, and every fowl of the air; and brought them unto Adam to see what he would call them. Genesis 2:19.

DECEMBER 22

The Dwarf Mongoose

Living in the Nyiri Desert of Southern Kenya is an animal that illustrates today's text. With temperatures reaching 116°F in the shade, the dwarf mongoose has to survive a grueling three-month summer. The desert's few waterholes are dry, and the only available moisture is in the insects and small rodents the mongoose eats.

Under such conditions every member in a family of dwarf mongooses is extremely important. The average size of a family group is 12, and every member must pull his or her weight. There can be no shirking.

The primary task of the family is finding enough food, but it has other chores to perform along the way. Depending to some extent on the age and sex of the individual, each mongoose may serve the family as a baby-sitter, guard, warrior, or nurse. But any family member can take over any task as needed.

Baby-sitting is a big job, of course, because many predators would love to have baby mongoose for lunch. But perhaps the most crucial profession for a mongoose is to be a guard. The number of guards at any one time depends on the size of the family group and the rate of feeding. As many as six guards may be on watch. Guard duty lasts from 15 to 45 minutes. The guard is always alert, sitting on its hind legs, ready to sound the alarm that sends all the mongooses scurrying for cover.

The warriors fend off predators. They also chase away other mongoose groups that want to invade the family territory.

But it is nurse duty that sets the dwarf mongooses apart from other animals. With the exception of human beings and possibly some species of whales, no other species of mammal cares for its sick and injured. When a member of the dwarf mongoose family is ill or hurt, one or more of the healthy family members quickly takes up the task of caring for the ailing mongoose.

A WORD FROM OUR CREATOR

For I was an hungered, and ye gave me meat: I was thirsty, and ye gave me drink: I was a stranger, and ye took me in: naked, and ye clothed me.
Matthew 25:35, 36.

hen our friends the Nelsons were missionaries in Southeast Asia, they had two dogs, one named Blitz and the other Jogger. Both were Eskimo Spitzes—medium-sized dogs with snow-white fur, boundless energy, and tails that curled tightly over their backs.

One day Jogger, his tail drooping, stopped eating. He was sick. If they had been in the United States, the Nelsons would have taken the dog to a veterinarian, but none was available where they lived. As it happened, both Mr. and Mrs. Nelson were physicians, so Jogger was in the best of hands with the Doctors Nelson taking care of him.

The Nelsons checked Jogger's blood and found that his hemoglobin count was a very low 4! While they were at it, they also examined Blitz's blood—his hemoglobin was a healthy 17. Jogger had a serious infection that was destroying his blood cells faster than he could produce more. If something wasn't done fast, he would die.

The Nelson's gave Jogger the best remedy that they had available, an antibiotic that would destroy the infection if they could keep Jogger alive long enough for the medicine to work. The next day, however, Jogger was so weak that he couldn't even walk. He would die if something more wasn't done.

The Nelsons quickly decided that if they gave some of Blitz's healthy blood to Jogger, he might live long enough to fight the disease. The Nelsons led Blitz to an empty storeroom in the hospital in which they worked, and put him to sleep. Using a hypodermic needle, they drew some of Blitz's blood. When Blitz woke up, he would be weak, but his healthy body would quickly produce new blood.

The Nelsons injected Jogger with Blitz's blood. By the time all the blood had run into Jogger's veins, he was feeling better. As he jumped up, his tail went up into a curl over his back. He was a new dog—thanks to Blitz!

Blitz sacrificed some of his blood so that Jogger could live. And without the blood of Jesus, we are sick unto death, with no hope. By accepting the sacrifice of Jesus, we are made new.

Blitz Saves Jogger

A Word From Our Creator

Therefore if any man be in Christ, he is a new creature: old things are passed away; behold, all things are become new. 2 Corinthians 5:17.

December 24

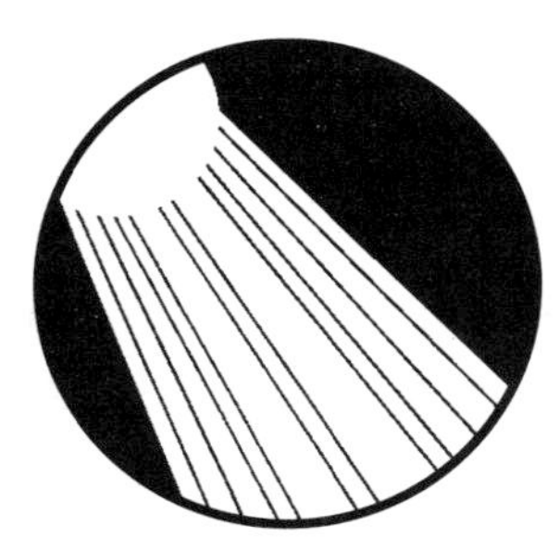

The Glory of the Lord

At Christmastime people string lights to celebrate the season. Many communities award prizes for the most brilliantly and artistically lighted houses and yards in town. The names of the winners appear in the newspaper for all to read. But wait! Aren't Christmas lights supposed to remind us of the birth of the Christ child?

On the night when Jesus was born, some very special lights filled the sky. There was the light of the star that the Wise Men were following. And there was the light that surrounded the shepherds when the angels announced the birth of the Messiah. It was as though the heavenly host wanted to shout from the mountaintops: "Hear ye! Hear ye! The King of the universe is born today! He is lying in a manger behind the inn in Bethlehem. Won't somebody notice?"

But no one was interested; no one cared. Well, no one except a few shepherds and some strangers from a faraway country. The people on whom Jesus had showered His richest blessings, the people who were His chosen nation of all the peoples on earth—too many of those people had forgotten that He was coming. How strange that must have seemed to those watching the scene from throughout the heavens.

The angel messengers couldn't contain themselves. They *had* to tell someone! So they told the shepherds. But their voices terrified the shepherds. Finally, after calming their fears, the angel gave the official announcement: "Unto you is born this day in the city of David a Saviour, which is Christ the Lord" (Luke 2:11). The shepherds could hardly believe their ears. But the host of heaven wasn't satisfied.

"And suddenly there was with the angel a multitude of the heavenly host praising God, and saying, Glory to God in the highest, and on earth peace, good will toward men" (verses 13, 14).

On that night no lights brought glory to the owner of the house. It was the glory of the Lord that shone round about them—the light of the first day of Creation. The Light of the world had arrived again to give light to the darkness, "and the darkness comprehended it not" (John 1:5).

A Word From Our Creator

And there were in the same country shepherds abiding in the field. . . . And, lo, the angel of the Lord came upon them, and the glory of the Lord shone round about them.
Luke 2:8, 9.

It was the world's darkest hour, a time that prophecy had foretold: "Darkness shall cover the earth, and gross darkness the people" (Isaiah 60:2). Earth was doomed to become a dead planet. Humanity had sinned, and "the wages of sin is death" (Romans 6:23). Death to the dark planet—that was the immutable law of God Himself. It could not be rescinded. Every living thing on earth was destined for the cosmic trash heap.

But then God gave! Out of the depths of unsearchable love, God presented His Son. When we were without hope, Jesus offered us His place in the kingdom. It's impossible to fathom the value of that gift.

But that's not all. To make it easier for us to understand and accept His gift, God brought us still another gift. The second gift is a gift from Jesus. He asked the Father to give us a spiritual power often symbolized by atmospheric heaven, the power of the wind and the rain: His own Holy Spirit. "But the Comforter, which is the Holy Ghost, whom the Father will send in my name, he shall teach you all things, and bring all things to your remembrance, whatsoever I have said unto you" (John 14:26). God's Spirit comes to us in two forms, one like the wind and the other like the rain.

When "the earth was without form, and void; and darkness was upon the face of the deep," "the spirit of God moved upon the face of the waters" (Genesis 1:2), and a whole new world began to emerge as God's Spirit translated His love into action. When Jesus came to earth as our Saviour, darkness again covered the planet, and again the Creator provided His Spirit. "And suddenly there came a sound from heaven as of a rushing mighty wind, and it filled all the house where they were sitting. . . . And they were all filled with the Holy Ghost" (Acts 2:2-4).

After the wind comes the rain. Just as the rain soaks in to soften and water the soil, so the Holy Spirit softens and waters the soul. "Seek the Lord, till he come and rain righteousness upon you" (Hosea 10:12).

God's gift is a combination: He gives you His Son, who gives you His Spirit, who gives you His righteousness.

December 25

What Jesus Gave You

A Word From Our Creator

For God so loved the world, that he gave his only begotten Son, that whosoever believeth in him should not perish, but have everlasting life. John 3:16.

December 26

Leaves—God's Natural Air Filters

A Word From Our Creator

In the midst of the street of it, . . . was there the tree of life, which bare twelve manner of fruits, . . . and the leaves of the tree were for the healing of the nations. Revelation 22:2.

We can't imagine the wonderful things that Jesus has prepared for us in heaven. In our text John tells us that the leaves of the tree of life keep the nations healthy. I suspect that the tree of life in heaven is very much like the one that the Creator put on this earth in the Garden of Eden, don't you? And if that's true, then the leaves of that tree—and probably the leaves of all plants—were created with health-giving properties.

Plants are essential to our health. Not only do they give us our best food, but they are actually small factories that make our planet a safe place to live. They convert the carbon dioxide that we exhale back into pure oxygen for us to breathe.

But plants help us to survive in many more ways, and the National Space Agency (NASA) has been studying how plants purify the air we breathe. For example, formaldehyde is a very common—and dangerous—by-product of many modern building substances. We must control this gas that gets released into the air of our homes and other buildings so that it will not harm us. Because it's always best to find natural solutions to our environmental problems, NASA scientists tested the effect of putting houseplants into a room filled with formaldehyde gas and discovered that they reduced the amount of gas by more than half within six hours. After testing several kinds of houseplants, they also found that the most effective of the natural air cleaners studied was the spider plant. Within one day one plant eliminated 90 percent of the poisonous gas. How do ordinary plants purify air? The leaves "breathe" in the polluted air, filter it, and release pure oxygen, holding the poisons in their cells.

If Jesus can create plants that clean our air, you can be sure that He can purify our lives as well. After all, is He not the source of the breath of life?

DECEMBER 27

The Day of the Lord

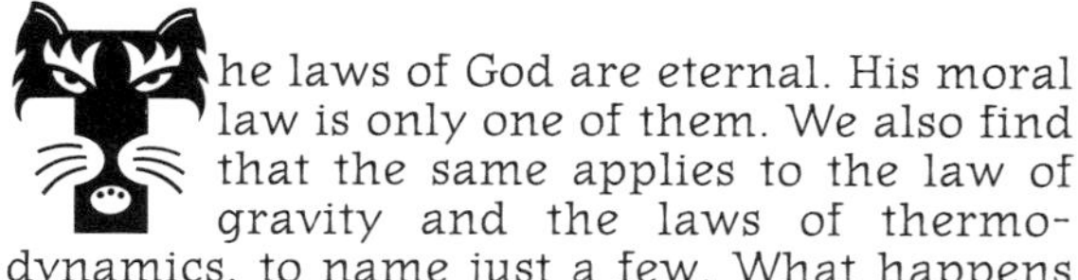

he laws of God are eternal. His moral law is only one of them. We also find that the same applies to the law of gravity and the laws of thermodynamics, to name just a few. What happens when someone defies the law of gravity? If you jump off of a tall building, you'll fall—it is the law! And what happens when you hit the ground? The impact dictates your probable death. You can't defy the laws of God's universe without paying the consequences.

For reasons that we may not understand from this side of eternity, sin caused earth and its people to fall under the dictates of the "law of sin and death" (Romans 8:2). The results are inescapable. The earth will come to a fiery end.

According to the apostle Peter, it will be as spectacular an event as you can imagine: "The heavens shall pass away with a great noise, and the elements shall melt with fervent heat, the earth also and the works that are therein shall be burned up. . . . The heavens being on fire shall be dissolved, and the elements shall melt" (2 Peter 3:10-12). No ordinary explosion, it's clear that the event includes the earth, but is somehow not limited to our planet. The *heavens* (plural) shall pass away. Peter's description of such an explosion reminds us of what astronomers call a supernova.

A supernova is an exploding star. The most well-known example is a heavenly object known as the Crab Nebula. Located in the constellation Taurus, this star exploded for all the world to see in A.D. 1054. For a while it was the third brightest object in the sky, exceeded only by the sun and the moon. The Crab Nebula is only 4,500 light-years away, which means that the actual explosion took place about 3,500 B.C.

But Peter wasn't trying to scare anyone. He was giving us a powerful message: "Seeing then that all these things shall be dissolved, what manner of persons ought ye to be . . . ?" (verses 11, 12). Peter answers his own question: "Seeing ye know these things before, beware lest ye also, being led away with the error of the wicked, fall from your own stedfastness. But grow in grace, and in the knowledge of our Lord and Saviour Jesus Christ" (verses 17, 18).

A WORD FROM OUR CREATOR

Knowest thou the ordinances of heaven? canst thou set the dominion thereof in the earth?
Job 38:33.

December 28

The Breaking of the Day

Many birds awaken and begin to sing long before daylight. Ornithologists call this singing the "dawn chorus." But scientists aren't sure what triggers the songfest.

Because birds sleep through the night with their heads tucked under their wings, the predawn twilight doesn't awaken them. It seems that an internal clock rouses the birds while it's still dark, then they sit in the darkness, waiting silently for the coming of the dawn. And then, as though brought to attention by some invisible director, they break out in a chorus that's never out of key and never off tempo. It begins with a few birds and then swells as others join. Some species have special dawn songs that they sing only before and during daybreak.

What inspires the birds to sing at the daybreak? Even though no one really knows, we believe that the Creator provided the dawn chorus in the Garden of Eden to welcome the dawn. We also believe that the dawn chorus reminds us of the soon coming of Jesus. In the words of the hymn:

> " 'Tis almost time for the Lord to come,
> I hear the people say;
> The stars of heaven are growing dim,
> It must be the breaking of the day.
> O it must be the breaking of the day!
> O it must be the breaking of the day!
> The night is almost gone,
> The day is coming on;
> O it must be the breaking of the day!"

One morning in the not-too-distant future a hush will spread throughout the universe as Jesus and all the angels approach Planet Earth. Suddenly we will hear the sound of a trumpet from the skies, and we will look up and shout in a mighty dawn chorus, "Lo, this is our God; we have waited for him, and he will save us" (Isaiah 25:9).

A Word From Our Creator

Lo, this is our God; we have waited for him, and he will save us: this is the Lord; we have waited for him, we will be glad and rejoice in his salvation. Isaiah 25:9.

DECEMBER 29

The Hornbill Alarm Clock

In East Africa individuals of two species of hornbills spend almost every day with the family groups of the dwarf mongoose. The diet of the Von der Decken's hornbill and the yellow-billed hornbill consists of insects and small rodents. And as it happens, the dwarf mongoose's choice of food is also insects, along with an occasional mouse. The hornbills aren't adept at finding such food, but as the mongooses scurry through the grass and weeds they have no trouble stirring up plenty of food—enough for themselves and for the flock of hornbills as well.

The mongooses, on the other hand, need protection from birds of prey. When not accompanied by the hornbills, the mongooses have to deploy up to half their family to watch for avian predators. But as it happens, the birds that prey on the mongooses also prey on the hornbills, so the hornbills are constantly on the alert. With both the hornbills and mongooses on the lookout, the chance of seeing a hungry hawk before it spots them thus increases. So the hornbills and the mongooses work together for their mutual benefit.

The dwarf mongoose family retires for the night into the ventilation tunnels of active termite mounds. The hornbills go to a roost tree some distance away. But early the next morning the hornbills arrive at the termite mounds, where they sit patiently in the trees for up to 45 minutes for the mongooses to emerge. Then they wait for up to 30 minutes more while the mongooses perform their morning grooming and territorial marking. Then it's off for the day's feeding foray.

Once in a while the mongooses oversleep. But there's a limit to the hornbills' patience. If the hornbills have to wait as long as an hour for the mongooses to emerge, they become very agitated. They fly down to the base of the termite mounds, peer into the ventilation shafts, and call "wok-wok-wok." The mongooses tumble out immediately and head off on the hunt within four minutes.

Jesus is coming soon. He has invited us to His coronation banquet. Are we ready, or do we need a wake-up call?

A WORD FROM OUR CREATOR

And . . . now it is high time to awake out of sleep: for now is our salvation nearer than when we believed. Romans 13:11.

December 30

Deciding to Be Born

It is said that being born is the only thing in life that you can't control. Well, if two scientists at Cornell University are correct, we may have to revise that idea. While studying the birth of sheep, Dr. Nathanielsz and Dr. McDonald have learned that an unborn lamb determines when it will be born. The message comes from the lamb's own brain. This is how the process works. When the time is right, somewhere in the lamb's hypothalamus (hy-po-THAL-a-mus), a part of its brain, cells produce a special messenger hormone. This hormone triggers the birth process. If the message isn't sent, the lamb won't be born.

The hormonal messenger emerges from the paraventricular nucleus (par-ven-TRIK-u-lar NU-clee-us), a section of the hypothalamus, and heads for the pituitary (pi-TU-i-tare-ee) gland, another part of the brain. The pituitary gland receives the message and translates it into another hormone, which in turn goes to the adrenal (a-DREE-nal) gland in the rear portion of the lamb's body. The adrenal gland takes the information and produces yet another hormone called cortisol (CORT-i-sol). Cortisol acts as a message from the unborn lamb to the mother. It passes through the umbilical cord to the mother's womb. Translated into words, the hormone message might say, "I am ready to be born!"

The womb receives the cortisol and translates it into the production of another hormone called estrogen (ES-tro-gen), which stimulates the muscles of the mother's womb—and the lamb is born! Some evidence suggests that human babies give similar signals to their mothers.

Nicodemus didn't know all these chemical details, though he believed that Jesus was talking about physical birth. But Jesus gently instructed Nicodemus that the process of spiritual birth was the same. "Jesus answered, Verily, verily, I say unto thee, Except a man be born of water and of the Spirit, he cannot enter into the kingdom of God" (John 3:5).

You see, in your response to Jesus, you decide to be born again. Like the lamb, only you can make that decision.

A Word From Our Creator

Nicodemus saith unto him, How can a man be born when he is old? can he enter the second time into his mother's womb, and be born? John 3:4.

December 31

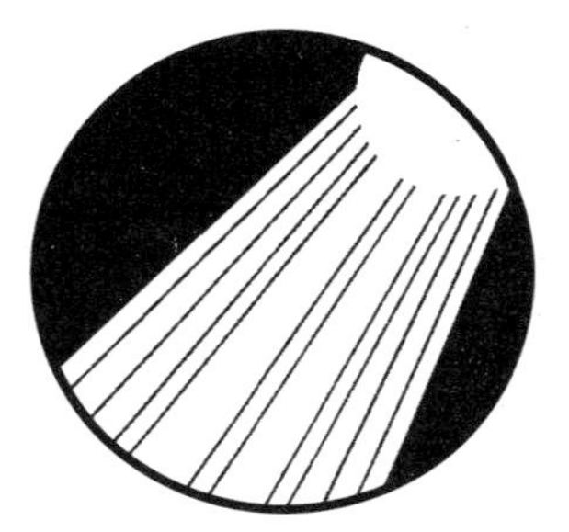

God Gives You Light

Very soon a day is coming when Jesus will return again. The heavens will light up with the brightness of His third coming! Yes, we usually refer to it as His second coming, but when Jesus appears in the clouds of heaven to take us home, it will be the third time He performs a worldwide act of creation and redemption, the third time He brings the light of the world to a dark planet.

At His first advent Jesus came as a light-bearing Creator to a planet enshrouded in darkness. He said, "Let there be light: and there was light" (Genesis 1:3). Jesus created people, and those people forsook Him to follow a false light—Lucifer had been the light bearer, but now was Satan, the prince of darkness.

The next time Jesus returned to earth He was a human being. Again it was at a time when darkness shrouded the earth and gross darkness the people (Isaiah 60:2). Satan ruled. And again Jesus came as the light of the world (John 8:12). Once more the people forsook Him. "The light shineth in darkness; and the darkness comprehended it not" (John 1:5). In darkness He died on the cross to save us. But in a brilliance brighter than that of the sun, He came forth from the tomb to begin a new work for humanity—preparing a people to meet Him at His *next* coming. "Spread the word," He told His disciples. "Tell everybody. I am coming back for you. Get ready! Be ready!"

This time His people will not forsake Him. Those who of their own free will reject Jesus will have chosen to be destroyed by the brightness of His coming (2 Thessalonians 2:8). "But ye are a chosen generation, a royal priesthood, an holy nation, a peculiar people; that ye should shew forth the praises of him who hath called you out of darkness into his marvellous light" (1 Peter 2:9). "Let your light so shine before men, that they may see your good works, and glorify your Father which is in heaven" (Matthew 5:16).

"And, behold, I come quickly; and my reward is with me, to give every man according as his work shall be. I am Alpha and Omega, the beginning and the end, the first and the last" (Revelation 22:12, 13).

A Word From Our Creator

And there shall be no night there; and they need no candle, neither light of the sun; for the Lord God giveth them light: and they shall reign for ever and ever. Revelation 22:5.

SCRIPTURE INDEX

GENESIS
1:1-3 Jan. 1
1:6 Jan. 2
1:11 Jan. 3
1:14 Jan. 4
1:16 June 28
1:20 Jan. 5
1:21 Apr. 13, Nov. 16
1:25 Feb. 17
1:26 Jan. 6, Dec. 15
1:30 Sep. 5
2:2, 3 Jan. 7
2:7 June 19, Aug. 1
2:9 Nov. 12
2:16, 17 Sep. 26
2:19 Dec. 21
2:20 Jan. 10
2:22 Sep. 14
3:4, 5 Nov. 21
3:6 July 11
3:13 Aug. 19
3:15 Jan. 21
6:14 Mar. 7
9:2 Feb. 18
9:13-16 Nov. 6

EXODUS
2:23 July 29
10:23 Feb. 5
14:13 May 25
16:14 Dec. 4
19:16 Mar. 6
33:17 Aug. 4

NUMBERS
32:23 Oct. 23

DEUTERONOMY
4:30, 31 Oct. 14
6:6 July 1
11:16, 17 May 1
31:6 May 20
32:2 Sep. 11

JUDGES
5:20 Mar. 15

1 SAMUEL
13:6 Apr. 10
17:47 Apr. 27

2 SAMUEL
22:2 Dec. 8

1 KINGS
4:29-33 Mar. 4
18:45 Sep. 25

1 CHRONICLES
4:40 Sep. 22

2 CHRONICLES
1:12 Sep. 15

NEHEMIAH
9:6 May 31

JOB
1:6, 7 June 13
6:15, 16 June 5
7:2 July 16
10:11 Oct. 20
11:7, 8 Oct. 16
12:7 Aug. 3
24:13 July 26
26:7 May 17
26:8 Jan. 30
37:5 Oct. 9
37:16, 17 Jan. 22
37:9 Apr. 17
37:18 Feb. 6
38:3 Oct. 11
38:19, 20 Oct. 1
38:22 Dec. 11
38:33 Dec. 27
38:34 July 19
38:28, 29 Feb. 13
38:29 May 15
38:31 Mar. 29, Oct. 4
38:32 Mar. 8
39:26 June 26

PSALMS
1:1 May 19
1:3 Jan. 17, Aug. 22
1:6 Oct. 12
8:3 May 10
8:3, 4 Jan. 25
10:9 Mar. 10
11:2 Apr. 6
18:15 Aug. 14
19:1, 2 Feb. 12
19:1-3 Aug. 6
19:6 Sep. 27
23:2 Sep. 10
25:17 July 18
27:1 Jan. 15
32:7 Dec. 9
33:7 Mar. 27
33:8 Aug. 23
34:8 Oct. 26
35:20 June 30
36:6, 7 Sep. 9
37:7 Nov. 23
37:40 Nov. 17
38:10 Mar. 26
40:3 Oct. 5
46:1-3 Jan. 20
50:15 Sep. 23
51:7 Oct. 10
55:6 July 13
62:6 Nov. 30
66:18, 19 May 11
69:22 May 2
73:22 June 23
77:19 Aug. 24
89:5 Apr. 5
89:34-37 Nov. 29
89:37 Aug. 16
90:2 July 5
90:10 Oct. 13
91:5, 6 Feb. 23
93:4 Aug. 21
94:22 July 15
96:11 Nov. 22
97:2 Nov. 13
97:6 June 21
104:2 Feb. 26

104:3 July 24
104:14 Feb. 14, June 16
107:23, 24 Feb. 2
119:1, 2 Jan. 28
119:101 Mar. 11
119:105 July 2
119:130 Feb. 19, Dec. 3
121:5, 6 Feb. 1
133:1 Nov. 8
135:7 Oct. 2
136:7-9 June 7
136:23 Feb. 16
136:26 Apr. 12
139:12 Nov. 5
147:4 Feb. 22
147:5 June 25
147:16-18 Mar. 21
148:1 Aug. 2
148:1-3 Aug. 9
148:4 Mar. 22
148:7, 8 May 29

PROVERBS

6:6-8 Sep. 8
6:30 Mar. 2
11:30 Dec. 16
12:22 Sep. 28
14:15 Nov. 4
14:26, 27 Mar. 30
17:22 June 3
20:1 Oct. 6
21:25 Mar. 24
22:15 Sep. 2
22:26 Mar. 25
28:1 Nov. 2

ECCLESIASTES

1:6 July 12, Dec. 18
3:1-5 Feb. 11
3:11 June 22, Oct. 29
7:11 Sep. 12
9:10 May 27
10:1 Dec. 6

SONG OF SOLOMON

2:4 Apr. 19
2:12 June 27

ISAIAH

1:18 Aug. 15
2:2 May 22
2:4 Apr. 18
11:9 Aug. 11
14:12 May 3
25:29 Dec. 28
28:16 July 3
33:24 May 13
35:1, 2 Apr. 11
40:8 Apr. 25
40:12 Feb. 20
42:5 Mar. 1
44:22 Sep. 18
45:13 July 28
45:18 Aug. 30
48:18 July 10
49:10 Aug. 29
51:6 Aug. 17
55:12 Dec. 19
58:8 Dec. 17
59:2 July 7
60:1 July 9
65:21 July 27
66:13 Feb. 24

JEREMIAH

11:19 May 12
13:23 Feb. 10
17:1 Aug. 28
17:9 Nov. 11
17:14 Feb. 21
23:24 Sep. 13
27:5 Mar. 5
31:37 Oct. 25
32:17 Mar. 12, 23
33:3 Feb. 15
33:22 Jan. 11

LAMENTATIONS

3:6 Oct. 17

EZEKIEL

34:28 July 14

DANIEL

2:22 May 7
12:3 Sep. 4

HOSEA

14:9 Feb. 4

AMOS

3:3 Apr. 7

JONAH

2:7 Aug. 31

MALACHI

3:6 July 17
3:17 June 11

MATTHEW

2:1, 2 Dec. 20
5:5 Nov. 10
5:13 Jan. 23
5:16 Apr. 9
6:4 May 8
6:11 May 18
6:23 Aug. 27
7:13 Aug. 13
7:15 Apr. 28
7:20 Feb. 28, Oct. 3
7:21 Feb. 25
9:38 July 21
11:28 Jan. 13, May 6, July 8
13:45, 46 Oct. 21
16:2, 3 June 12
18:21 Sep. 19
20:34 July 23
21:19 Jan. 31
24:23 June 18
24:27 Apr. 30
25:13 Sep. 13
25:21 Sep. 24
25:35, 36 Dec. 22
27:51 Apr. 14
28:2, 3 Apr. 16

MARK

1:35 July 22
4:28 Oct. 31
4:41 Apr. 3
8:18 Apr. 22
8:36 June 10
13:32 Mar. 16

LUKE

1:78, 79 May 14
2:8, 9 Dec. 24
3:9 Dec. 12
8:11 June 20
9:23 Apr. 24
9:58 July 20
10:36, 37 Jan. 26
10:41, 42 May 4
11:34 Oct. 15
18:11 Aug. 25
19:10 Oct. 28
21:28 Sep. 16
22:24 Nov. 14

JOHN

1:5-10 Apr. 15
3:4 Dec. 30
3:16 Dec. 25
3:19 Dec. 10
3:21 Jan. 29
4:10 Jan. 16
4:29 Oct. 7
10:9 Aug. 5
11:11, 12 June 17
14:1 Dec. 1
14:2 Feb. 3
14:2, 3 Oct. 19
14:3 Nov. 15
15:5 Aug. 8
16:33 Nov. 24
16:13 Jan. 12
16:33 Aug. 18
21:6 May 26

ACTS

2:2 May 21
3:6-8 June 4
10:34 Apr. 4
17:24 Sep. 6
17:27 Feb. 9
20:35 July 4
26:13 May 28

ROMANS

1:20 Jan. 14
5:3 May 5
6:23 Oct. 30
8:28 Dec. 14
10:17 Apr. 20
10:18 Aug. 20
11:33 June 2
12:4, 5 Aug. 10
13:11 Dec. 29

1 CORINTHIANS

6:20 Sep. 30
12:14-27 Sep. 29
15:41 Nov. 1
15:51, 52 June 1
15:56, 57 Sep. 21

2 CORINTHIANS

3:18 Apr. 2
4:6 Jan. 8
5:17 Dec. 23
11:13, 14 Mar. 3
11:14 Oct. 8

GALATIANS

3:27 June 6
5:14, 15 Mar. 31
6:7 May 9

EPHESIANS

1:17, 18 Oct. 22
2:20 Mar. 28
3:17-19 Mar. 14
4:14 June 15
5:2 Oct. 27, Nov. 3
5:9, 10 Oct. 24
6:11 Nov. 25

PHILIPPIANS

1:6 Mar. 18
1:10 June 24
2:8 July 6
2:15 Mar. 19, Nov. 19, Nov. 26
3:13, 14 Jan. 24
3:14 Nov. 20
4:13 Dec. 7

COLOSSIANS

1:16, 17 June 14
2:6,7 Nov. 28
2:21 May 23

1 THESSALONIANS

1:3 Nov. 18
4:17 May 24
5:2, 3 Mar. 13
5:16,18 June 29

1 TIMOTHY

4:7, 8 Mar. 9

2 TIMOTHY

1:9 Aug. 26
4:17 Dec. 2

TITUS

1:7 July 31

HEBREWS

7:25 Apr. 29
9:28 June 8
10:23 Dec. 5
11:3 Feb. 8
13:8 Sep. 20

JAMES

1:6 Jan. 19
1:26 Sep. 1
3:12 Aug. 7

1 PETER

1:17 May 16
1:24 July 25
2:2 Sep. 7
2:24 May 30

2 PETER

1:19 Sep. 17
3:7 Feb. 27
3:8 Mar. 5

1 JOHN

1:5, 6 Aug. 13
5:4 Apr. 23

REVELATION

2:21 Jan. 9
3:11 June 9, Oct. 18
7:1 Mar. 20
10:5, 6 Dec. 13
12:7, 8 Nov. 7

12:12	Jan. 18	21:4	Jan. 27, Apr. 8	22:2	Feb. 7, Dec. 26
12:17	Nov. 9	21:6	Apr. 21	22:5	Dec. 31
14:3	Apr. 1	21:23	July 30	22:16	Apr. 26